THE
KINCAIDS
Southern Seduction

New money. New passions. Old secrets.

Two seductive reads from wonderful writers
Kathie DeNosky and Rachel Bailey

D0493928

The Kincaids Collection

THE
KINCAIDS
Southern Seduction

KATHIE
DENOSKY

RACHEL
BAILEY

First published in Great Britain 2013
by Mills & Boon, an imprint of Harlequin (UK) Limited, Eton House,
18-24 Paradise Road, Richmond, Surrey TW9 1SR

THE KINCAIDS: SOUTHERN SEDUCTION
© Harlequin Enterprises II B.V./S.à.r.l. 2012

Sex, Lies and the Southern Belle © Harlequin Books S.A. 2012
What Happens in Charleston... © Harlequin Books S.A. 2012

Special thanks and acknowledgment to Kathie DeNosky and Rachel Bailey for their contributions to the Dynasties: The Kincaids miniseries.

ISBN: 978 0 263 90588 5

009-0313

Printed and bound by
CPI Group (UK) Ltd, Croydon, CR0 4YY

SEX, LIES AND
THE SOUTHERN BELLE

KATHIE
DeNOSKY

Kathie DeNosky lives in her native southern Illinois with her big, loveable Bernese mountain dog, Nemo. Writing highly sensual stories with a generous amount of humour, Kathie's books have appeared on the Waldenbooks bestseller list and received a Write Touch Readers Award and a National Readers' Choice Award. Kathie enjoys going to rodeos, travelling to research settings for her books and listening to country music. Readers may contact Kathie at PO Box 2064, Herrin, Illinois 62948-5264, USA or email her at kathie@kathiedenosky.com. They can also visit her website, www.kathiedenosky.com.

Dear Reader,

When I was invited to write the first book in the new Dynasties mini-series, I was absolutely thrilled. I love working with other authors on these special projects and this one was no different. I mean, who wouldn't enjoy collaborating with such talented ladies?

And, as impossible as it might seem, as I wrote *Sex, Lies and the Southern Belle*, my enthusiasm grew even more. Researching Charleston, South Carolina, and specifically the historic homes in the Battery, I fell in love with the antebellum architecture and the beauty of a city so rich with history.

That's one of the reasons the antebellum mansion Lily inherits on Battery Street plays a major role in the telling of their story. As grand as any castle, the gorgeous historic home is where Lily and Daniel work to overcome the secrets of the past and together find a love that will stand the test of time.

As you read about the modern South and get acquainted with all of the Kincaid siblings, it is my fervent hope that you enjoy these stories as much as we, the authors, enjoyed writing them.

All the best,

Kathie DeNosky

This book is dedicated to the wonderful authors I worked with on this series. It was a real pleasure, ladies!

And to Charles Griemsman. I look forward to working with you on many more in the future.

One

A knot began to form in Lily Kincaid's stomach as she looked around the conference table at her family and the three strangers who had attended her father's funeral the day before. They were gathered for the reading of Reginald Kincaid's will and as difficult as it was to believe her beloved father was gone, the fact that he had led a secret double life for the past three decades was almost impossible for her to grasp. It was just beyond comprehension to think that he'd had a second family up in Greenville all these years.

When Harold Parsons, her father's attorney, walked into the room with a thick file and sat down at the head of the table, then removed several envelopes and papers from the folder, her apprehension grew. She hated that her father had been taken from her, hated that his life's work was about to be divided up into shares. More than that, she hated that the perception she had of him had been nothing more than an illusion—an illusion that had been shattered with seemingly no way for it to ever be repaired.

"Before we begin, I would like to express my sincere condolences for your loss," Mr. Parsons said, his normally gruff voice softened with sincerity. "I knew Reginald for many years and will sorely miss his sense of humor and quick wit. I can remember the time—"

Lily bit her lower lip to keep it from trembling when the man claiming to be her half brother, Jack Sinclair, rudely cleared his throat and glanced at his watch as if he wanted to hurry things along. How could a man as warm and loving as her father had been have spawned such a cold, unfeeling son?

Her oldest brother RJ's scowl was formidable. "In a hurry to be somewhere, Sinclair?"

"As a matter of fact, I am," Jack stated flatly. "How long is this going to take, Parsons?"

Mr. Parsons's bushy white eyebrows met in a disapproving frown above his reading glasses. "It will take as long as it takes, young man."

"Please don't, Jack," Angela Sinclair begged, her voice trembling as she placed her hand on her son's arm. Her chin-length blond hair swayed slightly as she shook her head. "Please don't make this any more difficult than it already is."

If circumstances had been different, Lily would have probably felt sorry for the woman. It had been apparent yesterday at the funeral and today as they sat awaiting the reading of the will that she was taking the death of Reginald Kincaid extremely hard. But considering the nurse had been her father's mistress for the past thirty years and had shown up to mourn his death as if she and her sons were a legitimate part of the family, it was almost more than Lily could bear. Angela Sinclair either didn't realize or didn't care about what a shock and devastation it would be for the Kincaid family.

"You'll have to excuse my brother's impatience," Alan Sinclair spoke up, giving Lily and her family a sympathetic smile. "I'm afraid Jack is still trying to come to grips with Reginald's death."

Angela's youngest son, Alan, seemed to be the exact opposite of his older half-brother in every way. While Jack was tall, with dark hair, blue eyes and a cold, ruthless demeanor, Alan was shorter, had dark blond hair and hazel eyes like his mother, and appeared to be sympathetic to the shock and disbelief the Kincaids were going through. Not only were they having to cope with the death of their father, possibly by his own hand, they had been blindsided by the ugly truth of his clandestine life.

"Don't apologize for me," Jack growled, turning his hard stare on the younger man. There was such animosity in his expression, it was obvious there was no love lost between the two. "I have nothing to be sorry about."

"Enough!" RJ said, his voice deadly. Turning to the lawyer, he nodded. "Please continue, Mr. Parsons."

"If Sinclair doesn't want to stick around for the details, I'm sure you can send him a letter outlining what our father wished to leave him," Matt said, backing up RJ.

Only a few years older than herself, her brother Matt had already seen his share of heartache. It had been only a year since he had buried his wife, Grace, and been left to raise their young son, Flynn, on his own. Losing their father so soon after her passing had to bring up some very painful memories for him.

Lily glanced at her mother to see how she was holding up through this latest upheaval. The epitome of a true Southern lady, Elizabeth Kincaid had maintained an elegant calm about her throughout this whole ordeal that Lily couldn't help but envy. It appeared her mother was faring much better than Lily and her two sisters. Laurel, Lily's oldest sister, kept dabbing at her tears with a lace-edged hankie, while Kara looked as if she was in a state of total shock.

"Please continue, Harold," her mother said, smoothing a strand of short, dark auburn hair into place.

"Very well, Miss Elizabeth," Mr. Parsons said, using "miss" the way most older Southern gentlemen did with any lady, single or married. He read aloud the preliminary legalese, then clearing his throat, began to go through the list of her father's assets. "'Regarding my personal properties, I would like for them to be divided as such. To my son RJ, I leave the Great Oak Lodge in the Smoky Mountains. To my daughter Laurel, I leave my beach house on the Outer Banks. To my daughter Kara, I leave my vacation home on Hilton Head Island. To my son Matthew, I leave the Kincaid family farmhouse where we used to spend holidays. And to my daughter Lily, I leave the Colonel Samuel Beauchamp House in the Battery.'"

Tears filled Lily's eyes. Her father had known how much she loved the historic homes in the Battery. It was one of the prettiest sections in Charleston and quite possibly the entire state of South Carolina. But she had been completely unaware that he owned one of the stately mansions in that area.

After outlining the money and properties her father wished to bequeath to Elizabeth and Angela, Mr. Parsons added, "When Reginald updated his will, he wrote these letters and asked me to give them to you at this time." He passed each person in the room, except Elizabeth, a sealed envelope with their name on the front before he continued, "As for Reginald's business holdings, they are to be divided up as follows. 'RJ, Laurel, Kara, Matthew and Lily are each to receive nine percent interest in The Kincaid Group. My oldest son, Jack Sinclair, will receive forty-five percent interest.'"

Silence reigned for several long, uncomfortable moments as the gravity of her father's last wishes sank in.

"What the hell!" RJ's expression was a mixture of barely suppressed fury and total disbelief.

Lily gasped and the knot in her stomach turned to a sickening ache. How could their father do that to his children and especially to RJ, his oldest legitimate son? RJ had worked tirelessly for years as the executive vice president of The Kincaid Group and had been led to believe he would one day take over as president of the vast enterprise when their father decided it was time for him to retire. The news that their father had given the majority of the shares in the family business to Jack Sinclair was hard for all the Kincaid children to take, but it had to be completely devastating for RJ.

"That's only ninety percent," RJ said, his frown formidable. "Where's the other ten?"

Mr. Parsons shook his head. "Due to attorney/client confidentiality, I'm not at liberty to say."

The room erupted with heated allegations and threats

of legal retaliation from both sides of the table and Lily felt as if the walls were closing in on her. She knew if she didn't leave, she was going to be physically ill.

"I need...some air," she said to no one in particular.

Rising to her feet, she stuffed the unopened letter from her father into her purse and blindly ran from the room. She wasn't certain whether it was the news of her father's complete betrayal of his legitimate family or the new life growing inside her that caused her to feel sick, but she had to escape the law office.

As she hurried down the hall to the reception area, she wasn't paying attention and suddenly ran into someone standing as if rooted to the spot. Strong hands immediately came down on her shoulders to keep her from falling and when she looked up, her heart skipped several beats.

Of all the people she could have met up with in the law office, why did she have to run headlong into the owner and CEO of Addison Industries?

Daniel Addison was not only The Kincaid Group's fiercest business competitor, he was the father of her unborn child. A baby he knew absolutely nothing about.

"Where's the fire, sweetheart?" Daniel asked as he steadied the woman who, in the past couple of weeks, had treated him as if he had the plague.

"I need...air," Lily said, her voice barely more than a whisper.

Her unnatural pallor and the desperate look haunting her vibrant blue eyes caused his heart to stall. Yesterday afternoon when he attended Reginald Kincaid's funeral, he had seen her upset. But this went beyond the grief of losing a loved one. Lily looked as if her whole world was crashing down around her.

"Come on," he said, placing his arm around her shoulders and leading her toward the office exit.

"My family… I can't leave," she gasped.

Stopping at the receptionist's desk, he quickly told the woman he would call and reschedule his appointment, then instructed her to get word to the Kincaid family that he was taking Lily home. As he led her out the double glass doors and onto the sidewalk, he watched her gulp in the cool January air and knew that she was seconds away from losing her breakfast. Guiding her over to a trash can, he held her long, red hair back while she was sick.

"Please, go away and let me die in peace," she said when she finally raised her head.

"You're not going to die, Lily," he said, gently cupping her chin with one hand while he wiped the tears from her eyes with his handkerchief.

"I'm pretty sure you're wrong." She took a deep breath. "Right now I feel like death…would be a blessing."

"Did you drive your car?" he asked.

"No, I rode…with Momma," she said, her voice sounding a bit more steady.

He put his arm around her and tucked her to his side as he ushered her toward the parking garage across the street. "Good. I won't have to send someone back to get it."

"I can't leave," she said, starting to turn back toward the law offices of Parsons, Gilbert and Humbolt.

He held her firmly to his side. "This isn't negotiable, Lily. You're upset to the point of making yourself sick."

Opening the passenger door of his diamond-white Mercedes for her, Daniel nodded toward the inside of the car. "Get in. I'm taking you home."

"You're being a bully about this," she said stubbornly.

Daniel shook his head. "No, I'm making an executive decision. Now, will you please get into the car or am I going to have to pick you up and put you there?"

She glared at him. "You wouldn't."

"Try me, sweetheart."

They stared at each other for several seconds in a test of wills before she finally moved to sit down in the leather bucket seat. "Fine. Take me home and then you can be on your way."

He closed the door and walked around the car to slide into the driver's seat. "We'll see about that."

Considering her emotions at the moment, Daniel wasn't about to upset her further by telling her that he wasn't leaving her alone until he was certain she was going to be okay. He might be many things—ruthless in business, arrogant and fierce when he was in competition for a new client and jaded about most things in life—but he wasn't an uncaring bastard who left an obviously distraught female to fend for herself. Especially when that female was Lily Kincaid.

For reasons he couldn't explain, he had been drawn to her from the moment he laid eyes on her last fall at the Children's Hospital Autumn Charity Ball that his mother had helped organize. Young, vivacious and with a zest for life that he found utterly charming, he had introduced himself and asked her to dance, then asked her out to dinner. He hadn't really expected her to say yes, considering the thirteen-year difference in their ages, but to his delight she had accepted. That had been over three months ago and until the past couple of weeks, they had seen each other almost every night.

When he realized that Lily had fallen asleep, Daniel reached over to cover her delicate hand with his. He hadn't intended for things to progress between them so quickly, but he couldn't really say he was sorry they had. She was the most exciting woman he had ever met and the time they spent together had made him feel more alive and less cynical than he had in years. What he couldn't understand was why out of the clear blue sky, she stopped taking his calls and started making excuses not to go out with him.

As he turned the car into the driveway and drove around the Kincaid family home to the carriage house where Lily had an apartment, Daniel shook his head. He didn't know what had happened or why she suddenly wanted nothing to do with him, but he had every intention of finding out.

Parking the car, he reached over to trail his fingers along her smooth cheek. "You're home, sweetheart."

Her eyes fluttered open and she slowly sat up straight to look around. "Thank you for bringing me home, Daniel. I'm sure you have somewhere else you would rather be."

Before she had the chance to reach for the handle, he was out of the car and opening the door for her. "Give me your key," he said as he helped her from the vehicle.

"Really, I'll be fine." She shook her head. "You don't have to see me in."

"What kind of gentleman would I be if I didn't see you safely inside?" he asked, smiling.

For the first time since running into her in the law

office, she looked him directly in the eye. "Give me a break, Mr. Addison. It's midmorning and I seriously doubt that there's a safety issue for you to be concerned with."

He reached up to trail his index finger along her creamy cheek. "So now it's Mr. Addison? I thought we were a lot closer than that, sweetheart."

"I...uh, at one time...I suppose we were," she said, clearly uncomfortable with his observation.

Daniel had heard about someone looking as if they were a deer caught in headlights, but until that moment he hadn't seen it for himself. But that was the only way to describe the expression on Lily's pretty face. She looked trapped and desperate.

The question was, why? What had made her so clearly uncomfortable about being in his presence?

Unfortunately, he was going to have to bide his time until she was feeling a little more in control before he got to the bottom of what was going on with her and why she had ended their affair. The past few days had been a nightmare for her and her family and he wasn't going to add more stress by interrogating her as to what had changed between them.

Placing his hand at the small of her back, he felt a slight tremor course through her and instinctively knew it had nothing to do with the mild winter weather Charleston was experiencing. Good. At least she hadn't developed a complete immunity to him.

"I know that all this has been extremely hard on you, Lily," he said, meaning it. "For my own peace of mind, I want to see that you're all right before I leave."

"There's nothing I can say that's going to dissuade you, is there?" she asked, sighing heavily.

"No."

She looked more tired and world-weary than he had ever seen her and he hated that the events of the past several days had suppressed her fun-loving, free spirit. Whether she realized it or not, Lily needed someone to help her get through one of the toughest times in her life and he had every intention of being the one she turned to.

"Why don't you sit down and put your feet up while I make coffee?" he said when they walked into the living room and he helped her out of her coat.

"No caffeine for me." Her long wavy hair swayed as she shook her head. "I, um, haven't been sleeping well."

"I can understand that." He nodded as he removed his overcoat, then guided her to the couch. "You've been through a lot in the past few days, sweetheart."

"You have no idea," she said as she sank onto the cushions. Tears filled her pretty blue eyes as she looked up at him. "Why did he do it?"

If the account of Reginald's death in the newspaper had been correct, the man had used one of the antique guns in his collection to take his own life. Daniel knew for a fact that Lily and her father had been very close and his apparent suicide had to have been extremely difficult for her to cope with.

"I can't tell you why things happened the way they did, Lily," he said, sitting down beside her to take her into his arms. "It might never be clear why your dad felt compelled to end things in such a drastic way. But once the shock has worn off, I'm sure you'll be able to put this behind you and look back at the good times you shared together."

She stubbornly shook her head. "I'm not so sure. Not

when everything I thought I knew about my father has turned out to be a total lie."

He had meant to console her, not upset her further. "Give yourself some time. Right now your emotions are still too raw to see things clearly."

"You don't understand, Daniel." She pulled away from him to meet his gaze head-on. "I mean literally—everything about Daddy was a lie."

Something about her impassioned statement told him there was a lot more to the story than what the media had reported and she needed to get it out or risk going into emotional meltdown. "What leads you to believe that, Lily?"

She hesitated for a moment as first one tear, then another, spilled down her cheeks. "I might as well tell you. It's going to be the talk of Charleston by the end of the week."

"I'm listening."

"Did you notice that older blonde woman and the two men with her that sat just behind my family at the funeral?" she asked.

He nodded. "Are they relatives from out of town?"

"No. Yes." She swiped at her tears with the back of her hand. "To tell you the truth, I'm not sure what I should call them."

"Slow down, Lily." He didn't like that she was becoming more agitated. "Who are they?"

"That was my father's second family," she said as if the words tasted bitter. "For the past thirty years, all of his out-of-town business trips were nothing more than excuses to travel up to Greenville to spend time with that woman and her two sons."

Of all the things Lily could have told him about

Reginald Kincaid, that was the last thing Daniel expected. "Let me get this straight," he said slowly, trying to digest the revelation. "Your father had another wife and two kids up in Greenville that you're just finding out about?"

Lily nodded. "Actually, Angela Sinclair was my father's first love and her oldest son, Jack, is my half brother. Her youngest son, Alan, belonged to her late husband."

"Jack Sinclair is your half brother?" He had heard of the man and the resounding success Sinclair had made of his start-up company, Carolina Shipping, but Daniel hadn't had the opportunity to meet the man or do business with him. "But didn't you just say he was the oldest? How could his younger brother belong to another man?"

"My dad and Angela were involved when they were very young, but my grandparents didn't think she was the right type of girl for him," Lily explained, rising to pace the floor. "The way I understand it, my grandfather was building his shipping business into what The Kincaid Group is today. He and my grandmother wanted my father to marry someone who could further their standing with the social set of Charleston."

Daniel knew all too well how the bastions of Southern high society worked. His mother came from old money and was well-entrenched in the ranks of the social elite. She and her so-called friends looked down on anyone whose fortune didn't go back at least four generations, or whose family tree didn't include at least one or two officers from the Civil War.

"As an act of rebellion, Daddy joined the army to escape their matchmaking and since he was in a Special

Ops unit, there were months at a time that no one could communicate with him," Lily went on. "From what was said yesterday at the funeral, Angela tried to get word to him that she was expecting his child, but by the time Daddy was wounded and sent back here, Angela had seemingly dropped off the face of the earth. He thought she got tired of waiting for him and moved on."

"So when he couldn't find her, he gave in to his parents and married your mother?" Daniel guessed.

Lily nodded. "The Winthrops were an old, well-established family in Charleston, but by the mid-seventies their fortune had dwindled to almost nothing and they were desperate to maintain their lifestyle and place within their social circle."

Although Daniel hated the snobbery and pretentiousness of it all, it was the social order he had been born into and knew exactly how it worked. He had seen many of the old Southern families swallow their pride and encourage their sons or daughters to marry one of the nouveau riche. If they didn't, their lack of means effectively ostracized them from the wealthy social community.

"So it was advantageous for both families when your mother and father got married," he said, nodding. "Your dad's parents went up several notches on the social register and your mother's family gained someone to help them financially, as well as prop up their position in high society."

"I think that sums it up perfectly," Lily agreed.

"How did your dad and Angela get back together?" Daniel asked, wondering how Reginald had managed to find the woman after all those years when he hadn't been able to before. "And what about her husband? Where does he figure into the equation?"

"Apparently, her parents gave her a choice of marrying Richard Sinclair or giving up her child." Lily shook her head. "Given no other choice, I would have done the same thing and married a man I didn't love to keep my baby."

Daniel frowned. "What about Sinclair? What happened to him?"

"After they married and moved out of state, Angela gave birth to Jack and then several years later, she and Richard Sinclair had a son they named Alan." She shrugged one slender shoulder. "I'm not sure if it was an accident or if he became ill, but Richard died not long after that."

"So he's out of the picture and your dad finds Angela again," Daniel thought aloud.

Lily sighed heavily. "I don't know how he did it, but when he found her and discovered that she had given birth to his son, Daddy set up her and the two boys in a house in Greenville. Apparently she had been struggling to make ends meet on her nurse's salary and life got a lot easier for them when Daddy came on the scene. After that, he starting going on frequent business trips, which were actually visits to spend time with her and her sons."

Daniel shook his head as he tried to digest the story. "And you found this out yesterday at the funeral?"

A tear slid down her cheek and she bit her lower lip to keep it from trembling a moment before she answered. "Y-yes. But what we learned this morning at the reading of the will just compounded the hurt and betrayal we were feeling about his second family."

"What's that, sweetheart?" He couldn't imagine how the situation could get more complicated.

"Daddy left the majority of The Kincaid Group to Jack Sinclair, while my siblings and I were each given nine percent interest," she said swiping another tear from her cheek. "My father led RJ and Matthew to believe they would be running TKG one day. How could he betray Momma this way? And, for that matter, how could he betray all of us?"

Daniel didn't hesitate to stand up, walk over to her and take Lily into his arms. He knew how crushing the loss of her father had to have been for her, but finding out that he had led a secret life for so many years, then handed control of his business to someone the family hadn't even been aware existed had to increase the emotional pain ten times over. Pulling her against him, he held her as he tried to lend her his strength and support.

His compassion seemed to open the floodgates and he tightened his embrace as she sobbed against his chest. He didn't like seeing a woman cry. It always made him uncomfortable and at a loss as to what he should do. Lily's tears made him feel more useless than ever. He wanted to help, wanted to make the hurt she was suffering go away.

Unfortunately, only the passage of time could heal the pain and anguish of losing a loved one. He knew that firsthand from losing his own father to a heart attack fifteen years ago. But the disillusionment she was feeling over her father's indisputable betrayal might never go away.

"I'm okay now," she finally said, pulling from his arms.

"Are you sure?" he asked, reluctant to let her go. Although he hated what she was going through, he liked having Lily in his arms.

Nodding, she walked over to the couch, then curled up in the corner of it. "Thank you for bringing me home, Daniel. But I'm really tired. Could you please lock the door as you let yourself out?"

He had been dismissed and it didn't sit any better this time than it had for the past couple of weeks. But he knew she was completely exhausted from lack of sleep and the emotional turmoil she had been going through. Now wasn't the time to get into why she suddenly had no time for him.

"I'll be back this evening to check on you," he said, reaching for his overcoat.

"I appreciate your concern, but I'll be okay," she said, hiding a yawn behind her delicate hand. She snuggled down to lay her head on a plush pillow. "There's no need for you to go to the trouble of stopping by later. Really, I'll be fine."

Shrugging into his coat, he shook his head as he started toward the door. "It's not a problem. I'll pick something up for dinner and see you around six."

He expected her to protest, but when he turned around, Daniel discovered that Lily's eyes were closed and she was sound asleep. Good, he thought as he walked over to the couch to remove a colorful crocheted afghan from the back, then covered her with it. At least she couldn't tell him not to bother.

"Get some rest, sweetheart," he said quietly as he leaned down to kiss her forehead. "I'll be back in a few hours."

She murmured what sounded like his name, but she

didn't wake up to protest his returning and, as far as he was concerned, that was as good as her consent.

As he let himself out the front door and walked to his car, Daniel knew he was taking advantage of the situation. Lily had made it perfectly clear that she wanted nothing more to do with him and up until this morning, he had respected her wishes and backed off. But for some reason, he couldn't let it go, couldn't walk away without an explanation of why she'd had a change of heart about their affair.

Opening the driver's door and sliding in behind the steering wheel, he sat and stared at the carriage house for several long minutes. Considering his feelings on love and relationships, he was mystified why it even mattered. Maybe it was the fact that Lily had broken things off between them without telling him why and he was allowing curiosity to get the better of him. Or more likely, it was his stubborn pride that wouldn't allow him to drop the matter without making her tell him what had caused her to stop seeing him.

Whatever the reason, he was going to help Lily weather the emotional storm of losing her father and the family scandal that was about to erupt. Then he fully intended to get his answers from her and move on.

Two

After waking up to find Daniel had done as she asked and left her alone, Lily frowned at her feelings of disappointment. "Get a grip on yourself," she muttered as she pushed the afghan aside and sat up.

Daniel Addison was all wrong for her and the sooner she came to terms with that fact, the better off she would be. She had known when they first started seeing each other that it would end one day. It had to. They were exact opposites and wanted entirely different things out of life.

She wanted love, marriage and babies. But after going through a bitter divorce from his wife, Charisma, several years ago, those were the last things Daniel wanted. All he cared about were short-term affairs devoid of deep emotions, commitment and children. And if Lily hadn't known that from the gossip she had heard at some of the social functions around Charleston, she had certainly found out when his mother took great pleasure in telling her.

A shiver slithered down Lily's spine when she thought of how poorly she had been treated at the dinner party she and Daniel attended at Addison House, just before Christmas. His mother was, without a shadow of a doubt, the coldest, most unpleasant woman Lily had ever had the misfortune to meet. The woman had even gone so far as to accuse Lily of trying to elevate her social standing by being associated with Daniel—implying that because her father's fortune didn't go back several generations, Lily wasn't worthy of circulating among those considered to come from "old money."

She shuddered at the thought of ever being near the woman again. But more upsetting was that Charlotte Addison was the paternal grandmother of Lily's child.

Lily nibbled on her lower lip as she tried to calm the butterflies in her stomach. She was having Daniel's baby and at some point she was going to have to tell him. But how? How was she going to break the news to a man who had no interest in ever having a child of his own that whether he wanted to or not, he was going to be a daddy? And considering his feelings about children, would he try to get her to end the pregnancy?

She placed a protective hand over her still flat stomach. She truly didn't think he would ask that of her, but it wouldn't matter if he did. This baby was hers and she loved it with all of her heart.

Rising to her feet, she wandered into her studio and glanced at the drawings for the latest children's book she was illustrating. Children were so very important to her and she couldn't imagine anyone not wanting to have a child to enrich their life.

She released a shuddering breath. It would just be his loss, she thought sadly. Whether he wanted anything to do with the baby or not, it was only right to let him know about her pregnancy, and as soon as she found a good time, she fully intended to do just that.

As she stood there pondering how to go about telling him that he had fathered a child, the phone rang. When she answered, she wasn't at all surprised to hear her oldest sister's concerned voice.

"Are you all right, Lily?" Laurel asked.

"I'm fine now," Lily said, smiling.

She loved her family and the closeness they shared. But she hadn't told them about her pregnancy and she wasn't sure how to broach the subject. It was a given they would be supportive, but they were all busy with their own lives and she hated to add her problems to theirs. As public relations director for The Kincaid Group, Laurel was going to have to handle the media frenzy the scandal was sure to cause, as well as get ready for her upcoming wedding. Thankfully, their sister Kara was using her skills as a wedding and party planner to pull it all together for Laurel, but at the same time she was booked up with jobs for her thriving business, Prestige Events.

Lily could always turn to her brothers for advice, but they were no less busy than her sisters. Until today, RJ had his hands full being interim CEO of The Kincaid Group since their father's death, but she suspected he would soon be turning his attention to a legal battle as he tried to regain control of the business now that Jack

Sinclair held the majority of the shares. That left Matt. Poor Matt was so busy trying to juggle his job as director of New Business at TKG and being a single father, that he didn't have time for himself, let alone to give her advice on how she should handle this new twist in her life.

"You left so quickly this morning, I wanted to make sure that you're feeling better," Laurel went on.

"I just needed some air," Lily said, sorry for the worry she had caused her sibling. "I still can't believe that Daddy left the biggest part of the company to that awful man."

"I know," Laurel agreed, sounding as disillusioned as Lily. "We're looking into finding who owns the missing ten percent. If we can get whoever it is to vote with us, then as a whole, we'll have controlling interest in TKG. And at this point, that's imperative. After you left, Jack smugly told RJ and Matt that he expected a full report of assets, expenses, projected growth and a comprehensive customer list for TKG by the end of the month."

"What is he going to do with it?" Lily asked, alarmed. Did he intend to sell his shares back to the Kincaids at a ridiculously high price? Or was he planning to split the company and sell it off piece by piece?

"At this point, it's anyone's guess what he'll do with the information." Laurel's sigh echoed in Lily's ear. "But RJ and Matt are going to be busy working practically around the clock to get things together."

"I can only imagine how frustrated and angry RJ feels about all this." RJ was not the type of man to put up with Jack Sinclair's arrogance any longer than it took him to find a way to defeat him.

"RJ doesn't have a choice," Laurel said. "But I don't want you to worry about any of this, Lily. RJ and Matt will figure it out and if there's a way for us to regain control of TKG, they'll find it."

"Asking me not to worry is like asking me to make the sun rise in the west tomorrow morning. But I do promise I'll try." A knock on the front door had her walking out of her studio. "I have to go, Laurel. Someone's at the door. I'll talk to you tomorrow. Love you."

"Love you, too," Laurel said, ending the conversation.

Lily put the cordless unit on the charger, then continued to the door. It was probably one of her other siblings dropping by to check on her. After the way she'd fled Mr. Parsons's office this morning, she really wasn't surprised. Since she was the youngest in the family, her brothers and sisters had always watched out for her and she loved them all the more for it.

But when she opened the door, she found Daniel standing on the other side with a large paper bag in one hand and a bottle of wine in the other. "I was beginning to think you might still be napping," he said as he brushed past her and walked toward the dining area at the opposite end of the room.

"What are you doing here, Daniel?" she asked, closing the door to follow him.

Looking over his shoulder, he gave her an indulgent smile. "Don't you remember? I told you I would be back with dinner around six."

She frowned. "I remember telling you that you didn't need to bother stopping by, but I don't recall anything about you bringing dinner."

"You might have fallen asleep by that time," he said,

pulling cartons of delicious-smelling food from the paper bag to place them on the table.

"Might have?" She shook her head. "It's more likely that you purposely waited until I had gone to sleep to mention bringing dinner."

He shrugged as he removed his coat, then walked over to lay it on the back of one of the armchairs. "Either way, I did mention it." He returned to the table and picked up the bottle of wine. "Besides, you have to eat and I didn't think you would feel like making something for yourself."

Even though the food he had brought smelled heavenly and she was ravenous, she wasn't willing to give in so easily. "I might have plans," she said stubbornly.

"But you don't." He gave her a smile that caused her to feel warm all over. "Now, why don't we sit down and enjoy this before it gets cold?"

If there was one thing about Daniel Addison that she had learned in the past several months, it was that he never lacked confidence. She only wished she could say the same for herself, especially now that she was going to have to find a way to tell him about her pregnancy.

When he reached for two wineglasses on top of her small liquor cabinet, she shook her head. "I'm going to have a glass of milk."

He nodded as he removed the corkscrew from the cabinet drawer and popped the cork on the wine bottle. "Considering how sick you were this morning, that's probably a good idea."

She didn't comment as she walked into the kitchen and opened the refrigerator. It would probably be best if he was sitting down when she told him the reason behind her illness this morning and why she wasn't drinking wine with her meal.

When she returned to the dining area, she wasn't surprised that he had gotten plates from the china cabinet and was setting their places at the table. He was a man who took charge and was hands on when he saw something that had to be done. A tiny tingle coursed through her when she remembered his hands on her and the magic he created whenever he...

"Lily, are you all right?" he asked, bringing her back to the present.

"Um...of course, why do you ask?" She had to stop thinking about what they had shared in the past because there was absolutely no future in it.

A shadow of concern clouded his dark blue eyes. "You're not acting like yourself, sweetheart. You seem distracted by something."

The endearment Daniel always used made her long to go back a few months to when they first began seeing each other and everything was much simpler. His mother hadn't said those mean things to her and she hadn't known that her beloved father had been leading a double life since before she was born.

"I was just thinking about how everything was before Christmas." She shook her head as the gravity of all that had happened settled across her shoulders. "We had no way of knowing that it would be our last holiday with Daddy or that we would start out the new year with his funeral and a family scandal that will undoubtedly be talked about for years to come."

When Daniel took her glass of milk from her to set it on the table, then reached out to wrap his arms around her, Lily placed her hands on his broad chest to push away from him. Her whole world had changed in ways she could have never imagined and it was almost more than she could take in. But she couldn't allow herself to be drawn back under his spell.

"Please, Daniel," she said, trying to hold herself away from him.

"Hush, sweetheart," he whispered. "You need someone to lean on right now."

"Not literally," she said, unwilling to give up so easily.

His deep chuckle sent a shiver straight through her. "I think literal has its merits."

Unfortunately, Daniel was much stronger and the more she pushed, the closer he drew her to him. Suddenly too emotionally exhausted to resist any longer, she rested her head against his broad chest. Just for a moment, she wanted to forget that the past few weeks had happened and pretend that her life was the same as it had always been—carefree and happy.

But the feel of his hard muscles against her cheek, the steady beat of his heart and the solid strength of his arms around her, caused a longing to build inside her that had nothing to do with comfort and support. She had missed this man more than she had thought was possible, and it would be in her best interest to put distance between them.

Looking up into his navy eyes, Lily started to pull away, but just as a night creature often became trapped in the headlights of an oncoming car, she couldn't seem to look away as he slowly began to lower his head. He was going to kiss her and, for the life of her, she couldn't remember why she shouldn't let him. But the sudden rumbling of her stomach reminded both of them that she hadn't eaten anything since breakfast.

Daniel took a deep breath, kissed her forehead and smiled. "It would probably be a good idea if you eat something, sweetheart."

"I think you're right," she said, thankful that hunger had intervened and kept her from doing something she would regret later. The last thing she needed to do was fall under his spell again. Stepping back, she turned to pull out one of the chairs at the table and sat down. "What smells so delicious?"

"When I stopped by Miss Pauline's Southern Cupboard, I wasn't sure which you would prefer, baked chicken or roast beef," he said, seating himself at the head of the table. "So I got both."

"I'm positively starved," she said, meaning it. She might have been sick every morning for the past couple of weeks, but every evening, her appetite seemed to return with a vengeance. "I think I'll have a little of both. I love Miss Pauline's food."

"We also have mashed potatoes with gravy, green beans, corn fritters and fresh-made corn bread," he said, reaching for her plate. "And be sure to save room for apple pie."

"It all sounds heavenly," she said, watching him fill her plate. "I have some vanilla ice cream in the freezer that would be fantastic with the pie."

They both fell silent for several minutes as they enjoyed the delicious food. But the longer Daniel watched Lily eat, the more fascinated he became. They'd shared many meals, but he didn't think he had ever seen her quite so hungry. She was eating like a longshoreman after a full day's work at the docks of Port Charleston.

"When was the last time you ate?" he asked, watching her put another corn fritter on her plate, then reach for the carton of green beans.

She nibbled on her lower lip a moment as if trying to decide what to say. "I couldn't stand the thought of breakfast this morning," she said tentatively. "I only had a few crackers and a cup of tea. Then I slept through lunch and only woke up about an hour before you arrived with dinner."

He could understand her inability to eat earlier in the day. Knowing that she was going to come face-to-face with her father's second family for the reading of his will was enough to cause anyone to lose their appetite. And as exhausted as she had been, Daniel wasn't at all surprised that she had missed lunch. But it appeared she was making up for it now.

"Don't forget to leave room for the pie and ice cream," he said, smiling as he watched her enjoy another bite of roast beef.

"I know that the amount of butter Miss Pauline uses when she cooks is probably not the most healthy. But she has the best food in South Carolina." He watched Lily smile blissfully as a forkful of the buttery mashed potatoes disappeared into her mouth.

"I don't think it does any harm to eat like this occasionally," he said, amazed that she still had room for another bite of corn bread. "It's having food like this every day that isn't good for you. It clogs arteries and can add several pounds."

As soon as he said it, Daniel wished he could call the words back. If he had learned nothing else in his disastrous marriage, it was definitely not to mention gaining weight to a woman.

Lily slowly laid her fork on the edge of her plate

and gave him a penetrating look. "Do I look as if I've gained weight?"

Damn, Addison! Way to stick your foot in your mouth. How are you going to talk your way out of this one? Mentioning weight gain to a woman was the best way in the world to have her hand a man his head on a silver platter.

"I didn't say you looked like you had gained weight," he said, choosing his words carefully. "Just that if a person ate this way all the time, they would."

Instead of tearing into him for mentioning weight at all, as he thought she would, to his surprise Lily smiled as she shrugged one shoulder. "I suppose gaining a little weight isn't the end of the world."

It was all Daniel could do to keep his mouth from dropping open. If he had made the same blunder with Charisma, his ex-wife would have made his life a living hell for at least a month and it would have cost him an expensive piece of jewelry or a whole new wardrobe of designer clothes to pay for his sins. Then, every time they had any kind of disagreement, she would have dragged his comment on gaining weight into the fray. But Lily seemed to take it in stride and didn't act at all concerned about it. Amazing!

Deciding there was no sense in pushing his luck any further, he stood up to carry their plates into the kitchen. "I'll get the pie and ice cream."

"I'll help," she said, starting to rise from her chair.

Smiling, he shook his head. "Just sit there and relax. You've had a rough day and although I'm lost about most things in a kitchen, I'm pretty sure I can handle dipping a scoop of ice cream onto a piece of pie."

When he returned a couple of minutes later and

placed the dessert in front of her, Lily smiled as she picked up her spoon. "For a man who doesn't know his way around a kitchen, you did pretty well. It looks delicious."

He chuckled. "I'm afraid this is as far as my culinary skills go. Why do you think I took you out to eat all those times?"

"I really hadn't thought much about it," she said, closing her eyes as she savored the combined flavors of vanilla, cinnamon and apple.

As Daniel watched, her expression changed to one of pure pleasure and he couldn't help but remember the times he had seen a similar look come over her as he made love to her. A spark ignited in his lower belly at the thought of how responsive she had been, how passionate.

He swallowed hard and tried to think of something innocuous. He might have succeeded had it not been for Lily slowly licking a drop of melted ice cream from her lips. The action reminded him of other talents she had with that perfect little tongue and had him shifting to relieve the mounting pressure of his suddenly too-tight trousers.

When had the simple act of eating a piece of pie become so damn erotic?

"Don't you want yours?" she asked, unaware of his wayward thoughts.

Daniel stared down at the dessert in front of him. Oh, he wanted, all right, but it wasn't pie that he was craving. It was the memory of her delicious body pressed to his that fueled his hunger and caused his mouth to feel as if it had been stuffed with cotton.

Taking a gulp of his wine, he forced his body to

relax. He had no doubt that at any other time, he would find Miss Pauline's pie quite tasty. At the moment, it might as well have been a piece of rubber on his plate.

"Are you okay?" Lily asked, reaching over to steal a spoonful of his ice cream.

Nodding, he did his best to focus on Lily and her seemingly insatiable appetite. She had finished her pie and ice cream and now it appeared she was starting on his.

"I'm not all that hungry, why don't we share?" he said, picking up his spoon. He dipped it into the melting ice cream, then held it to her lips.

Her eyes met his as she opened her mouth and he immediately knew he had made a huge error in judgment. In all of his thirty-eight years, he didn't think he had experienced anything more provocative than having her gaze locked with his as her lips slowly closed around the bite of ice cream. His libido kicked into overdrive, reminding him that it had been the better part of three weeks since they had made love.

"I really hate to cut the evening short," he said suddenly, making a show of glancing at his watch. "But I just remembered I have to make an overseas call as soon as the Japanese markets open."

Lily had been on an emotional roller coaster for the past several days, and taking advantage of a woman's vulnerability to seduce her had never been his style. But if he didn't get out of there and damn quick, that was exactly what was going to happen.

"Thank you for bringing supper," she said, placing her napkin on the table beside her plate. "It really was delicious."

"It looked as if you might have been happy with my choices," he said dryly.

Confident that he had his body back under control, Daniel rose to his feet, quickly helped Lily clear the table, then walked into the living room to find his coat. "I'll come by tomorrow to see how you're doing."

Lily followed him to the door. "Thank you for your concern, Daniel. I do appreciate it. But it really isn't necessary. It may take some time, but I'm going to be fine. Really."

It appeared she was back to giving him the brush-off and that didn't sit well with him one bit. Turning back, he didn't think twice about reaching up to run the back of his hand along her smooth cheek. As he searched her upturned face for what she might be thinking, Lily swayed ever so slightly and leaned into his touch. He could tell it wasn't a conscious action on her part, but it was all the indication he needed that she still desired him. Taking her into his arms, he gathered her to him.

"Daniel, don't—"

"Hush, sweetheart," he said, brushing her mouth with his. He intended to remind her of how responsive she had always been to his touch.

Teasing her with feathery kisses, he nibbled at her perfect lips to test her willingness to allow him to continue. When she moaned softly and brought her hands up to his chest to grasp the fabric of his shirt as if to steady herself, elated satisfaction coursed through him. Whatever her reason had been for trying to distance herself from him the past few weeks, it wasn't because she no longer wanted him.

As difficult as it was, Daniel fought the urge to deepen the kiss. He had proven his point and although he fully intended for them to become lovers once again, he wanted to build her frustration to the degree that she could no longer deny her need for him.

"I'll see you tomorrow, Lily," he said, untangling her fingers from his shirt to take a step back.

The confusion on her pretty face and the disappointment she couldn't quite hide caused him to smile and, before she had the chance to find her voice and protest, he opened the door and stepped out into the cool January night. His body throbbed with longing and Daniel knew as surely as he knew his own name, he was in for a miserable, sleepless night. But in the long run, it was going to be well worth whatever hell he had to go through to have Lily back in his life and in his bed.

He just hoped he didn't go completely insane before that happened.

Staring at the closed door, Lily couldn't believe the myriad of emotions roiling inside her. She had wanted Daniel to actually kiss her, not just tease her to the point of utter frustration. But that was exactly what had happened and her disappointment that he hadn't kissed her senseless led to a deep annoyance with herself for wishing that he had.

She shook her head as she turned to walk into the kitchen to load the dishwasher. She couldn't believe how easy it would have been for her to throw common sense out the window and lose herself in Daniel's arms. Thank heavens he had backed off and hadn't taken things any further. She wouldn't have been able to resist him and that was something she had to do at all costs. Calling a halt to their seeing each other had been one of the hardest things she had ever done, but it was the only way to ensure she didn't suffer more hurt when he found out about the baby and walked away. They wanted different things in life, and it was best to stop now before she lost her heart completely.

But that didn't explain why she had failed to let him know about the baby when he noticed her voracious appetite. It had been the perfect opportunity to explain why she ate more than usual and that she fully expected to gain weight as her pregnancy progressed.

Her pregnancy hormones had to be responsible for her mixed emotions as well as her reluctance to let him know he was going to be a father. Either that or it was the dread of telling him and knowing for certain that his interest in her would come to a swift and permanent end.

Sighing, Lily started the dishwasher and wandered into the living room. She supposed she should work on the new children's book she had been commissioned to illustrate. But when the family had been informed that her father had died of an apparent self-inflicted gunshot wound at his TKG office, she had put work on hold and hadn't been able to concentrate on it since.

She still couldn't believe all that had happened over the past several days—especially what had taken place during the reading of her father's will just that morning. But as she thought about her father's betrayal of his legitimate family, she remembered the letters Mr. Parsons had given to them. She had forgotten about them after running into Daniel at the law office.

Lily stared at her purse, which was lying on the end table, and her hand shook when she finally worked up the courage to reach for it. She wasn't at all certain she was prepared to read her father's last thoughts to her.

But then, she didn't think she would ever be ready for what was probably his final goodbye.

For several long moments after retrieving the envelope from her bag, she simply sat there holding it while she stared at her name in her father's handwriting on the front. Given all that she had learned about him in the past several days, could she even believe what he had to say to her?

Finally, she decided that whether she believed what he had written or not, the only way to know would be to open the envelope. Taking a deep breath, she turned it over and, using her fingernail, lifted the sealed flap. When she pulled out the letter and unfolded it, her breath caught on a sob when she noticed the date. It was only a few days before he died.

My dearest Lily,

One of the greatest joys in my life has always been that you thought of me as your knight in shining armor. Whether it was chasing away the monsters from your closet when you were three, kissing a skinned elbow to make the hurt go away when you were eight or listening to your hopes and dreams as you got ready to go off to college, every second of the time we spent together has been very special and I never wanted you to see me as anything but your hero. Unfortunately, Lily-girl, I'm just a man with a man's faults.

By now you've discovered that your dear old dad had feet of clay and wasn't quite the champion you thought me to be. I never meant to disappoint you and I hope one day you can find it in your heart to forgive me for my weaknesses. No matter what you hear about me and my transgressions, please know that the bond between us was not only real, but very precious to me.

One of the many things that you and I shared together was a love of the historic district of Charleston. That's why I'm leaving you the Colonel Samuel Beauchamp House in the Battery. It's one of the city's finest examples of Southern architecture and I know from the Saturday afternoons we spent in White Point Gardens when you were a child that it's your favorite. You may meet with a bit of resistance from the former owner, Charlotte Addison, but stand your ground, Lily. You're a strong, capable young woman and whatever decision you make concerning the property, I know it will be the right one for you.

I love you, Lily, and I have no doubt that without me you'll find the strength to weather whatever challenges life brings your way. From the moment you were born, you have been my little princess—the ray of sunshine that brightened my life and I feel very blessed that you are my daughter.

With love,
Daddy

Tears streamed down Lily's face as she slowly folded the letter and returned it to the envelope. Deep down she had known that the closeness between her and her father couldn't have been a lie, but the hurt and disillusionment of the past few days had overshadowed their relationship and caused her to question what she knew in her heart to be true. No matter what he had done, her father had loved her.

Unfortunately, it was going to take her some time to get past his handing over controlling interest in TKG to Jack Sinclair, while more or less cutting his legitimate children out of the picture. Lily sighed heavily. Then there was his betrayal of her mother, even though Elizabeth Kincaid didn't seem to be nearly as upset about the disturbing revelations as Lily would have thought.

"What were you thinking, Daddy?" she murmured aloud.

As she sat there wondering what her father could have possibly thought to accomplish by what she could only describe as inexcusable choices, something she had read in the letter caused her to catch her breath.

Quickly removing the letter from the envelope, she reread what her father had left her and the name of the Beauchamp mansion's former owner—Daniel's unpleasant, ill-tempered mother. Dear heavens, what had he gotten her into?

Three

After a miserable couple of hours waiting for her morning sickness to subside, Lily sat with her elbow propped on her art table, her chin cupped in her palm. She wasn't accomplishing anything by staring off into space, but she couldn't seem to settle down to work. All she had been able to think about since reading her father's letter the night before was what she was going to do with the Beauchamp property.

She had never been inside the structure, but from the outside the beautiful four-story antebellum mansion had always captured her eye. With three levels of piazzas overlooking White Point Gardens and Charleston Harbor beyond, she was almost certain that the Sullivan's Island Lighthouse and Fort Sumter could be seen in the distance.

She smiled wistfully. As a child, whenever she had

passed by the stately double house, she had imagined how wonderful it would be to stand in the cupola on top of the tall roof and pretend to be a princess, surveying her kingdom below. And now the home she had thought to be as grand as any castle was actually hers.

What on earth was she going to do with it? It was such a big house and she didn't need all that space. Of course, when the baby came there would be the two of them, but it was still going to be much more room than they would need.

As she pondered what to do with the mansion, she was reminded of her father's warning. What had he meant when he told her that she would meet with opposition from Charlotte Addison? What was that all about?

Deciding she wasn't getting anything done anyway, Lily left her art table and walked over to the laptop on her desk. With everything being accessible online these days, she should be able to find out some of the mansion's history and the connection that Daniel's mother had with the place. A few of the homes in the Battery had been passed from one generation to the next, never being occupied by anyone outside of the family who built them. A sense of dread began to settle in the pit of Lily's stomach.

Her suspicions were confirmed when the first link she clicked on was a twenty-year-old article on homes in the Battery. According to the reporter from the *Post and Courier,* Charleston's newspaper, the mansion had been in Colonel Samuel Beauchamp's family since it was built in the late 1700s. It went on to read that the home had been passed down to his descendants and, at the time the article was written, belonged to Mrs. Charlotte Beauchamp-Addison, who anticipated keeping it in the family when she eventually passed it on to her son, Daniel.

A chill traveled the length of Lily's spine. No wonder Charlotte Addison had treated her so poorly when she had shown up with Daniel at the dinner party. She obviously resented the fact that Reginald Kincaid, one of the nouveau riche, as the woman had called him, had purchased her ancestral home. Lily had been condemned simply because she was his daughter. If the mansion had meant so much to her, what could have possibly caused Charlotte to sell it to him?

Lily suddenly caught her breath. Did Daniel know about all this? Was he aware that her father had bought the home he was supposed to own one day and could that be the reason he had become interested in her to begin with? Had he hoped to somehow use his association with her to get the Beauchamp mansion back into his family?

Frowning, she nibbled on her lower lip. She didn't think that was the case. He had told her on more than one occasion that he loved the new condo he'd bought after his divorce. It was close to the Addison Industries office building and within walking distance of Charleston's French Quarter.

Trying to unravel her tangled thoughts, Lily jumped when the phone rang. "Hello Matt," she said, recognizing her brother's office number on the caller ID.

"Lily, could you do me a favor and watch Flynn one night a week for the next several weeks?" Her brother sounded rushed and she could only imagine the tremendous amount of stress he was under after hearing that

Jack Sinclair was going to be in control of The Kincaid Group.

"Of course," she said, smiling. "You know how much I love my nephew."

"Great. RJ and I are going to be working late for who knows how long and I'm trying to line up babysitters," Matt explained.

"What nights do you need me?" Lily asked. She loved spending time with Flynn and found that playing with him had inspired some of her best illustrations.

"Are you free Thursday evenings?" he asked. "Laurel is watching him Mondays and Kara has Tuesdays and Wednesdays covered."

"That's fine. What about the weekends?"

"He's going to spend Friday nights and all day on Saturdays with Mom." Lily heard him shuffle papers and realized Matt was trying to work and arrange child care at the same time. "I've already told RJ that Jack Sinclair can wait on the reports he wants until hell freezes over if need be, but Sundays are mine with Flynn and I'm not going to give that up for Sinclair or anyone else."

"Good for you," Lily said, meaning it. "Is there anything else I can do to help?"

She heard her brother sigh heavily. "Not unless you can figure out a way to add several more hours to the day."

"Sorry, Matt, but I don't think anyone has figured out how to do that just yet. What time do you need me on Thursday evenings?" When he named a time, she added, "Please take care of yourself. Whatever is going to happen, it's not worth sacrificing your health."

"Thanks, sis," he said, sounding tired. "I'll try to keep that in mind."

After ending the call, Lily started to return to her worktable to try to get something done, when the phone rang again.

"Good afternoon, sweetheart," Daniel said cheerfully. "I'm about five minutes away. Would you like to start setting the table for lunch?"

"Daniel, I'm not sure—"

"Have you eaten yet?"

"No, but—"

"Then set the table," he said, breaking the connection.

Lily stared at the phone in her hand for several seconds before placing it on the desk to go set the table. She thought about calling Daniel back and insisting that he respect her wishes to be left alone. But she did need to talk to him and try to find out how much he knew about the sale of the Beauchamp mansion to her father as well as try to find a way to tell him about the baby.

Maybe then she would know more about what kind of battle her father had gotten her into with the Addisons. And how Daniel was going to react when he learned about the baby.

As Daniel steered his Mercedes around the Kincaid mansion to the carriage house in the back, he couldn't help but smile. After having lunch with Lily, she had asked him to stay for a bit so they could talk, but he'd had to decline because of an afternoon meeting with the president of the dockworkers' union. He had, however, managed to convince her to let him pick her up after the meeting for a trip to check out the most recently renovated exhibit at the aquarium, then have an early dinner at the little bistro she loved in the French Quarter. As far as he was concerned, that was progress in getting things back to the way they had been before his mother's dinner party.

Parking the car, he hesitated before opening the driver's door. Everything had been going great between them until the night of the party. But immediately afterward, Lily had decided to be conveniently busy whenever he asked her out. Could his mother have possibly said something to Lily that evening, causing her to have a sudden change of heart about seeing him? Or had the thirteen-year difference in their ages suddenly become a problem for her?

He dismissed the latter thought outright. Surely he would have had an indication if age had become an issue. They both enjoyed most of the same things and there had never been any sort of gap in conversation when they discussed the kind of music they liked to listen to, the books they had read or type of movies they preferred. No, the problem had to have been generated by his mother. He narrowed his eyes. It wouldn't surprise him if she had said something to insult or hurt Lily. In the past, when Charlotte Addison felt that someone was beneath her, she had never hesitated to let that person know all about just who she was in the pecking order of society. On more than one occasion, he had witnessed her boasting about her family pedigree and the fact that the Beauchamps were considered to be in the highest echelon of Charleston's social order.

But when could she have had the chance that evening to talk to Lily alone? He had purposely tried to keep

Lily at his side throughout the evening, anticipating that his mother might say something insulting. And he had been certain that given the chance, she would. Not only was The Kincaid Group the chief rival of Addison Industries, his mother seemed to have a huge problem with Reginald Kincaid in particular.

As he got out of the car and walked toward Lily's door, Daniel decided that by dinner he fully intended to have his questions answered and things straightened out between them. Then at his earliest possible convenience, he would confront his mother and firmly suggest that she mind her own business and stop meddling in his social life.

"I see you're ready to go," Daniel said when Lily stepped out of the carriage house before he reached the door.

"Actually, I had just returned from checking on my mother to see how she's doing when I heard you arrive," Lily said as she walked toward his car.

"How is your mother faring?" he asked, knowing the entire family had been dealing with one shock after another since their ordeal began.

"Momma is holding up surprisingly well," Lily said, frowning. "It makes me wonder if she might not be in a state of shock and everything that's happened will come crashing down on top of her later."

Opening the passenger door, Daniel helped her into the car, then walked around to slide into the driver's seat. "Sometimes grief brings out a strength in people they never knew they had," he suggested, suspecting that might be the case. With a quiet grace about her, Elizabeth Kincaid had always impressed him as having the heart and soul of a steel magnolia lying just beneath the surface of her soft-spoken, genteel exterior.

"I think you might be right," Lily said. "It's like she's become the rock that the rest of us are leaning on."

Reaching over, he covered her hand with his. "And don't forget. I'm here for you too, sweetheart."

Lily gave him an odd look before she finally nodded. "Thank you, Daniel. I appreciate your compassion, but as I've told you, I'm going to be fine."

Neither had a lot to say on the drive to the aquarium and Daniel hoped that the exhibit he wanted to show her would help relieve some of her tension and stress. "When I heard the plans for renovating this area of the aquarium, I knew it was something you would enjoy," he said as he bought two cups of shrimp from Gilligan's Shrimp Shack not far from the entrance to the exhibit.

Lily eyed the two plastic feeding sticks the attendant handed him as they walked toward the Saltmarsh Aviary. "What are we supposed to do with those?"

"We're going to feed the stingrays," he said, anticipating her reaction. He wasn't disappointed when her eyes brightened with almost childlike excitement.

"I've always thought stingrays look so graceful as they swim," Lily said as they walked up to the enormous tank.

He placed a shrimp on the end of one of the sticks, and handed it to her. "Just stick it down into the water and wait."

As he watched, Lily did as he instructed and in no time a large ray glided up to the stick and ate the shrimp. "Oh, Daniel, this is definitely my new favorite thing about the aquarium."

Her enthusiasm was infectious and by the time both

shrimp cups were empty, Daniel felt as if he were a good ten years younger. It was always this way when he was with Lily. Her zest for life never failed to improve his mood and he found that his outlook wasn't nearly as jaded and cynical as it had been just a few hours ago.

"Thank you for bringing me," Lily said as they walked on to view the puffer fish and diamondback terrapins in the mock saltmarsh tidal creek.

He shook his head. "No, I'm the one who should be thanking you." Reaching down, he took her hand in his and brought it to his lips to kiss the back. "Seeing all this wouldn't have been nearly as much fun without you."

By the time they left the aquarium, Lily looked more relaxed and he gave himself a mental pat on the back for thinking to bring her to the exhibit. "What do you have planned for after dinner?" he asked on the short drive to her favorite bistro.

For the second time that afternoon, she gave him a look as if trying to decide what she wanted to say. "Mr. Parsons stopped by my mother's this morning to drop off the keys to the different properties my father left to me and my siblings. I thought I would go take a look at the home I inherited."

"Where's it located?"

"In the Battery."

"Nice area," he said, meaning it. He had been raised in the Battery, and it was where some of the finest homes in Charleston were located. Steering the car into the restaurant's parking lot, he switched off the engine and turned to face her. "Since we're already out, why don't I drive you over there after we eat?"

She gave him that look again—the one she had been

giving him all afternoon. If he didn't know better, he would swear she suspected him of something. But he didn't have a clue what he could have done to deserve it.

"That might be a good idea," she finally said. "I think I'd like to get your opinion on what I should do with the place."

As he guided her into the bistro, Daniel grinned. "If you want to know how to pack it, ship it or liquidate it, I'm your guy. Decorating? Not so much."

After a scrumptious dinner, Daniel drove along South Battery Street toward the Beauchamp mansion, and Lily couldn't help but feel a bit apprehensive about touring the house with him. She purposely hadn't told him that the home she inherited was once owned by his mother—the very house that was supposed to one day be his. She wasn't sure why she had omitted the information, other than she had a feeling his immediate reaction when he saw the place would tell her if he was interested in getting it back or really didn't care about it.

"That's it," she said, pointing to the stately home up ahead.

"You inherited Colonel Sam's old place?" Daniel asked, clearly astounded. "Up until fifteen years ago, this used to belong to my mother."

His surprise was genuine and Lily was almost certain that Daniel was unaware her father had bought the home. "I've always thought it was one of the most beautiful mansions in the Battery," she said, smiling.

He shrugged as he turned the car into the driveway. "I guess it's all right."

"Don't you like historic homes?" she asked, wondering how anyone could resist the charm and beauty of antebellum architecture.

"I think they're great when someone takes the time to keep them up," he answered, getting out of the car. When he came around to open her door for her, he added, "It's when they're allowed to fall into a state of disrepair that they look like any other old house that's been let go."

"The outside looks as if someone has been taking good care of this one," she said, crossing her fingers that the inside looked just as nice.

"I hope for your sake they have," he said, guiding her up the steps onto the piazza. "The last time I was in this place it was in need of some serious renovations and looked to me like it could turn into a bottomless money pit."

Reaching into her handbag, Lily removed the set of keys Mr. Parsons had tagged as belonging to the house. "I hope the electricity is on. Otherwise, I'll have to come back tomorrow in the daylight to see what needs to be done."

Daniel took the keys from her and, unlocking the door, stepped inside ahead of her. "Let me find the switch and we'll see if the lights work."

When the foyer's crystal chandelier sparkled to life, Lily crossed the threshold and felt as if she had indeed entered the princess's castle. Apparently her father had seen to it that the mansion had been completely restored to its original grandeur.

"This is everything I thought it would be and more," Lily said, in awe of her surroundings.

The walls, wainscoting and ornate dentiled ceiling cornice had been painted a rich cream that glowed warmly in the chandelier's light and contrasted perfectly with the highly polished heart-pine floor. A graceful sweeping staircase with a black cypress banister and steps ascended to the upper floors and Lily could only imagine how beautiful the rest of the house had to be.

"Wow," Daniel said, looking around. "I'm impressed. Your dad spent a small fortune to bring this old place back to life. I've never seen it look this good."

"I can't believe it's mine," Lily said, falling in love with the house all over again.

"Let's check out the rest of it," he said, taking her by the hand.

As he led her through the mansion, Lily marveled at the attention that had been paid to detail. Every room was fully furnished and although the furniture was new, it had been chosen to complement the antebellum style, while still projecting a comfortable homey atmosphere.

Whoever designed the master suite had pulled out all the stops to make it the most luxurious room in the house. From the balcony off the sitting room overlooking the courtyard below, to the his-and-her bathrooms, the interior designer had outdone himself.

By the time she and Daniel had toured all the rooms and walked out onto the lighted terrace, Lily had to ask, "How could your mother part with such a beautiful place?"

"It didn't look anything like this when she owned it and besides, she really didn't have a choice." Putting his arm around her shoulders, he led her across the yard toward the carriage house. "Right after I graduated from college, my dad died and I had to take over Addison Industries. That's when we discovered that he wasn't the best of managers. The business was in such bad shape financially, it took her selling off the summer home on Hilton Head Island, as well as parting with this place, just for her to survive until I could get the business back in the black and out of the danger of bankruptcy."

"I'm so sorry, Daniel." Lily couldn't begin to imagine how stressful the situation had to have been for him. "You've done an amazing job of bringing it back. I've heard RJ and my father talk about Addison Industries being TKG's toughest competitor."

He shrugged. "It wasn't easy, but I think it was harder on my mom than anyone else. For the first time in her life, she had to adhere to a strict budget and she was scared to death that some of her snooty friends would find out that she was on the verge of being destitute."

Lily couldn't help but wonder how Charlotte Addison's pride had survived such a devastating blow. "Did you know she had sold the home to my father?"

"I had my hands full with getting Addison Industries back on its feet," he said, shaking his head. "I didn't have time, nor did I care what she did with this place, just as long as I didn't have to deal with it." His adamant tone convinced Lily that Daniel truly had no idea who had bought the mansion or that he had any interest in getting it back.

As he started to unlock the door to the carriage house, she turned and, rising on tiptoe, impulsively kissed his cheek.

"What was that for?" he asked, chuckling as he turned and wrapped her in his arms.

"I'm just happy," she said, not wanting to explain about her unfounded suspicions. "Do you mind?"

"You're not going to get any complaints out of me," he said, using his index finger to trace her jawline.

His gentle touch reminded her of how tender he could be, how much care he took when he made love to her. "Daniel, I'm not certain—"

"I'll be sure for both of us," he said, lowering his head to brush her lips with his.

When his mouth settled over hers, Lily brought her hands up to his chest to push away from him, to put distance between herself and the temptation he posed. The issue of how much he knew about her father buying the house had been settled, but she had yet to tell him the news that would no doubt put a permanent end to his attraction to her.

But as his arms tightened around her and he traced her lips with his tongue, she abandoned all thought and allowed him to kiss her the way she had wanted him to do the night before. There would be plenty of time within the next few days to tell him about the baby and face the future without Daniel in her life.

As he explored her with a thoroughness that threatened to turn her insides to warm pudding, a tingling sensation began to spread throughout her body and she welcomed his deepening of the kiss. It had been the better part of three weeks since he had held her like this, made her feel as if she was the most cherished creature on earth. And heaven help her, she didn't want him to stop.

He pulled her closer and the feel of his hard, muscular body pressed to hers sent a flash of heat racing from the top of her head to the soles of her feet. His chest muscles beneath her hands flexed as she clutched his shirt and she could feel his heart pounding against her fingertips.

"I've missed you, sweetheart," he said, easing away from the kiss. "I've missed holding you like this."

"Me, too."

Lily could have denied that she had missed him, but what was the point? Her response to him had been every bit as eager as it had always been and there was no sense in her lying to either one of them.

"What happened, Lily?" he whispered close to her ear. "Why did you stop seeing me?"

"Please, not now," she begged, not wanting reality to intrude. She kissed the exposed skin at his open collar. "Could we please leave this for another time?"

Just when she thought he was going to press the issue, he leaned back and, staring down into her eyes for several long moments, finally nodded. "It can wait for now." He gave her a smile that made her feel warm all over. "Why don't we check out the carriage house, then lock up and go back to your place."

"It sounds like we have a plan, Mr. Addison," she agreed. "You can drop me off and then go home."

He gave her an exasperated look, but didn't comment.

She knew he was confused by her insistence that she wanted to be left alone, then her allowing him to hold her, kiss her. But she was doing her best to distance herself from him and if he wasn't such a source of temptation for her, she would be able to do that. Unfortunately, from the moment he took her into his arms at the Autumn Ball, she had discovered a weakness within herself that she hadn't known existed. Whenever Daniel touched her, she seemed to lose a will of her own. It was something she needed to work on—had to work on—or risk losing her sanity when he found out about the baby and lost interest in her.

When they entered the carriage house, they found that her father had turned it into a studio with huge floor-to-ceiling windows to let in plenty of natural light. "It looks like your dad had planned on an artist using this," Daniel said, giving her a knowing wink as they looked around the spacious work area.

Lily had a hard time blinking back her tears. It was clear her father had her in mind when he'd commissioned the renovations of the property, meaning that he had planned for some time to make her childhood dream of living here come true.

"When I was a little girl, Daddy used to take me to White Point Gardens across the street. We would sit for hours on one of the benches staring at this place and I would tell him stories I made up about the princess who lived here."

"I'll bet she had red hair and blue eyes," Daniel teased, walking up behind her to put his arms around her.

She nodded as she indulged herself just one more time and leaned back against him. "The princess would stand in the cupola and look out at Charleston Harbor."

"What was she looking for?" His deep baritone vibrated against her back and caused a delightful fluttering in her lower belly.

"She was watching for her prince to sail into Charleston Harbor and come home to live with her in the castle," Lily answered.

"Of course," he murmured close to her ear. "Any princess worth her salt always waits for her prince, whether he's sailing up in a ship or riding a big white horse."

"Now you're making fun of me," she said, smiling as she turned in his arms to face him.

"Maybe just a little," he said, grinning. "Have you ever thought of writing children's books, instead of just illustrating them?"

"My father always thought I should," she said, doing her best to stifle a yawn. She had missed the afternoon nap that she had been taking since becoming pregnant. "But since college, the major children's publishers have kept me so busy illustrating for others, I haven't had time to think much about it."

"You should," he said, kissing her forehead. "Now, why don't I walk you to my car and then I'll go back and lock up. You're starting to look pretty tired."

She nodded as they left the carriage house. "It has been a long day."

While Lily waited in the car for Daniel to return from turning off lights and locking the house, she couldn't help but think about what her father had said in his letter. She was a strong, capable woman who he was confident would make the right decision about the mansion. He hadn't insisted that she keep the property, but he had everything in place for her, anticipating that she would want to.

Staring up at the stately home, she knew it was foolish for one person to even contemplate living alone in a house with more than ten thousand square feet of living space. But her father had spared no expense in getting it ready for her. He had given her her dream and, wise or not, she was going to take it.

"I've made a decision about what I'm going to do with the mansion," Lily said when Daniel returned to the car.

"And just what might that be?" he asked, starting the car and driving it down the driveway to the street.

"It's going to take me a week or so to make arrangements, but as soon as I can get things packed up, I'm going to move in and live here."

Four

For the next week after touring the mansion with Lily, Daniel found himself embroiled in a labor dispute with the dockworkers that left little time for anything but a few hurried phone calls and a standing order at the local florist for a daily bouquet of flowers to be delivered to her apartment. Lily hadn't asked him to stop calling and seemed to appreciate all of the flowers, but they still weren't completely back to where they had been with their affair before Christmas. That was the first thing he intended to remedy as soon as possible.

It would already have been taken care of by now, if not for the snag that had developed with the labor force. He had thought he and the union president had worked things out the day he had taken Lily to the aquarium, but apparently the rank and file had other ideas. Just that afternoon, he had been able to come to an agreement with the dockworkers and anticipated being able to spend a lot more time with her.

Unfortunately, tonight was not one of those times. In one of their phone conversations, Lily had explained that she would be babysitting her nephew on Thursday evenings for the next few weeks, while her brothers worked on getting reports ready for Jack Sinclair. So what was he going to do with his evening?

As he sat at his desk contemplating his options, his cell phone rang. "Daniel Addison," he said, answering the call.

"Daniel, I'm so glad I caught you."

"Hello, Charlotte." At her request, he hadn't called her "Mom" or "Mother" in years.

"I haven't talked to you since Christmas Day and I was wondering when I may expect a visit," she said in her usual formal tone.

"I'm free this evening," he answered, deciding not to put her off. He did want to talk to his mother about the night of the dinner party and what she might have said to Lily. This evening seemed as good a time as any to do that.

"I think that would be marvelous, Daniel. Shall I have Cook set an extra place for dinner?" she asked.

Barely able to keep from rolling his eyes at her pretentiousness, he sighed heavily. "Sure, why not."

"I'll expect you at six then." His mother ended the call as she always did, without saying goodbye.

Twenty minutes later, as he drove to the home he had grown up in on East Battery Street, just half a mile from the Beauchamp mansion, Daniel couldn't help but think about how vastly different his childhood had been from Lily's. She had been raised in a loving home with several brothers and sisters, who remained quite close as adults.

He, on the other hand, had been the only child of a frequently aloof mother and a father who could only be described as a dreamer. To say his parents were a mismatched couple was an understatement and Daniel couldn't understand how they had managed to stay together for over twenty-five years of marriage.

Charlotte Beauchamp-Addison was all about maintaining her standing in society and feeling superior among her circle of so-called friends, while George Addison had drifted through life with a laid-back, "whatever will be, will be" attitude. Daniel sometimes even wondered if his father had purposely ignored the signs of an impending heart attack, in order to die and get away from the pretentiousness and snobbery of life with Charlotte.

When he parked his car, Daniel entered through the back door of the house. He had always liked coming in through the kitchen. At least he got a warm greeting from Rosemary, the housekeeper and cook who had worked for his parents for as long as he could remember. It hadn't been easy, but he had managed to see that the woman remained on the job, even through the times when he hadn't been sure he would be able to bring Addison Industries back to solvency. But the woman was, and always had been, considered part of the family.

"How's my favorite girl?" Daniel asked, smiling as he walked over to where the gray-haired woman stood, stirring something in a pot on the stove.

"I'm mad at you, Daniel Addison," she said, her attention never wavering from what she was cooking.

"You haven't been by to see me in almost three weeks. Do you know how hard it is for a woman my age not seeing the boy I helped raised? I could very well die of a broken heart."

Daniel chuckled as he kissed the woman's wrinkled cheek. "I'm sorry, Rosemary, but there's been a lot going on since Christmas. Will it make you feel better if I try to do better in the future?"

She turned to give him a sympathetic look. "I heard about Miss Lily's daddy. How is that poor child doing?"

"As well as can be expected under the circumstances," he answered. The woman had only met Lily once, at the dinner party before the holidays, but she and Lily had hit it off right away.

"My heart goes out to that girl, losing him the way she did," Rosemary said, her kind brown eyes shining with unshed tears. "You be sure to tell her that I've got her and her family in my thoughts and prayers."

"I'll do that," he said, knowing the kind-hearted woman his mother insisted on calling "Cook" was completely sincere with her sympathy.

Continuing into the sitting room, he found Charlotte posed by the window, staring out at Charleston Harbor. It was her favorite place to be when receiving guests.

"I don't know why you insist on coming in the back way like a common servant, Daniel," she admonished, turning to face him.

"Hello to you too, Charlotte," he said, sitting down in one of the chairs by the fireplace. "How have you been?"

His question was all it took to get his mother started on the various charity functions she was helping to plan and the latest gossip circulating through the garden club. Barely listening, something she said suddenly caught his attention.

"What was that?" he asked, sitting up straight in the chair.

"I said that Madelyn Worthington told me all about poor Elizabeth Kincaid's betrayal by that wretched man," Charlotte said, patting an imaginary out-of-place hair back into place. "I've known for years that Reginald Kincaid was nothing but a low-bred scoundrel and I'm not the least bit surprised he turned out to be such an embarrassment to his family. Having a mistress and two bastard children in Greenville is just a disgrace."

"Only one of the woman's sons belongs to Kincaid," he corrected. "And when did you start feeling sorry for Elizabeth Kincaid?" He distinctly remembered Charlotte referring to the woman as being a fool for marrying beneath her station.

His mother ignored the question, asking one of her own. "Are you still keeping company with that youngest Kincaid girl?"

"As a matter of fact, I am," he said proudly.

Charlotte looked anything but pleased. "Really? I thought the two of you had a parting of the ways just before Christmas."

Daniel narrowed his eyes. Now he knew his mother had something to do with his and Lily's breakup. Otherwise, how would she have known?

"We stopped seeing each other for a few weeks, but just recently started dating again." Technically they had only gone out once since running into each other at the lawyer's office, but he fully intended for their trip to the aquarium to be the first of many outings they shared. "Why do you ask?"

"Oh, the night of my dinner party it seemed like she was losing interest in continuing your association," his mother said calmly.

With years of practice at being a master manipulator, he wasn't fooled by Charlotte's disinterested demeanor. His mother knew a lot more about why Lily tried to end their affair than he did and he intended to find out what that was.

"What did you say to her?" he asked. "And don't tell me you don't know what I'm talking about, Charlotte. I know exactly how you operate."

She didn't so much as flinch at his accusation. "I just pointed out that since your divorce, you've made it no secret that you aren't interested in anything long-term with a woman or marrying to carry on the family name." Her smug smile caused him to clench his back teeth together so hard, he was surprised it didn't break his jaw. "She comes from a large family and I'm sure that she has ideas of raising a brood of her own one day. It's better that she knows now that isn't what you're interested in than to give her false hope for the future. Besides, she doesn't have the breeding of a young woman suited for a man with your standing in the community."

"And I guess Charisma did?" Daniel retorted.

"I'll admit that Charisma was a bit high-strung, but you can't deny she had a suitable background," Charlotte answered as if the issue was as important to him as it was to her. "Her family has been a part of Charleston society almost as long as the Beauchamps and Addisons. She would have passed along the traits you would want in an offspring."

"I shouldn't be surprised that you thought she was good wife material," he said, unable to keep the bitter tone from his voice. "She's just like you, and I think that the traits you seem to think are so important would be better off not polluting the next generation."

"Charisma is like me, isn't she?" Charlotte said, smiling as if he had paid her a compliment and completely ignoring his disdain for the qualities her grandchild might inherit. She shook her head. "She was my best hope for a grandchild to carry on the family's esteemed name."

"Yeah, the two of you were as alike as I've ever seen—sweet as honey when things are going your way, but when they aren't, you turn as vicious as a shark in a feeding frenzy." He shook his head. "If I had wanted to carry on the family name, it certainly wouldn't have been with Charisma."

"Then why did you bother marrying her in the first place?" Charlotte asked, raising one darkly penciled eyebrow.

"Because, like you, she only showed the side of herself that she wanted me to see until she got her hooks in me," he said, disgusted with himself for not seeing through his ex-wife's facade sooner. "By the time she showed her true colors, it was too late. We had already walked down the aisle."

"But you must have cared for her at some point," his mother persisted. "The two of you were married for almost three years."

"I tried to make things work, but I'm not like my father," he stated flatly. "I finally faced the reality of the situation and realized that no matter what I did or how I did it, it was never going to keep her from making my life a living hell. I chose the peace and freedom of being single over a life of the abject misery Dad suffered."

"Your father needed a strong woman to guide him," Charlotte said, unabashed by her son's observations.

"Well, I don't." He glared at his mother. "I prefer a woman to be my equal, not one who tells me every move to make and how to make it."

"Do you honestly believe that Kincaid girl is your equal?" Charlotte scoffed.

"Yes, I do. But that is absolutely none of your concern." Daniel had heard enough and he didn't think he could stomach much more of his mother's arrogance. "I think I'll take a rain check on that dinner, Charlotte." He rose to leave. "And I'm giving you fair warning. In the future, you would do well to keep your nose out of my business and your opinions to yourself. I'll see who the hell I want for as long as I want and I don't intend to listen to another word about it from you."

Without waiting for his mother's reaction, he walked out of the room. On his way through the kitchen, he apologized to Rosemary for skipping her delicious meal, then headed home to the peace and quiet of his condo. Eating alone was preferable to listening to Charlotte extol the virtues of his cold, intractable ex-wife's pedigree, while running down a warm, caring woman like Lily.

To keep from saying anything against his mother, Lily had simply stopped seeing him rather than cause a rift between them. That was the kind of class and breeding Charlotte should applaud and strive for—not run down.

Lily Kincaid was twice the woman his mother or his ex-wife would ever be and if he hadn't known that before, he certainly did now.

* * *

"Are you sure that living in that huge house all by yourself is what you really want?" Kara asked, clearly worried.

"Yes." Lily knew her sister was voicing the concern of her entire family when she stopped by to pick up some extra rolls of Bubble Wrap Kara kept at her shop. "I've always loved that house and now that I've seen the inside, I can't think of anywhere else I'd rather live."

"I haven't driven up to Hilton Head to see about my property yet," Kara said, handing Lily a box filled with several rolls of the packing material. "I've been so busy trying to get everything ready for Laurel and Eli's wedding, I just haven't had the time."

"Has Laurel chosen the colors she wants to use for the wedding and reception?" Lily asked, hoping her sister chose a shade for the bridesmaids' dresses that didn't clash with red hair.

"She's leaving it up to me and Eli to decide." Kara shook her head. "I don't think I've ever had a bride who didn't care what color scheme was used at her wedding or who encouraged the groom to help the planner make all the choices for her."

"Well, she is rather busy now that she's handling the press releases for the family, as well as public relations for TKG," Lily said, wondering if that was all there was to Laurel's disinterest. At times it seemed that Kara was more excited about their sister's wedding to Eli Houghton, owner of a luxury resort on Seabrook Island in the Outer Banks, than Laurel was.

"I'm sure that her hands are full," Kara agreed. "But still—" When the phone rang, she stopped and held up her finger as she picked it up. "Prestige Events, may I put you on hold for just a moment?"

"I'll let you get back to work," Lily said, smiling when her sister muted the call. "My dishes and I thank you for the Bubble Wrap."

"If you need more packing materials or someone to help you move, just let me know," Kara said, already pressing the button to return to the call.

As Lily drove back to the carriage house from Kara's shop, she went through a mental checklist of all that she wanted to accomplish for the day. She needed to sketch out a few more scenes for the new children's book she was illustrating and pack more of her things for her move to the Beauchamp mansion. And, of course, somewhere between drawing a mouse wearing a fedora and wrapping china with Bubble Wrap, she would need to take a nap.

She smiled as she turned into the driveway leading back to the carriage house. Once filled with almost boundless energy, since becoming pregnant she required a nap around the same time every afternoon. The doctor had told her that the fatigue was common and would probably disappear after the first trimester only to return during the last few weeks before giving birth. But as out of character as it was for her to sleep during the day, she fully intended to enjoy every minute of her pregnancy even if she had to do it without the baby's father.

Thinking about Daniel, she sighed wistfully. She hadn't seen him for the past week, and whether it was smart or not, she had missed him. He had called her as often as he could and sent flowers every day, but it wasn't the same as being with him. And that was dangerous to her peace of mind.

She wished things could be different—that he wanted what she wanted. But he didn't, and all the wishing in the world wasn't going to change that. She was going to have to tell him about the baby, and as soon as she got moved into the Beauchamp House, that was exactly what she was going to do.

When she drove around her parents' home to the carriage house in back, she found Daniel waiting for her. Parking her Mini Cooper next to his white Mercedes, her heart sped up. "Speak of the devil," she murmured.

"Don't you have to work today?" she asked as they both got out of their cars. Opening the back of the Mini to remove the box of Bubble Wrap, she started toward the front door. "I thought you had another meeting with the dockworkers."

"It was canceled," he said, walking over to take the box from her. "We were able to get things resolved late yesterday afternoon."

"It must be a relief to have that over with." She knew from listening to her father and brothers how disruptive the labor force walking off the job could be to an international shipping company.

"But don't you have other duties to attend to as CEO of Addison Industries?" she asked, not at all pleased with herself for being so happy to see him.

The trip to the aquarium and the kiss they shared at the mansion were wonderful, but they changed nothing. He was still a man who was completely turned off by commitment and having children. And she still wanted the happily-ever-after—a loving husband, marriage and a big family.

But it was going to be a serious test of her will-power not to fall for him all over again. He just looked so darned good. In a suit and tie, he was drop-dead gorgeous. Daniel Addison wearing blue jeans, a black T-shirt and a brown leather blazer was positively devastating. It was all she could do to keep from abandoning her resolve and throwing herself into his arms.

"That's the beauty of being the boss," Daniel said, oblivious to her inner struggle. Easily handling the lightweight box with one arm, he held up a sack from a nearby Chinese restaurant with the other. "I can take off for an early start to the weekend whenever I want to."

Opening her front door, Lily led the way into the apartment, then took the box of Bubble Wrap from him. "As you can see, everything is in a state of total chaos right now," she said, finding an empty place next to a bouquet of flowers on the coffee table to set the box.

"I see you have quite a few things packed." She watched him look around at the cartons and boxes already sealed and stacked for the move. "You aren't taking the furniture, are you?"

Lily shook her head. "Since Daddy had the mansion fully furnished, there wouldn't be anywhere to put any of it." She threaded her way around a pile of empty containers to the dining table on the far side of the room. "I thought I would leave my furniture here in case Momma wants to let one of the servants move in or if she decides to rent it out to someone."

He set the sack of takeout on the table. "When do you plan on moving?"

"Over the next three days." She walked into the kitchen to get a couple of disposable plates and plastic cutlery. "I thought I would take the lighter boxes over there tomorrow and Sunday. Then, when the movers get the heavier things on Monday, all that should be left to do is find where I want to put things at the mansion."

"I have an idea," he said, taking food from the sack. "Why don't we move some of this over there this afternoon. Since I'm off for the rest of the day, I can carry boxes inside while you start putting things away."

Lily nibbled on her lower lip as she thought about his offer. "It would be nice if some of this mess was cleared out of the way."

Daniel looked over at the tall stack of moving cartons in the living room. "I'm going to go so far as to say it would be a hell of a lot less dangerous, too."

"It is going to take several trips," she thought aloud as they sat down to eat. "My little car can only hold so much, even with the backseats folded down, and I'll probably need the extra afternoon to get everything moved."

"Do you actually enjoy driving that little toy?" Daniel asked, handing her a carton of sweet-and-sour chicken.

"You sound just like my brother," she said, frowning. "RJ keeps telling me I should replace it with a real car."

He raised one eyebrow. "I take it that isn't something you want to do?"

"I love my Mini Cooper," she said, defending her little car. "I could easily afford to replace it with a larger, more expensive model, but I don't want to. It's fun to drive and I think it suits my personality."

"Okay," Daniel said slowly, as if knowing he was treading on a sensitive subject. "We'll use it and my car this afternoon, then tomorrow I'll get one of my company pickup trucks to move what's left."

Having his help would greatly cut down on the amount of time it took her to move. But the more she was with Daniel, the bigger threat he posed to her peace of mind. If she continued to be around him, there was a very real danger of her falling for him again, and it would make things that much harder for her when she told him about the baby and he walked out of her life for good.

"I can't ask you to do that," she said regretfully. "I'm sure you have other things you need to be doing."

"Nope. And besides, you didn't ask." Reaching across the table, he covered her hand with his, sending a tingling awareness spiraling throughout her body. "I wouldn't have offered if I didn't want to help, sweetheart."

"I don't want—"

"Just say yes, Lily," he commanded with the same smile that never failed to make her heart skip a beat.

Lily stared at him for a few seconds longer as she began to realize that she had already lost the battle she had been waging within herself. Sighing, she gave in to what they both wanted. "All right. Yes, you can help me move."

Daniel carried the last box of art supplies into the studio in the Beauchamp carriage house just as daylight was starting to fade to dusk. He and Lily had made several trips from her parents' place over to the mansion and reduced the amount of boxes piled in her living room to just a few. They had even managed to move most of her clothes and toiletries.

"It shouldn't take long to move the rest of your things tomorrow," he said, watching her lay out drawings of a mouse wearing a trench coat and fedora across her worktable. "We'll be able to move twice as many boxes with the truck. You'll probably even be able to cancel the movers for Monday."

"Thank you for all the help, Daniel. I really appreciate it." When she looked up, her vivid blue eyes brightened and he could practically see the wheels turning in her pretty head. "If I wanted to, I could even start staying here tonight."

"You could," he said, nodding. "But by the time we have dinner and you got back over here, it would be time for bed. Wouldn't it be better to get a good night's sleep at the apartment, then you'll already be there to finish the move when I come by tomorrow morning with the truck."

"I suppose you're right," she said, putting the last of her drawing pencils into a holder on the worktable.

Wrapping his arms around her, he pulled her to him. "Why don't we go back to your place, have a pizza delivered and open a bottle of wine to celebrate your move."

"That sounds nice, but I think I'll pass on the wine," she said, resting her head against his chest. She was too tired to pull away and besides, it felt good to be in his arms. "I think I'd rather have the pizza and then a big bowl of ice cream with lots of chocolate syrup and peanut butter mixed in with it for dessert."

He leaned back to see the expression on her face. "You're serious?"

"Absolutely," she said, grinning. "I've had ice cream,

chocolate and peanut butter almost every night for the past few weeks."

"Really?"

She nodded. "Why do you think I keep that large carton of vanilla ice cream in the freezer?"

"Okay, I'll give it a try. We'll have ice cream to celebrate," he said, laughing. He kissed her forehead. "Then I'll run an extra couple of miles tomorrow morning just to work it off."

Ten minutes later as they turned the corner onto the street where the Kincaid home was located, Daniel slowed the car to a stop and swore under his breath at the sight a couple of blocks ahead. "What the hell's going on?"

Lily gasped. "Are all those vans and cars parked in front of my mother's house?"

"It looks that way," he said, deciding to drive on past the media circus. "Why don't you call to see what's up before we try to get past them to your apartment."

"I'm almost afraid to." When she took her cell phone from her purse, he noticed that her hands were shaking. "I'm not sure I want to know."

He could understand her apprehension. Although he hadn't been with her when the family had been notified of her father's death, Daniel had seen the news-footage reporting from in front of the Kincaid mansion. He imagined it had to have been something like the scene up ahead of them.

"The line is busy. I'll try RJ's number," she said as they sped past the reporters and cameramen from all the area television stations. "RJ, what on earth is going on at Momma's?" she asked when her brother answered.

Daniel had a gut feeling that whatever was going on, it wasn't going to be good news.

"Oh, my God! You can't be serious."

One glance at Lily and Daniel steered the car over to the curb. Her peaches-and-cream complexion had bleached to a ghostly white and her eyes were bright with tears.

Looking over at him, she nodded. "Yes, I'm with Daniel. We moved most of my things to the mansion this afternoon." She paused. "Yes, of course. I'm sure I'll be fine at the Beauchamp house tonight. Do you think the media will be gone by morning?" She paused for her brother's answer, then added, "I promise I'll wait for you to call tomorrow before I try to go back to the carriage house."

"What's happened?" Daniel asked when she ended the call.

"The police just released a report stating that my father's death has been ruled a…homicide," she said, the single word catching on a sob. "RJ strongly suggested that I stay at the Beauchamp house tonight if I want to avoid being accosted by the media when I try to get back home."

"You could stay at my place," Daniel offered.

"I'd rather not," she said, shaking her head. "It wasn't a secret that we were seeing each other before Christmas and I'm not entirely certain some photographer trying to get a story won't be lurking in the shadows."

What she said made sense. They had been featured on the society page of the newspaper more times than he cared to count during their three-month affair, and with the breaking news that Reginald Kincaid had been murdered, there was a very real possibility that his condo would be on the media's radar as well.

"I'm staying with you," Daniel said, steering the car back onto the street. "I don't want you being alone until things quiet down."

"I'll b-be okay," she said through chattering teeth that had nothing to do with the mild winter temperature. "I don't w-want—"

"This isn't negotiable," he said firmly. "If you're concerned about the sleeping arrangements, don't be. I understand that things between us moved a bit fast when we first started seeing each other. We haven't been intimate for several weeks and you're not ready to make love with me again. I get that. But there are five guest bedrooms in that house and I'm sure I can find a comfortable place to sleep."

When she fell silent, he took that as a yes, and after a quick detour to his condo for a change of clothes, Daniel drove them back to the Battery and, parking at the rear entrance of the house, used Lily's key to let them in the back door. He didn't want to use the front entrance for obvious reasons. It wasn't common knowledge that Lily had inherited the mansion, but he wasn't going to take any chances that a stray member of the paparazzi had recognized his car when they drove past her mother's place and followed them.

As soon as he had the door secured behind them and the alarm system turned on, Daniel took Lily into his arms. "I'm so sorry all this is happening, sweetheart. If I could make it all go away, I would."

"I can't believe someone...murdered my father," she said, wrapping her arms around his waist as if he was a lifeline. "Who would do that? Why would they do that?"

"I don't know." He held her close. "But I'm sure the authorities will find whoever it is and bring them to justice."

"I hope so," she said, trembling against him. "RJ said that after the police interview the security team at TKG and get preliminary results from the autopsy, they're going to interview each member of the family. Does that mean we're all under suspicion?"

Daniel didn't want to tell her that was most likely the case. She'd had enough upset and he wasn't going to cause her more by confirming her assumption.

Thinking quickly, he shook his head. "It's probably just a matter of investigative procedure. There might be something that you or one of your siblings could tell the detectives that would give them a lead to follow or a clue who the killer might be."

"I suppose you're right," she said, sounding emotionally spent.

"One of those boxes we brought over contained towels, didn't it?" he asked. When she nodded, he guided her toward the back stairs, leading from the kitchen to the second floor. "Let's go upstairs and get you into a warm bath. Maybe it will relieve some of the tension and help you sleep."

While Lily took a nice soaking bath in one of the two master bathrooms, Daniel took a quick shower in the other. As he toweled himself dry, he wondered who could have killed Reginald Kincaid and why.

It was a fact of life that men in high corporate positions weren't without their share of enemies. Whether it was a disgruntled employee, a business rival or a radical member of a special interest group, there was always someone who didn't agree with the way a CEO conducted business and the decisions he had to make for the welfare of the company. But who would have taken their grievance to the extreme and resorted to murder?

Pulling on a pair of boxer briefs, Daniel walked into the bedroom and sat on the edge of the king-size bed as he waited for Lily to finish her bath. He didn't like that she was having to relive the loss of her father. She had just started to adjust to losing the man and now the uncertainty of what had happened, and why, was starting all over again.

But he liked even less that there was an unknown murderer on the loose and there was no way of knowing if he intended to target another member of the Kincaid family.

Five

When Lily came out of the bathroom, she stopped short at the sight of Daniel sitting on the edge of the bed wearing nothing but a pair of dark blue boxer briefs. She had seen his body many times during their three-month affair and it never failed to cause her pulse to race. But tonight? With learning that her father had been murdered and seeing reporters camped in front of her mother's house, how could she possibly be distracted by how sexy he looked?

But that was exactly what she was thinking. With broad muscular shoulders, well-developed pectoral muscles and enough ripples on his abdomen to make a bodybuilder proud, Daniel Addison exuded over six feet of pure sex appeal.

"Feeling more relaxed?" he asked as she walked over to the side of the bed.

"A little," she said, wishing that she could close her eyes and things would be the way they were before his mother's dinner party. Her father would still be alive and she wouldn't be getting ready to have the talk that she knew would send Daniel running in the opposite direction from her. But then, that would mean she wasn't pregnant. And no matter how strained things became between them when she told him about the baby, her pregnancy was something she wouldn't wish away for anything in the world.

Rising to his feet, he walked around to where she stood and pulled her to him. "I'm sure things will look a little brighter in the morning when you're more rested."

"Daniel, there's something we need to discuss," she said, loving the feel of his bare chest pressed to her cheek. She had put off telling him long enough. He might not want a child but he was going to have one, and it was past time that she told him about the baby. "It's really important."

"Not tonight." He shook his head and, reaching down, pulled the comforter back for her to get into bed. "You need sleep and there's nothing that can't wait until tomorrow."

"But if I don't tell you now, I might not—"

He put his index finger to her lips to stop her. "Whatever it is, you can tell me in the morning."

Too tired to argue, she simply nodded and climbed into bed. Daniel was right. Her news had waited this long, it could wait another eight hours.

"I'll be on the couch in the sitting room if you need me," he said, pulling the comforter over her.

"I thought you were going to sleep down the hall in

one of the other bedrooms," she said, unable to stifle a yawn.

Leaning down, he gave her a quick kiss. "I decided that was too far away. Now try to get some rest, sweetheart."

As she watched him walk through the open French doors and into the sitting room, she couldn't help but feel disappointed that he had stuck to his word about sleeping in another room. She shouldn't be, she told herself, rolling to her side. Being held by him throughout the night, even if they didn't make love, would only complicate things and make it that much harder for her when they finally did discuss her pregnancy tomorrow morning.

Unable to stop thinking about how she should tell him that he was going to be a daddy in seven months, she must have drifted off to sleep. The next thing she knew, Daniel was stretching out on the bed beside her and gathering her into his arms.

"It's all right, Lily," he said, cradling her to his bare chest. He wiped the tears from her cheeks with the pad of his thumb. "I'm here, sweetheart. Everything is going to be fine. It was just a nightmare."

Leaning back to look at him, she couldn't tell him that it might have been a bad dream, but it was one that she feared would turn out to be all too prophetic. In the dream, she had told him about the baby and watched the attraction in his eyes turn to utter contempt.

When she had ended their affair, she might have told herself that she was calling a halt to things before she got in too deep and suffered a broken heart when he lost interest in seeing her after learning about the baby. But the truth of the matter was, she had already fallen in love with Daniel, had most likely loved him from the moment they met.

She knew it was foolish and that she would suffer more emotional pain when he learned her secret and severed all ties with her, but she couldn't resist wanting one more night in his arms. Snuggling against his solid strength, she asked, "Will you please keep holding me, Daniel?"

"I'm not going anywhere, sweetheart," he promised as he ran his hands up and down her back. "Not until you tell me to."

Lily rested her head on his shoulder and her hand on his broad chest. With the steady beat of his heart beneath her palm and his strong arms wrapped around her, she felt more content, more secure than she had in several weeks. It felt as if in his arms was where she belonged, where she would always belong.

"Lily, don't get me wrong," he said, his voice a bit rusty. "I love the way your hand feels on my body. But if you keep that up, I can't guarantee that I'll be able to continue being a gentleman for much longer."

Realizing that she had been moving her fingers over his pectoral muscles and the upper part of his abdomen, she stopped immediately. "I'm sorry. I didn't realize..."

When she started to pull her hand away, he covered it with his and, holding it to him, gave her a kiss that sent heat streaking to the darkest corners of her soul. "I've missed holding you, Lily. I've missed you touching me like this and me touching you. It's all I've been able to think about for three weeks. But you've had a lot of trauma in the past several days and I won't take advantage of that. I came in here to comfort you and I promise that's all that's going to happen."

As she stared up at him, she realized that he was trying to do what he felt was honorable. But was that what she wanted? To simply be held by the man she loved? Possibly for the last time?

Considering his views on love and having children, they had no future together. She knew that and, although it made her sad, she had accepted the inevitable. Could she resist one last night of knowing the strength of his lovemaking and the ecstasy of their bodies coming together as one heart, one soul?

"You wouldn't be taking advantage of the situation," she said, realizing that her decision had already been made. "I want you to make me forget that outside the doors of this house there's a world waiting to intrude." She kissed his strong jaw. "I want you to make love to me, Daniel."

She watched him tightly close his eyes and swallow hard before opening them again as he eased her to her back. "Are you sure that's what you want?" he asked, propping himself on one elbow to stare down at her. "I'd rather go take a dozen cold showers than to have you regret one minute of my making love to you."

"There are a lot of things I'm not certain of," she said honestly. "But I do know that no matter what tomorrow brings, I won't regret being with you tonight."

It was apparently all the assurance he needed to hear, because, without hesitation, Daniel lowered his head to capture her lips with his. Teasing and coaxing, he masterfully built her anticipation of deepening the kiss and when he did take it to the next level, his tongue stroking hers sent a tingling wave of excitement flowing throughout her entire body.

As he explored her inner recesses, he moved his

hand down her side to the tail of her nightshirt. His fingertips grazing her thigh as he slowly inched the garment upward caused a shiver of pure delight to race up her spine and she had to remind herself to breathe. But when he continued up her side to the swell of her breast, then paused to worry her taut nipple with the pad of his thumb, heated sensations spread to every cell in her being.

Unable to lie still, Lily raised her shoulders to help him remove the nightshirt. She wanted to feel his hands over every part of her and she wanted to touch all of him as well. In one smooth motion, he tossed her night-shirt over the side of the bed, and the feel of her sensitive skin pressed to his bare flesh caused the stirrings of an empty ache deep in her core.

Running her hands over his chest and abdomen, she reacquainted herself with the width of his shoulders and the dormant power lying just beneath his smooth skin. She loved his body, loved that it contrasted so perfectly with her softer feminine form.

"I'm going to love every inch of you," he murmured against her skin as he nibbled his way down to her collarbone and beyond. "And when I get done, there won't be a doubt left in your mind how much I've wanted and missed you these past few weeks."

The promise in his voice caused a quiver of anticipation to course through her. When he reached the slope of her breast, then kissed his way to the sensitive tip, her breath caught and a coil of need began to tighten deep inside her. She held his head to her when he took her into his warm mouth. Unable to stop a tiny moan of pure pleasure from escaping, she reveled in the many sensations he was creating inside her. He was driving her completely insane and she loved every minute of it.

"Does that feel good, Lily?" he asked as he trailed his lips down her abdomen to her stomach.

"Y-yes."

He traced the elastic waistband of her panties with his finger. "Do you want me to stop?"

"I-if you do…I'll never forgive you," she said, gasping for breath.

His deep chuckle seemed to vibrate all the way to her soul. "Sweetheart, there's no way I could stop now." When he slid his hand down inside her panties, she automatically raised her hips to help him and in no time, the scrap of silk and lace joined her nightshirt on the floor. "Those three weeks without you have felt like a lifetime."

Before she could tell him that she felt that way too, he caressed her side, her hip and the inner part of her thigh. Her heart pounded against her ribs as she waited for his touch. When he finally cupped the soft curls at her apex, then slipped his fingers inside to stroke her with tender care, the aching desire he created was almost more than she could bear.

"P-please…Daniel," she gasped, reaching down to find him. She gave to him as he was giving to her, but she wanted more. She wanted him to fill the empty ache that threatened to consume her. "I…need you now."

Lily felt him shift as he removed his underwear, then the feel of his body pressed to hers, his arousal strong against her thigh, caused an answering flutter in her lower belly. She wanted him to join their bodies, to make them one heart, one mind, one soul.

"Sweetheart, I got so carried away, I forgot that I

don't have anything to protect you," he said, his voice filled with regret.

"There's, um, no need…to worry about that," she assured him.

"It's a safe time of the month?" he asked as his fingers continued to excite her in ways that she could have never imagined.

"Mmm."

She knew she was being evasive and that it was unfair not to tell him that there was no need to protect them from what had already happened. But she wanted this one last time with him, wanted to store up the memory for the empty nights that lay ahead of her.

With no hesitation, he parted her legs with his knee, then levered himself over her. Reaching down, she guided him to her and Lily closed her eyes as she savored the exquisite feelings of becoming one with the man she loved.

"Open your eyes, sweetheart," he commanded when their bodies were fused completely. "I want to watch your pleasure build until you can't wait any longer. Then I want to watch you the moment I take you over the edge."

Gazing into his eyes as he slowly began to move within her, she felt as if she might drown in the dark blue depths. Heat spiraled throughout her being and ribbons of excitement threaded their way to the ever-tightening coil deep within her as her body responded to his rhythmic thrusts. Holding on to his broad shoulders to keep from being lost, Lily felt her feminine muscles begin to contract around him as Daniel fulfilled his promise of creating a passion in her so strong that she lost sight of where he ended and she began.

Time seemed to stand still as the tension inside her built to a crescendo, then suddenly broke free to send waves of pleasure coursing all the way to her soul. Moments later, Daniel groaned and she felt him stiffen inside her as he found his own shuddering release. When he buried his head in her shoulder and collapsed on top of her, Lily held him close as they both slowly drifted back to reality.

Loving the feel of him still inside her and the weight of his large body covering hers, when his breathing eased and Daniel moved to her side, she felt a deep sense of loss.

"Are you all right?" he asked, pulling her close.

She wanted to tell him that she loved him—would always love him—but it wasn't what he wanted to hear. Instead, she nodded. "That was perfect."

"Oh, I still have a few tricks up my sleeve that will make it even better the next time," he said, kissing the top of her head.

"You're not wearing a shirt," she teased. "How could you possibly have anything up sleeves that don't exist?"

"Hush, woman," he said, laughing. "Rest assured, I have more ammunition in my sensual arsenal that I'm going to take great pleasure in showing you."

She knew that once he learned about the baby, that would change. But snuggling against him, she decided to face that in the light of day, along with all the other recent harsh realities of her life.

The first light of day had just started to peek through a part in the bedroom drapes when Daniel lay his arm over Lily's stomach to draw her close. He smiled at the feel of her soft curves nestled at his side. Last night had been mind-blowing and he still couldn't get over how much he had missed Lily's uninhibited response to his lovemaking. She was so receptive to his touch, and the fact that she wasn't the least bit shy about touching him in return never failed to arouse him in ways a man could only dream of.

He propped himself up on his elbow to stare down at her sleeping so peacefully beside him. He had even missed waking up in the mornings with her warm bare skin against his hair-roughened flesh. Not that they had spent the entire night together all that often, but he had forgotten how pleasant it was to wake up with her the few times that they had.

Watching her sleep, he frowned. He wasn't entirely sure he was comfortable with how easily he had gotten used to the little things like waking up next to Lily or how cute he found her propensity to crowd him on his side of the bed. It certainly wasn't something he missed about his ex-wife. Of course, Charisma would have had to sleep with him more than a few times a month for him to have become accustomed to having her next to him in bed.

Daniel lay back and pillowed his head on his folded arms. His ex-wife had used sex as a bargaining tool—a way to coerce him into buying her a new pair of diamond earrings or the little red Ferrari she just had to have for her trips to the mall. Otherwise, she slept in the master bedroom, while he was perfectly content to sleep in a room down the hall.

But that was one thing he never had to worry about again, he thought contentedly. He was single and intended to stay that way.

He glanced over at the sleeping woman beside him.

Whatever he and Lily had going on between them was special and, without outside interference from his mother, they would be together for as long as it lasted. Then, when the time came for them to stop seeing each other, he would go his way and she would go hers. No hard feelings and no emotional pain for either of them.

As he lay there patting himself on the back for keeping his life simple, Lily moaned and stirred next to him. He wondered if she was having another nightmare until she sat straight up in bed, threw back the covers and bolted for the bathroom.

"What the hell?" He grabbed his underwear from the pile of clothing on the floor and pulled them on, then knocked on the closed bathroom door. "Are you all right, sweetheart?"

When she failed to answer, he tried the knob. The door was locked.

"Lily, what's going on?" he demanded.

"P-please go…away," she said a moment before he heard the sounds of her being sick.

"As soon as you're able, open the door," he said, wondering what could have caused the upset.

Retrieving her pink fluffy robe from the closet, every possible reason that might have caused her to be sick ran through his mind as he waited outside the closed door. It couldn't be a case of food poisoning because they had both had the same thing for lunch and skipped dinner and he was fine. Of course, she might be sick because she hadn't eaten. Or maybe it was a delayed reaction to learning that her father had been murdered. That coupled with the media circus outside her mother's place and the fact that the police intended to question the family was enough to cause anyone's nerves to get the better of them.

When he finally heard the click of the lock being released, he was waiting for her when she opened the bathroom door and after helping her into her robe, walked her over to sit on the end of the bed. "I'll be right back," he said, going into the bathroom to wet a washcloth. Returning to the bedroom, he knelt in front of her and patted the cool, damp terry cloth over her cheeks and forehead. "Feeling better now?"

She nodded. "Daniel…" She paused to take a deep breath. "We have to talk."

"Why don't you lie down and rest a little more?" he suggested. "We can discuss whatever you like after you're feeling better."

"I have to tell you now," she said shaking her head. "Otherwise, I might lose my nerve."

Something in her tone caused the hairs on the back of his neck to stand straight up. "What?"

He watched her close her eyes, then she took another deep breath and looked him square in the eyes as she announced, "I'm pregnant."

"Pregnant."

A mixture of shock and disbelief coursed through him and it suddenly felt as if all the oxygen had been sucked out of the room. Slowly rising to his feet, he walked over to sit in the chair across the room. Propping his forearms on his knees, he stared down at his loosely clasped hands as he tried to wrap his mind around the single most life-changing word of his life.

"You're pregnant," he repeated, knowing he sounded like a damn parrot, but unable to stop himself.

It had been the last thing he expected her to say. Lily

was pregnant and there wasn't a doubt in his mind it was his baby.

"The baby is the reason I've been sick in the mornings but ravenous the rest of the day," she said, her tone a bit unsure. "It's also the reason I've been so tired and have to take naps in the afternoon."

Daniel opened and closed his mouth several times as he tried to decide what to ask first. Should he question her about when she discovered the pregnancy? Should he ask when the baby was due? Or should he find out how she wanted to handle things? How the hell was a man supposed to deal with something he thought he'd never face?

"How did this happen?" he finally asked when he found his voice. When she gave him a look that suggested she thought he might be a little simpleminded, he immediately shook his head. "Strike that. I know the biology. I'm just trying to figure out when it could have happened. We were always careful."

"I think it might have been the night after Thanksgiving." She sighed. "If you'll remember, we got so carried away we didn't think about protection until after the fact."

He nodded. "That was the only time it could have happened. But when did you find out about the pregnancy?"

"The morning of your mother's dinner party," she said, sounding a bit hesitant. "I was going to tell you that night after the party, but—"

"Charlotte had her little talk with you first."

"How did you know about that?" Lily shook her head. "I didn't say anything."

"You didn't have to," he said, getting up to pace

the floor. "After I thought about it, I realized that you had stopped taking my calls and refused to go anywhere with me right after the party. And knowing my mother's penchant for snide comments and sticking her nose where it doesn't belong, it all added up. Then, when I asked her about it, she admitted it." He stopped pacing as a thought occurred. "If we hadn't run into each other in the lawyer's office the day your father's will was read, would you have told me about the pregnancy?"

She stared down at her hands, but there was no hesitation when she nodded. "I was going to tell you right after the holidays, but with Daddy dying and all that has happened since, I could never seem to find the right time."

"Lily, we both know better than that," he said, shaking his head. "There were plenty of times in the past week that you could have told me."

When she looked at him directly, there was a defiance in her expression that he had never seen before. "You're right. I could have told you, but I wasn't sure your knowing was in my best interest until the pregnancy was a little further along."

It suddenly dawned on him what she meant. "You thought I would ask you to put an end to it, didn't you?"

"I wasn't sure," she said, shaking her head. "But I wasn't going to give you the chance to try to talk me out of having my baby."

Walking over to kneel in front of her, he took her hands in his. "Lily, you have to believe me. I wouldn't ask you to do anything like that. It's true that I never intended to have a child, but that doesn't mean I won't take responsibility for the baby if you choose to have it."

She suddenly straightened her shoulders as her expression changed to one of pure defiance, then rising to her feet, she picked her nightshirt off the floor. "That isn't necessary, Daniel. I'm perfectly capable of loving and raising my baby on my own without your help." She motioned for him to look around as she walked over to the dresser and removed some clothes. "As you can see, I have a huge house now with more than enough room for half a dozen children if I want them. And believe me, I won't think of a single one of them as a responsibility. Having a child is a blessing and one that I'm really looking forward to."

Before Daniel could react, she walked into the bathroom and slammed the door. The sound seemed to echo throughout the room and galvanized him into action. He needed to think, needed to decide how to handle this latest development.

Taking a quick shower, he dressed and went downstairs to see if they had brought coffee when they moved most of Lily's food the day before. As he waited for the coffeemaker to work its magic, he wandered out onto the terrace. The January sun shone brightly across the backyard and highlighted the quaint beauty of the paved courtyard. He saw none of it.

Lily was having his baby. Un-freaking-believable.

What he found even more incredible was that he wasn't nearly as upset with the idea of being a father as he had always thought he would be. Was he still in a state of shock? Or was he just mellowing with age?

Having never entertained the idea of fatherhood, he had really never given thought to how he would react if he did impregnate a woman. He was sure as hell giving it his undivided attention now.

What kind of father would he be? Given that he was an only child, raised by two people who had no business procreating, he really didn't have an example of what parenting was all about. Hell, since becoming an adult, he had never even been around kids, let alone a baby.

He ran his hand over the tension building at the back of his neck. It wasn't like getting a car. At least vehicles came with extensive instruction manuals and directions on where things were located and how to troubleshoot certain problems. The last he heard, the hospital might send a few pamphlets along when parents took a new baby home from the hospital, but otherwise they were on their own to figure things out.

And how were he and Lily going to manage custody of the child? Whether he had intended to be a daddy or not, he wanted to be a part of his kid's life and he didn't care much for the idea of having contact with him or her only a few days a week.

No, if he was going to be a father, he was going to do this right. And he knew just what that meant.

Taking a deep breath, he walked back into the kitchen and eyed the wine rack. He could use a drink and if it were a little later in the day, he would definitely pop the cork on a bottle of merlot. Instead, he would have to rely on a good strong cup of coffee to get him through what he had to do.

Twenty minutes later when Lily entered the kitchen, he sat at the table sipping his coffee and wondering how she was going to react when he told her about his decision. "Are you feeling better?"

"A little." She filled a teakettle with water, set it on

the countertop range, then opening one of the cabinets, reached for a box of crackers on the top shelf.

Daniel quickly left the table and got the box for her. "Is this all you're having for breakfast?" he asked, frowning. "Shouldn't you be eating something a little healthier?"

"Weak tea and crackers sometimes helps to settle the queasiness," she explained, taking a tea bag from one of the canisters on the counter.

"Why don't you sit down and let me make the tea for you?" He gave her what he hoped was an encouraging smile. "I can tell you still aren't feeling one hundred percent."

For a moment he thought she was going to refuse, but, shrugging, she put a few crackers on a small plate and walked over to sit at the table. "The nausea usually runs its course by midmorning," she said, nibbling on one of the crackers.

Once he had the tea made and took his seat across the table from her, he asked, "Are you up to discussing your announcement?"

She finished the cracker, then took a sip of tea before she answered. "I don't know that there's anything to talk about, Daniel. To me this baby is a precious gift. But all you see is an inconvenient obligation."

"Sweetheart, you have to understand," he said, reaching across the table to cover her hand with his. "Being a father is something that had never crossed my mind and it came as a shock that I'm actually going to have a child. I've never been around kids and I'm man enough to admit that I'm going to be treading in unfamiliar waters. But when I said I would take responsibility, what I meant was that I intend to do my best to man up and be a good parent."

"That's not the way it came across when you said it," she murmured, her expression dubious.

"I'm sorry for that," he said, meaning it. "But I give you my word that, even though we didn't plan on this happening, I'm going to do the right thing by you and the baby."

She stared at him a moment, before she vigorously shook her head. "No. Don't you dare—"

"You're going to be the mother of my baby," he interrupted her. "And as soon as the arrangements can be made, I'm going to make you my wife."

Six

"Oh no you're not," Lily said, pulling her hand from his. "Up until an hour ago, making me or any other woman your wife wasn't even a consideration for you. You can't sit there and tell me that your views on marriage have suddenly taken a hundred-and-eighty-degree turn just because I told you I'm pregnant."

"Sweetheart, I don't think you should be getting this upset." He sounded so calm, so self-assured, that she wanted to bop him across the top of the head with something. "I'm sure it's not good for you or the baby."

"You don't have the slightest idea of what is or isn't good for us," she stated flatly.

"I'm going to take care of that with a trip to the mall as soon as it opens," he said, apparently undaunted by her accusation. "I'll buy every book I can find on pregnancy and taking care of an infant. Rest assured, by the time you give birth, I'll know everything that's going on with you and the baby."

Unable to sit still, she rose from the table. "Daniel, I think it's admirable that you want to learn all you can about babies and that you want to be a good parent. But marriage isn't a requirement to do that."

"I realize that, Lily," he said, standing to face her. "But our getting married is what I want."

Placing her fingertips to her temples, she massaged the tension that was building into a pounding headache. "No, Daniel, getting married is not what you want and if you weren't so stubborn, you would admit it."

"A baby needs both its parents together," he insisted. "And you and I already have a lot going for us."

She barely kept her mouth from dropping open. "Like what? Making love?"

The rat had the audacity to grin. "Well, there's that. You can't deny that we both enjoy what we have together in bed."

"There's a whole lot more to a marriage than pleasing each other sexually." How on earth could he think it was that simple?

"It's a good start," he said, reaching out to take her into his arms.

"You're actually serious, aren't you?" She couldn't believe they were having this conversation. "What about trust and mutual respect?"

"If you didn't trust me, you would have never gone to bed with me, Lily," he said reasonably. "And it's out of respect that I'm asking you to marry me."

"Oh, yeah, that's what every woman wants to hear," she said, not even trying to keep the sarcasm from her voice. Pulling from his arms, she put distance between them as she held up her hand to tick off the reasons she was refusing his offer. "Number one, I won't marry you because you didn't ask. You *told* me that was what we were going to do."

"Would you prefer I get down on one knee?" he asked, smiling.

She ignored his glib question. If she didn't, she might do him bodily harm. "Number two, I wasn't born yesterday. Knowing your views on the subject, I'm not fool enough to believe that you had a miraculous turnaround when you heard the word *pregnant*." She held up another finger. "Number three, and for me, the most important reason of all that I refuse to marry you, is that you don't love me."

"I don't believe that love is a requirement for marriage," he said, straightening his shoulders as if bracing himself for battle.

"And I believe it is," she said, knowing that they had reached an impasse. Suddenly feeling defeated, she shook her head. "I'm going upstairs to lie down before I call to see if the media has stopped camping out on my mother's front lawn. Please, lock the door and set the alarm when you leave."

"I'll get the truck on my way back from the bookstore," he called after her as she walked from the room. "We'll talk more this afternoon while we move the rest of your things. But make no mistake about it, Lily, we will be together."

Lily didn't bother telling him that there wasn't anything left to be said. She had taken a stand and she wasn't going to back down. Besides, he wasn't listening anyway.

Lying down on the bed, she hugged one of the pillows close to her chest in an effort to stop her heart from feeling as if it were breaking. She had known from the gossip at the many charity events she'd attended the past few years that Daniel Addison wasn't the type of man a woman pinned her hopes and dreams on. He didn't want a home, a loving wife and children. He was perfectly content leading the life of one of Charleston's most eligible bachelors. But when he introduced himself and asked her to dance that night at the Children's Hospital Autumn Charity Ball, the moment he took her into his arms, she had foolishly fallen in love with him.

Now he was telling her he wanted them to be married, but it wasn't for the right reasons. She wanted the fairy tale of love and happily-ever-after, while all he wanted was to do what he deemed to be socially acceptable.

Tears filled her eyes and ran down her cheeks. She didn't want a marriage like the one her mother had apparently had with her father, didn't want to wake up one day and find that Daniel had a second family in another town.

Turning to her side, she squeezed her eyes tightly shut against the thought. She didn't think Daniel had a long-lost love he was searching for, but then that had probably never crossed her mother's mind about her father, either.

The scent of Daniel's clean masculine body on the pillow caused her tears to fall faster. He'd held her, made love to her, and as much as she would like to pretend that he was the prince she would one day share the castle with, he wasn't.

Daniel didn't love her and probably never would. And she refused to settle for anything less from him.

When he unlocked the door to the Beauchamp mansion and reset the alarm, Daniel set the bag of books and the suitcase full of his clothes on the hall bench and headed straight for the master suite upstairs. He had waited to leave until he was sure Lily had fallen asleep and he was fairly certain she wouldn't awaken until he returned from his trip to the mall bookstore. He had intended to get one of the Addison Industries pickup trucks to move the rest of her things on the way back, but once he saw the headlines on the front page of the Charleston newspaper and a report from the morning news crew stationed on the Kincaids's lawn, he had decided against it.

The media seemed determined to get a comment from one of the family members about the latest development in Reginald Kincaid's death and confirmation on the rumor that he had been leading a double life for several decades before the homicide. Daniel was just as determined that Lily was not going to be the one they harassed. She had enough to deal with. Not only was she having to get used to the fact that someone had murdered her father, she was pregnant and having to adjust to the idea of becoming his wife. She didn't need the added stress of being pursued by a horde of reporters as they tried to scoop each other on the story.

When he entered the master suite and walked through the sitting room, the French doors opened to the bedroom beyond alerted him that Lily was already awake. "How are you feeling after your nap?" When she didn't answer, he checked the rest of the suite. She wasn't there. "Lily?" he called, hurrying out into the hall.

His voice was met with silence and he wasn't sure whether he should start looking for her on the floor above or take a chance that she was out in the carriage house. Deciding to search the entire house before he headed outside to see if she was in her studio, he climbed the stairs leading to the third floor.

"Lily, sweetheart, are you up here?"

Nothing.

He wasn't a man who was prone to worry, but he was becoming more concerned with each passing minute as he went from one bedroom to the next, looking for her. Her car was still at her mother's place, therefore it was unlikely that she had left on her own. He quickened his steps. He didn't even want to think about the fact that Reginald Kincaid's killer was on the loose with few clues as to who it was or if the person intended to target anyone else in the Kincaid family.

When he turned to start back down the stairs, he noticed that the door at the end of the hall, the one leading up to the cupola, was open. Taking the steps two at a time, he was relieved when he found her standing at the windows, staring out at Charleston Harbor.

"Isn't this breathtaking?" she said, pointing out at the view. "I can see the Sullivan's Island Lighthouse and Fort Sumter."

Daniel glanced out over White Point Gardens at the harbor beyond. The scenery was nice, but he liked the view inside the cupola a whole lot better.

Lily looked amazing. She had pulled her long red hair up into a ponytail with some kind of puffy, dark green fabric band, exposing the smooth, creamy skin of her slender neck. He barely resisted the urge to pull her close and kiss every inch of it. Instead, he concentrated on the bulky emerald sweater and snug jeans she was wearing. The sweater looked soft and the color complemented her hair and vivid blue eyes perfectly. But when she bent over to pick up her sketch pad and pencil from the floor, the denim pulling tight across her shapely backside caused the air to lodge in his lungs and sent his blood pressure soaring.

"Did you get the truck?" she asked, straightening to face him. "I haven't heard from RJ, but I'm sure the media must have cleared out by now."

"I don't think that's the case," Daniel said, shaking his head to clear it. "When I stopped by my place after going to the bookstore, I saw a live report from your mother's front lawn on the news. The press is still trying to get an interview with a member of your family and I don't think they're going anywhere until they do."

"Why are they being so persistent?" she asked, frowning. "We don't know any more about what happened to Daddy than what the police released in their statement yesterday evening."

"I'm not sure, sweetheart." He couldn't resist touching her smooth cheek as he tried to decide whether to tell her that the media had also gotten wind of Reginald's secret life up in Greenville. "When a man as successful as your father is found at his office desk with a bullet in his head, whether it was self-inflicted or a homicide, investigative reporters are going to try to dig up everything they can."

"Was there anything in the paper about Angela Sinclair and her two sons?" she asked hesitantly. He knew she was hoping that part of the story would stay under wraps for a bit longer.

Daniel reluctantly nodded. "Right now, it's being reported as a rumor they are trying to verify."

"But it won't take long before that happens," she said, her expression not at all happy. "I just wish everyone would leave us alone long enough to deal with Daddy's loss and the revelations about the Sinclairs."

He didn't hesitate to put his arm around her shoulders and pull her to his side. "I wish it could be that way, too."

She wasn't pulling away from him and he hoped she had come to the conclusion that their getting married was for the best. But he wasn't stupid enough to bring up the subject this soon. He would give her a little more time to realize that it was the perfect solution.

"So I'm going to have to hide out here for a while longer before I'm able to move the rest of my things?" she asked, oblivious to his speculation.

"I would say it will be the first part of the week before we're able to move what's left." He shrugged. "If you want to get out of the house for a while, we could always go back to the aquarium and feed the stingrays. You enjoyed that."

"Thank you for the offer, but I think I'd rather stay here and finish putting things away." She shook her head. "But don't think you have to stay with me. I found a small stepladder in the basement. If I need to put something on one of the top shelves, I can always use that."

"Like hell you will." He turned her to face him and, putting his hands on her shoulders, met her startled gaze. "You're not getting anywhere near that ladder. Is that clear?"

"Oh, really?" Her eyes narrowed. "What gives you the right to tell me what to do?"

"I'll be the first to admit that I know next to nothing about pregnant women, but do you really think that a fall would be good for you or the baby?" He knew if she thought about it she wouldn't take the chance of something happening that might jeopardize the pregnancy. But her heated response was an indication that she still wasn't happy with him.

"I hadn't thought of that," she admitted grudgingly. "But don't feel that you have to stay here with me. I'm sure you have other things you'd rather be doing."

He blew out a frustrated breath. "Lily, I'm not going anywhere now or in the future. While I was out, I stopped by the condo and picked up some of my clothes—"

She glared at him. "Don't you think that was rather presumptuous of you?"

"When I told you this morning that we're going to be together, I meant it," he said, unconcerned by her protests.

He wasn't about to upset her further by telling her that he wouldn't even consider leaving her alone at night until after her father's killer had been caught. For that matter, he wasn't all that happy about having to leave her alone during the day to go to his office, but there was no way around it. His only consolation was that during daylight hours, there would be too many witnesses in the park across the street.

"And I told you—"

"Hush," he said, pulling her to his chest as he lowered his mouth to hers.

At first Lily started to push away from him, but as he moved his lips over hers, he could feel her body relax until she dropped her sketch pad and sagged against him. Deepening the kiss, he marveled at her eager response and the sweet taste of her desire. She might still be upset with him, but she couldn't resist him any more than he could resist her.

The thought had him aroused in two seconds flat and if he didn't put a little distance between them, he wasn't entirely certain he could keep from making love to her right there in the cupola. Considering there was nowhere but the floor to do that, Daniel reluctantly broke the kiss.

When he lifted his head and took a step back to gaze down at her upturned face, he didn't think he had ever seen her look more beautiful. With her cheeks rosy from the blush of desire and her eyes bright with passion, it took every bit of willpower he had not to take her back into his arms.

Deciding that he needed a diversion, he bent to pick up the sketch pad at their feet. He eyed the drawing of the cupola's interior. "What's this?"

She blinked as if coming out of a trance before pointing to the sketch. "I thought that having a window seat around the entire perimeter in here would be a nice addition. I could sit up here and sketch or just watch the ships and boats in the harbor."

He glanced at the pad of paper, then looked around the area inside the cupola. "There should be just enough room if it's not too wide," he said, nodding. "When are you going to have it built?"

She shrugged as she started down the stairs to the floor below. "Probably not until spring."

An idea began to take shape as he followed her downstairs to the kitchen. It shouldn't take more than a day to get the project completed. If he could find a way to get her out of the house long enough, having it built would be a nice surprise for her and quite possibly get him back in her good graces.

"What do you have planned for the last Saturday of the month?" he asked, thinking of a contractor friend of his who owed him a favor.

"I have an exhibit of my illustrations at the mall bookstore for a couple of hours that afternoon," she said as she pulled the makings for sub sandwiches from the refrigerator. "Why?"

"I thought it might be fun to plan a day seeing some of the sights," he said, thinking quickly. "We could take one of the tour boats out to Fort Sumter in the morning and then visit the Charleston Museum in the afternoon."

"I haven't been to those places in a few years," she said thoughtfully. "It might be nice to visit before the tourist season starts."

"Why don't we plan the outing for a week from today then," he said. It was going to cost him extra for his friend to build the window seat on such short notice, but if it made Lily happy, then it would be well worth whatever he had to pay.

She stopped making sandwiches to meet his gaze. "Daniel, it's not going to work."

"What?"

"If you think moving in here and taking me places is going to get me to change my mind about marrying you, you're wrong." She shook her head. "I know what

I want and it's something you can't or won't give me. Either way, I'm not settling for anything less."

"Let's just go and have a good time," he suggested. "I give you my word that I won't pressure you to do anything you don't want to do."

As they ate lunch, Daniel thought about what Lily said. He knew she wanted him to love her, but how could he give her what he wasn't even sure existed? Love was something he hadn't experienced much of throughout his life and certainly not during his disastrous marriage.

He supposed his mother loved him as much as she was capable of loving, but when he was growing up, her idea of showing him how she felt had been to pat him on the head, hand him a hundred-dollar bill and send him off to the arcade. His father had been even worse at showing how he felt about his only son. The few times George Addison had tried to be affectionate, more times than not the gestures had been awkward and clearly embarrassed the hell out of the man. Of course, their cook Rosemary had always made it clear that she was extremely fond of him, but Daniel had never heard her verbalize that she actually loved him.

Staring across the table at Lily, he knew he cared for her. There was certainly no question that he desired her. But love?

"Daniel, are you listening to me?" she asked, interrupting his disturbing introspection.

"I'm sorry, I was thinking about something at the office," he lied. "What were you saying?"

"I asked if you would like to go to my brother's with me on Thursday evening to babysit my three-year-old nephew," she said, taking a sip from her glass of milk.

More comfortable with her question than with his own thoughts, he concentrated on answering her. "Do you think your brother would mind me tagging along?"

She shook her head. "I can't see why Matt would have any objections. Besides, this will give you a glimpse of what it's like to care for a child and how you relate to one."

He knew she expected him to decline the invitation and up until learning he was going to be a father, he probably would have. But he wanted her to see that he really was serious about being a good parent and it couldn't hurt to see what he should expect down the road when their child was a bit older.

Giving her an agreeable smile, he nodded. "Helping you babysit sounds like a great idea. I think I would like that. A lot."

As Lily watched Daniel get down on the floor to help Flynn build a skyscraper made of oversize Lego bricks, she couldn't help but marvel at how well he was doing with her nephew. From the moment they had walked into Matt's house, Flynn seemed to charm the socks off Daniel and she could tell Daniel was having a good time interacting with the little boy. For a man who had never spent time around a child, he seemed to be thoroughly enjoying the experience.

"It's almost time for bed," Lily said, checking her watch. "While I make your bedtime snack, why don't you show Daniel how well you put your toys away, Flynn."

Always well behaved, Flynn nodded and started putting the blocks into their plastic canister. "Dannel, help pick up the blocks, please," Flynn instructed, managing Daniel's name as best he could. Flynn's vocabulary was excellent for a child his age, but he still had a little trouble with some words.

When Lily stepped to the door to tell them the snack was ready, she smiled as she watched the exchange between her nephew and his new best friend.

"Here you go," Daniel said, picking up the last of the blocks, then getting up from the floor to stretch.

"Come on, Dannel," Flynn said, holding his hand up to take Daniel's. "Time for my snack."

As Lily watched, Flynn led Daniel past her into the kitchen. "I share," Flynn said when they were all seated. He picked up his spoon and dipped it into the small cup of pudding in front of him. "I a good sharer."

"Thank you, Flynn, but I'm not really hungry," Daniel said, ruffling her nephew's dark brown hair. "But I promise the next time I come over I'll have some pudding and milk with you. Will that be all right?"

With a spoonful of pudding in his mouth, Flynn nodded vigorously.

While her nephew ate his snack, Lily smiled at Daniel. "You looked as if you enjoyed yourself this evening."

Daniel glanced over at Flynn shoveling more pudding into his mouth. "This little guy makes it easy to have fun." He gave her a grin that made her feel warm all over. "Thank you for letting me help you babysit."

"You're very welcome," she said, smiling back as she wiped Flynn's hands and mouth. Picking up her nephew from his booster seat, she kissed his baby-soft cheek. "Are you ready to take your bath and get your pajamas on before I read your bedtime story?"

Throwing his arms around her neck, Flynn gave her

a hug. "Your book, Aunt Lily." When she set him on his feet, he walked over to where Daniel sat at the table, his expression serious. "You stay for the story."

"I'm going to be here as long as your Aunt Lily," Daniel reassured the child.

"C'mon, Aunt Lily," Flynn said, taking her hand to tug her along. "Dannel wants to hear the story."

"We'll only be a few minutes," Lily said, amazed that Flynn had taken to Daniel so quickly.

Ten minutes later, as they walked back into the family room with Flynn dressed in his pajamas and holding the book he had picked out, Lily watched as the little boy crawled up into Daniel's lap. "Do you want Daniel to read the story this evening?" she asked.

"No. You," Flynn answered, resting his head back against Daniel's shoulder.

With her nephew sitting on his lap and Daniel cradling the little boy with one arm, Lily was touched by the sight. What was there about a man being so attentive and gentle with a child that she found sexy?

Opening the book, she decided that her pregnancy hormones must be working overtime. She was finding everything about the way Daniel dealt with her nephew to be heartwarming and she looked forward to seeing him with their own child.

As she read the story, she kept glancing over at Flynn and watched as his eyes began to droop. When she was sure he had fallen asleep, she closed the book and started to get up.

"What happens next?" Daniel asked, grinning. "Did the puppy find his way back home?"

"Of course." She laughed softly. "Children's books always have happy endings. But why did you want to know how the story ends? You didn't get that caught up in it, did you?"

"I wanted to know what to tell him if he quizzes me the next time we babysit," Daniel answered as he got up from the chair and shifted her nephew to where Flynn's head rested against his shoulder. "If you'll lead the way, I'll carry him to bed for you."

He intended to accompany her the next time she had to babysit?

Lily shook her head as she walked down the hall ahead of him and her sleeping nephew. Daniel was apparently very serious about learning to deal with children so that he could be a good parent and she was glad. She wanted him to love their child, even if he couldn't love her.

When they tucked Flynn into his bed and walked back to the family room, Daniel sat down in the armchair while she seated herself on the couch. "So what do you think?" she asked. "Do you feel a little more relaxed about being around children?"

"Absolutely," he said, smiling. "I wasn't sure how the evening would go, but I really did have fun. Flynn is a great kid."

"I think so," Lily said, "but then I'm prejudiced because he's my nephew and I love him to pieces."

They fell silent a moment before Daniel asked, "Where's his mother?"

"Grace was killed in a plane crash about a year ago," Lily said sadly. "She was on her way for a weekend visit with her parents when the chartered plane went down, and my heart aches for both her and Flynn. She wanted him so desperately, but she was robbed of the opportunity to see him grow up. And although Matt is trying to keep her memory alive for him, Flynn won't know his mother except in pictures and on video."

"That's tragic," Daniel said, his tone filled with compassion. He frowned. "You made it sound as if it wasn't easy for them to have the little boy. Was there a problem with her getting pregnant?"

"I'm not exactly sure what was wrong, but Grace wasn't able to conceive and I'm not sure that she would have been able to continue the pregnancy if she had," Lily said, yawning as she curled up in the corner of the couch. "That's why they finally decided to go with in vitro fertilization and use a surrogate to carry a baby to term."

He rose from the chair and, walking around the coffee table, joined her on the couch to put his arm around her. "I'm sure it's been hard on your brother. Losing his wife and trying to juggle being a single father with all that's going on now at The Kincaid Group couldn't possibly be easy."

"It really has been difficult for him, and I'm worried about him." Her heart ached for Matt and all the tragedy that he had been through in the past year. "He was devastated when Grace was killed and now he's torn between being with Flynn and working practically day and night to get these reports ready for..." She paused as she tried to hide another yawn. "Jack Sinclair."

"Why don't you give up and take a little nap?" Daniel suggested.

"I can't go to sleep. I'm babysitting," she said, unable to resist laying her head on his shoulder.

"I'm awake." He kissed the top of her head. "If there's a problem I can't handle, I'll let you know, sweetheart."

"Well, I might close my eyes for just a few minutes," she said reluctantly.

She hated to shirk her duties as a babysitter, but Daniel was there to wake her in case Flynn needed her. And she was having such a hard time keeping her eyes open that maybe resting them for a bit would help.

Daniel smiled. He knew as soon as Lily closed her eyes that she had fallen asleep. From everything he'd been reading in the books he had bought at the mall, it was quite common for a woman to need extra rest in the first few months of her pregnancy, then again the last month or so before she gave birth.

Gazing down at the woman who was going to have his baby, he couldn't believe how drastically his views had changed in such a short amount of time. If someone had told him just a week ago that he would be embracing the idea of becoming a father and doing his best to convince a woman to marry him, he would have laughed his head off. But now?

After spending time with Lily's nephew and finding that he wasn't a complete washout with kids, Daniel found that he was actually looking forward to the day when he could sit on the floor and do things like build a Lego skyscraper with his own son or daughter. It was something his own father had never even attempted when Daniel was a boy and he couldn't help feeling they had both come out losers because of it. His father had missed the opportunity of knowing the wonder of the world as seen through the eyes of a child and Daniel had missed out on having a real dad, not just a man who only made a halfhearted attempt to relate to him.

Placing his hand on Lily's still-flat stomach, he

thought about what an amazing mother she was going to be, too. As he watched her with Flynn throughout the evening, he had marveled at how kind and patient she was—suggesting that he pick up his toys instead of ordering him to do it and allowing him to make choices of the book he wanted to read and who he wanted to read it. And she wasn't the least bit uncomfortable showing the toddler plenty of affection.

Several times in the past few days, he had wondered what kind of parents they were going to be. But not anymore. They were going to make a great team, raising this child. And that led him to a more immediate problem. How was he going to convince Lily to marry him?

He had been true to his word when he told her that he wouldn't pressure her into doing anything she didn't want to do when he started staying with her at the mansion. But he was finding that he wasn't a patient man when the stakes were this high. He wanted their baby to have a set of parents who not only worked together to raise him or her, he wanted their child to have a mother and father who bore the same last name.

He had made up his mind and, although it hadn't been an easy decision, come to terms with the fact that he was again going to wade into the pool of matrimony. Now all he had to do was find a subtle way to convince Lily to get her feet wet with him.

And as far as he was concerned, the sooner that happened, the better.

Seven

"Who on earth could that be?" Lily muttered as she hurried down the hall. No one but her family and Daniel knew she lived here and he had left over an hour ago to go to his office.

Crossing the foyer, she hoped it wasn't someone from the newspaper or television stations. The reporters had been relentless trying to get an interview and forced her mother to make the decision to cancel the family's Sunday dinner last week, as well as the coming week's get-together. A day or two after the news broke that her father had been murdered, Laurel had released a statement that the family didn't know anything more than the police and asked that they please respect the Kincaids's privacy as they mourned the death of their loved one. Instead of quieting things down, the press release only seemed to fuel the media frenzy.

Looking through the peephole in the center of the door, she half expected to see a member of the press standing on the piazza. What she didn't expect was to see Charlotte Addison standing on the other side.

Lily was almost tempted to pretend she wasn't home or that she hadn't heard the doorbell. Her father had warned her that she would have to deal with Daniel's mother at some point and putting it off wasn't going to make it any easier. She took a deep breath and steeled herself for an unpleasant confrontation.

"Hello, Mrs. Addison," she said, opening the door.

The woman looked taken aback. "What are you doing here?" she asked, raising one disapproving eyebrow.

"I moved in a week ago," Lily answered, noticing there wasn't a car in the driveway or one parked along the street in front of the house. Had the woman walked the half mile from her home on East Battery?

"I saw lights on last night when I returned from a meeting of the planning committee for this year's Read and Write charity event, but I just assumed someone had rented..." She shook her head. "It's not important. What does your mother intend to do with this place?"

Lily would have liked to tell the woman that it was none of her business. But she couldn't ignore the years of Southern etiquette her mother had taught her from the time Lily was old enough to listen—always show elders respect and courtesy even in the face of other people's rude behavior.

"My mother doesn't own the mansion, Mrs. Addison," Lily said, trying her best to keep her irritation in check. "I do. My father left it to me in his will."

To Lily's surprise, Charlotte Addison smiled. "Then

we shouldn't have any problem coming to an agreement."

Lily had no idea what the woman was talking about. "Excuse me?"

"This is my ancestral home and I want it back," the woman said as if Lily's father had stolen it from her.

"It's not for sale, Mrs. Addison," she said firmly. She might have allowed the woman to bully her into doing what she wanted once, when Charlotte wanted Lily to stop seeing Daniel, but Lily wasn't going to let it happen a second time. "I've loved and admired this house all my life and it was my father's wish that I have it."

Charlotte's expression darkened. "How could you possibly care so much for a piece of property that you have no ties to?"

"But I do." Lily pointed to White Point Gardens across the street. "When I was a little girl, my father used to take me for walks in the park and I would spend hours sitting on that bench across the way, staring at this house and dreaming of living here."

"A child's fancy," the woman scoffed, but her complexion had turned a bit pale and Lily noticed that she looked as if she wasn't feeling well.

"Are you all right, Mrs. Addison?" she asked, growing concerned.

"I…think I need to sit down for a moment," Charlotte said, sounding a bit shaky. She kept staring at Lily as if transfixed.

"Please, come in and I'll get you something to drink," Lily said, taking the woman's arm to help support her.

No matter how Charlotte Addison had talked to her

in the past, she was Daniel's mother and the grandmother of the baby Lily was carrying. Besides the fact that she had been brought up to lend her assistance to someone when there was a need, Lily really didn't want to see anything bad happen to her.

Once Lily had Charlotte comfortably seated on the couch in the formal sitting room just off the foyer, she hurried to get the woman a glass of water. When she returned, Mrs. Addison looked as if she might be feeling a lot better.

"Do you need to put your feet up, Mrs. Addison?" Lily asked, handing her the glass. "Should I call Daniel?"

"No," the woman said a little too quickly. There was a hint of panic in the one word and Lily sensed that Mrs. Addison didn't want Daniel knowing she had paid Lily a visit. "My blood sugar or my blood pressure might be a bit low," Charlotte said, taking a sip of water. "I'll be fine. Really."

Having had a childhood friend with juvenile diabetes, Lily knew that if it was low blood glucose, Charlotte needed to eat something. "I was just making a turkey sandwich for myself. Why don't you come into the kitchen and I'll make one for you as well."

For the first time since Lily had met her, Mrs. Addison looked a bit unsure. "I don't…want to impose."

"Nonsense," Lily said, helping her to her feet. "It's no trouble at all." As she escorted Charlotte down the hall, she wondered how on earth she managed to get herself into situations like the one she was currently in. But she couldn't in good conscience send the woman on her way without making sure she was going to be all right.

While Lily made sandwiches for them, she noticed that Mrs. Addison, although silent, kept looking around at the renovations that had been made to the mansion. "Do you like the restoration my father commissioned?" she asked, setting the food in front of Charlotte.

"Yes, it looks…surprisingly nice," the woman said begrudgingly.

"If you're up to taking a tour after we eat, I'll show you the rest of the house," Lily offered.

She wasn't certain why it should matter to her, but she wanted Charlotte to see that the man she had more or less accused of stealing the home from her had cared enough about the place to see that the once-elegant antebellum mansion had been restored to its original grandeur. Lily fully expected her to refuse, considering Charlotte's bitterness toward Lily's father, but she felt compelled to try to vindicate him in the woman's eyes, if only a little.

"Yes," Mrs. Addison said, surprising her. "I think I would like that very much."

When Daniel walked through the rear entrance of the Beauchamp house, he thought he might be hallucinating. Seated at the table in the kitchen with Lily was his contemptuous, opinionated mother. What the hell was she up to this time?

"Hello, Daniel," Charlotte said, surprising him with her almost congenial tone.

"Charlotte," he said, giving her a slow nod of acknowledgment. What was going on?

Glancing at Lily, he tried to judge her mood. His mother had a knack for rubbing people the wrong way with little or no effort. Knowing how Charlotte felt about Lily and her family, he fully expected that she had dialed up her condescension several notches once she learned a Kincaid was living in Beauchamp House. But Lily didn't seem the least bit upset. In fact, just the opposite. She appeared to be quite relaxed and at ease with his mother.

"Lily, could I see you in the foyer for a moment?" Turning his attention to Charlotte, he added, "We'll only be a few minutes."

When Lily followed him down the hall to the entryway and well out of earshot of Charlotte, he asked, "Why is she here?"

"It's all right, Daniel," Lily assured him. "Your mother stopped by on her morning walk to inquire about the house and I invited her to come in when she seemed to become lightheaded."

"Is she all right?" He had never known Charlotte to be sick a day in her life, but she was a little over sixty and could be developing problems.

"She's fine now," Lily said, assuring him. "I asked her if she would like to have lunch. After we ate, I showed her the renovations that Daddy had made."

"She hasn't been giving you attitude over your dad or our seeing each other?" he asked, unable to believe that was all there was to his mother's visit.

"Not really." She shook her head. "She did tell me that she wanted to buy the mansion back, but I told her it wasn't for sale."

"And Charlotte accepted that?" he asked.

"Not at first." Lily shrugged. "I told her that I loved this place and about how long I've dreamed of living here. After she saw how much time and effort went into the renovations, I think she realized I was serious about my feelings for it and accepted that I won't be selling it." She glanced down the hall toward the kitchen. "We really should get back to her. It's rude to leave someone alone like this."

Daniel shook his head to clear it as he and Lily returned to the kitchen where his mother sat gazing out of the floor-to-ceiling windows at the courtyard beyond. What could have caused Charlotte's turnaround? And why?

He didn't believe for a minute that she had shown up on Lily's doorstep to inquire if the place was for sale, then gave up that easily. Nor was he buying her sudden change of heart about the Kincaids. Charlotte didn't operate that way.

After sitting at the table listening to Lily and his mother exchange polite conversation while he ate lunch, he wasn't entirely certain he hadn't somehow landed in the twilight zone. Charlotte was being quite civil and he knew his mother well enough to know that her tone was completely sincere. She was actually enjoying herself. Unreal!

When he finished eating, he checked his watch. "I hate to eat and run, but I have a meeting in about an hour and I need to get back to the office," he said, rising to his feet. He picked up his suit jacket from the back of the chair and put it on. "I'll be going past your place if you'd like a ride home, Charlotte."

"Yes, I think I'll take you up on that offer," she said as she stood up. Turning to Lily, she smiled. "Thank you for lunch. It's been nice chatting with you. You and Daniel will have to come over sometime for dinner."

"That would be nice," Lily said, smiling

The exchange between the two women in his life

was almost more than he could comprehend and Daniel couldn't wait to get Charlotte into his car. A change in attitude that drastic had to have been brought about by something and he wanted to know what it was.

Escorting his mother to the car, he quickly slid in behind the steering wheel. "What was that all about, Charlotte?"

To his mother's credit, she didn't try to act as if she didn't know what he meant. "She really does love Beauchamp House, doesn't she?"

"Yes, she does," Daniel answered as he drove the car out onto the street. "Living in Colonel Sam's old place has been a dream of Lily's her entire life."

"If not entirely happy about it, I can be content with her owning the property as long as I know she cares that much about it," Charlotte said decisively.

"Who are you and what have you done with my mother?" he asked, meaning it. "I would have thought a Kincaid living there would have sent you into orbit."

"I'll admit that at first I was livid to learn that Reginald's daughter had inherited the property, but she is Elizabeth Winthrop's daughter, too, and that counts for something," Charlotte explained. "The Winthrops have been in Charleston as long as the Beauchamps, and until Elizabeth married that scoundrel, their background was impeccable. Now that Kincaid is gone, I suppose her error in judgment can be overlooked."

"And that's all it takes to make Lily living there okay with you?" he asked, unable to get over his mother's screwed-up reasoning. "Kincaid is dead and that restores Elizabeth's standing in the social pecking order?"

Charlotte shrugged. "That and the fact that the girl

is pregnant with a Beauchamp descendant who will be residing in the mansion with her."

Shocked that his mother knew about Lily's pregnancy, Daniel steered the car over to the curb, to turn and stare at his mother. "Lily told you about the baby?"

"Oh, no," she said, shaking her head. "Lily didn't say a word. She didn't have to."

"Then how—"

"Have you ever heard of the 'pregnancy glow'?" Charlotte interrupted.

He shook his head. It sounded like something made up. "No, I can't say that I have."

"It's more pronounced with some women than it is with others," Charlotte went on quite seriously. "It has something to do with the hormonal changes and a woman's complexion. Lily definitely has it."

Now Daniel knew he had entered another realm. Never in a million years would he have believed he would ever be listening to Charlotte explain the changes caused by pregnancy.

"When may I expect my first grandchild?" Charlotte asked.

"Mid or late August," he heard himself tell her. The whole conversation was so surreal, Daniel wasn't entirely certain he wasn't dreaming.

"And when are you going to make an honest woman of Lily?" his mother asked as calmly as if they were discussing the weather.

"That's hard to say," he answered, steering the car back into traffic. "You did a lot of damage with your meddling before Christmas and she isn't overly receptive to the idea just yet. But I'm working on it."

"Is there anything I can do to help things along?" Charlotte asked, shocking him yet again.

"Good God, no." The last thing he needed was his mother's interference.

"This could be my only grandchild, Daniel," Charlotte said sternly. "I don't want him or her to be born on the wrong side of the blanket, nor do I want us to be strangers."

"You really mean that, don't you?" he asked.

Charlotte nodded. "I thought that after you and Charisma divorced, my chances for becoming a grandmother had died along with your marriage." She turned in the bucket seat to face him. "No matter what you believe about me, most of which is probably true, I do care and want to be part of your child's life."

"I'm glad to hear that, Charlotte, but this is between me and Lily. Whether we get married is our decision. I want you to stay out of it. I do, however, give you my word that you will get to know the child." Parking the car outside Charlotte's home, he got out and opened the door for her. "It's not common knowledge that Lily's pregnant and I'd rather you not say anything to anyone about it until we're ready to announce the news ourselves."

"I won't." She raised one eyebrow. "Does Elizabeth know?"

"Not that I'm aware of." Walking her up the front steps to the wide porch, he noticed that his mother wore a smug expression. He almost groaned. "What's going on in that devious head of yours this time, Charlotte?"

"It appears that I'm the first of the grandmothers to

know about the baby," she said, sounding somewhat triumphant.

Shaking his head, Daniel walked back to his car. Some things never changed. He should have known that Charlotte would somehow find a way to feel superior to Elizabeth Kincaid.

At the moment, his mother's head games were the least of his worries. He had to make a trip to the contractor's office to drop off a key to the Beauchamp house for the builders to add a window seat to the cupola, then he had to get to his meeting with Lily's sister.

Kara Kincaid had built a solid reputation as an event-planning genius and he was in desperate need of her help. If she could assist him in setting up and initiating something to convince Lily to accept his proposal of marriage and become his wife, he would forever be grateful to her. And he was finding that getting Lily to say yes was becoming more important to him with each passing day.

"Have you seen this, Daniel?" Lily asked as they walked through the natural history exhibit at the museum. "I wasn't aware that we had so many prehistoric animals in Charleston."

"Yeah, about twenty-eight million years ago," he answered, laughing. "Haven't you ever been through this part of the museum before?"

She shook her head. "When I was little, all these mounted skeletons gave me nightmares."

"Boys must be a lot different about these kinds of things than girls," he said thoughtfully. "The dinosaur bones were always my favorite part of coming to the museum when I was young. I even thought I wanted to be a paleontologist when I grew up."

"My favorite exhibits are the ones with the dresses and jewelry." She couldn't help but smile. "I love seeing how women used to dress. Can you imagine how grand it must have been with all those beautiful gowns twirling around the dance floor at a ball and all the jewels sparkling in the glow of the candlelight?"

"No. Not really."

She smiled at the frown on his handsome face. "No, I don't suppose boys care much about hoopskirts and necklaces made of precious gems."

"Are you sure you don't have time to write children's books?" he asked, grinning. "You certainly have the imagination for making up stories any little girl would love to read." He took her hand in his and brought it to his lips. "If our baby's a girl, I'll let you take the lead on teaching her about dresses and jewelry. I'll take care of coaching her softball team."

"And if the baby's a boy?" she asked.

His grin made her feel warm all over. "We won't make you suffer through looking at the bones of an eighteen-foot-long crocodile or the primitive toothed whale skeleton."

"Thank you. You have yourself a deal." She couldn't help but shudder at how horrible the animals had to have been when they were roaming the area. "I think I can safely say I won't be changing my mind about that, either."

Strolling through the museum with Daniel, Lily couldn't help but think about how wonderful it had been since he moved into the mansion with her. He had kept his word and hadn't put any pressure on her to invite him back into the master suite or agree to marry him, giving them time to learn even more about each other. She would have never dreamed that he liked classic movies or that he wasn't a big fan of sailing.

But their time together had also taken a toll—at least on her. Loving him the way she did, it had been extremely difficult to have him kiss her goodnight, then watch him walk down the hall to one of the guest bedrooms, while she entered the master suite alone.

She sighed. How much longer could she go on being so close to him without having him touch her? Love her?

As they continued on through the museum, she realized they had wandered into the room displaying examples of historic weaponry of the past three hundred years. "This is another area where you can take the lead," she said as a chill ran the length of her spine. "If you don't mind I think I'll skip this and meet you later by the entrance."

"Don't like swords and muskets, huh?"

"Not particularly."

His expression suddenly became remorseful and he immediately took her by the elbow to guide her out of the room. "Lily, I'm sorry. I should have realized this exhibit would drag up painful emotions."

"I suppose antique guns won't always remind me that my father was killed with one," she said, glad to be away from the weaponry area. "But right now, it's just a bit too soon."

Moving from one glass case to another in the textile section, Lily forced herself to forget about the guns and concentrate on the elaborate ball gowns. She couldn't help but wonder if their baby would be a girl or a boy. It really didn't matter to her which gender the baby was just as long as he or she was healthy. Although, it would be fun to share the beauty of the historic dresses with her daughter.

"Do you want a boy?" she asked as they strolled toward the exit of the museum.

Daniel shrugged. "I think every man would like to have a son." When they stepped out into the fading sunlight of late afternoon, he took her into his arms. "But I would be just as happy with a little red-haired girl with her mother's blue eyes."

"Perfect answer, Mr. Addison. You're going to be a wonderful father."

Lily couldn't resist raising up on tiptoe and kissing him soundly.

As she stared into his navy blue eyes, she knew she had lost the battle she had waged with herself for the past week. She wanted Daniel, had never stopped wanting him and she knew in her heart that would never change.

She nibbled on her lower lip a moment before she whispered, "I've missed having you hold me."

The heat in his gaze indicated that he knew exactly what she meant. "I've missed making love to you, too. But why did you have to tell me that now?" he asked, groaning as he rested his forehead against hers. "Now I'm going to rush you through dinner so that we can get back to the mansion."

"Why?" She knew, but she couldn't resist teasing him. "I thought you made reservations at that new five-star restaurant you've been wanting to try."

Nodding, he put his arm around her waist and pulled her to his side as they walked toward his car. "No matter how good the food is, I'm not going to know whether I'm having beef bourguignon or filet of boot leather."

"Really?" She laughed. "What makes you think that?"

He opened the car door for her to get in, then leaning inside, gave her a kiss that curled her toes. "Because all I'll be able to think about is taking you in my arms and loving you all night long."

Throughout dinner, Daniel seized every opportunity to touch her hand, give her meaningful glances and tell her how much he wanted her. By the time they walked out of the elegant French restaurant, Lily wasn't sure which one of them was more eager to get home—him or her.

Several minutes later when they arrived at her house, instead of taking her right upstairs to the master suite as she anticipated, Daniel took her hand in his and led her to the flight of stairs going up to the third floor.

"Where on earth are we going?" she asked, following him.

"You'll see," he said, opening the door to the steps leading up to the cupola. When they reached the top, he instructed, "Now close your eyes. I have something I want to show you."

She had no idea what he was up to, but she could tell he was impatient for her to see whatever it was. Closing her eyes, she heard him flip on the light switch a moment before he led her up the last step to the cupola.

"Open your eyes, Lily."

When she did, she caught her breath at the sight

of the beautiful window seat encircling the perimeter of the tiny room. "Oh, Daniel, I love them," she said, touching the aqua print fabric of the plush cushions. "This is exactly what I envisioned." Turning to put her arms around his neck, she gave him a quick kiss. "Was this the reason you insisted we stay out the entire day?"

"I had to make sure the contractor had plenty of time to get them finished," he said.

With his arms around her waist, holding her close against his solid frame, she felt as if she could stay that way forever. "I love everything about them and I love… that you thought to do this for me."

Gazing into his blue eyes, she watched them darken to navy as he gave her a smile that stole her breath. "I'm glad you like them, sweetheart."

She had wanted to tell him she loved him, but sadly, it wasn't what he wanted to hear. "Please kiss me, Daniel."

"Sweetheart, I thought you'd never ask," he said a moment before he took a step back to turn off the lights to ensure privacy.

When he returned to her, his mouth settled over hers and Lily gave herself up to the mastery of his kiss. Daniel might not love her, might never feel the emotion that filled every cell of her being, but that didn't stop her from loving him.

She knew she was playing with fire and there was a very real possibility that she would end up getting burned. But she couldn't seem to stop herself. No matter how much she wanted to protect herself from the emotional pain she might suffer, he was, and probably always would be, her biggest weakness.

As he deepened the kiss, she abandoned all thought

and reveled in his exploration. Compelled to do a little exploring of her own, she engaged him in a game of advance and retreat, tracing his lips, then slipping past them to stroke his tongue as he had done hers. His answering groan sent heat streaking throughout her entire being. She wanted him to know how she felt, needed him to feel the strength and power without her saying the words. She belonged to him as she would belong to no other man and she intended for him to know that.

When he slid his hand down along her side, then tugged the tail of her silk blouse from the waistband of her skirt, Lily anticipated the touch of his hands on her sensitized skin. Helping him to free the garment, she reached for his belt buckle.

"Just a minute, sweetheart," he said, breaking the kiss.

He put just enough distance between them to unbuckle the strap of leather at his waist, then pulled his shirt from the band of his trousers. Taking her back into his arms, he slipped his hand beneath her blouse and skimmed it along her ribs to the swell of her breast. When he covered her with his warm palm, her heart skipped several beats and she felt as if her knees were going to give way.

She suddenly felt herself being lifted off her feet and she realized when he placed her on his lap that he had settled them both on the new window seat. The feel of his strong arousal pressed to the side of her hip and the touch of his hand as he gently caressed her breast caused her head to spin, and the need growing within her became almost unbearable. She wanted him— needed him. Now.

"Hey, where are you…going?" he asked when she pulled from his arms to stand up.

She glanced at the windows of the cupola and the night sky outside that was so dark she could barely see her hand in front of her face. Reassured that they were concealed from prying eyes, she smiled as she knelt in front of him to release the closure at the top of his waistband, then reached for the tab at his fly.

"Lily…are you sure about…this?" He sounded as if he had run a marathon.

She nodded as she slowly ran her fingernail down the zipper and the bulge beneath straining to be freed. There were a lot of things that she was unsure of, but loving him wasn't one of them. If she couldn't tell him how she felt, she intended to show him.

"You are about to get so-o-o lucky, Mr. Addison."

Daniel held his breath as tooth by tooth, Lily eased the zipper down, releasing him from the confines of his pants. One of the many reasons he had been attracted to her had been her free spirit, her spontaneity. But never in his wildest dreams would he have imagined the circumstances in which he found himself at that moment. Every man had his share of fantasies, but all his paled in comparison to the reality of what was happening to him now.

When Lily had the zipper completely lowered, he felt as if his head might fly right off his shoulders when she used her index finger to trace him through the cotton of his boxer briefs. He had never experienced anything more erotic in his entire life as from base to tip, she painstakingly measured his length and girth. By the time she reached the elastic at his waist and he raised his hips to help her pull his underwear down his thighs, Daniel decided if he died at that very moment, he would leave the world a very happy man.

When he reached for her, Lily surprised him when she shook her head. "Not yet, darling."

He was smoldering hot and it appeared she was getting ready to add more fuel to the flames. "Sweetheart, I think I'd better…warn you. You're playing… with fire," he said through clenched teeth.

The touch of her hand on his heated body caused his heart to race, but the first touch of her lips kissing him intimately drove his blood pressure into stroke range. Daniel squeezed his eyes shut and tried to concentrate on maintaining his control, but it was damn difficult with Lily slowly driving him to the brink of insanity.

Unable to remain passive any longer, he reached down to lift her to her feet. "Let's go downstairs to the master suite."

She surprised him when she shook her head. "I need you now."

When she slipped her hands beneath her skirt to remove her panties, then straddled his hips, he thought he might die of ecstasy as her body slowly consumed his. "Don't…move," he warned.

"Why?" Her warm breath feathering over his ear almost sent him into total meltdown.

"Because if you don't remain completely still, there's a very real possibility this could be the shortest lucky streak on record," he said, knowing it was going to take every ounce of his stamina to keep that from happening.

When he felt he had regained enough control to ensure her pleasure, he kissed her, then placing his hands on her hips, urged her into a rocking motion against him. Heat suffused every fiber of his being and he knew he had never experienced with any other woman the degree of passion, the deep insatiable hunger, that he did with Lily. She made him feel whole for the first time in his life.

Deciding not to delve into what that might mean, Daniel concentrated on Lily's body tightening around him and he knew she was close to reaching the pinnacle. Just when he thought he might lose the battle he had been waging with himself, he heard her soft moan at the same time her body intimately caressed his.

Daniel groaned deeply as her pleasure unleashed the tide that had been building inside him. Holding her tightly against him, he wasn't sure he could keep from passing out as the intensity of his release sent waves of pleasure surging through him.

Never before had making love been as powerful, as all-encompassing. He felt in his heart it never would with any other woman. Only Lily.

And that's when he knew. He had finally found the emotion that had escaped him all his adult life—the feeling that he hadn't even been sure existed.

He had fallen hopelessly in love with Lily Kincaid.

Eight

On Monday, Lily nervously sat in police headquarters in downtown Charleston, waiting to be interviewed about her father's homicide. "Please state your name, age and your relationship to the deceased, Miss Kincaid."

"I'm Lily Kincaid, I'm twenty-five and the youngest daughter of Reginald Kincaid," she said, surprised that her voice sounded so steady, considering the state of her jangled nerves.

"Where were you on the evening of December thirtieth, the night your father was murdered?" Detective McDonough asked.

As the lead detective on her father's murder investigation, Charles McDonough had explained in advance that her statement would be recorded and that his questions would be straightforward and to the point. He had told her that he wanted her answers to be just as concise.

But she hadn't expected him to be so blunt. Hearing the word *murder* to describe her father's death was almost more than she could bear. At times she still found it difficult to believe her father was gone, let alone that someone had taken his life.

A chill ran the length of her entire body as she reflected on how her father had to have known his killer and had most likely let whoever it was into the office building that night. The security at TKG was too tight for him not to have let the person inside. Either that or the murderer had access to the alarm system codes and knew the security guard's scheduled rounds. Either way, it left her with a horrible sense of dread. Could she know the killer?

"I was at the bookstore in the Shops at Charleston Place mall," she answered, pulling herself out of her disturbing speculation.

"What time were you there?" Detective McDonough asked.

"I arrived at the mall around six that evening and didn't leave until the store closed at nine." She remembered exactly when she had left because she and the bookstore manager had walked out to their cars together.

"Is there anyone who can corroborate your story?" McDonough asked.

"Yes, the manager of the bookstore, Mona Peterson, and several of her employees were present," she answered. How could it possibly be that the homicide detective managed to make her feel as if she were keeping something from him when she had absolutely nothing to hide?

Detective McDonough nodded. "What was the nature of your business at the bookstore?"

She had no idea what that had to do with catching her father's killer, but she supposed it was standard procedure for him to ask. "I'm an illustrator of children's books and I was helping to arrange an exhibit of my work to be displayed until this Saturday, when the author of the book will join me for a book signing."

She had considered canceling the appearance, but as Daniel had pointed out, her father's life was the one that had ended. Her life had to go on.

"Do you know of an acquaintance, either personal or professional, who might have threatened your father or have a motive for killing him?" the man asked, his expression stoic.

"No." She shook her head. "My father never discussed business with me and I really don't know of anyone who would want to do him harm."

"What about your family?" McDonough persisted. "Were there any strained relationships or estrangements?"

"No."

The man paused a moment. "What about his mistress and her two sons from up in Greenville?"

Lily hadn't expected the detective's questions to be easy, but she hadn't been prepared for him to ask her about her father's secret life. "I really don't know anything about them," she answered honestly. "The first I learned that they even existed was when they showed up at my father's funeral."

Detective McDonough stared at her for several long moments as if trying to judge if she was telling the truth. "Well, I think that's about it," he said, closing a file on top of the table in front of her. He gave her a pointed look. "We will be checking out your story to see if you were where you indicated. If you have any changes you wish to make to your statement, now would be the time to do it."

Relieved that the interrogation was finally over, Lily shook her head. "No. To the best of my knowledge, everything I've told you is correct."

"Thank you for coming in to make your statement, Miss Kincaid." When she rose to leave, he opened the door to the small room where the interview had taken place. "If I have any more questions, I'll be in touch." Seemingly as an afterthought, he added, "If you think of anything that might help us with the investigation, please don't hesitate to give me a call."

As Lily left the police station and drove back to the Beauchamp house, she couldn't help but be relieved that her part in the investigation was over. The detective had told her that he would be interviewing everyone in her family separately and it appeared that he had started with her first.

She really didn't have anything to contribute to the investigation, but at least Detective McDonough knew she had an airtight alibi and could eliminate her as a possible suspect. Maybe once they whittled down the list of people who might have had contact with her father in his final hours, they would then be able to zero in on the horrible person who had committed the crime.

Steering her car into the driveway of the mansion,

Lily was surprised to see Charlotte Addison sitting on the piazza in one of the white wicker chairs by the front door, apparently waiting for her to return home. "Hello, Mrs. Addison," she said, getting out of her car. "I wasn't aware you were dropping by today. I hope you haven't been waiting long."

"No, I've only been here a few minutes," the woman said, surprising Lily with an actual smile.

Lily had no idea what caused Charlotte Addison's change of attitude toward her, but whatever it was, it had happened the day she stopped by to see if Lily was going to sell the mansion. But she wasn't going to question the about-face. Mrs. Addison was the mother of the man Lily loved and anything was better than the hostility the woman had displayed at the dinner party she'd hosted the week before Christmas.

"Would you like to come in?" Lily asked, not knowing what else to say when Charlotte fell silent.

"Well, maybe for just a few minutes." When Lily unlocked the door and stepped back, Mrs. Addison entered the house ahead of her. "I do have something I need to discuss with you."

"Would you like some tea?" Lily asked as they walked into the formal sitting room just off the foyer.

"No, thank you." Charlotte sat down on the edge of the couch, then directly met Lily's questioning gaze. "I know that in the past I may have been a little…shall we say, hasty with my opinion of you and your family," she said as if choosing her words carefully. "But I think that's behind us now and I feel we should forget about it and move on."

It appeared that Charlotte's acknowledgment that there had been a problem was as close to an apology as she was going to get. Lily really hadn't expected even that much from the woman.

"I think that would be best," Lily agreed. She thought they had moved past the issue when the woman dropped by the house while she was out walking the week before. Apparently Charlotte felt compelled to reiterate that she'd had a change of heart.

"The reason for my coming by today is to ask a favor of you," Charlotte said, finally getting to the point of her visit. "I think I mentioned the other day when I was here that I'm on the planning committee for the Read and Write charity event?"

"Yes, I remember you mentioning it."

The woman patted her perfectly coiffed hair as if putting it back into place. "Our maxim is 'promoting literacy in everyone from five to ninety-five,' and this year we've decided to hold a bachelor auction to raise funds for our programs." She frowned. "I wasn't altogether pleased with the idea of auctioning off men in order to raise money for such a worthy cause, but every bit of the proceeds will go to Read and Write, so I suppose it will be all right." She shook her head. "But I didn't stop by to tell you how undignified I think our means of raising money is this year. I wanted to ask if you would be willing to assist us."

"I think a bachelor auction will be all right, Mrs. Addison. It sounds like an excellent way to raise money." Lily approved of any cause to help further literacy and bachelor auctions were always popular. "What can I do to help out?"

"If possible, we need the use of this house." Charlotte's smile brightened as she explained further. "We often like to set some of our more elegant events in historic homes and since the renovations, the Colonel Samuel Beauchamp House would be perfect. The balcony just off the sitting room in the master suite here would be a lovely place for our bachelors to be spotlighted when they walk out for the bidding. They would be easily seen by everyone and the paved courtyard and large backyard could accommodate all our guests."

Lily nodded. Her privacy would only be invaded for one night and it was for a cause close to her heart. "I don't have a problem with that at all, Mrs. Addison. Is there anything else I can do to help out?"

"Excellent. And no need to worry, I think that we have everything else under control," Charlotte said, rising to her feet. "We'll have a tent set up with refreshments, so we won't need the use of the kitchen." As she walked across the foyer to the door, she turned back. "By the way, how are you feeling?"

"I'm doing just fine," Lily answered, wondering what could have caused the woman's concern. "Why do you ask?"

"Oh, no reason." Charlotte gave Lily a smile as if they shared a secret. "It's just that the other day you looked…a bit peaked."

The woman's knowing expression caused Lily to wonder if Daniel had told his mother about the baby. Could that be the reason Charlotte seemed concerned about her health?

"I'm doing fine. Really." Until she talked to Daniel and found out for sure, she wasn't about to discuss her pregnancy with his mother. Instead, she asked, "How are you doing? Any more problems with feeling lightheaded?"

The woman looked puzzled for a moment before she

shook her head, dismissing it as if it wasn't an issue. "I couldn't be healthier."

"That's good to hear, Mrs. Addison."

"Please, call me Charlotte," she said, shocking Lily even more when she gave Lily's arm an affectionate pat. "After all, you are…" She paused as if trying to find the right way to phrase what she wanted to say. "With my son now."

As the woman walked across the piazza and down the steps, Lily stared. Charlotte Addison was unreal. It had barely been a month ago that she had told Lily how unsuitable she was for Daniel. Now she was practically putting her stamp of approval on their being together?

There had to be a reason behind the woman's sudden change and when Daniel got home from the office, Lily intended to find out what it might be. She hadn't asked him not to tell anyone about the pregnancy, but she had assumed he would let her decide who they told and when they shared the news. And it wouldn't be long before she had to make that decision.

She nibbled on her lower lip as she closed the door and headed toward the kitchen for a snack before her nap. Her entire family was going to be at the bookstore on Saturday to show her their support, and because some of the more persistent reporters were still dropping by her mother's from time to time, they had decided to stop by the mansion after the signing for a family get-together. With all of them gathered, it would be the perfect opportunity to make her announcement about the baby.

Placing her hand on her stomach, she smiled. "You've got a big family who is going to be thrilled to hear that you're on the way." She almost laughed as another thought occurred. "And it appears you have a paternal grandmother who is pretty happy about you, too. Either that or she suffers from multiple personalities."

Seated in the reception area of The Kincaid Group offices, Daniel flipped through a magazine, then losing interest, tossed it on the coffee table in front of him as he waited for his meeting with RJ and Matt Kincaid. He was on a mission and as soon as he talked to Lily's brothers, his plans for this Saturday should come together nicely.

His meeting with her sister last week had been postponed at the last minute and he was glad that it had. At the time, he really hadn't had any ideas of what he wanted to do to convince Lily they should be married and hoped Kara would be able to think of something. But after acknowledging to himself how he felt about Lily, he knew exactly what he wanted to do and once he contacted Kara with the details, she had assured him that she would make it happen.

"Mr. Addison, RJ and Matt Kincaid will see you now," the secretary advised him.

Rising to his feet, he walked into the executive office to face Lily's brothers. "Thank you for seeing me on such short notice," he said, shaking both men's hands.

The brothers remained silent and Daniel could tell they were suspicious of him. He couldn't say he blamed them. Addison Industries was their chief rival and it probably felt as if the enemy had entered their camp. They had no idea he was paying them a visit for an entirely different reason than business.

"I suppose you're wondering why I wanted to meet

with both of you," he said, settling himself into a chair in front of RJ's wide desk.

"It did cross our minds," RJ said dryly as he sat down on the other side. The oldest of the Kincaid siblings, RJ was closest to his age and since Daniel's divorce, they had met up several times on the social scene. If there was a bigger player than Daniel had been before he met Lily, he would put his money on it being RJ.

"What can we do for you today, Addison?" Matt asked, standing just to the side of his older brother.

Both men's ties had been loosened and the buttons at the top of their collars had been unfastened. They looked overworked and extremely tired. Daniel could only guess how much pressure they had been under since the reading of their father's will.

Respecting the fact that RJ and Matt's time was at a premium due to the fact they were having to dance to Jack Sinclair's tune these days, Daniel got right to the point. "You both know I've been seeing your sister for the past several months and that I've been staying with her at the Beauchamp House. Since your father is gone, I thought I would talk to you and find out if either of you have a problem with me asking Lily to be my wife."

He could tell by the look on both their faces that he had taken the Kincaid brothers by surprise. But as Lily's sister Kara had pointed out, the plan they had come up with to convince Lily to marry him had a better chance of working if the entire Kincaid clan was on board with it.

A slow smile began to turn up the corners of Matt's mouth. "I don't have a problem with it and I know Flynn won't." He shook his head. "You're all my son has talked about since you and Lily babysat the other night."

"He's a great kid," Daniel said sincerely. "You should be very proud."

"I am," Matt agreed, beaming.

"As long as you're what Lily wants and she's happy, I don't have any objections," RJ said, grinning. "But I think I'd better warn you, Addison. Give her one minute of grief and you and I will have a come-to-Jesus meeting you won't soon forget."

"I wouldn't expect anything less from you, Kincaid," Daniel said, knowing how much Lily meant to her older siblings.

Outlining what he and Kara had planned and asking the brothers to participate, Daniel rose to leave. "I'll see you on Saturday."

"Good luck," both men called after him as Daniel left the office.

He purposely hadn't told any of Lily's siblings about her being pregnant. That would be up to her when and how she wanted to break the news to her family. Besides, he didn't want her thinking that he was trying to use the baby as leverage to get her family to convince her to marry him. She needed to know the reason he wanted to marry her was because he loved her, not because she was pregnant with his child.

As he drove from The Kincaid Group offices to the mansion, he went over his plan again. He hoped that he wasn't about to make a fool of himself in front of her family, as well as many of the good citizens of Charleston. Finding a way to tell her he loved her and getting her to believe him, then laying his heart on the line and asking her to marry him, came at no small risk to his pride, as well as his heart.

He had rejected the idea of love for so long that he knew Lily wouldn't believe him unless he could think of something that would convince her beyond a shadow of a doubt that he was sincere and ready to make the commitment of a lifetime. That's why he was pulling out all the stops to give her the rest of her dream.

Feeling pleased with himself for thinking up the idea, when he walked into the mansion ten minutes later, he stopped dead in his tracks. Lily stood on a chair in the middle of the foyer dressed in a long white dress with gold-and-purple trim, while her sister Kara knelt in front of her using pins to adjust the hem of the gown. Lily looked just like a princess.

"What's going on?" he asked, not happy with the whole damn scenario.

First off, he didn't like that his pregnant girlfriend was standing on a chair that could tip over with one wrong step. And second, he couldn't help but wonder if Kara or one of her other siblings had slipped up and told Lily about his elaborate plan. The whole idea hinged on surprise and he hoped it hadn't been ruined.

Lily smiled. "The bookstore manager called to ask if the author and I would mind dressing like characters from the book for the signing on Saturday." She laughed. "Since he wouldn't look right in a princess costume, I got the job. Fortunately, when I called Kara to see where I could get a dress on such short notice, she had one in her shop."

Relieved that she was none the wiser to the scheme, he couldn't help but grin. "So is the author going as a frog?"

"That's what I asked," Kara said around the pins she held between her lips.

"Since there isn't a frog in the book, that's doubtful," Lily said, turning for her sister to finish pinning the hem. "I think he's probably going to be dressed as the wise old wizard or maybe one of the ducks."

Daniel walked over to make sure Lily didn't fall from the chair. "If I were him, I'd opt for the wizard," he said, taking her hand to make sure she was steady. "It's a little more dignified than a duck." He had never been the type to hover over someone, but where Lily was concerned, he was finding it more difficult to resist with each passing day.

"Well, I think that does it," Kara said, sitting back on her heels. She started putting the rest of the pins back into a little plastic box. "As soon as you change, I'll take the gown with me and drop it off with the seamstress for her to hem. Then I think you should be all set for Saturday."

Lifting Lily down from the chair, Daniel waited until he was sure she had gone upstairs to the master suite to change before he asked Kara, "Is this dress-up thing for the bookstore real?"

"Well, it is now," she said, rising to her feet. Her green eyes twinkled mischievously as she confided, "I called and explained everything to the manager. She was more than happy to request that Lily and the author dress in character."

"Brilliant idea. Thanks." He could well understand now why Kara had built a solid reputation for being the best event planner in Charleston. Her ideas were extremely creative and her eye for detail was amazing.

"Oh, I almost forgot to tell you," she said, putting

the box of pins in her purse. "I did as you requested and told our mother all about your plan. She's going to be there, too."

"Excellent." When he heard Lily coming back down the stairs, he seized the opportunity to change the subject before she asked what they had been discussing. "How's your mother doing?"

"Surprisingly well." Kara shook her head. "Don't get me wrong, I'm proud of how well she's handled losing our dad, but I worry that she might not be dealing with all that's happened."

"I know what you mean," Lily said, handing her sister the gown. "I don't know about you, but to me, she didn't seem all that surprised when Angela Sinclair and her two sons showed up at the funeral."

Kara shook her head. "It's not just you, Lily. Laurel and I noticed that, too." She checked her watch. "Sorry to cut this short, but I'd better get going. I have just enough time to get this to the seamstress before she closes for the day. Then I have an anniversary dinner to oversee on Sullivan's Island this evening."

"Thank you for helping with my costume," Lily said, hugging her sister.

Kara hugged her back. "You know I'm happy to help. I'll see you on Saturday afternoon at the bookstore."

Daniel watched the exchange between the two sisters with interest. Being an only child he had often wondered what it would have been like to have a sibling—someone he shared a childhood history with. Watching Lily with her family, he couldn't help but think that life might not have been quite as lonely in the Addison household if he'd had a brother or sister.

"Your mother dropped by again today," Lily said when she closed the door behind Kara.

He groaned. "What was the nature of her visit this time?"

"It was actually quite pleasant." Lily told him about the charity event for literacy and his mother's request to use the house, then giving him an odd look, added, "Have you told your mother about the baby?"

"I didn't have to. Charlotte told me," he said, shaking his head. "Why? Did she say something?"

"Not really. She just kept smiling and asking how I feel." Lily frowned. "But how would she know—"

"When I took her home the other day, Charlotte told me that you have 'the glow.'" He put his arms around Lily to draw her to him. "I didn't believe her until I looked it up on the internet and sure enough, there it was." He shrugged. "It has something to do with hormonal changes causing a woman's complexion to look as if it's glowing. Apparently Charlotte knew what it looked like."

"I thought that was an old wives' tale." She looked a bit worried. "Do you think your mother has told anyone? I'd rather my family hear about the baby from me than to learn about it through the rumor mill."

"I asked her not to say anything," he assured Lily. "Charlotte might be intractable and at times downright obnoxious, but she's always respected my privacy when I've asked her to."

"That's good to know," she said, melting against him.

He loved the feel of her curvaceous body against his. Hell, he was finding that once he acknowledged the emotion's existence, he loved everything about Lily.

But if he told her now, he knew she wouldn't believe him. She would no doubt think he was just telling her what she wanted to hear to get her to agree to marry him. Even though that was exactly what he wanted her to do, he needed her to believe that he was sincere about his feelings for her, as well. He just hoped that what he had planned for Saturday was enough to convince her.

Later that night, after making love with Daniel, Lily snuggled close within the circle of his strong arms. "Did I tell you that my entire family will be coming to the bookstore this weekend, then stopping here for coffee and dessert afterward?"

"No, I don't remember you mentioning it," he said, sounding sleepy.

"Since Momma's had to cancel our family dinners the past two Sundays because of a few overly zealous reporters, she suggested the get-together." Lily pressed her lips to his shoulder. "I thought it might be a good time to let them all know about the baby."

He was silent for a moment and she thought he might have fallen asleep, when he finally said, "I'm sorry I won't be here when you tell them."

"You won't?"

He shook his head. "I won't be able to make it to the bookstore, either. I have an out-of-town meeting that I need to attend."

"How long will you be away?" she asked. A cold dread began to fill her chest.

"I probably…" he paused to yawn "…won't be back until sometime Monday."

She had never known Daniel to schedule a meeting

out of town or for that matter on a weekend. "Is this something that just came up?"

He nodded. "I met up with an old college friend I hadn't seen in years and we're going to spend the time catching up."

Pulling from his arms, Lily sat up and threw back the covers.

"Hey, where are you going?" he asked when she got out of bed to put on her robe.

"I…um, I'm hungry," she lied. When he started to get up with her, she shook her head. "You have to go into the office tomorrow morning. Go ahead and get your rest."

"Are you sure?" he asked, yawning.

Tying the sash on her robe, she nodded. "I'll be fine."

As she descended the stairs, Lily's heart thumped against her ribs and a sinking feeling settled in the pit of her stomach. Daniel's reasons for not attending the event at the bookstore and for skipping her family gathering sounded too much like the excuse her father had always used for his frequent trips out of town.

Tears filled her eyes. He knew how important the exhibit and signing at the bookstore were for her career and that she wanted him to be there with her. Why couldn't he have postponed the meeting with his friend until next weekend?

She had no reason to believe that what Daniel told her was anything more than what he said it was. To her knowledge, he had never lied to her, never led her to believe that he was anything but trustworthy. But how could she know for sure? Her mother had believed her father for three decades, only to learn of his betrayal when his mistress showed up at the funeral with her two sons.

Was she overreacting to the situation? Had learning about the double life her father had led for all those years affected her more than she realized?

Sitting down at the kitchen table, Lily stared down at her tightly clasped hands. She needed advice and she knew just the person to help her sort through her fears.

When she glanced at the clock on the microwave oven, she realized it was too late to call tonight. But when Daniel left for the office tomorrow morning, Lily was going to visit the woman she had turned to all her life when she needed guidance. She was going to talk to her mother.

Nine

"Momma, could we talk for a few minutes?" Lily asked when she found her mother sitting in the den reading a book.

"Of course, Lily." Her mother's smile and welcoming hug were already making Lily feel a little better. "What's bothering you, darling? You look as if you're carrying the weight of the world on your shoulders."

Lily wasn't surprised her mother knew something was wrong. Elizabeth Kincaid always knew when her children were upset and in need of her comfort and advice.

Sitting on the couch beside her mother, Lily couldn't seem to find a way to ask her mother what she wanted to know without it sounding as if she was prying. "Momma, did you ever suspect that Daddy had a secret life?" she finally asked.

Her mother remained quiet for a moment, then closing her book, took Lily's hands in hers. "Lily, I think deep down I've always known that your father's heart wasn't entirely mine. But I do believe he cared for me. And I know he loved all you children so very much." She gave Lily's hand a gentle squeeze. "Why do you ask?"

"I'm in love with Daniel Addison," Lily said, not knowing where else to start.

"I know, darling." Elizabeth smiled warmly. "Call it a mother's intuition if you like, but I've known for some time that Daniel is the one for you."

Lily shook her head. "I wish I could be as confident of that as you are."

"What makes you think differently?" her mother asked gently.

"He thinks we should get married, but he doesn't love me," Lily said, biting her lower lip to keep it from trembling.

"Oh, I'm sure you're wrong, darling," Elizabeth said, putting her arm around Lily's shoulders.

Deciding to tell her mother everything, she confided, "I'm pregnant."

"That's wonderful," Elizabeth said, hugging Lily close. "I'm thrilled that I'm going to be a grandmother again."

Lily knew her mother would be happy to hear about the baby. Family was everything to Elizabeth. "I thought Daniel and I could tell everyone after the bookstore event, but he's not going to be there with me. He has other plans."

Elizabeth lovingly kissed her cheek. "Where's he going to be?"

"He said he's going out of town to meet a college friend and…" Tears filled Lily's eyes. "It just sounds so much like what Daddy told you—told all of us—for all those years."

Her mother slowly shook her head. "Lily, you can't make Daniel pay for the mistakes your father made. It isn't fair to either one of you."

Was that what she was doing? Lily wondered. Had she suddenly started doubting Daniel simply because of what her father had done to her mother?

"The baby was the only reason Daniel told me he thought we should get married." Lily shook her head. "And he hasn't even mentioned that in the past couple of weeks."

"Daniel Addison has never impressed me as being a man who changed his mind so easily." Her mother nodded. "I'm sure he still wants to marry you. Maybe he's just giving you the space you need to decide that's what you want, too."

"I do want that." Unable to sit still, Lily rose to her feet and walked over to stare out the window at her mother's garden. "But is it asking too much for me to want him to love me?"

"I'm sure you're wrong about him not loving you." Her mother smiled. "I noticed the way he looked at you that first night when he asked you to dance at the Autumn Charity Ball for the Children's Hospital. I know in my heart it was love at first sight for him, Lily."

She feared her mother was wrong. "I wish I could believe that, Momma. But I don't think so. He doesn't believe in love and I won't settle for anything less from him."

"That's what he might think, darling," Elizabeth said, smiling. She left the couch to join Lily at the window. "Trust me on this. A mother knows these things. Daniel loves you with all his heart."

"But—"

"Give him time." Her mother gave her a comforting hug. "You'll see that I'm right."

On Saturday afternoon, Lily smiled until her face hurt as child after child insisted on having their picture taken with the Princess of Ducks. Not even the author of the book they were promoting, dressed as the wise old wizard, got as many requests. "Are you ready to leave?" Kara asked when the last child in line walked back to his mother.

"More than ready." Lily massaged her face with her fingertips. "I think I have a cramp in my cheeks from smiling so much."

"You make a beautiful princess," Elizabeth said, joining her daughters.

"Thank you, Momma," Lily said, hugging her mother. "But I think you're just a bit prejudiced."

"Aunt Lily a princess," Flynn said proudly as he and Matt walked over to them.

Bending down, Lily kissed her nephew. "Are you ready to go back to my house for ice cream and cake?"

"I don't know about Flynn, but I sure am," Matt said, grinning. "RJ and I worked through lunch so we could take off early to be here and I'm starving."

"Are you about finished gathering the information Jack Sinclair wants?" Lily asked, concerned. Both of her brothers looked tired and she knew they were under a tremendous amount of stress as they got the reports ready. Yet they had made the time to be there for her, while Daniel seemed to seize an excuse not to.

"We just have a few more things left," Matt said. "Then we'll have to wait and see what Sinclair has to say."

"Let's not discuss business today," Elizabeth suggested. "This is a day to celebrate Lily's accomplishments and success."

Lily could understand her mother's reluctance to listen to the details of yet another betrayal by their father. The fact that he had given the majority of TKG to his illegitimate son, while dividing up the rest between her children had to hurt their mother deeply, probably more than any of them realized.

"Lily, are you riding back to your place with Kara?" Laurel asked as she and RJ joined the rest of the family.

Lily nodded. "Kara brought me." Laughing, she added, "And unless she intends to make me walk home, she's stuck taking me back."

She still couldn't understand why her sister had been so persistent about driving her to the bookstore. But the moment Kara learned that Daniel wasn't going to be attending the event, she had insisted that she come by to get Lily.

As she and her family left the bookstore, Lily noticed that her mother and siblings all drove away from the parking area, while Kara seemed preoccupied with sending a text message on her cell phone. "Someone wanting you to plan their party?" Lily asked.

"Business is good," Kara said evasively as she smiled and started the car.

When they drove from the parking area, Lily couldn't help but feel sad. As much as she loved having her family at the event, the one person she wanted most of all to be there with her wasn't. Daniel had left early that morning for his trip and she didn't anticipate seeing him again for a couple of days.

"You're awfully quiet," Kara said as she drove them toward the Beauchamp house. "Is something wrong?"

"I was just thinking about how nice it was to have everyone there today." She did appreciate her family being there for her, but it was overshadowed by Daniel's absence.

"It would have been nicer if Daniel had been there, right?" Kara guessed.

"Yes." Apparently she hadn't been able to hide her disappointment as well as she thought.

When Kara parked the car in her driveway, Lily looked around. "Where is the rest of the family? They left before we did."

Shrugging, Kara followed her into the house. "Maybe they stopped to pick up something for our little get-together."

"Everyone drove separately," Lily said, shaking her head. "Why would all of them stop?"

"I don't know. Maybe they took a different route and they're held up in traffic." Kara motioned toward the stairs. "I didn't get a chance to see the house when I was here the other day. Why don't you give me the grand tour while we're waiting on them?"

"Sure. Just let me change and I'll show you around," Lily said as they climbed the stairs.

Her sister shook her head. "I'd rather you didn't take the dress off just yet. I'd like to get a picture of the entire family gathered around you still in costume."

Lily frowned. "Why?"

"For my scrapbook." Kara gave Lily a beseeching look. "Please?"

"Oh, all right," Lily said, giving in. She wasn't aware her sister had the time for scrapbooking. "We're already upstairs. Where would you like to start with the tour?"

"Why don't we start with the cupola and then work our way down?" Kara suggested. "I'd like to see the new window seat."

"How did you know about those?" She hadn't told anyone about Daniel having them built for her.

Kara looked a little startled. "I… Uh, Daniel mentioned them the other day. While you were changing out of the dress for me to take to the seamstress." Her cell phone chirped, indicating that she had another text message. When she checked the message, she smiled. "Lead the way. I'm dying to see the view."

"Don't you need to answer that?" Lily asked as they climbed the steps to the cupola.

"No, it was just a client letting me know his event is running on schedule," she said, pocketing the phone.

"If you have an event going on, why aren't you there?" Normally Kara was present at the parties she planned to see that things went off without a hitch.

"The view here is absolutely gorgeous," Kara said, instead of answering Lily. "You can see all the boats in the harbor."

Lily nodded as she gazed out at the big oceangoing ships and a few sailboats. "I'm assuming there will be more of the smaller boats in the spring and summer when it's warmer."

"Oh, look," Kara said, pointing toward the harbor. "Does that boat have something written on the mainsail?"

Looking in the direction her sister pointed, Lily squinted her eyes to try to focus on the boat sailing across the harbor. "How can you see that far away? Did you get new glasses?"

"Here." Her sister wore a knowing grin as she handed Lily a pair of binoculars she had removed from her purse. "Use these."

Lily frowned. "When did you start carrying binoculars?"

"Will you stop asking questions and just look?" Kara asked, grinning.

A bubble of hope began to rise in Lily's chest and her hands began to tremble as she took the binoculars from Kara. She had seen that look on her sister's face too many times not to know something was up. Looking through the lenses, she searched for the boat Kara mentioned and when she found it, her heart began to race and her knees began to tremble.

Daniel, dressed in a black tuxedo, stood on the deck. The message written in bold block letters on the pristine white mainsail read: I LOVE YOU, PRINCESS LILY.

Dropping the binoculars on the window-seat cushion, tears filled her eyes and she couldn't seem to stop shaking. "Daniel…loves me?"

Kara put her arm around Lily's shoulder. "Yes, he does."

"He doesn't like sailing," Lily said, picking up the binoculars for another look.

"He apparently loves you more than he hates being on a boat." She took the binoculars from Lily and ushered her toward the stairs. "Now, let's get down to the marina to welcome your prince when the boat arrives."

Her heart was so full of emotion it felt as if it might burst from her chest as Kara drove her the short distance to the marina. "When did the two of you… I mean, how did you manage…"

"Daniel got in touch with me almost a week ago," Kara said as she parked her car at the marina. "He knew exactly what he wanted and left it up to me to make it happen."

"I had no idea." Lily couldn't believe they had managed to arrange such an elaborate stunt in such a short time or that she had been none the wiser to the scheme. "Are you the one who arranged for me to be a princess today at the bookstore?"

"Guilty," Kara said, laughing. "I filled the manager in on everything. She and the author both thought it sounded like a lot of fun and after the success of the signing today, I wouldn't be surprised if more children's authors and illustrators are asked to dress in character."

As she and Kara hurried toward one of the slips where the sailboat would dock, tears streamed down Lily's cheeks at the sight of her family, Charlotte Addison and a crowd of curious boat owners lining the pier. At the end of the planked walkway, an arch made of gold, white and purple balloons marked the spot where Daniel would disembark.

When she saw the sailboat enter the marina, then lower the sails to slowly cruise its way to the slip, a thought crossed her mind. Did Daniel really love her? Or was this just a ploy to get her to agree to marry him?

She immediately pushed the ludicrous idea to the back of her mind. No man went to the lengths Daniel had to convince her that he loved her if he didn't mean it.

Watching him step off the boat, she lifted her long

skirt and ran the short distance to meet him under the balloon arch. As she gazed into his eyes, the love she saw shining in their navy depths stole her breath. "You really mean it, don't you?"

"I really do," he said, nodding. Wrapping his arms around her, he pulled her to him for a kiss that left them both gasping for breath. "I love you, Lily Kincaid."

The crowd behind them burst into applause.

As they walked past her mother on the way back up the pier, Lily stopped to give Elizabeth a hug. "You were right, Momma. He does love me."

Her mother nodded at she dabbed at her eyes with a lace-edged handkerchief. "I know, darling." Elizabeth hugged Daniel. "I'm so very happy for both of you."

Not to be outdone, Charlotte Addison kissed Lily's cheek. "Thank you for making my son more happy than I've ever seen him," she whispered. Turning to her son, she smiled. "You were right, Daniel. Equal in every way."

"Thank you, Charlotte," Daniel answered. "That means a lot."

"What did your mother mean by that?" Lily asked as they moved on through the crowd.

"I'll explain later." He grinned. "There's more to come. The surprise isn't over with just yet. "

"It isn't?" She couldn't imagine what he could possibly do to top the message on the sailboat.

When they reached Kara, he asked, "Is it here?"

"Right this way," her sister said, as she raised her hand to wave. A horse-drawn Victorian-style carriage immediately rolled up in front of them at her sister's signal. "We'll meet you back at the Beauchamp House."

Once she and Daniel were seated in the carriage and

it was slowly making its way down East Battery, Lily turned to kiss his cheek. "I can't believe you did all this for me."

"I had to, Lily," he said, putting his arm around her shoulders and tucking her to his side to shield her from the chill of the late-afternoon air. "I knew if I just told you that I love you, you wouldn't believe me."

She shook her head. "Probably not. You had me convinced that you didn't believe in love."

"I didn't." He kissed her forehead. "At least not until I asked a beautiful princess with long red hair and the prettiest blue eyes I've ever seen to dance with me at the Autumn Charity Ball. The moment I took her into my arms, I fell in love. I was just too stubborn to admit it."

Lowering his head, Daniel settled his lips over hers. There was such emotion, such love in his kiss that it brought tears to her eyes. Daniel did love her and she loved him with every fiber of her being.

When the carriage stopped in front of the mansion, her family and Charlotte were waiting for them and, escorting them in, Daniel led the way to the formal dining room. A huge cake with a prince-and-princess figurine on top sat in the middle of the long dining table. It had Congratulations, Lily and Daniel written in purple on the white icing.

"Congratulations?" Lily asked, looking around at her smiling family. "For what?"

Daniel had only professed his love. He hadn't proposed. Not really. His pragmatic suggestion that they get married a couple of weeks ago didn't count.

Before she realized what was happening, Daniel dropped to one knee and, in front of her family and his mother, took her hand in his. "Lily Kincaid, I love you more than life itself. Will you do me the honor of marrying me?"

Until that moment, she hadn't noticed the beautiful diamond solitaire he had poised to slip on the third finger of her left hand. "Y-yes!" One by one tears began to roll slowly down her cheeks. "I love you so much. Yes, I'll marry you, Daniel."

Sliding the white-gold ring into place, he rose to his feet and pulled her into his arms. "Do you want to tell everyone the rest of our news now?" he whispered close to her ear.

"They're all here. I think now would be a good time," she said.

"Lily and I have a little more news we'd like to share with you," Daniel said, smiling down at her.

"We're going to have a baby toward the end of summer," Lily said, gazing up at the man she loved.

A collective cheer went up from her family, and Lily was amazed to see her mother and Charlotte locked in a tearful hug. Both women may have already known about the pregnancy, but now they were able to celebrate freely the upcoming birth of their grandchild.

"I'm so happy for you about getting married and having a baby on the way," Kara said, hugging Lily. "Please tell me you'll let me plan your wedding and baby shower."

"I wouldn't think of having anyone else," Lily said honestly. "I can't believe the lengths you went to make today so perfect."

"Yes, thank you for everything, Kara," Daniel added, his expression grateful. "When I called you the other day to tell you what I had in mind, you took my idea and ran with it." He smiled. "Believe me, you outdid yourself. Today went above and beyond any of my expectations."

Kara looked extremely pleased. "I was glad to do it and I'm thrilled you liked the results." Turning to Lily, she advised, "When you decide on a date, let me know. It's never too early to start planning."

"We'll let you know as soon as we do," Lily promised.

Long after his mother and Lily's family left, Daniel sat with his arms around Lily on the new window seat in the cupola. "I love you, Lily," he said, kissing her temple. "More than you'll ever know."

Now that he had acknowledged his feelings for her, he couldn't seem to stop telling her. But he didn't think she minded. Each time he told her, the love he saw in her vivid blue eyes shined a little brighter.

"When do you want to get married?" she asked, leaning back against his chest as they gazed out at the star-studded night sky.

"As soon as possible," he said without hesitation.

Lily nodded. "I'll have to check with Kara on dates she has available."

"I was thinking that we might go ahead and get married right away and then have a big wedding sometime this fall after the baby is born," he said, hoping she was receptive to the idea.

She was silent for a moment and he thought he might have made her angry with his suggestion. "Actually, I like that idea," she finally said. "I think I would like to have a mid-October wedding—around the same time we met last year at the Autumn Charity Ball."

"Sounds good to me," he said, meaning it. "October is my lucky month."

She turned her head to look up over her shoulder at him. "Really? I wasn't aware you had one of those."

"I didn't until last year," he said, grinning. "When I met you and asked you to dance."

"Good answer, Addison." She kissed his chin. "Are you trying to get lucky again?"

He chuckled. "Not until morning, sweetheart. You've had a big day and I'm pretty sure when we go downstairs to the master suite, you're going to fall asleep the minute your head hits the pillow."

"You're probably right," she said, hiding a yawn behind her hand.

They both fell silent for some time, before she spoke again. "Thank you for giving me my dream."

Turning her in his arms, he shook his head as he gazed at the woman he loved more than life itself. "Your dad gave the princess her castle."

"That's true." Lily cupped his cheek with her soft hand. "But you gave me the prince I had been standing in the cupola waiting to see sail into Charleston Harbor. The man who will live with me in the castle and help me fill it with happy little princes and princesses." She kissed him. "I love you, Daniel Addison."

"And I love you, Lily Kincaid. For the rest of our lives."

* * * * *

Turn the page for an exclusive short story

*By USA TODAY bestselling author
Day Leclaire.*

The Kincaids: Jack and Nikki, Part 1

She emerged from cold, velvety blackness into a pool of firelight thrown from torches positioned strategically around the impeccably landscaped backyard and patio of the Colonel Samuel Beauchamp House. Even though she'd arrived late to the charity event, she didn't hurry. From his position on the second-floor balcony Jack Sinclair caught sight of her before anyone else in the gathering below. And he didn't think he'd ever seen anyone more beautiful.

"What am I offered for this fine bachelor?" the auctioneer called out, a hint of sarcasm underscoring his final two words. Clearly not a fan of his, Jack surmised. "Come on, folks. Remember, this is for charity."

The woman moved with the grace and power of a

goddess, hair as dark as a midnight sky falling from a center part to gently cup her shoulders. A wintry breeze gusted, lifting the feathered fringe across her brow and blowing it away from a classic, aristocratic face featuring high, elegant cheekbones and arching brows. Her gently curved chin spoke of a stubborn nature, while full, lush lips begged for a lover's kiss.

The goddess kept coming, moving through the crowd without breaking stride, her tall, lean shape encased in formfitting black wool, all she needed to hold Charleston's unusually temperate winter weather at bay. She paused beneath the balcony where he stood and tilted her head to stare up at him. Her gaze held a feminine challenge that aroused his most primitive desires, and even from a solid twenty feet away he could see that her eyes possessed all the glitter and brilliance of a flawless sapphire.

Jack looked…and he hungered.

"Someone? Anyone?" the auctioneer persisted. "One entire evening of fancy dining and dancing for the low, low price of fifty dollars. Do I hear twenty-five? Every penny goes to support Read and Write, promoting literacy in everyone from five to ninety-five."

His plea was met with a silence that roiled and seethed with each passing second, tumbling viciously through the men and women gathered below, all of whom smiled at the unmistakable message their silence sent. *You don't belong. You're not one of us. You have been tried, judged and found wanting.*

Grouped to one side stood his family. Fine. Not his family. They were the "Legitimates." The sons and daughters of his father's legally wedded-and-bedded wife, Elizabeth, while Jack was Reginald Kincaid's bastard son, forced to carry the name of his mother's late husband, Richard Sinclair, even though they didn't share a blood relationship. He allowed a brief, cold smile to cut through his carefully dispassionate expression. Hell, even his half brother, Alan Sinclair— another "Legitimate," though from the Sinclair side of his family—had aligned himself with the Kincaids. No surprise there.

Of course, the only reason Jack had been allowed to step foot on his half sister's property was because he sat on the board of Read and Write and had been talked into this ridiculous stunt long before the venue had been set. Otherwise, he was willing to bet Lily Kincaid would have barred him from attending. And now he'd pay the price. No one would bid on him and he'd be forced to suffer the public humiliation.

Well, screw 'em. Screw their fine, aristocratic backgrounds. Screw their hunger to put an upstart bastard in his place. Screw their cruelty. If it weren't for the children, he'd walk away and never look back. But he knew what harm illiteracy could cause. It was a war he believed in and would fight every day of his life, regardless of a little humiliation.

"Final call for bids," the auctioneer said, an edge of desperation to his voice. "Who will make an offer? Anyone? Twenty dollars? Ten dollars?"

"One thousand dollars!"

Those three words rang through the crowd. If it had been silent before, now that silence deepened, ringing with a shock so profound Jack could have heard the proverbial pin drop. As though acknowledging that fact, his goddess smiled. "But I expect value for my money," she called up to him. "Is dinner and dancing all you're offering?"

He allowed a brief grin to come and go. "What more would you like?"

"Anything?"

"Name it and it's yours."

Now, where the hell had that offer come from? Jack had been a businessman long enough to know better than to make such an unconditional proposal. He'd learned to look at every angle and all potential outcomes, to close every loophole and employ a ruthlessness that had earned him the nickname "the Bastard" in business, as well as birth. But it had only taken one blue-eyed, come-hither look from a face capable of making angels weep, and he'd offered the woman a loophole the size of Montana.

The murmur of voices rippled through the crowd, the sound slowly escalating with each passing second. Not that his goddess noticed. Her full attention remained fixed on him. Slowly, she smiled. Not a calculating look like so many of the women he'd known, but a warm, teasing expression that delighted in his offer.

"Then what I want is one wish to be fulfilled whenever and wherever I say," she informed him. "I think that's worth a thousand dollars."

Well, hell. "And then some."

"You made the offer." She shrugged. "I merely accepted your terms."

And with that, she turned on her heel and disappeared into the crowd, the shouted "Sold!" washing behind in her wake. He tracked her progress until the darkness swallowed her once again, darkness melting into darkness. The auctioneer gestured for him to surrender his place to the next bachelor in line. He didn't hesitate. He plunged through the open doorway into the salon off the master bedroom and threaded his way through the house.

He had a goddess to find.

Nikki could sense his approach, feel the punch that came from a man who exuded power both physically as well as through strength of personality. What in the world had she done? Not two hours after returning from an amazing two-week vacation, she'd hightailed it over to the bachelor auction she'd promised to attend before leaving for Aruba…and bid on a complete stranger. Worse, she'd flirted with him in front of half of the movers and shakers that dominated Charleston high society. No doubt her mother's phone would be ringing off the hook within the hour.

He came after her out of the darkness, a shaft of moonlight silvering his dark brown hair and catching in the unnerving robin's egg blue of his eyes. At six foot two he topped her by a solid five inches…or would if her boot heels didn't gift her with an extra few precious inches. She was more accustomed to looking men directly in the eye. Preferred it. But with this one, she needed to look up—up over a fabulous physique that began with powerful legs, a backside just rounded enough to give definition to his trousers, a tux jacket that emphasized mile-wide shoulders and finally his face. Tough. Ruthless. Shrewd. The entire package was mouthwatering and then some.

"Are you a cop?" The thoughtless question escaped before she could prevent it. Even though she'd learned long ago to think before speaking, sometimes her control slipped. Like now.

He stiffened, those powerful eyes narrowing. "No. Are you concerned you might need one?"

Uh-oh. Somehow she'd offended him. She dismissed his question with a careless shrug and attempted to backpedal. "I suppose my question didn't come out quite right."

"Then why don't you rephrase." It wasn't a question.

"You just have the look of a cop." She gestured toward his face. "You know, that 'I'll get my man no matter what it takes' sort of intensity. Plus, you were able to track me down. Not easy in the dark."

"It also wasn't hard. People looked at me, then looked in the direction you'd taken." He examined her in a focused way, as though attempting to dissect who and what she was. Still coplike and she should know, considering her father had worn the uniform. "I'm Jack, by the way."

"Nikki," she supplied, offering her hand.

He took it, swallowed it in a huge paw that made her look downright dainty in comparison, something not easy to do. His grip also filled her with an unexpected warmth, the hold almost protective. How strange. Ever since her father had died, she'd always been the protector of the family, the go-to person whenever an emergency cropped up or a difficult decision needed to be made. The strong one. And yet, she'd bet every last penny of the thousand dollars she'd just spent that Jack would do all that and more. For some reason, she found the thought deeply unsettling.

"I suppose we should exchange cell numbers in

order to set up our dinner," she suggested, tugging her hand free.

He released her and reached inside his tux jacket, removing a sleek, black PDA. "Not to mention the wish you managed to throw into the bargain. Clever of you."

"Mmm. A thousand dollars' worth of clever. Still," she added with a shrug, "I don't mind since I consider it money well spent. I'm a huge advocate of literacy."

"As am I."

Something in Jack's voice warned that it hit on a personal level. Interesting. Maybe something to pursue during their dinner date. Nikki exchanged numbers with him, adding him to her contacts list. They stood far too close, something she did her best to ignore though it proved an almost impossible challenge.

Heaven help her, but his scent was amazing, combining a quiet masculine fragrance with what she suspected he'd smell like fresh and naked from the shower. Authority exuded from him, an innate cloak of form and personality, intensely and overwhelmingly male. And she could feel the slow assault to her softer, more feminine defenses, the tremble of crumbling walls before the impending breach. She needed to find a way to reinforce those defenses, to hold herself at a safe distance. After all, hadn't she learned that powerful men weren't to be trusted? Of course she had. She'd learned that brutal fact in the most devastating way possible.

She spared Jack a swift look. As reluctant as she was to set them at odds with each other so early in their acquaintance, she didn't have any choice. She needed to protect herself first and foremost. And she knew just how to build a bulwark between them. One simple question was all it would take to drop it into place.

"Why wouldn't anyone bid on you?" she asked with seeming casualness.

He stepped back and she froze at the fierce expression in his eyes. She'd hoped to create some breathing room between them. She hadn't expected to stir such an intense reaction. "Don't you know?" he demanded softly.

"No."

His disbelieving gaze swept over her. She'd seen that sort of flat, penetrating look before. Her father had possessed it, along with the hard, cold cop eyes that went with it. So did his ex-partner, Charles McDonough, now a detective on the Charleston police force. Jack examined her inch by inch, appraising the cost of her clothing, the quality of the designer. Then he stripped her. Weighed her. Calculated her worth as a person, identified her background and education. Her intellect and personality. Her brand new tan, courtesy of her trip to Aruba.

"You're one of them," he said at last.

She didn't deny it. Couldn't. "My mother's family is." Her mouth curved to one side. "I guess you could say I straddle the line."

His intensity eased somewhat. "How?" he asked simply.

"My father's family all served in the military or law enforcement in one capacity or another. Blue-collar to a man, while mother's kin are old Southern aristocracy. It made for an…odd upbringing, to say the least."

To her surprise he actually returned her smile. "An upbringing we share."

She gestured in the direction of the charity auction, still ongoing, the sounds distant and muted from their position by the Beauchamp carriage house. "That's what they hold against you?" she asked, the question shaded with doubt. "You aren't part of Charleston aristocracy? That seems a little extreme, even for them."

"That's only one among many sins attributed to me, none of which need worry you."

"What should worry me?" she asked dryly.

The moon chose that moment to slip behind a bank of clouds, throwing his expression into shadow at the very instant she needed to see it the most. His voice issued from the darkness, want making it ripe and deep, sinking into her pores like a searing caress. "Only one thing."

Jack wrapped his fists around Nikki's soft lamb's wool collar and jerked her closer. Her body collided with his, pliant capitulating to unforgiving. Her walls trembled once again beneath the unexpected assault, breached by heat and need, and she teetered on the edge of yielding.

She knew what he intended, just as she knew she could escape if she struggled. But she didn't want to struggle. Curiosity filled her, a trait that had cursed womankind from the creation of Eve. It had been so long since she'd had a man's hands on her, known his touch. His possession. His kiss. She suspected Jack would excel at the art. There was only one way to find out for certain.

She lifted her face, allowed a shard of moonlight to splinter across her surrender. Without another word, he leaned in, took her mouth. Took her. She went under for the first count, swamped by a wave of desire higher and more powerful than she ever thought possible. His mouth felt firm against hers. In control. Oh, God...delicious! She came up for air just long enough to sigh out his name before the second wave slammed into her, sending her plummeting into desire again. Her lips parted and he swept inward, driving her insane with a tantalizing duel that filled her with a sharp, almost painful yearning. So long. So painfully long since a man had held her. Wanted her. Made her forget propriety and lessons learned.

A slight noise shattered the silence, penetrating the mist of passion that enclosed them, coming from somewhere between where they stood near the front doors of the carriage house and the courtyard. It almost had Nikki surfacing again. But at the last instant she went under for the third and final time, all too happy to drown in Jack's embrace.

"Hello?" came a woman's voice. "Who's there?"

It bothered Nikki to no end that she wasn't the one to terminate the kiss. Jack did, had the self-possession to pull back and regard her with a smile of masculine amusement. "I believe that's my cue to leave," he murmured.

A woman stepped into the intimate circle—one of the Kincaids, if Nikki wasn't mistaken. Her startled look flickered from Jack to Nikki and back again. Then her blue eyes narrowed in open displeasure.

"You have my number," he informed Nikki. "Call me when you're ready to pick up where we left off. Lily," he greeted the woman, tossing her a smile of open amusement—and possibly a hint of challenge—before melting into the darkness.

Dear God, what the hell had he been thinking, allowing lust to override common sense?

Jack worked his way around the crowd toward the front of Beauchamp House, his features set in a hard, ruthless expression that held all possible intruders at bay. And they would have approached, he knew it for a fact. Their fascination and curiosity, particularly in response to Nikki's outrageous bid, threatened to overcome their wariness. He refused to give them the opportunity, particularly after his reception at the charity auction…or lack thereof.

Of course, not everyone had been unwelcoming. His thoughts flashed to the woman who'd bid on him. Nikki. Now that he thought about it, he hadn't asked for her last name. What sort of fool did that make him? Ah, well. He had her phone number. So long as she wasn't a Kincaid—or affiliated with them—he didn't give a damn what her name was.

He did find one thing intriguing. Clearly, Nikki didn't recognize him, didn't associate him with the scandal that had broken early in January, following on the heels of his father's death—now ruled a murder. Didn't realize that he was Reginald Kincaid's bastard son.

Jack doubted it had even occurred to her to ask his full name, any more than he had hers, or chances were excellent she'd have made the connection. Would she still have bid on him if she'd known? When she found out the truth would she cancel their dinner date? Because guaranteed, someone would be all too happy to break the news, probably Lily.

He'd just have to deal with the possibility of her canceling if, or more likely when, it occurred. For some reason the knowledge that she'd follow the lead of the rest of Charleston's high society filled him with impotent fury, which didn't make the least sense. He'd known Nikki for less than an hour. Considering the craziness of the past month, he couldn't afford any distractions, particularly those of the female persuasion. Even so...

Man, she was gorgeous. Everything about her appealed, from the long-legged length of her, to the raven's wing sweep of hair, to the elegant features dominated by eyes jewel-blue bright. And then there was that kiss. He could still taste the delicate ripeness of her mouth. Still feel the lingering effects of the fragrant warmth of her body against his, the feminine curves that he'd have given just about anything to explore with a slow thoroughness that would end in only one way.

With the delicious Nikki in his bed.

Maybe he could handle one additional complication in his life. Dealing with the headaches—and opportunities—created by his inheritance of a forty-five-percent share of The Kincaid Group, in addition to the demands of his own business, Carolina Shipping, made for a very full plate. But maybe Nikki would offer a tantalizing dessert.

And everyone saved room for dessert, right?

"It's Nikki Thomas, isn't it?" the woman who'd interrupted Jack's kiss asked. Her gaze strayed in the direction Jack had taken, an odd expression flitting across her face.

Nikki nodded, vaguely recognizing the other woman from the various social functions they'd both attended. Recognizing, too, that she was a Kincaid. "That's right. You're Laurel's sister...Lily? Or is it Kara?" She offered an apologetic smile. "Sorry. I know Laurel from work, but haven't quite gotten the rest of the family straight."

"I'm Lily. The youngest. Laurel is oldest, then Kara—short brown hair, not quite as curly as mine? You might not have met her since she doesn't work for The Kincaid Group. Then there's me." Amusement gleamed in her blue eyes. "Not to mention two brothers thrown into the mix at various points between, of course."

"RJ and Matthew. Yes, I run into them at work, as well."

"That's right." Lily spared another glance over her shoulder. Clearly, something about Jack's presence bothered her. "Are you a friend of Jack's?" she asked hesitantly.

"I met him for the first time tonight. Why?"

Shock replaced Lily's amusement. "Then, what in the world made you bid a thousand dollars for him?"

Okay. There was something going on here. Something Nikki hadn't quite gotten a handle on. "No one else seemed willing to and I felt sorry for the guy. So, tell me. Why was he getting the cold-shoulder treatment?"

Lily gave her an odd look. "You don't know?"

"Clearly not." A sense of unease filled her. "What? He's an ex-con? A gigolo? Swindles little old ladies out of their fortunes?"

"I wouldn't put any of those things past him," Lily stunned Nikki by admitting. "Though that's not what I have against him."

"Which is…?" Nikki prompted.

"I thought you worked for TKG."

"I do. I'm your family's corporate investigator."

"Then you must know about Jack, know he's in direct competition with our family's business. The rumors about him have been flying ever since my father died." Pain flashed across her face. "Was murdered," she corrected carefully.

Nikki froze. "Wait." Oh, God. She couldn't have made such a hideous mistake. Granted, she'd been in Aruba for the past two weeks, which had put her totally out of the loop. Still… Her heart rate kicked up a notch and a knot formed in the pit of her stomach. She moistened lips gone bone dry. "Are you saying that Jack, the Jack I just bid on is—"

Lily nodded. "Jack Sinclair. My father's illegitimate son."

* * * * *

WHAT HAPPENS
IN CHARLESTON...

RACHEL
BAILEY

Rachel Bailey developed a serious book addiction at a young age (via Peter Rabbit and Jemima Puddleduck) and has never recovered. Just how she likes it. She went on to earn degrees in psychology and social work, but is now living her dream—writing romance for a living.

She lives on a piece of paradise on Australia's Sunshine Coast with her hero and four dogs, where she loves to sit with a dog or two, overlooking the trees and reading books from her evergrowing to-be-read pile.

Rachel would love to hear from you and can be contacted through her website, www.rachelbailey.com.

Dear Reader,

I was thrilled to be invited to contribute to Dynasties: The Kincaids—the opportunity to work with a stellar bunch of authors was far too good to pass up. And when I was told it was Matthew Kincaid's story I'd be writing, I couldn't have been more excited.

Matthew is such a fabulous character—strong, noble and a loving father—that I was keen to spend time delving into his life and helping him meet his destiny in Susannah Parrish. And little Flynn? He just crawled right into my heart and didn't leave.

I also loved immersing myself in South Carolina and Charleston culture. I watched a heap of movies filmed there (a great excuse for a movie marathon!), listened to southern bands when I was writing, researched the history and poured over blogs and webcams from Charleston. Now I have a teensy obsession and am planning to visit one day!

Special thanks to Kathie DeNosky, Jennifer Lewis, Heidi Betts, Tessa Radley and Day Leclaire for being a brilliant group of women to brainstorm and explore the lives of the Kincaids with, and thanks to Charles Griemsman for his most excellent guidance on the Kincaids series.

I hope you enjoy meeting Matthew, Susannah and Flynn as much as I did!

Cheers,

Rachel

For Cathy Bay,
who handed me my first category romance novel (see
what you think, she said); who was the first person to say,
you should write a book; who introduced me to Romance
Writers of Australia; who read and critiqued my first
writing efforts; and who has given me the gift of sixteen
years of friendship. Cathy, this book (and the ones before
it) literally would never have eventuated without you.

Thanks to Barbara Jeffcott Geris, Robyn Grady and
Sharon Archer for reading drafts of this book and making
it better. I appreciate you all more than I can say.

Thanks to Charles Griemsman for the superb editing
and to Jenn Schober for her agenting skills.

One

With his cell phone in a white-knuckled grip, Matthew Kincaid watched his son through the glass panel of the hospital room's door.

Three-year-old Flynn sat up against his pillows, his halo of dark hair haphazardly framing his little face. Two of his aunts, Matt's sisters Lily and Laurel, sat on either side of his bed, talking and playing with him. Since his wife's death a year ago, Matt's family had been extraordinary. They'd rallied around and given Matt and Flynn any extra support they'd needed.

It wouldn't be enough this time.

And all the wealth the Kincaids had amassed over three generations in shipping meant little in that room where his son was confined.

Despite the pale tone to Flynn's skin and the tired smudges under his eyes, onlookers might not guess how compromised his health currently was. Might not guess that his aunts had been through a decontamination process before being allowed in the private room, to avoid any germs gaining access to his weakened immune system.

As he watched his son try to learn the hand game Lily was teaching him—such a nice, normal activity for a little kid—Matt fought back the ball of emotion rising in this throat. He'd just come from a meeting with the doctors who'd laid out some chilling facts: Flynn's little body was still struggling to recover from the aplastic anemia. If his blood work didn't improve with the treatments they'd been using so far, they'd have to look at more drastic options.

Including a bone-marrow transplant.

A layer of ice settled over his skin, as it had done when the awful words had first been mentioned. Flynn was so young—too young to be facing such a procedure. And that was assuming they could even locate a compatible donor. The ideal option would be a sibling, but Flynn had none. Next best was a parent, but Matt's penicillin allergy had relegated him to being a last resort. The doctors didn't want to risk transferring the potentially life-threatening allergy to a three-year-old. Antibiotics were Flynn's only hope if he developed an infection.

Intellectually Matt could understand why the doctors didn't want to gamble on losing such a basic treatment—they'd explained in detail about documented cases of allergies transferred with marrow transplant. But it didn't make him feel any better. He wanted to be able to do something, *anything,* to help his little boy.

He curled his hand into a fist and pressed it to his solar plexus in a futile attempt to relieve the ache. When his son needed him the most, he'd failed him, and the knowledge was almost too much to bear.

He knew his brother and sisters would insist on being tested to see if they were a match, and Matt would welcome their offers, but the doctors had been pessimistic about the likelihood of a match being found there.

Which left only one option. One other person who had that primary link with Flynn. His biological mother.

He gripped the phone more tightly, took one last look at his little boy playing with his aunts and walked down the corridor to find some privacy.

Checking her watch, Susannah reached for the pages spurting from her printer. Twelve minutes till the meeting with the directors of the bank and the other key teams—since it was in an office down the hall, she'd easily make it. She'd stayed up late all week working on the new public-relations plan for the bank's rebranding, and was quietly confident they'd love it. Rebranding was a big move for the bank, and the PR angle was the biggest project Susannah and her team had handled, but they'd created strategies that were sure to get the reach they needed and generate a strong community buzz.

Her cell chirruped and she grabbed it as she slid the other arm into her jacket.

"Susannah Parrish," she said, scanning her desk to ensure she had everything for her presentation.

"Good morning, Susannah." The unfamiliar male voice was strained. "This is Matthew Kincaid."

The name immediately stilled her, brought a heaviness to her chest. Matthew Kincaid. Husband of Grace Kincaid, the woman to whom she'd handed her newborn baby. Memories of that day, of that special time in her life, crowded in, past the barrier she'd erected to keep them at bay—those few short hours she'd had with the newborn boy, his precious warmth and softness pressed against her. A sliver of time before she'd passed him to his new parents forever, giving them the gift of a baby, and saving her own mother from financial ruin.

Then her brain kicked into high gear.

"The baby," she whispered, her heart clutched tight. "Something's happened to the baby." There was no other reason he could be calling.

An uneven breath came down the line. "He's sick."

Sick? Her stomach swooped. He would only have turned three a couple of months ago. She dropped the folder on her desk and sank into her chair.

"What's wrong with him?" Though she hoped for something simple, logic dictated he wouldn't be calling over a head cold.

"He's had a virus," Matthew said, his voice sounding unnaturally rough, "and his body hasn't recovered properly."

That tiny little baby she'd nurtured in her womb was suffering. The thought was almost intolerable. "What can I do?"

"I was hoping you'd ask. There's an outside chance he might need a bone-marrow transplant. The best place to find a good match is a sibling or a parent, but I'm not an ideal donor." He paused and cleared his throat before continuing. "My brother and sisters will want to help, but—"

"How soon do you need me there?" she said without needing to think it through.

"You'll come," he said, as if confirming it aloud. And in those words she heard the massive relief he must be feeling.

"Of course I'll come. How soon?"

"The transplant isn't a definite yet—the doctors want to get the tests done and be ready to move if it does become necessary." There was a slight hesitation before he added, "But I'd appreciate it if you could come as soon as you can get away."

Pulse pounding through her body, she looked around her office, then at her watch again. She was owed time off, and her assistant was up-to-date and capable of covering for her. Taking leave without advance notice might cost her career a few points, but if that precious baby needed her, there was no contest. She could make this presentation, then hand everything over to her assistant and make a flight this afternoon.

She opened her bottom drawer and withdrew a vacation request form. "You're still in Charleston?" she asked.

"Yes. You're not?"

"Georgia now. I'll arrange leave immediately and get an afternoon flight." Her head was already buzzing with the arrangements and what she'd have to hand over to her assistant before she left the building.

"We could arrange for you to have the tests in Georgia." He spoke the words slowly and she heard his reluctance before he admitted, "But I'd prefer you to be here in case there's a crisis."

"I'd want that, too." Besides, she wouldn't be able to focus on anything here if she stayed while waiting on results. "Which hospital?"

"St. Andrew's, but send me your flight details and I'll pick you up from the airport."

Form in hand, she was on her feet, heading down the hall to her boss's office to get the request lodged before the presentation. "I'll ensure I'm there today."

"I'll see you then. And, Susannah," he said, voice deeper once again with emotion, "thank you."

"No need," she said as she knocked on her manager's office door, and ended the call.

Several hours later, she was wheeling her carry-on suitcase through the arrivals gate when she caught sight of Matthew Kincaid. At just over six feet, with closely cropped dark hair and a swimmer's body encased in a deep navy business suit, he was hard to miss. She remembered him clearly from a meeting she'd had with him and Grace before they'd signed the contract for surrogacy, and now, as then, he stole her breath.

However, she dismissed the reaction—it was irrelevant to her reason for being here.

His son.

Matthew saw her as she drew closer and gave her a tight nod of acknowledgment then reached for her suitcase. "I appreciate you coming so quickly."

"I'm glad to do it," she said truthfully.

The walk to the car was made in silence—she had too many questions to know where to start and Matthew appeared to be lost in his own world. During the pregnancy, she'd had much more contact with his wife—Grace's excitement about the baby had made her easy to talk to. Perhaps it would be best to save her questions for Grace.

She looked up at the blue Charleston sky. It had been almost three years since she'd been back. Georgia was where she chose to live, but Charleston was where she'd been born, where she'd grown up—it would always be home.

Once they were in his car and fastening seat belts, she asked, "Grace's with him now?"

A shudder seemed to race through his body, and then the only movement was the rise and fall of his chest as he looked through the windshield at the other parked cars, sunglasses hiding his eyes. He didn't turn to her as he spoke. "My mother is with him. Two of my sisters were there this morning but my mother swapped with them at lunchtime." A muscle in his jaw worked—he was so tense that she worried he would shatter into shards. Then he added, "Grace passed away a year ago."

Of its own volition, her hand lifted to cover her mouth, to smother the gasp that would otherwise have escaped. "How?" she asked from between her fingers then regretted it. The how was irrelevant when a man had lost his wife, and a little boy had lost his mother.

"Small plane crash." Still, he didn't look at her or make a move to start the car, simply sitting motionless in the shadowed light of the car's interior.

"Oh, Matthew, I'm sorry." She'd always thought of them as the perfect couple, a husband and wife with the world at their feet—gorgeous, rich, successful and in love. It seemed to go against the laws of nature for them to be so cruelly separated by death.

"Don't be sorry. It's not your fault." His words were loaded—he blamed someone for his wife's death, that much was clear. It was on the tip of her tongue to ask, but she had no right to pry any further into a topic that must cause intolerable pain. Having carried a child for this man did not alter the fact that she was a stranger. A stranger who needed to remember her boundaries and not be lulled into a false sense of intimacy because they had one thing in common. Matthew Kincaid deserved privacy in his grief for his wife.

Taking a mental step back, she sat up straighter in the plush passenger seat and brought the conversation around to the most pressing issue. "Tell me what's happening with Flynn."

With restless fingers, he tapped a rhythm on the steering wheel. "He had a parvovirus."

"I thought—" Feeling a little foolish, she stopped.

He tilted his head and looked at her. "That it was a virus dogs caught?" He gave a small, humorless smile. "I thought the same. There are lots of them, apparently, and Flynn caught a different strain. In children it can cause slapped-cheek syndrome. And that's just what it looked like—as though someone had slapped the poor kid's cheeks. Apart from that it seemed like he had pretty mild flu symptoms. Nothing out of the ordinary."

"But…?" she asked when he paused.

He rubbed a thumb across the grooves indented in his forehead. "But he didn't recover fully. He was lethargic and tired and just not himself. When I took him to the doctor they did some tests and found his white blood cells were low. Not critical, but by the next test they were even lower. They just kept dropping. The doctors said they expected the problem to be transient. That his bone marrow would start producing again." He grimaced. "But it hasn't."

"Have they tried other treatments?" she asked, but knew they must have if they were contemplating something this drastic.

Matthew nodded once. "They haven't had much effect so far. The doctors suggested screening the family for a compatible donor. In these cases the best possibility for a match is a sibling with the same parents. Next best chance are parents. After that the chances of compatibility get less."

"Which is where I come in."

"Which is where you come in," he echoed, lifting his sunglasses to sit on his head and turning to her. "He doesn't have a sibling and my penicillin allergy means they're reluctant to even consider me as a match at this stage." He spoke the last words almost through gritted teeth.

"You need his biological mother," she said, then bit down on her lip, feeling strange. She hadn't used that term to describe herself since the day she'd given birth to him and needed to fill out forms. She'd always felt good about giving him to such a loving couple, and considered him Grace and Matthew's child.

Now, just Matthew's.

His jaw clenched and released. "In retrospect, it was lucky Grace's eggs wouldn't take and we used yours. If they had, our options would be greatly reduced."

She swallowed. Grace had been hit hard by her inability to carry a child, but finding she couldn't use her own eggs, that she wouldn't be the biological mother of her own child, had devastated her. Grace had come to her, offering more money to contribute her eggs, but it hadn't been the extra money that had swayed her. Having lost a baby when she was younger, Susannah knew the value of the gift of life.

Matthew cleared his throat. "There's one more thing."

His tone sent a wave of trepidation through her veins. "Something else is wrong?"

"Not with Flynn. My family—and Grace's parents—believe that, although we used a surrogate, Grace was..." The shadowed skin of his jaw and throat pulled tight as he clenched the muscles there. "Grace wanted people to believe he was her baby in every way."

Having seen Grace's all-encompassing need to be a mother, she wasn't surprised that this was how they'd handled it. "It's okay, I understand."

His dark brows swooped low over green eyes sparkling with an intense honesty. "We meant no disrespect to you."

"None taken." She found a smile to reassure him. On this

point, at least, she could offer solace. "I'm not a part of his life, and Grace wanted him so very much."

"She did," he said, but the words were anything but simple. They carried a crushing weight with them. Her chest ached to witness such pain.

She looked more closely at this man who was raising the child she gave birth to. His broad shoulders were as rigid and set as if they'd been carved from marble. How heavy a load had they been carrying? Every instinct inside her demanded she reach out, to soothe. Instead she folded her hands in her lap to ensure they didn't move.

"Honestly, Matthew, I don't mind. I handed over that little baby to you and Grace with love. You don't need to explain anything to me about the decisions you've made."

"I appreciate that. Because I have something else to ask." He drew in a long breath and held it for a moment. "If you cross paths with my family, you'll find they can be…curious. Protective. And if they ask questions, you'll have the lead-in to tell them about your connection to Flynn." He turned to her, expression inscrutable. "I need you to keep Grace's secret."

Lie about not being the biological mother to keep the stability of a little family intact? With Flynn's health in question, instability and confusion were the last things they needed.

"Of course," she said. She offered a small smile to show she truly meant it.

Some of the tension fell from his shoulders and one corner of his mouth lifted in a cheerless version of a grateful smile, then he dropped the glasses back over his eyes and turned the key in the ignition. As the engine roared to life, her heart bled for the anguish she'd just seen in the depths of his eyes. She forced herself to look out the window—she was here to help the boy, not the father. As much as everything inside her longed to soothe the lines of pain around his eyes, it was simply not her role. Things were too complicated already.

* * *

Darkness was falling outside when Susannah made her way down the brightly lit hospital corridor to Flynn's room. Matthew had told her to find him there when her tests were over, and now she stood for a few moments observing them through the glass panel. Matthew's face was different with his son—the planes and angles looked softer, his smile easier. Yet the more tender version of Matthew Kincaid was just as compelling, perhaps more so. Her heart picked up speed and she couldn't tear her gaze away.

The little boy was facing away from her, so all she could see was a mop of dark brown hair and sweet little arms that reached out for his father's thumbs in whatever game they were playing. Then Matthew looked up and saw her and the tension seemed to pour into his body again until even his smile for Flynn seemed rigid. He said something to his son before pointing to the next room. She looked over and there was an interconnected door to Flynn's room so she headed over. Inside the anteroom was a washbasin, shelves of neatly folded gowns and boxes of masks and other paraphernalia.

The door opened and Matthew appeared. "He's being kept in semi-isolation," he said, answering her unasked question. "Before anyone goes in, they need to wash their hands up to the elbows and put on a gown." Something of her concern must have shown on her face because he shrugged one shoulder and said, "I'm just grateful he's not at the stage of needing us to wear a mask like the little girl in the room on the other side."

She looked through the glass panel to Flynn in his bed, curled up talking to a teddy bear. "He looks too small—too vulnerable—to be here."

Matthew didn't reply, but from the corner of her eye she saw him grimace. It must be beyond frustrating for him to watch his son in need and not be able to do anything about it. She fingered the strip of tape and bump of cotton on the inside of her elbow where they'd taken the blood, and prayed she'd be able to help if the transplant was needed.

"They're checking to see if I'm a tissue match now," she said, still watching the small boy interact with his teddy. "The woman who took the sample said they'd hurry it through and let us know preliminary results as soon as possible."

She felt Matthew nod, then they stood side by side for endless minutes, watching a three-year-old boy who'd already known too much pain in his short life, have a solemn conversation with a brown bear. The echoes of her hammering heart reverberated through her body, and the weight of all that rode on her tissue-matching test hung in the air, engulfing them in the small room.

"Would you like to meet him?" Matthew asked, his voice rough.

In one long whoosh, her lungs emptied. Even though she'd come here to help Flynn, she hadn't allowed herself a second's contemplation of being given the chance to meet him. Yet now the possibility was before her, as alluring as it was, she could see it was a bad idea. "It would just confuse things."

"We can keep it simple. We'll tell him you're a friend of mine and you wanted to say hello."

A little flame of excitement lit in her chest. Dare she meet this little boy? She'd willingly handed him to his new parents, never expecting to see him again—the situation of her own childhood had taught her it was better for children to have issues of custody and belonging mapped out and clear-cut.

But, he was within her sight—something she'd never dreamed would happen. And if they could keep it uncompli-cated and clear…

The flame of excitement in her chest flickered and grew.

Dare she?

She looked to Matthew for a sign, and he seemed happy enough to allow the meeting. To give her something she could always treasure—a sliver of time with the boy she'd carried for nine months.

A smile crept across her face and she bit down on her bottom lip in an attempt to contain it.

"Thank you. I'd love to meet him."

Two

Susannah tentatively followed Matthew into his son's hospital room with its sky-blue walls and bunches of shiny balloons. Flynn looked so small sitting on the bed in his teddy-bear pajamas. He had a cannula in the back of his little hand that was bandaged but wasn't connected to anything at the moment. The idea of an IV attached to him made her chest clench.

Flynn's little pale face looked up and he threw out his arms. "Daddeeee."

Matthew gently swung him up and planted a kiss on his cheek. "I told you I wouldn't be long," he said with such love it made her heart clench tight.

Flynn's gaze slid over to her and Susannah held her breath. He was a miniature version of Matthew down to the same shaped eyes, the same full bottom lip, but he had a dimple in his chin. Like the one that punctuated her own father's chin. Like the one she had. The floor tilted beneath her, but she didn't take her eyes from Flynn as the reality hit her hard.

This little boy was half *her*.

She'd been so glad to be able to give the gift of parenthood to two people who were desperate for a baby, and so adamant that she keep everything compartmentalized in her mind, that she'd never dwelled on the fact that Flynn was made from her flesh and blood. A part of the family line that came from her mother and her lost father.

Even when she'd been considering meeting him moments earlier, it had been as if talking about someone else's child, one she'd heard stories about. Not her mother's grandchild. Not her father's grandson.

Solemn blue eyes regarded her, then he asked his father in a loud whisper, "Who's that?"

And just like that, her heart was captured, and she had to blink back tears.

"This is a friend of mine." Matthew turned so Flynn was facing her. "Her name is Susannah."

"Hello, Flynn," she said past the lump in her throat.

"Hello, Sudann—" he frowned as he tried to wrap his tongue around the name "—Sood…"

"Maybe we could try something easier?" Matthew said, raising a dark eyebrow. It was a simple move, yet it transformed his face into something edgier, more alluring. Her mouth went dry. She looked back to Flynn, determined not to react to the innate appeal of his father, and found another Kincaid male who was hard to resist.

Interlacing her fingers over her belly so she wouldn't reach out to touch his little face, she smiled softly. "When I was little, my dad called me Suzi."

"Sudi," Flynn said.

She couldn't help but beam, hearing the baby she'd help create say her name. Or something approximating it. "Perfect."

Matthew put the little boy back down on his bed then leaned close to her. "Would you mind sitting with him for a few minutes?" he asked quietly, his breath warm on her ear. "I have to call the office and it might be tense. Flynn is pretty good at picking up things like that and it's the last thing he needs right now."

The crisp, clean scent of his aftershave curled around her, creating a powerful distraction from his words, and, although he wasn't touching her, the skin near her ear tingled as though he had.

She swallowed. "We'll be fine."

"Thanks." He dropped a kiss on the top of his son's head and spoke in a normal voice again. "I just have to call Uncle RJ. And while I'm gone, Suzi is going to stay with you."

"Okay," Flynn said, looking at her with those large eyes that she suspected saw too much.

Matthew paused at the door and smiled, but there was tension around his mouth, around his eyes. "I'll be quick."

After he left, Susannah stared down at the boy who was part her and part Matthew, and wanted so much to bundle him up and hug him tight. Instead she said, "So, Flynn, what can we do for fun in here? Got any good books?"

"A teddy-bear book," he said as if they were discussing a deadly serious topic.

"Why, I love teddy-bear books! Would you mind if I read it out loud?"

The little boy blinked then climbed down and retrieved a large hardcover with beautifully painted teddies on the front and deposited it in her lap. "It's an Aunty Lily book," he said and Susannah saw "Illustrated by Lily Kincaid" on the cover. Then he crawled back up on the bed and sat against the headboard, waiting.

Susannah read the story—sneaking glances at him whenever she could—and at the end, Flynn graced her with a blinding smile—the first he'd directed at her. "Thank you, Sudi."

Her heart stilled as if it couldn't take the beauty of that innocent smile, but it didn't take her long to regroup. She gathered his warm little body closer and pressed her lips to his forehead. Flynn relaxed into her embrace so she allowed herself to hold the kiss longer. Tears welled in her eyes, but she had her lids shut tight and wouldn't let them escape. She didn't need forever, but she was going to savor every moment she had with him now.

Eventually, not wanting to make Flynn uncomfortable, she took a breath and released him. He hadn't squirmed, and now he simply looked up at her with a curious expression. She smiled and blinked away the moisture in her eyes.

"What would you like to do?" she asked, looking at the toys and puzzles piled on a little table. "Would you like me to read you another book? Or we could do a puzzle?"

Flynn sucked his bottom lip into his mouth, clearly assessing her before sharing his thoughts. Then he curled a finger, inviting her to lean down. When her ear was level with his mouth, he whispered, "Can you sing me a song?"

Her singing talents owed more to enthusiasm than any semblance of skill, but she didn't think a three-year-old would mind. "Sure," she said brightly. "Twinkle, Twinkle?"

Slowly, not losing eye contact, he shook his head. The look on his face told her he had something specific in mind, so she waited.

His finger called her down for another secret. "Do you know Elvis?"

A smile tugged insistently at the corners of her mouth but he was so serious she restrained it. "Not personally, but I know his songs. Would you like me to sing one of them?"

Eyes so filled with hope that it made her heart ache, he nodded.

"Any song in particular?"

"I like them all," he said and she wondered exactly how many Elvis songs a three-year-old could possibly know.

"Okay, then." Her mind flicked through Elvis's songbook

and decided to try "Love Me Tender"—well-known and simple. As she sang the first couple of lines, a huge grin spread across Flynn's face and he snuggled into her side.

At the end of the first verse, she paused. "More of this song, or another one?"

"This one," he said with conviction. "Sudi, you sing it right."

She tilted her head to the side—her singing voice was hardly the best he would have heard, so what else could "right" mean? "Who doesn't sing it right?"

Warily he glanced over to the door then, apparently satisfied he wouldn't be overheard, he said in a stage whisper, "Aunty Lily sings it fast. And she dances."

Susannah had to hold back a laugh. Aunty Lily sounded fun. "So we don't want a dance version?"

He frowned as if that were an obvious point.

"Right, no dance versions of Elvis. Is Aunty Lily the only one who doesn't sing it the way you want?"

"Daddy sings them sad."

Without meaning to, she looked at the door where she'd last seen Matthew and her heart twisted. Why would Elvis make him sad? Perhaps an Elvis song had been Matthew and Grace's personal song? Or did he always sing sadly?

"Can you sing more?" Flynn asked, interrupting her thoughts.

"Sure I can, sweetie." She picked up the second verse, careful not to make it too fast or too sad, and her heart swelled when Flynn cuddled back into her side again.

As Matt strode down the corridor toward the anteroom, he caught a glimpse of a scene that had him slowing his steps then stilling. Susannah sat on his son's bed, Flynn curled against her slender body as she sang to him. Her head was dipped, her long blond hair partially curtaining them both. He couldn't hear the words, but knowing Flynn, he'd requested the Elvis songs Grace used to sing him. A chill crept across his skin.

The singing itself didn't surprise him—Flynn was remarkably proficient at convincing people to sing to him—it was his son's posture. Relaxed. Content. Trusting.

Since Grace's death, there hadn't been a single new person that Flynn had become affectionate with before he came to know them.

What had she said to inspire trust so quickly?

Part of him was glad that Flynn had found this ability to trust again, but another part wanted to drag Susannah away before his son became attached. The last thing that little boy needed was to lose someone else he'd come to love. The tight band that had been squeezing his chest for weeks now constricted that much more. Perhaps it had been a mistake to let her in his son's room.

He ran a hand through his hair and blew out a breath. He'd work out what to do about Susannah and Flynn's relationship later. For now, he had plans to make. He went in through the side room, washing his hands to the elbows, took a fresh gown, and when he slipped into the room, he found he'd been right about Elvis—Susannah was singing "Blue Suede Shoes." Her crystalline-blue eyes shone, her voice was sweet and she made him think of crisp, white sheets bathed in sunlight. Of stretching her out on those sheets and tasting the expanse of creamy skin he'd uncover.

Restraining a groan, he clenched his fists and forced the inappropriate thoughts from his mind. Not *this* woman, who his wife had envied but had understandably resented in equal measure. Nothing would betray his wife's memory more than him desiring Susannah Parrish.

Besides, between Flynn's hospitalization and Matt's recently discovering that his dead father had a second family on the side—and had left stock in the family business divided amongst the legitimate and illegitimate siblings—Matt didn't have the headspace to deal with one more thing. He needed to stay focused.

Susannah looked up and saw him but her singing didn't falter. Flynn's eyes were closed and when Matt crept closer, he saw his son had the deep, even breaths of sleep. He motioned to Susannah with a hand under the side of his head that Flynn was asleep then pointed to the other side of the room.

While she continued to sing, albeit in a softer voice, Matt picked his son up, moved him to the center of the bed and pulled the covers over him. This little boy was the most precious thing in his life and it killed him inside that he couldn't simply kiss him and make him better the way he'd been able to do until now. The doctors weren't even keen to let him be a donor because of his damn allergy. He brushed the hair off Flynn's pale face, pulled himself together, then crossed to the other side of the room with Susannah.

"I just spoke with the doctor," he said, digging his hands into his pockets. "They expect the results to be here in the morning."

Her long lashes swept down and her shoulders stiffened, as if bracing herself for tomorrow's outcome. "I'll meet you here first thing. My suitcase is in your car—just drop me at whichever hotel is closest."

Matt took a deep breath. The hospitality his mother had taught all her children wouldn't allow him to take her to a hotel. Not when she'd traveled interstate to help his son. But how comfortable would she be staying in a house alone with a man she barely knew? And should he ask a woman home who, with no effort, had brought his body back to life?

The most logical answer was to take her to his mother's house. His mother enjoyed hosting guests and, Pamela, the housekeeper who'd always been so much more, would appreciate having someone else to fuss over.

But he couldn't do that.

His mother—his entire family—believed Grace was Flynn's biological mother. He couldn't tell them why Susannah was here, or that she was being tissue matched to the youngest Kincaid.

When they ran into various members of his family, which they inevitably would if the tissue match was positive and she stayed longer, he'd use a cover story. But running into someone when he was by her side and staying in his mother's house were two totally different situations. Could he trust Susannah not to slip up under those circumstances? He didn't know much about her and had no idea how well she lied.

Best not to put her in a testing situation. Which only left one option.

He cleared his throat. "You can stay with me."

"No, I'll be fine at a hotel," she said, waving his suggestion away with a hand. "Honestly."

"Nonsense. My mother would be horrified if I made you stay at an impersonal hotel when I have plenty of room."

A line appeared between her eyebrows. "I—"

He rolled his shoulders back, not prepared to negotiate on this point. "I won't take no as an answer. My sister Kara will be here in about ten minutes to stay with Flynn for the evening, so we'll go then."

Her head tilted to the side. "You have a schedule?"

"Of course. Flynn is the only grandchild in our family. Everyone is concerned." It was breaking his heart that he couldn't be at the hospital full-time, but the family business was in serious trouble, both from lost business and potential hostile maneuverings, and Flynn loved his aunts, uncles and grandmother, so Matt had compromised by sharing the time with his family. From the corner of his eye, he saw his sister already in the anteroom next door, a little early as usual. "Kara made a timetable—her organizational skills are superb. Here she is."

The moment Kara stepped into the room, he wrapped her in a bear hug. "Thanks."

She held up an overstuffed bag. "We'll have fun—I made play dough and bought him his own set of highlighters for coloring. Hopefully that means he'll stop pinching mine." She grinned.

He grinned back. He could always count on Kara. "You know you're my favorite sister."

She laughed and rolled her eyes at Susannah. "He says that to all of us."

Susannah smiled as she looked back and forth from Kara to him. "How many sisters are there?"

"Three," Kara said. "We outnumber the brothers—there are only two of them."

As soon as she said it, she stiffened and Matt felt the same tension fill his muscles. There *had* been two brothers. Until his father's death, when they found they had a half brother they'd known nothing about. A secret big enough to become a betrayal of the entire family.

Shaking his head to dispel the thoughts, he touched a hand to Susannah's elbow. "Kara, this is Susannah, an old friend of Grace's."

Susannah didn't flinch at the way he'd introduced her, which he appreciated. He'd have liked to discuss their story before she met any of his family, but fortunately she seemed able to roll with the punches.

Kara reached out to shake her hand. "Nice to meet you, Susannah. Are you here to see Flynn?"

"Yes," Susannah said, no trace of artifice or nerves. "I was in town and gave Matthew a call. He mentioned Flynn was unwell and I wanted to visit."

A warmth glowed in his chest that stemmed from appreciation and respect for her quick thinking.

"Grace would have liked that," Kara said.

"Actually," Susannah said, "Matthew mentioned that you'd made a schedule to ensure someone is with Flynn. I'll be here at least a couple of days, maybe longer, depending on how a few things pan out, and I wouldn't mind helping out if you need someone else."

The tight band around his chest constricted. The more time

Susannah spent with Flynn, the more his son would become attached—laying the groundwork for a disaster when she left.

"That would be fabulous," Kara said. "Nights and weekends are no problem, but sometime during business hours would work well if that suits you? Our mother and Lily are the only ones who can easily arrange their days, so the schedule gets a bit tight then."

Matt rubbed the tight muscles at the back of his neck. How could he refuse an offer that would give his family a break? They were all going above and beyond for Flynn and he was more grateful than he could ever say. He dropped his hand from his neck and stuffed it in a pocket. It would only be a few days and he'd talk to Flynn if things got out of hand. He took a small step back to let them make the arrangements.

"I can start tomorrow," Susannah said.

"Great." Kara pulled an electronic organizer from her bag and began tapping buttons. "Just give me a number I can contact you on."

Before Susannah could revisit the idea of staying at a hotel, he cut in. "I've invited her to stay at my place while she's here. You can reach her there."

There was a flicker of a question in Kara's eyes before she seemed to dismiss it. "Perfect, I'll be in touch. But now, there's a gorgeous little boy just waking up, so I'd better go over and say hello."

Twenty minutes later, after he'd said goodbye to his son, he and Susannah were in his car, on the road to his house.

He squared his shoulders, ready to open a difficult conversation. "I apologize for lying about your relationship back there."

"Matthew," she said gently, "this is *your* family, your life— yours and Flynn's. I'm here to help. You do whatever you need to do and I'll fit in."

He wasn't used to such unqualified support. Grace had often been quite contrary, and his family was loving but opinionated—everyone having their two cents' worth at family lunches. Susannah's willingness to let him choose the path here, without question, was as welcome as it was novel.

He glanced over—her delicate features were relaxed and open, confirming there was no undercurrent to her words, and he had a feeling that what you saw was what you got with Susannah Parrish. "I appreciate that."

"Though, it would help if we talked about it so we're on the same page."

"Agreed," he said as he smoothly took a corner. "I should have mentioned it before we ran into Kara, but we covered well."

"So, I'm an old friend of Grace's?"

"It's not strictly a lie." He could feel her gaze on him and, after stopping at traffic lights, he turned to her. Her eyes were the blue of a summer's sky, and just as endless. It was the first thing he'd noticed when she'd approached him in the airport. A man could lose himself in eyes like those. He frowned and dragged his gaze back to the red light. "You and Grace spent time together several years ago."

"They don't know anything about Flynn's surrogate?"

"They don't know your name, so my family won't suspect it's you. Grace wanted details kept to a minimum since it reminded her too much of what she perceived as her failure." Nothing he'd said to her had been able to sway her from that assessment of herself. She'd been an excellent mother to Flynn. Genetics paled into insignificance compared to that.

The light turned green and he smoothly pressed down on the accelerator. "And if we tell them you're the surrogate, without telling them you're also the biological mother, they'll wonder why you're here since a normal surrogate wouldn't be needed in this situation."

"So we keep it simple?"

He'd put a lot of thought into this since the moment he'd known he'd have to call her. It was the only plan that seemed reasonable. "It's our best option."

"What if the tissue matching is positive and Flynn needs the transplant? Won't that make it harder to hide?"

"We'll cross that bridge if we have to." And he was praying like crazy that they never had to. He swallowed hard and his hands gripped the wheel tightly. "But my family—no one—can ever know that Grace isn't Flynn's biological mother."

He'd made a vow to Grace that he would not break. In fact, he was doubly bound to keep that vow—since he'd as good as killed her by making her take the fatal plane flight, the only means he had left to honor his college sweetheart was to protect her secret. He owed her this, and so much more.

The drive through Charleston brought back a multitude of memories from when she'd lived here. Susannah glimpsed the grand old houses the city was known for, standing tall and elegant as they passed; the bustle of downtown; the majestic trees draping the sidewalks. Sweet nostalgia filled her soul—she'd rarely been back to her hometown since the move to Georgia three years ago and she'd missed it.

A few blocks from where the Peninsula met the sea, Matthew pulled into the driveway of what looked like an overgrown stone cottage with large windows on both stories and a creeping vine covering large portions of the downstairs walls.

After opening the door, he stepped back to allow her to enter and Susannah took an uneven breath. She was merely staying with Flynn's father so she could be on hand if she was needed. It was a practical plan that made complete sense.

So why did it feel dangerous?

Some fanciful part of her was reacting as if an attractive man was inviting her back to his place because he was interested in her. Which was ridiculous. Just *how* ridiculous, she realized once she'd stepped over the threshold. The first thing that greeted her was a large framed photo of Grace, smiling beatifically, with baby Flynn in her arms. And, as he guided her through the house, she found more photos covering the walls.

Photos of Grace with Flynn, with Matthew, or the three of them together. Large and small; snapshots and portraits; laughing faces and soft, dreamy expressions.

This was not the house of a man who would ever invite another woman home. This was the house of a man still deeply in love with his wife.

Matthew stopped in front of a door, opened it and switched on the light. In the middle of the large room stood a four-poster bed, with lace fringing and a quilted cover in soft pinks and mauves.

"This is the guest bedroom. The bathroom is through there," he said, pointing to a door leading directly from the bedroom. "I'll give you a few minutes to freshen up, then, when you're ready I'll find us something to eat in the kitchen."

She'd eaten lunch on the plane, but nothing since. At his words, her stomach rumbled. "I can fix something if you want."

His gaze flicked to her stomach then back to her face with a faintly amused quirk at the edge of his full bottom lip. "No need. Pamela, my mother's housekeeper, keeps a stock of home-cooked meals in my freezer."

"That's sweet of her." For reasons she wasn't prepared to examine too closely, she was glad that Pamela and the Kincaid family were looking out for Matthew and Flynn.

"She's done it since Grace passed. I think she's worried I'm too busy to cook."

"And you're not?" she asked, thinking of all he had on his plate.

A rueful smile twitched on his lips. "Usually I am. I say a prayer of thanks often for Pamela's thoughtfulness."

"If I end up staying a few days," she said, seeing the answer to something that had been playing on her mind, "I'd like to pull my weight. I'll do the cooking."

"Susannah, I think what you've offered to do for Flynn more than 'pulls your weight.'" He smiled even as he frowned, and the unusual combination tugged at her. "Don't worry about it. Kitchen is down the stairs to the left—I'll see you in ten."

She watched his tall frame stride down the hall, entire body taut with the responsibility that sat astride his broad shoulders. How exhausting must it be for Matthew to be the sole caregiver for Flynn when he still grieved for his wife? If only she could—

Stopping the thought before it went any further, she slipped back into her temporary bedroom and changed her clothes then splashed water on her face. This little family unit wasn't part of her life. She'd be leaving soon. She twisted her long hair up into a knot and secured it with a clip.

Feeling refreshed, she followed the stairs down to the kitchen to find Matthew minus his tie and with sleeves rolled to a couple of inches above his wrists, stirring a pot on the stove. Those masculine wrists and the light covering of dark brown hair on the glimpse of his forearms were mesmerizing, and for timeless moments she couldn't drag her gaze away.

"I hope you like chili beans," he said as he looked up. "I'm reheating one of Pamela's specialties."

"Love them," she said, giving herself a shake to recover her equilibrium. She leaned closer to the pot. "Smells good. Can I do anything?"

He passed her an oven mitt. "The corn bread's ready to come out of the oven."

"I was serious, by the way," she said as she slid the tray of bread onto the marble kitchen island. "If I need to stay, I won't feel comfortable with you housing and feeding me unless I'm doing something. Besides, I've taken a week's leave and even with visiting Flynn sometimes at the hospital, I might go crazy with boredom."

"Well, I'd hate to cause someone to lose their sanity." An eyebrow arched in faint amusement. "I'm only willing to consider the possibility that the tissue matching will be positive, so, as far as I'm concerned, you're staying awhile. You can do some of the cooking. I'll leave the keys to Grace's Cadillac and a credit card. You'll need ingredients—we have the basics but you'll probably want more." He reached for a bowl, spooned a generous amount of beans and passed it to her. "If you're in Kara's schedule, you'll need the car to get to the hospital."

He picked up the second bowl he'd filled and the plate of corn bread, and indicated a breakfast table at one end of the large kitchen. "Is here okay with you?"

"Casual is good," she said, settling into the solid wooden chair. She tasted the chili beans and sighed. "It's possible that anything warm and home cooked would taste divine after a day of packing and traveling, but this is really good."

"We were raised eating Pamela's cooking." He glanced at the bread in his hand, a faraway look in his eyes. "It tastes like home to me."

They ate a few minutes in silence and the day's events played over in her mind.

"Can I ask you something?"

He glanced up, eyes wary. "Sure."

"Why does everyone sing Elvis songs to Flynn?"

A frown creased his forehead as he looked down at his bowl. "Grace was a big fan. She sang them to him instead of lullabies…."

"And now he asks for them," she finished for him.

"Yes."

It was one word, simply said, but it held an eternity of pain. It hurt to even watch so she tucked a stray piece of hair behind her ear and found a mischievous smile.

"I heard that not everyone sings them properly."

He glanced up sharply, his brilliant green eyes filled with confusion. "What do you mean?"

"He said that Aunty Lily sings her Elvis numbers too fast and occasionally dances to them, which is apparently inappropriate."

A reluctant smile tugged at the corners of his mouth. "That sounds like Lily."

And Daddy sings them sad.

The words pierced her heart. Of course he did—they reminded him of his beloved wife singing lullabies to their baby. It was amazing he could sing them at all. Unsure of what to say in the presence of so much grief, she ate another mouthful of chili.

"Susannah, there's something I want to ask of you, but…" Fine lines appeared around his eyes as pained reluctance overtook his face.

"Anything," she said softly. "Please, just ask and I'll do it." That's why she'd come. To help.

"It's not that kind of favor." He carefully placed his spoon in his bowl and steepled his hands together under his chin. "You'll be going home soon."

He paused so she said, "Yes," to fill the space.

"When I came back into the room this evening, and Flynn had fallen asleep, curled into your side…" He reached for his wine and had a mouthful, giving himself more time. "Flynn doesn't normally become affectionate with strangers, but he did with you for some reason, and if you spend more time with him—"

"You're worried that when I leave, he'll be hurt," she said, cutting in. She'd been tormented by the same thought.

"Basically." He picked up his spoon and stirred the food around his bowl before dropping the spoon back in and meeting her gaze. "I know I can't shelter him from every hurt, but if it's in my power to protect him, I will."

If only every child had a father who cared as much as Matthew. His love, his commitment to his son was etched in his every expression. "I promise I'll be careful when I spend time with him," she vowed. "I don't want to see him hurt, either."

"I know." There was certainty in his words, yet their time together today was the most they'd ever spent in each other's company—they were still virtually strangers.

So she couldn't help but ask, "You do?"

"I saw it in your eyes when you met him. You care."

She smoothed her skirt over her lap, gathering her thoughts—Matthew deserved to understand where she stood in regards to his son.

She looked back up and met his gaze. "When Flynn was handed to you and Grace at the maternity hospital, I was honestly pleased to be able to give you a baby. Grace was so desperate to be a mother, and I knew the two of you would make great parents. But, yes, I do still care about him. Want the best for him. So, please don't be concerned that I'll encourage an attachment that will hurt him when I leave."

A little of the tension seemed to leave his features as he nodded wordlessly and began to eat again.

After a few mouthfuls, the silence felt uncomfortable so she cast around for another topic.

"Do you have any allergies besides to penicillin?"

He arched an eyebrow and she realized she'd probably lost him by blurting out her question. "For when I buy ingredients tomorrow, I was wondering if you had a food allergy, like to peanuts or seafood," she added.

"I'm not fond of olives or oregano, but no, penicillin is my only allergy."

"It's tough that it might have stopped you from donating your bone marrow," she said without thinking, then cursed herself for reopening a painful subject.

A tortured look filled his eyes and she understood just how very much he'd wanted to be able to do that for his son. "Yes," he muttered.

The depths of pain she'd once again glimpsed called to her like a siren's song, demanding she ease the suffering.

"I'm sorry, Matthew."

He gave a small shrug. "I just wish I could be Flynn's first resort, not his last."

She wanted to ask how he was coping, but it was too intimate a question and she had no right to pry. He'd invited her into his home so she'd be nearby in case they needed her bone marrow. He didn't want her forming attachments to his son, or asking prying questions of him. She had to remember she was temporary. Nothing more.

Three

The next morning, Susannah was in the kitchen making toast when Matthew appeared, striding through the door, blowing her composure out the window. He wore trousers of darkest blue and a caramel business shirt—no jacket, no tie. The buttons at his neck and those leading down his chest weren't yet secured, giving an unfettered view of the strong column of his neck and his Adam's apple, then a glimpse of the smattering of dark chest hair. Her mouth suddenly went dry.

Until this morning, she'd seen his throat respectably outfitted in a collar and tie—even last night when he'd removed his tie, the collar had still covered the view now on display. Her heart thumped hard and erratically, which seemed an extreme reaction even considering this was the first time she'd seen his naked neck. Yet she couldn't tear her gaze away.

"Good morning, Susannah," he said, his voice smooth and deep. "Did you sleep well?"

She swallowed and determinedly looked back to the toaster. "Good morning. Yes, the room is lovely—I slept like a baby."

"You mean waking every two hours, feeling hungry?" She glanced back to see his green eyes had taken on a devilish glint.

The unexpected humor relaxed her and she smiled. "Flynn wasn't a good sleeper?"

"He was eight months before he slept through the night. But he's good now."

Matthew moved into the kitchen and reached toward a large silver machine. "I'm making coffee—do you want one?"

"Love one," she said on a happy sigh. She'd been eyeing the machine before he came down and wondering if she should attempt to work out how it operated, but was wary of breaking something on her first morning.

As she moved aside to give him more room, she noticed his feet were bare. Her breath caught. She'd seen plenty of naked male feet before—they were freely on show at any beach. But it was different seeing Matthew Kincaid's feet emerging from his suit trousers, moving around on his tiled kitchen floor. More intimate somehow. They were strong feet, broad with long toes and bluntly cut nails, and she had a vision of them sliding against her own feet. She shivered.

"How do you like yours?"

Her head jerked up to find him holding up a mug to highlight the question. His thoughts were innocent, it was hers that had been...best forgotten. That way lay danger.

"Black with one sugar," she rasped.

He pressed a button and a subtle mechanical noise filled the space between them, giving her a chance to recover her breath. Why was he affecting her so much? Was it the intense situation they faced? The false intimacy of staying in his house? Or something about Matthew Kincaid himself?

Abruptly the noise stopped and they were again two people standing in silence, alone in a kitchen.

"I'll make a proper breakfast tomorrow," she said, feigning normalcy, "but for today, do you want something other than toast?"

"Toast is fine. I usually make Flynn an omelet in the mornings but if I'm on my own, toast is all I bother with."

He leaned back against the counter, folding his arms over his muscled chest and crossing his naked feet at the ankles. She tried not to look as she slid two more pieces of bread into the toaster and moved to the fridge.

"Kara rang earlier," he said. "She wanted to know if you'd take the morning shift with Flynn. She was going to do it herself but there was some sort of wedding disaster she has to see to."

Delighted, she turned to him with butter in one hand and honey in the other. "She's getting married?" This family could do with something joyful to celebrate.

"Our sister Laurel is getting married. Kara is organizing the wedding. If it's a problem, I'll go. I'd planned on going into work this morning then spending the afternoon with Flynn, but—"

"It's no problem." She smiled, glad to be of use. "The only thing on my schedule was some shopping, and I'll do that later."

And the grateful smile that flashed across his face warmed her down to her toes and made any inconvenience worthwhile.

"Are you happy eating at the kitchen table?"

She glanced out through the glass doors to a little courtyard bathed in early morning sunlight. A wisp of serenity settled through her. "I saw a garden setting outside—would you mind if we ate out there?"

"Sure. It should be warm while the sun's hitting it," he said, walking over and unlocking the door. "In fact, it's been pretty warm this year."

She found a tray and piled it with plates, butter and spreads. Matthew put the coffees on the tray and leaned in front of her to lift it. The smell of clean skin and freshly laundered cotton surrounded her and her eyes drifted closed to savor the scent. When he moved away, her eyes flicked open again. Glad he hadn't seemed to have noticed, she grabbed some cutlery and followed him out onto the paved area that was warmed by the morning sun.

A light breeze played with the leaves on the bushy shrubs that enclosed the little courtyard. It was like a magical area, away from reality. Stepping away from the table, she turned her face to the sun, and, cutlery still grasped in one hand, spread her arms out to capture all the rays she could. The sunshine was so divine on her skin, the light breeze lovely as it lifted the edges of her hair, that she could have stayed for hours, soaking it all up. If she were alone.

She dropped her arms and turned to find Matthew standing a few feet away, watching her with an intensity that stole her breath. Telling herself there was no need to be self-conscious, she shrugged and laid the cutlery on the table.

"I like the fresh air," she said, a twinge of embarrassment still in her belly.

One corner of his mouth twitched. "I can see."

Ever since she was little, she'd searched out the sun and the wind, running outside on windy days to play. And now, as an adult, it was still something of a guilty pleasure.

"Working in an office all day and living in an apartment, I try to find time to be outside whenever I can. Just to feel the sun and the breeze touch my skin. It's...revitalizing."

The pulse at the base of his throat seemed to beat more strongly and his light tone was forced. "Sounds like a smart plan."

"I start to wilt if I stay inside too long," she said, aware her voice was breathier than it had been moments before.

A heavy silence fell, setting every nerve in her body on edge, until the tension drew out to become a physical thing between them. His eyes darkened, sending a shiver down her spine.

Finally he cleared his throat. "You're an interesting woman, Susannah Parrish."

"You don't like the outdoors?" Her uncooperative voice was close to a whisper.

"Love it," he said, stepping across to hold her chair for her. "I just never think of it as something I need. I take Flynn outside to play, and we go to parks, but it's something for him."

As she sank into the chair, she watched him move around the table to take his own seat. His tone had been matter-of-fact, but she sensed there was a clue here to understanding Matthew Kincaid. She picked up her coffee and sipped, turning the notion over in her mind.

"You can't live just for your work and Flynn. You have needs, too, Matthew."

He stilled, gaze locked on her and she suddenly regretted her choice of words—she had no right to be dishing out advice. She cast around for a way to make it right, to take the unintended provocative edge away, but came up with nothing.

His cell phone rang and he reached into his pocket, not breaking eye contact with her. Then he turned and headed for the glass door and into the house. "Matthew Kincaid," he said, closing the door behind him.

A trickle of relief flowed through her at the interruption. Though the courtyard was suddenly emptier, colder, without his presence. She rubbed her hands up and down her arms. In the short time since she'd arrived, she'd noticed that about him—he brought a room to life, as if there was a haze of…something… around him. Something almost magical. Even out here, outdoors, once he was gone, the air seemed flatter, the colors less vibrant.

The door opened and he reappeared. "That was the hospital."

Her heart skipped a beat. "Flynn?"

"No, it was the lab."

Her hands reached for the small table, and held firmly for support. "The tissue testing," she said and he nodded. "And?"

He grinned, and his face transformed. "They think you're a good match. It's the first piece of good news I've had since Flynn entered that hospital." He walked across to where she sat and took her hand, holding it between both of his. The touch of skin on skin was electric, sending a shimmer across every one of her nerve endings. "We finally have a backup plan, thanks to you."

"Oh, thank goodness," she said in a rush, partly from relief, partly from his hands still enclosing hers. She tightened her fingers around his.

"They're still not sure if he'll need it—" he dragged in a deep breath, and she could imagine the prayer he sent up "—but they'd like you to be available in case."

She didn't hesitate. "I've taken a week's leave. I'm yours."

Forty minutes later, she was entering Flynn's room, more nervous than she'd been yesterday. The first time she'd been alone with him, it'd been for a few minutes while Matthew made a call. This time, it would be several hours with a whole lot more expectation that she could be fun and entertaining. Which would be hard enough given her limited experience with children, but it also all needed to happen while not encouraging any attachment. She placed a hand over her belly to calm the butterflies that had taken up residence.

A tall woman with short, stylishly cut dark auburn hair hopped up from a chair against the wall and motioned with a finger against her lips that Flynn was sleeping while she tiptoed over. Her brilliant green eyes were the same shade as Matthew's, but she was too old to be a sister.

"You must be Susannah," the older woman said. "I'm Elizabeth, Flynn's grandmother. Thank you for filling in."

"It was no problem." As she turned and saw Flynn, her breath caught in her throat. His sweet little body was curled around the brown teddy, with the covers coming up to his waist. An almost physical pull beckoned her to his bedside, insisted she hold him.

The pull surprised her...and scared her. They'd been concerned about Flynn becoming attached to her—perhaps she should be as careful not to let herself become too emotionally involved with him, or risk breaking her own heart when she left.

"He's only been asleep for about ten minutes," Elizabeth said, "so he'll probably sleep a bit longer. It's hard to tell—he's tired all the time from the anemia so he'll probably want to nap a couple of times while you're here."

"I'll be fine." She spoke the words to Matthew's mother, but her gaze didn't waver from Flynn. "I'll let him set the pace, and I'll be sure to encourage him to rest if he seems tired."

"Kara said you were a friend of Grace's?" Elizabeth's tone was politely inquisitive, but Susannah understood her need to ask—this was a grandmother about to walk out and leave her only grandchild in the company of a stranger.

"Yes," she said, weighing up the amount of information to disclose. With a lie, it was best to stick as close to the truth as possible. "We knew each other a number of years ago. The last time I saw her was just after Flynn was born."

"You met Flynn?" the other woman asked, her head tilted to the side. "I'm sorry to sound so curious, it's just that I don't remember you from the baby shower."

"Just the once." At his birth. "I missed the shower—I was moving to Georgia about that time, then Grace and I lost touch. I was very sorry to hear about her passing."

Elizabeth turned a pained look to her grandson. "We all were. For Grace, for Flynn and for Matthew." She reached for her bag and, while her face was averted, brushed at her cheek. Susannah's heart clenched tight for the pain this family had been through.

When Elizabeth straightened, her face was composed, even if her eyes glistened. "Nice to meet you, Susannah. I hope to run into you again sometime."

"Likewise," she replied, and watched Matthew's mother slip out of the room.

Now she was alone, Susannah allowed herself a chance to stare at the little boy for timeless, heart-wrenching minutes. He was simply perfect.

Finally she dragged herself away and eased into the chair. She rummaged through her bag for a pen and notebook then began making notes to email her assistant later. After her presentation yesterday, the PR plan for the bank's rebranding had been given the green light. She might have left soon after, but her assistant and the rest of the team could handle the preliminary work, and Susannah would be home long before the launch to take control of the rest of the plan. And she would stay in regular contact via phone and email.

She tapped the pen against her chin. A week ago, this project had been the most important thing in her life, and now...her gaze drifted over to the sleeping child before she forced it back again.

And now it still needed to be. She'd be leaving Charleston soon, and when she did, her career would again be her main focus. She loved her job, and was proud of being in a senior position at only twenty-six. She had a tight group of friends at home, too—she hadn't had a chance to explain her trip to Charleston to them yet, just a quick text to all four saying she was out of town and would explain when she got back. It was a good life she'd built when she and her mother had moved there three years ago. A life that anchored her and pulled at her to return.

When she'd finished making the notes, her mind drifted to dinner. She didn't regularly make elaborate meals, since it was just herself at home, but when she had an excuse, cooking was something she enjoyed. The only thing she knew about Matthew's tastes was he liked chili beans. Did he like desserts, or did he prefer a second helping of savory? Rich flavors or mild? She'd have to wing it the first time and see what worked for him. Ideas started to form and she jotted them down to make the trip to the supermarket easier.

Movement at the edge of her vision caught her attention. Flynn stretched and yawned then his large, sleepy eyes locked on her.

"Hello, sweetie," she said, moving to sit on the side of the bed. "Your grandma had to go, so I thought I might spend some time here." She was sure Elizabeth would have briefed him, but she wasn't sure how disoriented he'd be after waking.

He nodded. "Hello, Sudi."

Then, he leaned into her and yawned again. His little body was still warm from sleep and she wrapped him in a protective embrace and laid a cheek on his silky mop of hair.

Without meaning to, she turned her face and pressed her lips against the top of his head in a kiss. In that moment, she didn't want to let him go—he was so warm and soft and trusting in this just-woken state. She held the kiss a few seconds longer, wanting to create a memory—the feel of his small body, his scent. A memory she could carry with her forever.

When she released him, he pulled back and slowly blinked at her, curiosity in his eyes. "Are you my new mommy?"

Her heart stilled in her chest and she couldn't get her throat to work. Flynn seemed unaffected by her silence; he simply continued to watch her with soulful eyes.

"Why would you think that, sweetie?"

"You kiss like a mommy," he said matter-of-factly.

She drew in a shaky breath. "That's just the way I kiss all little boys and girls."

He didn't seem put off. "You singed like a mommy last time."

She opened her mouth, but what could she say? *Think fast.* "Maybe that just means I'll be someone else's mommy one day," she said brightly. "If I'm lucky, they'll be as wonderful as you."

He looked far from convinced, so she sat farther into the bed, dragging a leg up to sit sideways. She needed to address this head-on. "Here's the thing, Flynn. New mommies sometimes come along, but it's up to daddies to choose them."

He considered this before shaking his head. "I fink the kids should choose them."

"You have a point." She tried to suppress a smile—his argument had logic, but this could be a problem later and she needed to take it seriously. "You know, I don't really know much about how it works. But there *is* someone who knows."

"Who?" he asked, his eyes becoming impossibly big.

"Your dad. He's a smart man. I think you should ask him."

Flynn stared at her for a moment, and butterflies quivered in her stomach as she waited to see whether he would let her off the hook or not.

Then he got up on his knees, reached to the side table and retrieved the bear book they'd read yesterday. He passed it to her, eyes hopeful.

"I was just in the mood for a book about teddy bears," she said on a relieved breath.

He gave her a contented smile and curled into her side.

At lunchtime when Matt stepped into the anteroom to spend the afternoon with his son, Susannah was walking in to meet him from the other side. As she moved, her long blond hair swung around her shoulders and, though she was smiling, concern was clear in her eyes.

He mirrored her smile as she slipped through the door in case Flynn was watching. "Is something wrong?"

"Nothing new about his condition." She paused and bit down on her lip and his eyes were drawn to the action. Such a plump lip, tailor-made for the nibbling it was currently having. He turned away. He shouldn't be thinking about Susannah Parrish's lip.

"But I wanted to forewarn you about a question you'll probably get."

Relief flowed through him, and he bent to wash his hands. "He's always been challenging with his questions."

"Flynn asked if I was his new mommy."

He snapped to attention and pivoted to face her, hands dripping on the floor. "How did that come up?"

"I swear, Matthew," she said, wrapping her arms around her middle, "I didn't encourage him."

That was true—Susannah could never cause anyone pain on

purpose, he knew that deep in his bones. He tapped the faucet off with his elbows and reached for a paper towel.

"I know." He threw the towel in the bin and took a breath. "But do you know where he got the idea?"

Her eyes flicked to Flynn through the window. "He says I kiss like a mommy, and sing like one, too."

He winced. Strong pieces of evidence to a three-year-old. "What did you tell him?"

"I said daddies were the ones to choose the new mommies and he should talk to you about it." Although her eyes were still worried, a grin peeped out. "He thinks kids should choose the new mommies."

Matt couldn't restrain a chuckle. "That sounds like our Flynn. Thanks for aiming him back to me—I'll handle it from here."

Not that he had any idea what he'd say to the kid who was too wise for his own good. As much as Matt had tried to protect him when Grace died, his son had changed. Now he saw too much. Thought too much.

And he deserved better than a father who was making it up as he went along. Grace had been the one who'd always known what to do with kids. Even when they'd been talking about a divorce, he'd still expected they would share custody afterward.

Now he was all Flynn had. He looked through the glass panel at his son flicking through his favorite teddy-bear book.

He would just have to do better.

Four

Susannah watched Matthew eat the last spoonful of her coffee and hazelnut cheesecake. A warm glow suffused her body when he made an appreciative sound. Cooking calmed her—somehow allowed her thoughts to fall into order—so she would have wanted to cook today regardless. But to have someone enthusiastically appreciate her food made it that bit more worthwhile. Especially when that someone was Matthew, whose opinion she'd come to respect.

"After a meal like that, I don't think you need to worry about pulling your weight," he said, leaning back into his chair and giving her a lazy appraisal.

"It's one of my mom's many recipes." Her mother had taught her to cook from when she was young—savory meals, desserts, cakes. They'd been the recipes her own mother had taught her, and maybe one day Susannah would have her own little girl or boy to teach them to. A picture of Flynn flashed in her mind, but she pushed it away. He was *Matthew's* son, not hers.

"I can see that you and your father ate well."

"My dad passed away when I was young, so it was mainly Mom and me." The familiar ache swelled to fill her chest. It'd been many years but she still missed her father immeasurably, missed his hugs, his radiant love for her mother and her.

"I'm sorry to hear that," he said, genuine concern in the fine lines around his eyes. "I lost my father not long ago."

Headlines in the local newspaper had screamed the new developments in the story to passersby when she'd been at the store earlier. She'd picked up a copy and read the first few lines about Reginald Kincaid's murder, then placed the paper back on the pile and moved on, unwilling to be another vulture, prying for details of something so intensely private.

For the rest of the afternoon, she hadn't been able to stop thinking about the story, her heart aching for Matthew. So much grief and burden—first his wife's tragic death and becoming a single parent to Flynn. Now losing his father, and discovering it was through murder.

The urge to reach out and touch his hand verged on irresistible—had there been anyone to comfort him? His wife was gone and each family member would have been suffering their own grief. She glanced at his broad shoulders, his strong frame. What would it be like, drawing him close and offering a consoling embrace? Her skin warmed. Probably less about giving comfort and more about her fascination with him, judging by her body's response to the mere thought.

She settled for wrapping her fingers around her wineglass. "Were you and your father close?"

He nodded once, his lips curving into a grim smile. "We're a close family." A frown line appeared on his forehead then grew while he studied his empty plate. "Well, I thought we were."

She remembered the obvious affection between Matthew and Kara, and the way he'd spoken about his other siblings. "What's made you question it?"

His gaze was on his empty plate but she knew he didn't see it. Even as he spoke, she knew his focus was a million miles away.

"After my father's death," he said through a tight jaw, "we discovered he had a second family. Complete with two extra sons—one biological and one informally adopted. Seems that, decades ago, he met up again with his first love to find she'd borne him a son, been married and had another son to her husband. By the time she met Dad again, the husband was gone, so Dad set her up as his mistress and created a second family for himself with her and the boys."

She leaned back in her chair, physically rocked by the revelation, despite not knowing his father. The betrayal, the anger, must have been overwhelming.

"You had no idea?" she whispered.

His eyes were bleak. "None at all."

"Oh, Matthew, I can't imagine how awful that must have been. Especially to find out that way."

"It was no picnic," he said and reached for his wineglass before taking a long sip.

"So, beyond the shock, is it a good thing getting two new brothers?"

He dragged a hand down his face. "I don't think the new brothers are looking to play happy families. Jack, my father's biological son, definitely isn't and the jury's still out on Alan. Also, the way my father divided the stock between both groups has left the family company in a precarious position."

"I'm so sorry. Sometimes life is simply unfair."

He gave her an ambiguous smile and stood to clear the plates. "Tell me about your mother."

She recognized the change of topic for what it was—he'd exposed too much for comfort to a virtual stranger—so she allowed him the preservation of his dignity.

"My mother is fun," she said and followed him to the sink with their wineglasses. "Always lively, always ready with a witty joke. It must have been hard for her after my father died, but she rarely let on."

He opened the dishwasher and looked up, genuine curiosity in his eyes before he stacked their crockery in the slots. "How old were you when he died?"

"Eight." She had no clear memories left of that time, just the overwhelming sense of sadness and despair. Poor Flynn must have experienced similar depths after losing Grace, and she wished with everything inside her she could have saved him that. At least he had Matthew, the way she had her mother.

"My parents were very much in love," she said, "but Mom pulled herself together quickly to ensure my world was stable. I see you've done the same thing for Flynn and I really respect that."

A quick grimace passed across his face before he turned away to grab a cooking pot. "Did you have much family around?" he asked.

"Mom's parents were interstate and they'd help where they could. Dad's parents were less helpful." The resentment that lived in the pit of her stomach threatened to simmer, but she wouldn't let it. She wouldn't let them ruin her mood all this time later.

He straightened and his green gaze narrowed on her. "Define 'less helpful.'"

Perceptive man, Matthew Kincaid. For an instant, she considered deflecting the question, or giving a half response, but he'd just shared a very personal story and she couldn't be less than honest in return.

"They sued for custody of me after Dad died."

Very slowly, he put the cutlery down and rested his hands low on his hips. "Were there any grounds?"

"Only in their imaginations. They'd never liked or approved of my mother. She was an outsider to their social scene. My father had provided a buffer for her when he was alive, but once he was gone, they pulled out all the stops."

Her father's family had money and influence—a lethal combination. It had taught her young that wealthy families who were used to getting their own way were dangerous. Her mother had been blinded by love when she'd married, but Susannah had learned from that mistake. Families like her father's—like the Kincaids—were full of secrets and maneuverings. She'd bet the Kincaids had a few more secrets up their sleeves, too. Families like theirs always did.

"Criminal," Matthew said, scowling. "To make it harder for you both while you were grieving is unforgivable."

The unqualified support loosened the knot in her chest where the memory lived and allowed a little more of the story to ease out. "Not just while we were grieving. When they lost the custody case, they wiped Mom. Wouldn't acknowledge she existed. Mom would drop me over on visits once a month, and they'd shower me with presents and try to convince me to live with them."

"I can't imagine Grace's parents doing something that selfish. They adore Flynn—they stay with us regularly, and ring him every Sunday. Thinking of them pulling Flynn away from me...it's just inconceivable." He shook his head. "Did you tell your mother?"

"No, I just put up with it." Until they went too far.

"How are they now?" he asked with a raised eyebrow, obviously being far too perceptive once again.

She hesitated before admitting, "I wouldn't know."

"You stood up to them," he said, warm approval in his eyes. "What was the tipping point?"

It was a time in her life that she avoided revisiting, and had never told anyone else about, yet, it seemed somehow natural to share with this man.

"Four years ago," she began, then moistened her lips, "my mother lost everything in a despicable scam. She'd trusted someone she worked with who disappeared after the scam went down. Lots of people were stung and despite the authorities being called in, there was no chance of recovering her money. She was going to lose the house she'd shared with my father. Her family didn't have a lot of money, so she made me promise not to tell them. But my father's family was rich, and she was their daughter-in-law."

"She didn't know you asked, did she?"

She shook her head.

"What did they say?"

"They were exquisitely polite and very sorry not to be able to help, but—" she flinched, remembering their falsely sympathetic faces "—the bottom line was they wouldn't spend the money on a woman they didn't care for and had never wanted in their family."

She'd learned something that day—something she'd already known but had been trying to avoid admitting. Wealth changed people. Especially families. When money was inherited, it changed the family dynamics. Made life into an "us and them" scenario. She wanted enough money to get by, but huge wealth wasn't something she wanted anything to do with. And she'd never marry into a rich family the way her mother had.

He moved forward the smallest of steps and ran his fingertips down her arm in a gesture that was comforting even as it made her pulse jump.

"Susannah, I'm sorry." His voice was deep with concern.

"One good thing came of it," she said, trying to ignore the fingers that now rested near her elbow. "I went home, legally changed my name to my mother's maiden name and haven't seen them since."

If she'd lost her father's name in the process, that was regrettable but ultimately it was okay—her father had hated the way his parents had treated his wife, so she knew he would have understood. And she had him living in her heart, which was more important than a name.

"Good for you." One corner of his mouth kicked up. "So what happened with your mother?"

"I took out a loan for as much as I could get approved, and I met Grace soon after. Your money for the surrogacy paid the balance on Mom's house. It's rented out for the time being to help with loan repayments, and we moved to Georgia so Mom could live with family till the bank is paid out."

His fingertips began to trace a pattern on her skin once more, causing her pulse to jump erratically. "The house was that important?"

"She'd worked her entire life and," she said around a tight ball of emotion in her throat, "after Dad died she worked two jobs to give me the best start in life she could manage. I couldn't let her lose her house, the home for her retirement, her one link back to the man she loved."

With sure hands, he pulled her into his arms. She resisted at first, she was used to dealing with things on her own and she'd only known this man a couple of days, but he held her with a gentle firmness until she relaxed into his warmth. He was offering his support so freely, and just this once, she allowed herself to simply absorb.

And yet, there was something else that thrummed between them, a dangerous craving that always seemed to be lurking just beneath the surface when they were together.

She knew she should move away, banish the craving.

But she didn't.

Lately Matt wasn't used to having any woman in his arms besides his mother or his sisters. Susannah Parrish didn't feel remotely like his sisters. Her eyes, filled with strength and hurt at the betrayal had been his undoing. He couldn't have stood another second with the distance between them. And, even though he rubbed a palm slowly up and down her back the way he might for Lily, Laurel or Kara, he couldn't begin to fool himself.

This wasn't platonic—her nearness was setting his skin on fire.

He'd never known why she'd carried his baby, what she'd

used the money for, but the story of her resilience was amazing. Could he have ever done something as difficult for similar reasons?

"If I'd known, we'd have paid you more." Heck, if he thought she'd take it, he'd give her more now.

"It was enough," she said softly. "But thank you for saying that."

"What if I give—"

She pulled back in his arms and he could see her face again. "Please don't offer. I'll be fine."

"Noble as well as generous and beautiful," he said, cupping her cheek in his hand. Her pupils dilated and her breath came faster, and he wanted to kiss her so badly that he ached with it. He leaned down, wanting…

"Matthew," she said, and he stopped close enough to feel her breath on his face as she spoke. "This isn't a good idea."

"It sure feels like a good idea," he said, not retreating an inch. And, God help him, at this moment he couldn't consider anything other than how her mouth would feel opening beneath his.

"Things," she began, then paused to swallow. "Things are too complicated already."

"It's just a kiss, Susannah," he told her…told himself. "It doesn't have to mean anything." He brushed his lips across hers lightly, needing to feel them. "Just—" over one corner of her mouth "—one—" then the other corner "—kiss."

On a sigh, her lips parted, and a shudder ripped through his body. He'd been trying to deny that he'd wanted her ever since she'd walked through the arrivals gate at the airport. In the past year, any flicker of desire—no matter how minor—had felt disloyal to Grace, and had been followed by a tidal wave of guilt. Despite the talks of divorce, they'd still been married when she'd died. Worse, if he hadn't suggested divorce in the first place, Grace would still be alive. The confusion had kept him closed to the idea of other women for twelve months.

But what Susannah stirred within him was too strong to deny.

Her mouth tasted of the sweet dessert, combined with an allure all of her own that drew him ever deeper.

He plowed his fingers through her silken hair, holding her for his kiss, unwilling to risk her withdrawal. The wet slide of her tongue against his was sinfully erotic, her teeth nibbling at his lip explosive.

Mindless, he found her hips and drew her closer. As close as he could get while clothes provided a barrier. Her hands skimmed over his shoulders and down his back, and he wanted nothing more than to feel those hands on bare skin. To have his hands on her bare skin. He wanted her with an all-consuming need that was beyond thought.

He reached for the first button on her blouse but before he could make any headway, she pulled back.

"Matthew," she rasped, resting her hands on his chest. "Please."

The rough edges in her voice reverberated through his body. "Please, what?" he asked with a smile.

"If you try to kiss me like that again—" she paused, as if gathering enough breath to continue "—I won't be able to resist."

His pulse leaped. "Good," he said and his head began a descent again.

"Flynn." The one word was all she said, but it broke through the sensual fog in his brain and he paused.

"What about Flynn?"

She stepped beyond the circle of his arms, and his hand drifted down from her shoulder, lingered at her elbow then, when he reached her hand, his fingers tangled with hers. She looked at their entwined fingers for so long he wondered if she would say anything. Then she looked up, and sucked her bottom lip into her mouth. Barely a minute ago, she'd done the same thing to his lip and this time, he wanted to drag hers into his own mouth. But he waited, holding himself in check until he could kiss her again.

"When I was young," she finally said, leaning back against the counter, "and my grandparents would ask me to live with them, they'd tell me it was what my father would have wanted. I missed him terribly and they used that to get what they wanted. I know this is a completely different situation, but I've never forgotten that feeling of being torn. Of the confusion."

He squeezed his eyes shut and held them closed as he tried to get his brain to follow the quick change from kissing her to talking about her childhood. Was she seriously thinking Flynn was at risk—from her?

He cocked his head to the side. "You'd never do something that despicable to Flynn."

"Never," she confirmed with a fierceness in her expression. "But I truly believe we need to keep the family arrangements clear so Flynn doesn't sense any confusion and read into it that he's getting a new mommy. He's very astute."

Matt released her fingers and scrubbed his hands through his hair. She was right—Flynn was very perceptive for his age. Some of the things that came out of that kid's mouth astounded him. And with all the upheavals in his family at the moment, following his grandfather's death, and two new "uncles" he hadn't yet met arriving on the scene, the last thing Flynn needed was any more uncertainty. He'd already asked if Susannah was his new mommy.

"All right." He blew out a long breath. "There's some chemistry between us, we can't deny that." In fact, it was baffling that he felt this strongly about someone he barely knew, but there was no ignoring anymore that he did. "Perhaps it would be better all-around if we didn't take it further."

"Yes," she whispered, watching his mouth. His skin heated.

"And if we're going to ignore it, it'd help enormously if you didn't look at me that way. I only have the willpower of one man."

Her gaze flicked to her feet and she shuffled back. "I'm sorry."

With a finger, he lifted her chin until he could see her eyes again. "Don't be sorry." Gently he smoothed her hair back from her face. "We won't act on this, but promise you'll never feel sorry for wanting me."

"Okay," she said, her voice tight.

"And I won't be sorry for wanting you," he said roughly then left the room before he forgot his promise and kissed her.

Matt stood in the anteroom to his son's hospital bedroom, washing his hands and watching Susannah. Flynn was asleep and she was curled in the visitor's chair, reading a book—her legs tucked beneath her, her hair falling forward to curtain her face. The air caught in his chest. Everything inside him demanded he finish what they'd started last night. But she'd been right to stop their kiss—it had been a monumentally stupid move on his part. As if things weren't already messy enough with keeping the secret about Flynn's biological mother from his family, and ensuring stability and clarity for Flynn.

And Grace had been so jealous of Susannah during the pregnancy—not only was she carrying their baby, but the baby was biologically a product of him and Susannah. How much worse would Grace have felt if she'd known he'd soon be lusting over Susannah? After creating the situation that had killed his wife, the very last person he should be thinking of bedding was Susannah Parrish.

So why was his body convinced otherwise? Annoyed with himself, he shook the water from his hands with a bit too much force, and turned to grab a paper towel. As he did, he caught sight of a man coming through the door. A man who made Matthew's fingers curl into fists.

Jack Sinclair.

His father's oldest child. The man their father had left forty-five percent of The Kincaid Group to in his will and who had made his dislike of his father's legitimate family abundantly clear. Jack had been playing his cards close to his chest so far, but no one doubted his intentions—to take over TKG and fold it into his own company, Carolina Shipping.

With frustration and resentment fueling his scowl, Matt thrust his hands on his hips. "What the heck makes you think you'd be welcome here?"

Jack met the glare with one of his own, feet solidly planted shoulder width apart. "Regardless of how we feel about each other, that little boy is my nephew. I spent a couple of months in the hospital myself when I was a child and I intend to see him."

A touch of humanity from the enemy...or a ploy? "I notice you didn't bother to call first."

"Would you have invited me to visit if I had?"

Before Matt could reply, the door opened again and a third man entered the room, completing the bizarre triangle of Reginald Kincaid's sons—Matt's brother RJ.

RJ froze midstride, looking from one man to the other before his furious gaze settled on Matt. "What the hell is he doing here?"

Matt was heartened by the support of his brother's outrage. "I was just asking the same thing."

As one, the brothers turned to face the interloper.

Jack rolled his shoulders back and held up a gift bag. "I've brought a toy. I'm a blood relation to the boy and I want to meet him."

The door to Flynn's room slid open and Susannah slipped through. Just seeing her face made a large chunk of Matt's stress evaporate, replaced by a tugging desire deep in his gut. Unable to help himself, he moved to her side and placed a hand at the small of her back, trying to ensure it appeared platonic, but feeling uncomfortably proprietorial in a room of three men.

"Susannah, this is my brother RJ. Susannah is an old friend of Grace's who's been visiting Flynn."

RJ leaned over to shake her hand, taking his gaze from Jack long enough to smile at her. "Nice to meet you, ma'am."

"Likewise," Susannah said.

Matt glanced up at Jack and narrowed his eyes. "And this is Jack Sinclair. My father's other son."

Susannah shook Jack's proffered hand. "Nice to meet you, Jack," she said, then faced down each man in turn. "I know you've both just met me, so this might seem out of line, but there's so much tension in this room, it's ready to smother me. And Flynn will feel it, too. You can't all go into his room together."

There was something of a mother lion in her eyes, and Matt knew that if his brothers tried to walk in, she wouldn't be afraid to stand in their way. His chest swelled. It was a beautiful thing to watch.

Jack again held his gift bag aloft. "I'd like to give this to the boy."

Susannah glanced over, raising her eyebrow the barest hint, yet he understood—she was asking if he'd let her take Jack in to Flynn's room, alone. He glanced over at Flynn through the glass wall—he was watching the interaction. If he tried to eject Jack, Flynn would see, and Matt would do anything to keep Flynn's world stable at the moment. No confrontations, no ripples in the pond.

And he had to admit, no matter how much it galled, this man was a blood relation to Flynn. Though why that would mean anything to Jack Sinclair, he had no idea.

He relaxed his body language for Flynn's sake, but he glared at his half brother with all the animosity inside. "This is a one-time deal, Sinclair. You go in, you give him the present, you leave again. And you don't come back."

Jack glared back and spoke through a tight jaw. "Understood."

He silently nodded to Susannah—she was right that they couldn't all go in together. The best environment for Flynn would be if Jack went with her. While she explained the gown and hand-washing routine to Jack, Matt steered RJ out into the hall.

He planted himself in front of the glass panel in the wall—he might have given the okay for Jack to go in, but at the first sign that Flynn was even slightly uncomfortable or unhappy, he'd throw the gate-crasher out himself.

"So, how is the little tyke?" RJ asked, concern clear in his voice.

"His blood work is a little better." He'd caught the doctor on the way in and heard the latest scores. Flynn wasn't out of the woods by any means, but any improvement, however small, was good news. It meant needing a bone-marrow transplant was less likely, and brought the day he could come home that bit closer.

"I can't tell you how glad I am," RJ said, clapping Matt on the back. "Let's hope it continues that way."

Matt allowed himself half a smile at the prospect. Unwilling to jinx it, he didn't want to dwell on Flynn's improvements too much—the blood work had improved before...then dived again. But his brother's enthusiasm allowed him the space for just a moment to consider that his little boy's health was really on the mend.

They watched Jack enter Flynn's room and Susannah perform the introductions and the atmosphere in the corridor changed. From the corner of his eye, he could see RJ mirroring his battle stance of straight back, hands low on hips and—he knew without looking—a scowl.

"Any news on who owns the last ten percent?" Matt asked. Their father had left forty-five percent of The Kincaid Group to be shared among his legitimate children, and another forty-five percent to Jack Sinclair. No one knew where the last ten percent was—the ownership had been hard to trace past the shares being sold to a now-defunct business—but they needed them fast.

Anger at his father burned in his gut—both for keeping his second family a secret and for giving Jack shares in the family company which had led to this predicament. Their father had left them a letter each, which most of them had opened at the will reading, hoping for an explanation of his actions. As far as he was aware, none of them had got one. Matt hadn't wanted to even touch his letter, let alone open it. Had his father stood in front of him that day, Matt would have turned and walked away. And the rage still seethed down deep. The last thing he wanted was to speak to a man who'd kept such monstrous secrets, had betrayed them so badly, even if it was only via a letter. Barely resisting crumpling the envelope and tossing it, he'd thrown it in a desk drawer in the unlikely event he changed his mind. He should have burnt it.

But he had to shove the emotions aside and strategize if they were to succeed. RJ was acting CEO, and Laurel, Kara, Lily and he would vote with RJ to install RJ as permanent CEO, but they needed the ten percent to outvote Jack if—when—he opposed. Until then, they were stuck in a stalemate.

"No news." RJ blew out a disgusted breath. "But I've put Nikki Thomas on the case. She's vowed to have the owner present when we vote."

"If anyone will find them, Nikki will." Their father had hired the corporate investigator not long before he died, and she'd managed to impress them already with her determination and ability to get results.

"Jack's given nothing away?" Matt asked. "I wouldn't put it past him to have located the shares and bought them already."

RJ shook his head. "He's playing his cards close to his chest, so if he has them, he wouldn't be sharing the information with us. He's a cold one. He'll be planning even now to get the ten percent and fold TKG into his own company."

Matt winced, but he'd had that exact thought himself. "What about Alan—any chance he's got them?" It seemed their father had taken his mistress's other son under his wing somewhat, yet not left him any stock in the will.

"I doubt it. If Dad had wanted to give him stock, it would have been at the same time as the rest of us. Though I have been thinking about Alan."

Through the glass panel, Matt surveyed Jack awkwardly

trying to make conversation with Flynn. "Alan seems like the better man of the two."

RJ grunted his agreement. "I'm wondering if Alan will want a job. At the next board meeting, Jack could use his shares to demand we employ his brother."

"Alan said he was between jobs, so he might want something," Matt said.

"And I don't think Jack will settle for a mere job. He's got his eye on the prize. Everything."

A lead weight dropped into his stomach as he acknowledged the truth in that. They stared at the scene through the glass panel for another couple of minutes as Jack awkwardly handed the gift bag over toward Flynn, who tentatively took it, one hand holding Susannah's fingers.

"One thing I can promise you," RJ said, "I won't let that man ruin TKG."

There was a fierceness in RJ's voice that was unusual. Matt turned to study his brother's face. The whole family had been thrown off balance, not only by their father's death, but the revelations about his second family, then the forty-five percent of company stock being willed to Jack. Even so, RJ had always been easygoing, even when he was in corporate shark mode.

He was about to ask what was going on, but inside Flynn's room, Jack moved to the door, and Matt needed to get inside to hold his son and make sure he was all right after meeting his new uncle. And he needed to see Susannah, to thank her for intervening, to ensure she was okay, as well. Analyzing RJ's mood change could wait.

Five

Five days later, Susannah was wandering the aisles of Matthew's basement wine cellar. Flynn had shown some definite improvement, but he wasn't yet past the risk that he might need the bone-marrow transplant, so she'd extended her leave for another week.

As the days had drifted on, she'd taken to slipping down to Matthew's wine cellar a few times a day for respite from the house—it was the only room that wasn't dominated by Grace's presence. Which was appropriate—this was Grace's house—and she hated herself for feeling a little jealous.

Down here it was shadowy and cool and strongly masculine. The shelving was made of dark wood, in straight lines and sharp angles.

She held a warm mug of tea between her hands as she perused the labels. Möet. Dom Pérignon. Krug. Veuve Clicquot.

"Thinking of taking up wine collecting?" The voice that caught her off guard was deep and smooth and faintly amused.

She turned to find Matthew casually leaning on the door frame, ankles crossed, hands deep in pockets.

Her heart turned over in her chest. It was a strange thing—she'd dated men before, had even flirted with the idea of marriage with one long-term boyfriend. But no man, boyfriend or otherwise, had ever affected her the way Matthew Kincaid could. All without a touch—he stood eight feet from her, but the heat of his gaze made her skin tighten. Made her want his kiss with a desperation that was alien to her.

She swallowed and found her voice. "How long have you been standing there?"

"Long enough to see how relaxed you are, perusing my collection." He pushed off the door frame and prowled toward her. "This isn't your first time in here, is it?"

An electric shiver raced up her spine. "Would you prefer I didn't come down?"

"You're welcome to explore any part of the house and grounds." He stopped within touching distance, his face in shadow, but she could hear that his breathing was a touch more rapid than normal. "I'm just interested why you chose a cellar over, say, the conservatory."

His nearness set off a series of pinprick sparks throughout her body. She rubbed her forearms, attempting to dispel the sensation, but it made no difference.

"Normally I would, but…things seem simpler down here," she said, attempting to explain what she only barely understood herself. "Clearer."

He turned and the muted light caught the planes of his face, making him look stark. Dangerous. Desirable.

"You're looking for simplicity?" he asked, voice low.

"Aren't you?"

He watched her mouth as he spoke. "I guess I am."

"And things between us would never be simple."

"Maybe not," he drawled, "but they'd be good."

A shiver of gooseflesh raced across her skin. Instinctively she knew it was the truth. That making love with Matthew Kincaid would be an exquisite experience. It had been in his kiss. It was in his heated gaze. It was in his slow, deliberate step closer.

"We agreed we wouldn't act on this," she said, her voice wavering.

He stopped mere inches from her, his Adam's apple bobbing slowly down then up. "We were stupid."

"We were thinking of Flynn," she said, trying to sound sure. "That he needs to know exactly where everyone fits in his life. No place for confusion."

He ran a finger down the side of her face. "He's not here. He's with Lily, probably playing games the nurses wouldn't approve of, if I know my sister."

The temptation was so strong, it was a physical force, drawing her ever closer into the magical aura that surrounded him. His lips—so close—beckoned. Their kiss had been playing on an unending replay loop for five days, driving her to distraction, reminding her of the delicious pressure of his mouth, the smooth eroticism of his tongue meeting hers. If she simply leaned forward, she could taste the pleasure again.

But the other image that had been replaying in her mind was Flynn's solemn, hopeful eyes when he'd asked if she was his new mommy. Each time she remembered, it broke her heart anew.

"If I come with you to your bed right now—" his eyes flared and she steeled herself against the allure "—we'd change in our interactions with each other afterward. Flynn doesn't *have* to be here now...he'll see us together later. He'll know something's changed."

His eyes drifted closed and squeezed tight, as if against a blow, before slowly opening again. "And he's already watching you too closely for comfort."

"I'm the last woman you can afford to get involved with."

There was silence for a heartbeat, two. Then he closed his eyes again and took a step back. "It's a shame you think ahead."

"A curse of working in public relations."

"Since we can only do things that are above reproach, would you like to help me choose a bottle of wine for dinner?"

She glanced around. "I don't know anything about wine."

"I'll teach you," he said, his voice too deep and smooth for a conversation about beverages. With a hand lightly resting on her waist, he guided her to another row. "You were in the champagne section. This is the first of the reds." He picked out a bottle and handed it to her. "That's a 1929 Burgundy."

Suddenly realizing the bottle must be worth a small fortune, she handed it back. "Are they all old bottles?"

"I'm more interested in drinking the wine than keeping it, but I do have a few, like this one, that are worth holding on to." He replaced it and they moved down the row before he pulled out another bottle. "This is a 2004 Pinot Noir. One of my favorites, so I pick up a few bottles wherever I see them." He shrugged one shoulder as if they were talking about collecting items no more expensive than her tea mug. "What do you usually drink?"

"If I'm at a restaurant, I follow the waiter's suggestions of what wine will go with the meal."

"We can do that. Tell me what was that heavenly scent that hit me when I walked in the door?"

"Crème brûlée for tonight." Her favorite—rich, creamy and decadent.

"Then I suggest—" he guided her several rows away with that heated palm at her lower back "—we open a dessert wine after the main meal." He scanned the rows before gently pulling out a dark, dusty bottle. "Perhaps this one."

As she took the bottle, she looked blindly at the label, but instead of reading, her full attention was on the aftershave that wrapped around her like a cloak, and under that, the scent of Matthew himself, robbing her of logical thought. He took the bottle from her hands and she focused on the action like a beacon, bringing her back to reality.

She moistened her lips. "Do you normally have wine with your dessert?"

"I don't usually have dessert," he said beside her ear, "but it's fast becoming my favorite time of day."

Before she could process the words, he turned and strode to a shelf along the wall that held an assortment of items and retrieved a bottle opener. She watched his strong hands work quickly and smoothly as he screwed the gadget into the cork, then eased the cork out. The man's hands were a work of art. How would they feel on her body...? The air around her thickened, becoming harder to draw into her lungs.

He replaced the bottle opener on the shelf and picked up a tasting glass. She watched, mesmerized, as he poured a small amount into the glass, swirled it a few times, then passed it to her.

"Taste," he softly commanded.

She took the glass and raised it to her lips. "It's sweet."

"Very," he agreed, his gaze on her mouth.

She tipped the glass and the wine flowed over her tongue, rich and sweet, with a depth of flavor. A small purr of approval escaped her throat.

"Now imagine you've had a spoonful of the crème brûlée first, and then sipped this."

She closed her eyes and focused on the flavors and how they would combine and the effect was positively sinful. Then other decadent images flooded into her mind—Matthew's powerfully built body stretched out before her on his bed; the feel of him pressed against her in passion; the sound he'd make when he found release....

As her eyes flicked open, she found him watching her, unblinking, his pupils large in his brilliant green eyes. More than anything, she wanted to lean into his strength, to take him up on the promise his eyes held. But there had been a reason not to do that—for the life of her, she couldn't think of it right now, but she was sure there had been one earlier.

"I—I—" She paused to gain control over the stammer that had suddenly appeared in her voice. "I'd better check on the dessert in the oven—it'd be a shame to ruin it now we have a wine to match it."

"Yes," he agreed, his voice like gravel. "You should check on that."

She turned and flew up the stairs to the safety of the kitchen, hoping like all hell that Matthew didn't follow her until her equilibrium had time to reestablish itself. And until she remembered that reason she couldn't crawl into his bed.

Matthew had suffered through the sumptuous dinner, trying to keep his growing fascination for Susannah under control. Yet he hadn't been able to avoid noticing every time her fork passed between her lips, every movement her creamy throat made as she swallowed. And as she'd walked across the kitchen to serve the dessert, the gentle sway of her hips had his skin tightening. Every night he came home to this torture and it was getting worse each time.

"I'll pour the wine." Desperate to find something for his hands to do, he pushed to his feet and grabbed the bottle of dessert wine he'd brought up from the wine cellar earlier.

The change was no improvement to his circumstances. He had to retrieve glasses, which were in a cupboard beside her. As he opened the door and curled his hands around two glasses, a sweet fragrance enveloped him and he stilled to breathe it more fully. Floral, perhaps jasmine. Maybe gardenia.

With a start, he realized he was standing beside her with his hand in an open cupboard and she was looking at him curiously. Her lips were slightly parted and he remembered tasting them as if it had been mere moments ago.

"I was going to serve the crème brûlée with whipped cream on the side," she said, her voice uncertain, as if filling the silence.

"Sounds good."

Roughly grabbing the bottle, he stalked across the room, and poured the wine. He had to stop obsessing about Susannah Parrish. Surely her effect on him was merely proximity? Being in his house, sleeping down the hall, making herself at home in his kitchen. Beside his family and his personal assistant, he hadn't spent this much time with any woman since Grace's death.

Whatever it was, it was purely physical. He would never develop any stronger feelings for a woman again. Wasn't sure he was even capable of it. But desire? Oh, yeah. He was sure capable of that right now. And then some.

She reached in front of him to lay his plate on the table, and he tracked the progress of her arm—the skin was smooth and pale, and he was certain it would feel soft. Luxuriant. Then, at the last moment, as she released the plate, he saw her hand tremble. He raked his gaze over her, noticing every detail and realized she held a tension in her body that matched his own. A flush spread from her neck down till it disappeared under her blouse.

He held back a curse. This would be so much easier to ignore if it was an unrequited desire.

She sank into her seat and gave him a tentative smile, and all he could do was offer a tight nod in return before sampling her brûlée.

The first taste slid over his tongue with wicked richness and he almost groaned. It was sex on a spoon. He glanced up at Susannah—did it have the same effect on her?—but her eyes were studiously focused on her plate as she ate.

Perversely wanting her to react, wanting to see if she was in the same hell he'd been condemned to, he lifted his glass. "Try the wine. It'll bring out the flavors."

She glanced up, her tongue darting out to lick a speck of sticky golden dessert from her bottom lip and the blood drained from his head. She lifted the glass and sipped, then took another spoonful into her mouth, and it was as if a cloud of bliss enveloped her. Her pupils dilated and her skin glowed.

He wanted that. Wanted to see her entire body reaching for nirvana.

With him deep inside her.

He held back the harshest oath he could think of and shoved the plate away. "You have a talent."

With skepticism clear in her gaze, she looked from the plate to his eyes. "Yet you didn't finish it."

"I'll have it later. I need to go for a run." If he pushed his body to the point of exhaustion, maybe he'd get some relief from the relentless need for her. There were shoes and running clothes in the car, he'd grab them on the way out. He stood and took his plate to the sink, heart thundering, then gripped the edges of the counter, summoning the strength to walk out the door.

"You've just eaten a full meal and you want to go for a run?" The soft voice came from behind him.

Unable to look at her, he focused on the shadowy trees out the window above the sink. "If I don't do something drastic and soon, I'll carry you to my bed."

He heard her gasp and turned to face her, not bothering to hide the hunger that filled his body. "Remind me again why it's such a bad idea? Tell me why we're fighting something we both want. Because unless you can give me a solid reason in the next seven seconds, I'm taking you upstairs."

Susannah shivered. He was serious. And she didn't want to stop him. She wanted all the raw passion that exuded from every square inch of him. But they'd had reasons for not taking this extra step, reasons that had made good sense earlier.

"Because…" She paused and cleared her throat. "Because I'm only here temporarily. And things are complicated enough between us, and Flynn, already that we don't want to confuse them any more." He prowled forward and she stepped back, stopping when she hit the counter.

"I'll be leaving soon…" she finished uncertainly. It had sounded much more convincing the last time she'd said it—now it seemed flimsy.

"New plan." He leaned fists on the counter on either side of her, holding her in place. "You come to my bed now."

She opened her mouth to protest, but he laid a finger across her lips. "We go into this with no illusions, and no one will be hurt. We'll keep it separate from Flynn and he'll never know. You're leaving soon, so this will be short-term. We're both adults, we can deal with that. What we can't deal with is fighting this attraction," he said fiercely. "It's too damn strong. At least, it is for me."

"Doubly so for me," she said through a dry throat. Yet, a rebel part of her mind protested…she'd never slept with someone knowing it would go no further—purely for the physical pleasure. Could she do it? Indulge her desire for him and not let her heart get involved?

If the choice was between never experiencing Matthew's lovemaking or trying something new in having a short-term physical relationship, then the decision wasn't difficult at all.

"All right." She met his gaze. "Let's go with your new plan."

A shudder racked his large frame. "For days, I've barely been able to look at you without imagining touching your skin. I've wanted to kiss you right here—" his lips touched the place where the column of her throat met her shoulder "—so badly it's been keeping me awake at night."

The heat of his tongue on the vulnerable skin was intoxicating, drawing her under his dark spell. She brought her hands up to his shoulders so she didn't fall…and for the simple pleasure of touching him.

"What's been keeping you awake at night?" he murmured against her skin.

An image flashed into her mind—the bare skin she'd glimpsed on his neck when his top buttons had been undone that first morning. With fumbling fingers, she undid his shirt buttons to halfway down his torso and splayed her fingers on the warm skin she uncovered.

"This," she whispered, running her fingertips over the crisp hairs that were scattered across his chest, the heat inside her building.

He drew a sharp breath between his teeth. "Just that?"

"Starting with that."

In one smooth motion, he grabbed the back of his shirt, pulled it over his head and discarded it. The expanse of muscled chest that stood before her sent sharp anticipation zinging through her veins. His arms slid around her waist, and she leaned forward and pressed her lips to the skin just above a flat brown nipple.

"Susannah," he rasped then pulled her face up to kiss her hungrily. It was as darkly decadent as their first kiss, but this time it was so much more. There was no need to hold back; she could give free rein to all the passion she'd been holding in check, all the primal need that reared up inside her.

Although this kiss wasn't merely about giving—it was about taking what she wanted. And she wanted Matthew.

He wrenched his mouth away and began making a damp trail down past her chin. His cheek, covered in evening stubble, created a delicious abrasiveness as it brushed along her throat. She was caught in a whorl of desire—fire licking her veins, sensual fog filling her mind. Had she ever needed anyone, anything this desperately, this deeply?

Her fingers found the smooth planes of his back; felt the flex and release of his muscles as he moved. When his teeth gently sampled the skin of her collarbone, she dug her nails into the flesh near his spine.

"Tell me you want this as much as I do," he said, his tone half entreaty, half demand.

She put her hand over his heart and found the beat—it thundered like hers. Then she took his hand and placed it over her heart. "Both hearts racing. I want you, Matthew."

He replaced his hand with the velvet brush of his lips, then his teeth as he softly bit the flesh on the slope of her breast through the fabric, before his fingers tugged impatiently at the buttons on her top. Once he'd parted the sides of her blouse, his hot gaze lingered on her breasts, his fingers tracing over the white lace of her bra. Pressure coiled out from her belly to every square inch of her body. She moaned softly, and he squeezed his eyes shut.

"Too much," he said, his jaw tight. "It's too much."

With gentle roughness, he swept her up, onto the large wooden kitchen table, bunching her skirt to her hips, and she wrapped her legs around his waist. He swore when she pressed herself against the bulge in his trousers, but he didn't move away. His darkened gaze locked on hers with unwavering intensity and time stood still as, disconcertingly, her heart unfurled a fraction. She struggled against any scrap of emotional connection—this was purely physical. They'd agreed. Then he pressed himself closer and the moment was thankfully lost to the sensual thrall he so easily incited.

Needing to feel him properly, she reached for the button on his trousers and released it before pushing the zipper down and letting them drop to the floor. He hooked his thumbs in the waistband of his boxers and pushed them down the same path and finally she could hold his silken heat in her hands. He groaned and she allowed her fingers to explore the rigidness, to play, to tease.

A hand clamped around her wrist. "I'm too close—if you keep doing that, I'll embarrass myself."

He was close? His breathing was ragged, his pupils dilated. Yes, she'd known he wanted her, but seeing the extent of his desire gave her a jolt of feminine power.

His arms were around her, releasing her bra. She shrugged out of it and tossed it over a chair. He filled his palms with her breasts and she pushed closer, wanting even more contact. She wanted everything he had to give. He leaned down and took the peak of one breast in his mouth and she moaned his name.

As he transferred the attention to the other breast, his hands worked her panties down her legs and thrust them aside before coming back for her skirt. Not waiting for him to find the zipper at her side, she loosened it and lifted her hips so he could pull it out from under her.

Once it was gone, he smoothed a hand over the delta of her thighs then parted her with his fingers. Hypersensitive from wanting him for days on end, the touch jolted her and she bucked against him. He slid his fingers against her, and she became boneless from the intensity, from the pleasure.

But he didn't linger—he was back kissing her again, his arms holding her firmly against his body, and this time when she wrapped her legs around his waist, there were no barriers between them.

"Don't move," he rasped then pulled away and disappeared for endless moments. Her skin began to cool and she hoped to heaven that he'd gone for protection—any other reason would be too devastating to consider. When he reappeared seconds later, he was sheathed and ready, and she went a little dizzy with longing. She reached for him, found his arm and dragged him closer, but he needed no encouragement. His head came down and kissed her with breathless urgency, while his hands slid under her hips, tilting her toward him.

He broke the kiss, and between ragged breaths, said, "I can't wait."

"Then don't," she said. She'd already been waiting too long for him—it might only have been days in real time, but it had felt like an eternity.

He slid inside her and all the breath left her body. He was everywhere—filling her vision, filling her body, filling her mind... Finding and matching his gliding rhythm, she clung to him, climbing higher.

One of his hands left her hips and snaked behind her shoulders to bring her up to meet his mouth. Her insides wound tighter, too tight, but she couldn't slow the momentum while Matthew's relentless, exquisite pace reigned.

Impossibly soon, she was on the edge, wanting to wait, to

linger, to relish every second, while also wanting to soar higher, but he took the decision away with his uncompromising pace and she burst free, floating above the world, boundless. Even as she soared, she felt him follow and reach his own summit with a guttural cry.

All she could do for a long time was cling to him, stunned by the intensity of their lovemaking. Still held against his panting body, she wondered if his thoughts were the same, before he eased her back down onto the table.

"I'm sorry, Susannah," he said, his voice laced with self-recrimination.

She blinked, bringing his face and his words into focus. "Sorry for what?" Thinking back, she couldn't remember him hurting her or anything else to apologize for—just an explosive experience she didn't think would ever be matched.

He eased back and turned to rest a hip on the table beside her. "I wanted to make it perfect for you, but I just couldn't slow down."

She chuckled at the ridiculousness of saying sorry about something so glorious. "Didn't it look like I had a good time?"

"I have to admit, toward the end there, I barely noticed." He winced and she realized how serious he was. "I don't remember ever losing control like that before."

She took his lightly stubbled cheeks between her hands. "Let me assure you, Matthew, it was good for me. Excellent, in fact. No—" she grinned "—incredibly excellent." Despite the frantic rush—or perhaps because of it?—it had easily been the best of her life.

His shoulders relaxed and a slow-burn smile spread across his face. "Even so, I'd like to make it up to you."

Blissful contentment still permeated every cell of her body, and she raised a playful eyebrow. "You thinking of flowers?"

Without warning, he was on his feet, had hoisted her into the air and was cradling her close. "Nope."

"Sappy greeting card?" she asked, casually ignoring the sudden change of being held high in his arms.

As they made their way to the staircase, he snatched a kiss. "Not even close."

"So, tell me, Matthew—" she ran a fingernail across his chest "—how do you plan to make it up to me?"

"I'm going to do it again." He pressed a kiss to her cheek. "Slower." A lingering kiss on her lips. "Better."

Her skin quivered. "I'm not sure I can handle 'better,'" she said, and meant it. Anything more might make her lose consciousness altogether.

He arched an eyebrow and lifted her higher in his arms. "We're about to find out."

At the top of the stairs, her happy mood evaporated as he turned left instead of right—they were going to his room. He'd mentioned his room—his bed—earlier, but she hadn't put the pieces together until this moment.

His room in the marital house…the room he'd shared with Grace.

Nausea swelled up from her stomach. She scrambled out of his arms and planted her feet on the floor. "Matthew, I'm sorry, but I can't."

He frowned and glanced downstairs, toward the kitchen. "It's a bit late for qualms about making love with me—that horse has well and truly bolted."

The door down the hall taunted her, and she laid a hand over her belly to quell the sick feeling. "I can't go in there." Surely he could understand?

Still frowning, his gaze swung from her to the door down the hall and back again. "I don't see—" Then his eyes widened as understanding dawned. "Susannah, this wasn't Grace's room." He took her hand and led her to the first door, then opened it. It was decorated in deep blues, with a blue-gray quilt. A very masculine room—it reminded her more of the wine cellar than anything else in the house.

"I moved in here after she died. Her room is the next one down the hall—I've left it as it was for Flynn. He likes to go in and hold her things."

Cautiously she took a step farther into the room. An enlarged photo of waves crashing into rocks dominated one wall, cupboards and drawers made from cherry wood on the opposing wall. Dominating the room was a large cherrywood bed. The tension in her belly dissolved. This was Matthew's room, no doubt about it. And she liked it—it was a room to feel comfortable in, a room that felt like him.

He came to stand behind her and threaded his fingers through hers. She felt his naked body press against her back. "You're the first woman I've brought in here."

It had been a year since his wife had died. Before she could censor herself, she asked, "Not even—"

"No one," he said with finality as he nuzzled the sensitive spot behind her ear.

Despite knowing that shouldn't mean anything to her—there was nothing more than the physical between them—it did. She turned in his arms. "I shouldn't admit it—" to herself *or* to him "—but I like that."

"Glad to oblige." His hands slid from her waist up her rib cage. "Now, back to the conversation we were having earlier."

As her breath hitched, she wrapped her arms around his neck, allowing his hands free rein. "Which conversation was that?"

His fingers continued their languid journey, down her sides, over the curve of her hips, in crazy patterns across her back. "I have some making up to do."

"Ah, yes. And not with flowers or a greeting card." She leaned closer and took his earlobe into her mouth, satisfied when he drew in a sharp breath. Then she leaned back, and found his green gaze again darkened with desire. "So, how do you plan to do it?"

"I thought I'd start by—" he picked her up and laid her out on the bed "—and then perhaps add a bit of—" Holding her ankle, he bent one of her legs up and kissed the inside of her knee.

Everything inside her wound tight, and his tongue lazily traced upward, along the sensitive flesh of her inner thigh. When he reached the center of her, raw electricity burst through her body.

"You know," she said, breathing hard, "I'm not sure slower will actually be better this time."

He glanced up and grinned. "It's a shame you think that way. I plan to make this last all night."

She melted into the pillows behind her and gave herself up to the sinfully delicious prospect.

Six

Susannah stretched contentedly in Matthew's bed, feeling the heavenly slide of his naked skin against hers. Over the past four days, they'd fallen into a habit of taking the dessert she'd made to his room. Tonight it was a triple-chocolate mousse and, after an hour of eating it both from the glass and Matthew's body, Susannah lay sated.

"There's something I need to ask," he said, his voice rumbling in his chest under her ear. He moved one arm behind his head and, with the other around her waist, he pulled her closer against his side.

"Whatever it is, you've chosen a good time." She smiled, feeling much like a cat in the sun.

"I spoke to Flynn's doctor today, and he said Flynn's blood work had maintained the improvement. He can come home tomorrow."

Suddenly her whole body, the room, the world, felt lighter. She pulled back a few inches to see his face. "And you're only just mentioning this now? That's fabulous news!"

A smile tugged his mouth. "He's doing great, and as long as I take him for regular checkups, they're optimistic that he'll recover one hundred percent."

Then another implication of Flynn's improvement sank in and her stomach hollowed. She wouldn't be needed as a standby bone-marrow donor. Her reason for being in Charleston, in Matthew's house, no longer existed. She'd always known this was temporary, and Matthew had said they'd be going into their physical relationship with no illusions, but still, a crazy kind of panic bubbled up into her chest.

Despite being unable to meet his eyes, she was determined to handle the situation with poise and found an accepting smile. "I'll leave for Georgia in the morning, before he gets home."

"That brings me to my question." He lifted her chin with a knuckle and waited until she looked up into his endless green eyes. "I want someone stay with us for a week—just an extra pair of eyes to keep watch on him while he's in the early stages of recovery. I told him it would be my mother, but he asked if it could be you."

Stay? She blinked slowly, absorbing the concept. Spend more time with Matthew and his son? They hadn't wanted to make love in the first place because Flynn would sense something was different and get his hopes up. If she stayed longer, wouldn't that compound the sin?

Yet a rebel part of her heart—a maternal corner she'd tried to keep silent—wanted desperately to stay a little longer and get to know Flynn. And then there were the extra nights it would allow in Matthew's bed…

"You think this is a good idea?" she asked tentatively.

He released her chin and shoved a hand through his dark hair. "One of the nurses mentioned that Flynn might find it something of an anticlimax when he gets home, because he's had so many visitors and staff fussing over him. Home will seem quiet and uneventful in comparison. I have to admit, having someone like you, someone he likes and who would be a novelty would probably help keep his spirits up while he makes the transition. And the hospital tells me that keeping his spirits up is important to his recovery." There was vulnerability in his eyes, a need to provide this for his child when he'd been blocked from providing so much recently.

Matthew stroked a finger along her spine. "Will the extra leave be a problem?"

They were at the end of the second week of her leave already—she'd extended it with the option of another extension. Her boss had been understanding about the circumstances. In the three years she'd been at the bank, she'd rarely taken leave, so there would be enough to cover this, and her assistant could continue leading the team for another week. And they'd given Matthew's family a cover story for her stay that would work for another week—that he'd offered Grace's old friend a place to stay while Susannah applied for jobs in Charleston. He'd told them she wanted to move back from Georgia and Grace would have expected him to help. His family had seemed to accept the story.

But they weren't the major issues. She laid her head back on his chest. "What about Flynn becoming attached to me?"

"We make sure all the signals project that you're just a visitor, and we emphasize that you'll be going home in a week, so his expectations are managed."

Could it work? Could she spend extra time with that precious little boy without setting him up for hurt? Her mind raced with the possibilities.

"Do you really think we can do that?"

He pulled her closer, flush along his side. "I'm sure we can. Say yes."

"Yes." Without thought, the word slipped from her mouth but as soon as it was said, her heart lifted.

"Thank you." His eyes darkened. "And that's seven more nights of you in my bed—though we'll have to pretend you're sleeping in your room." One corner of his mouth kicked up. "Or we could do it the other way around. I might like the chance to sneak into your bedroom late at night."

The tantalizing thought sent a shiver flashing across her skin, and brought out her brazen side. "What would you be wearing?"

"A robe. In case I was caught," he drawled and arched a lazy eyebrow.

"Sensible." She traced a fingernail over his pectoral muscles and smiled when he shuddered. "And under that?"

"You'd find me as naked as I am now." His hand slid under the sheet, then feather-soft over her abdomen.

Her pulse quickened. "I'm rather partial to you being naked."

"Glad to hear it." His fingers walked a slow, sensual path up her ribs, toward her shoulders. "Because there's something I'd like to do when I reach your room and it works much better without my clothes."

"Would I be dressed?" she asked, allowing the sheet to be tugged away when his fingers reached it.

"No, you'd definitely be *un*—" he placed a kiss in the valley between her breasts "—dressed."

She reached down, found him ready and one by one wrapped her fingers around him. "As it turns out, we're both naked now."

He drew in a sharp breath and the muscles in his neck tightened. "I believe you're right."

"Why don't you give me a preview?" She wriggled, aligning their bodies the way she wanted them, and twined her arms behind his neck.

He positioned himself between her thighs then leaned down on forearms either side of her head to whisper in her ear. "Now?"

"Yeah, now," she said, wrapping her legs around his waist, urging him on.

"It would be something along these lines…"

Ignoring the doubts at the back of her mind, she let herself become lost in this man while she still had him.

* * *

As Matt held Susannah's door open in the hospital parking lot, he couldn't draw his eyes away from the long shapely leg that emerged. It peeped out from beneath the hem of her long skirt, heating his blood and scrambling his mind. The moment she was standing free, he curled one hand behind her back and one around her neck, then leaned her against the car.

A smile curved her mouth. "I hadn't realized parking lots had this effect on you."

"You have this effect on me," he growled a second before lowering his head and seeking her mouth. She parted her lips without hesitation and he sank into her sweet depths and the sheer oblivion kissing Susannah granted. Her hands crept up to lock behind him, pulling him impossibly closer.

"Any reason for that?" she asked breathlessly when he wrenched away. "Not that I'm complaining, mind you."

He smoothed the hair back from her face, memorizing everything about her expression in this moment—eyes dark and sleepy, lips rosy and damp, cheeks flushed. He had one more week of Susannah in his bed, and he planned to make the most of it. But for now, things would be more circumspect during daylight hours.

"Once we walk in those doors," he said, placing a final, chaste kiss on her Cupid's bow lips, "we'll be on our best behavior. No clues for Flynn to pick up."

"So this was like a last fling." Her hands released their grip behind his back and, with a light touch across his skin, found their way back to her sides.

"Until he goes to bed."

"I'm looking forward to it already," she whispered, her gaze focused on his mouth.

For a long moment he considered giving in to his body's demand for another kiss, but if he did, they might not leave this parking lot for hours. And he was anxious to get Flynn. He'd missed the little guy more than he could ever have predicted before he'd become a father.

He drew in a steadying breath and moved away from the temptation of Susannah. "Let's go."

They walked side by side, but his hands itched to touch her. To twine their fingers together, or to place a palm at the small of her back. He resisted—they couldn't send mixed signals to Flynn and let him think he might be getting a new mommy. The poor kid had enough to deal with right now without the inevitable letdown if that happened then realizing Susannah really was leaving. When Flynn was around, Susannah was a friend of the family, no more. He had to keep his hands to himself.

As they walked past the nurses' station, one of the nurses waved him over. "Good morning, Mr. and Mrs. Kincaid."

Beside him, Susannah stiffened, and he winced, well aware that they probably looked like a family unit. If anything, they'd look more like a family than when he and Grace had been with Flynn, considering the dimpled chin his boy shared with Susannah. Guilt reared up from the pit of his stomach and swamped him.

No matter how much he, Susannah and Flynn might *look* like a family, they weren't. Grace was the one who belonged here. He'd stolen this from her, and he had no right to bring another woman into the equation. It was unfair to Susannah, and a betrayal to Grace's memory.

"Just Mr. Kincaid," he said with a smile to soften the correction. "This is Ms. Parrish."

"Oh, I'm sorry, Mr. Kincaid, Ms. Parrish. I just wanted to tell you how thrilled we all are that Flynn's going home. He's become quite a favorite here."

"Thank you. I'm looking forward to getting him home." In fact, now he was inside the hospital, he was more than restless to get to his son, and his fingers began tapping away on his thigh.

The nurse glanced down at the chart on her desk. "You've spoken to the doctor already?"

"On the phone last night." The doctor had said he wouldn't be available this morning, but had passed on instructions for once Flynn was at home, and said he'd see them at their follow-up appointment.

"Excellent," the nurse said. "I've started his discharge paperwork. If you just drop in on your way out and sign the forms, we should be right to go."

They walked to the anteroom, not needing to stop and gown up this time. Since he was going home, Flynn was ready to interact with people who hadn't been through the decontamination procedures. The doctor had recommended limiting his contact to just family members for a while longer, and to tell anyone who was sick to stay away. None of which would be a problem—Matt would have moved mountains to make the environment safe for his son.

Flynn scampered to the end of his bed and threw his arms out as they entered his room, his cheeks pink with a healthy flush. "Daddeee!"

Matt picked him up, and held him tight. "Hey, kiddo."

Flynn returned the hug for about three seconds before he pulled away to announce, "Daddy, I can go home today."

"I'm counting on it," Matt said, grinning.

Then Flynn reached for Susannah. "Sudi! I can go home today."

She put her arms out and Matt passed his son to her, and watched them talk, heads together. Susannah's face had a beautiful softness, her affection for Flynn shining clearly.

Another wave of guilt engulfed him, making it difficult to breathe. This was Grace's role—she should be here, bringing her son home. She'd loved Flynn with everything inside her, occasionally to the exclusion of all else. And Flynn had loved her back with the same devotion. It was Matt's fault they'd been torn away from each other—in pressuring her to take a doomed flight he may as well have killed her with his own hands. He cursed himself to hell and back, as he'd often done since that awful day twelve months ago.

The door to the anteroom opened behind him and he turned to see Alan Sinclair's dark blond head pop around the door frame.

"Do you mind if I come in?" he asked, with an easygoing smile.

Momentarily surprised, Matthew hesitated before remembering a call his personal assistant had taken a few days ago from Sinclair. Matthew had given permission for Sinclair to visit, though he couldn't see why he'd want to. Nonetheless, he appreciated being asked. Basic respect. Jack Sinclair had simply assumed he'd be given access to Flynn, but Alan's courtesy confirmed the opinion Matt had been developing—Alan was twice the man Jack was.

He covered the ground to the entrance and offered his hand to Alan. "You just caught us. We're taking him home today."

"Glad I didn't come this afternoon." Alan glanced over at Flynn who was watching the exchange from Susannah's arms. "Who would I have given this teddy to if you'd already gone home?"

Flynn's face lit up when he saw the chocolate-brown bear with large blue eyes. Susannah had moved closer so Flynn was within reaching distance but still kept a protectively firm hold on him.

Having backup was as novel as it was nice, but Matt knew he couldn't allow himself to rely on it, so he reached for Flynn and held him on his hip.

"This is your—" grandfather's mistress's son "—Uncle Alan."

"Hello, Flynn," Alan said warmly, handing over the bear. "Do you like bears?"

"Yes." With wide eyes, Flynn surveyed the bear from all angles, obviously pleased with what he found by the grin that stretched his face. Matt put him down on the bed so Flynn could play with his new toy.

"And this is Susannah, a friend of ours." Matt turned to Susannah. "This is Alan Sinclair. You met his brother, Jack, a few days ago."

Alan offered his hand to Susannah. "Pleased to meet you, Susannah."

Matt watched Alan as Susannah took his hand. Did he notice the similarities between her and Flynn, putting two and two together the way the nurse had? Did others in his family suspect the truth about Flynn's parentage? He sighed and retrieved Flynn's empty bag from the cupboard. Maybe no one noticed how much Flynn resembled Susannah and he was getting paranoid.

Through the glass, a nurse held up some papers and Matt nodded. She'd obviously finished the discharge forms.

He turned back to Alan. "I hate to rush you, but we're just on our way home."

"Not a problem," Alan said with an easy smile. "I just wanted to drop this off. Nice to meet you, Flynn." He turned to Susannah. "And you, too, Susannah."

After Alan left, they packed Flynn's bags to the soundtrack of Flynn detailing which of his toys would be played with on his return to his own bedroom. Susannah glanced up and their eyes met in a moment of shared humor and optimism. It was balm to his soul to hear his son's enthusiasm—such a turnaround from the lethargic boy he'd brought into hospital not too long ago.

They were ready in minutes, and Matt carried Flynn's bags while Susannah pushed Flynn in a child's wheelchair the nurses provided, stopping to sign the forms on the way out. They left the wheelchair at the front door and Susannah lifted his son into her arms.

Seeing the nurse again brought her mistake about them being a couple to mind. Yet, watching Susannah and Flynn chatting away on the short walk to the car, he couldn't help observing how *right* the three of them looked together. How easily Susannah had slipped into their lives. Into Flynn's heart. Into Matthew's own bed.

Maybe this was all falling into place so easily because it was meant to be?

Could it be that easy—or was he fooling himself with a convenient half-truth?

They reached his car and, after stowing the bags in the trunk, Matthew took his son and strapped him into his seat before depositing a kiss on the top of his head. Then he turned to the woman who was causing his confusion.

"Thanks for coming," he said. As they passed behind the car where Flynn couldn't see, he slipped his hand around hers for an illicit two-second touch. "Flynn liked having you here."

"I was glad to do it," she said, but he saw the same confusion, the same doubts that were pursuing him, reflected in her eyes.

He opened her door and after she was in, he closed it and made his way around to the driver's side. As he slid into his seat, he turned to survey his passengers. "Ready to go?" he asked them.

"Yes," Flynn replied, beaming.

He met Susannah's eyes in a moment of pure understanding—the elation of bringing Flynn home, healthy and happy. The second time this morning she'd given him the simple pleasure of sharing a parenting moment. He'd missed that beyond measure. Yet it was shadowed by the knowledge that they were playing with explosives, perhaps letting themselves be lured in too deep.

He turned the key, ready to drive this imitation family home.

Seven

Two hours later, Susannah was sitting with Matthew and Flynn around a garden setting in the glass conservatory eating banana and chocolate-chip muffins. Before sunrise, she'd been up baking an assortment of food she hoped might tempt a three-year-old. So far, given Flynn's enthusiastic reaction to the brunch picnic, it seemed she'd succeeded. Matthew had eaten more than she'd expected, and the fact that father and son were happily devouring her food made a contended joy rise higher than it should.

The phone rang, and Matthew reached for the cordless he'd brought with him and handed it to Flynn. "That will be Grandma."

Flynn's face beamed and he eagerly took the handset. "Grandma?" he asked into the receiver. The reply must have been affirmative, because then he was off, a stream of chatting, telling all his news about his hospital stay.

Matthew leaned over, his warm breath brushing the shell of

her ear as he spoke. "Grace's parents. They ring every Sunday at ten o'clock."

Even with her body's predictable response to his nearness, something she couldn't define twisted painfully in her belly. "That's great they take an interest in him."

"They adore him," he said, watching his son. "Grace was an only child, so now she's gone, Flynn is the only grandchild they'll ever have. They come and stay often, and never miss a Sunday call."

He didn't have to say the rest. It hung in the air between them—Grace's parents were another reason he could never disclose that Susannah was Flynn's biological mother. If he was the only grandchild they would ever have, then how could he tell them they had no genetic connection to the little boy? Rob them of their remaining link to the daughter they'd tragically lost? And she wouldn't want him to—it would be too cruel.

"Daddy," Flynn said, his face serious, obviously with an important mission.

Matthew turned to him, a gentle smile on his face. "Yes?"

"Grandma wants to talk wif you." He passed the phone to his father then turned to Susannah. "Can I have ano'ver muffin, please?"

"Sure, sweetie," she said.

She handed him one, and while he ate, she watched Matthew talking to his mother-in-law, her heart unexpectedly sinking. They were obviously on familiar and friendly terms—laughing and chatting casually. The scene zoomed out in her mind, leaving her dizzy then came into clear focus.

This was Grace's family. Grace's parents on the phone, who'd rung Grace's little boy. They were in Grace's house, and she was sleeping with Grace's husband.

Her vision swam and she dug her nails into her palms.

This wasn't her life—she'd simply slotted into a Grace-shaped hole in Flynn and Matthew's life.

At least there was a time limit—in a week she'd be back in

her own life in Georgia and Grace's family would go back to functioning without her. The thought wasn't as comforting as she'd hoped.

The next morning at breakfast, Matt was on top of the world. His son was home and on the mend, and he'd spent half the night making sweet, glorious love to Susannah. Things were looking up.

"Does anyone want more pancakes?" Susannah asked, glancing over to where he and Flynn sat at the kitchen table.

"Me!" Flynn called gleefully.

Matt took their plates to the stove where Susannah was making another batch of her blueberry-and-oat pancakes, pausing to admire how good she looked in his kitchen. He couldn't be here with her and not think of making love to her, her sumptuous curves draped over the table, clinging to him as she found release. His body heated now, not nearly sated enough even after the night they'd shared.

Drawing her into his arms wasn't an option when Flynn was in the room, but he'd be sure to make up for it the moment they had some privacy. Make up for it and then some.

"Here you go." Susannah flipped two pancakes onto each plate. Her cheeks were faintly flushed from the heat of the stove and all he could think about was how they took on the same flush when he was inside her.

He cleared his throat and hauled himself back into the present. "Have I mentioned these are the best pancakes I've tasted?" He put Flynn's plate in front of him and poured some more maple syrup over the golden creations.

"You might have," she said, winking at Flynn, "but I don't mind hearing it again."

The doorbell went, and Matt threw her a grin before heading out to answer it. When he pulled the front door open, his mother stood there and, without bothering with a greeting, he pulled her into a bear hug. She'd been great while Flynn was in the hospital—no, since Grace had passed—so it was good she was here now for Flynn's first breakfast at home.

When he let her go, she smoothed down his hair. "How's Flynn this morning?"

"Better," he said, closing the door behind her. "And eating like a trouper."

"Your omelets?" she asked with a dubious expression.

"Hey, he likes my omelets." He frowned in mock annoyance. "But, no, Susannah's still here. She made pancakes."

Her eyes were instantly alert. "That friend of Grace's?"

"That's the one." Before she could ask more questions, he ushered her through to the kitchen.

"Nanna!" Flynn called when he saw her. "Sudi made pancakes wif oats in them!"

"Did she?" His mother looked curiously at Susannah and back to her grandson then him. "That sounds marvelous." She walked over and deposited a kiss on Flynn's sticky cheek.

"You've already met Susannah?" he asked, wary of what was going on in his mother's mind. Perhaps it had been too much to hope that his family wouldn't question the story he'd fed them about Susannah's presence. At the time, helping out an old friend of Grace's while she looked for work back in Charleston had seemed a good enough reason to explain her stay. He hadn't worried too much about their reaction, which, in retrospect, could have been a mistake.

"Yes," his mother answered. "We met in the hospital."

Susannah turned and smiled brightly. "It's lovely to see you again, Mrs. Kincaid. Have you eaten breakfast, or can I offer you a pancake?"

Her smile hit him squarely in the chest, so to cover he headed for the coffeemaker. "And I was just about to make coffee."

He reached around Susannah for the jar of coffee grounds then glanced up at his mother for her answer, and found her watching him with that curious expression on her face again.

She started, as if realizing she'd been staring then smiled. "I'd love a coffee. And if you have a few minutes, Matthew, there's something I'd like to discuss."

Susannah moved around him with synchronicity as she put the empty pan in the sink and he continued with the coffee. "Flynn and I'll be okay on our own if you want some privacy."

"Thank you, dear," his mother said with a strange touch of self-satisfaction. "That's very thoughtful."

He finished the coffee, left one mug for Susannah, then took the other two and followed his mother into the parlor. She had far too much swing in her step for his peace of mind. She was planning something. They sank into facing couches and he handed her a cappuccino.

"You and Susannah," she began.

He rolled his shoulders back, ready to nip whatever she was thinking in the bud. "Are just friends."

She took a slow sip of her drink, watching him over the brim. "Somehow I expected you'd say that, yet why don't I believe you?"

"She was a—"

"Friend of Grace's. I've heard the story," she said with a dismissive wave of her hand. "But there's something more between you."

He opened his mouth to deny it, then changed tack and decided to pump her for information instead of the other way around. Casually he leaned back and rested an arm along the back of his couch. "Why do you say that?"

"A mother knows," she said, her tone flippant.

He leveled a sardonic stare at her and held it. It was a ploy that usually worked on her and he wasn't disappointed this time, either.

She shrugged and tried to hide her grin. "How about we say that when you look at each other, the sparks that fly are strong enough to light the whole of Charleston." Her expression sobered into an expression of pure parental reprimand. "However,

I won't lie and say I'm happy that she's here under your roof. How about she comes to stay with me and—"

"Not going to happen," Matthew said, cutting that idea off before it was fully voiced. Susannah was staying right here with him for however many days she had left in Charleston. "Do you think anyone else has noticed?"

"I doubt it," she said soothingly and took another sip of her cappuccino. "You're my son, and I can't help but keep an eye on you."

Visions rose of his entire family knowing and taking every opportunity to tease him then rumors leaking back to Flynn. He needed to end this now. "She's leaving soon, so we'd rather this didn't become public knowledge."

"Don't let her go."

The words had been so simply, so starkly delivered that he did a double take. "Pardon?"

"There's been something different about you lately. You've been worried sick about Flynn, I've seen that, but there has also been a…glow from the inside. It's like you're waking up from a deep sleep."

Matt groaned. His mother was well on her way to creating an epic romance for him with Susannah. He rubbed a finger across his forehead. "Don't get your hopes up."

"Darling," she said, her tone suddenly more serious, "we have something awful in common. We've both lost a spouse to death." She paused and he recognized the confused flash of conflicting emotions that played across her face from when he'd felt the same. "It's not something I'd ever wish for one of my children, and I would have done anything to spare you the last twelve months."

He put his coffee down on a side table and leaned forward to capture her hands between his. "I know you would. And I love you for that."

"Then promise me one thing."

"Okay," he said warily.

"If you're in love with her, don't hide it." Her voice faltered, but she regrouped then her chin kicked up. "Just promise me you won't hide it."

There was more to what she was saying. He frowned, trying to read her expression. Perhaps she was thinking about his father's hidden affection for Angela Sinclair?

"I'm not in love with her, and that won't change." He'd given his heart away once and it was decimated when things fell apart with Grace. He'd never offer it again. Whatever was— temporarily—going on between him and Susannah, it did not, would not, involve his heart.

"If you say so." There was a resigned affection in her voice that he remembered her using when he was a boy and she hadn't believed him.

He released her hands and picked up his mug of coffee again. "What did you want to talk to me about?"

She reached into her handbag and withdrew two tickets. "You've been courting Arnold Larrimore from Larrimore Industries as new business for TKG, haven't you?"

"I have." Getting his business would go a long way to plugging the hole that was created when people jumped ship after the scandal about his father had hit the papers.

"I happen to know he'll be at the Barclays' fundraiser on Sunday." She waggled the tickets in her hand triumphantly. "I managed to get us invited."

His mother's social connections through her charity work had been of great value to Matt's role as Director of New Business for TKG. She procured introductions, tickets to events, dinner party invitations and general access to a social scene the family didn't normally mix in. And since Grace died, his mother had accompanied him to any of the events where he needed a plus one.

"Great scouting." He'd do most anything to be able to announce to the board that he'd snared Arnold Larrimore's account and put TKG back on more solid footing.

"There's only one problem," she said, handing him the tickets.

He took them, with a sinking sensation in his stomach—he had a feeling where this was going. "Which is?"

"I don't think I can make it." Her face fell—a picture of tragic disappointment. "I've turned my ankle, and couldn't possibly spend an entire night in heels."

He glanced down at her perfectly normal ankle and back up again. "It seemed fine when you walked in here."

"It's been a strange injury." Her eyelids fluttered in feigned distress. "It comes and goes. In fact, I can feel it starting to ache now."

He narrowed his eyes. His mother was a good liar, but this had to be the lamest story she'd ever concocted. Obviously she'd created it on the spot. "Perhaps you should stay here for the day with it elevated. I'll put ice on it now then wrap it later."

"I think I'd be better heading for home. Pamela will know what to do. But you really should go to the Barclays' fundraiser." She pretended to think. "I know, take Susannah! I can stay with Flynn—a little turned ankle will be fine here with him."

"Mother," he growled, "you're trying to set me up."

She stood, and picked up her handbag. "I have no idea what you're talking about. Must dash," she said, leaning to kiss his cheek.

She took three steps before she remembered to limp. Matt shook his head and showed her out.

Later that night, Susannah opened her bedroom door to a light knock, to find Matt lounging in the doorway, one arm behind his back and a sexy grin on his face. His closely cropped hair was damp. Seemed he'd showered then pulled on a polo shirt and loose trousers afterward. Her entire body tingled with anticipation. How would she ever leave this man when the time came?

"Evening," he said, then drew her against him with one arm, capturing her mouth with the ease of a predator assured of his prey. She fell into the kiss with no regard for anything but tasting his essence, of dissolving into him. His lips were so warm, exerting just the right pressure. She gripped the front of his shirt as her knees wobbled. Reality ceased to exist—she was in a blissful place outside time and space that she only found with Matthew.

After an eternity, he slowly drew back, chest heaving, pupils large in his luminescent green eyes. He held up a bottle of wine and two sparkling glasses. "Fancy a nightcap?"

Still gripping his shirt, she attempted to reorient herself to her surroundings. To breathing. She released him then opened the door wider to let him through. "Let's start with that."

He poured a glass each then sprawled on her bed. Propped on one elbow, he looked far too comfortable and desirable. She took a memory picture to keep with her after she left Charleston that could sustain her in what she suspected would be long, lonely nights without him.

"My mother guessed there's something between us," he said with a rueful smile.

Her hand flew to her mouth. She'd thought they'd been careful. "Oh, I'm sorry, Matthew."

"She won't tell anyone." He held out a hand and when she took it, he dragged her down to sit on the bed with him. "And she still thinks you're just one of Grace's friends."

Grace. Her stomach lurched. In this family, with this man, everything always came back to Grace. It always would, which—she straightened her back—was just how it should be. Her sensitivity to being sidelined shouldn't affect how Matthew and his family operated. She was temporary—soon, she'd be returning to the life waiting for her in Georgia, her mother, her friends and a senior position at the bank.

"She left two tickets for a fundraiser on Sunday," Matthew said, pulling one of her feet onto his lap. "I need to go for work—I'm targeting a new account. Do you want to come?"

The magic his fingers were producing on the soles of her feet momentarily distracted her, which was dangerous. If she wasn't on her guard, she might actually agree to go.

"Where is it?" she asked, stalling for time.

He reached for her other foot and began to give it the same attention as the first. "At the Barclays' mansion on one of the islands of the Outer Banks."

She wrapped one arm around herself and sipped her wine. When she'd been a teenager, her grandparents had often taken her to society parties and elite fundraising events, and she'd hated each and every one of them. The feeling of not quite belonging, of being an impostor wearing a pretty dress and pretending to be as cultured and sophisticated as the other guests. She wouldn't return to that world. It was soul-destroying.

She shrugged apologetically and shook her head. "I'm sorry, I haven't brought anything with me I could possibly wear to an event like that."

"Not a problem," he said without missing a beat. "I'll buy you something."

Her skin cooled. Pulling her feet from his lap, she turned to face him. "You can't buy me a dress, Matthew." It would be far too…bizarre. Inappropriate. If he bought her things while she was having a physical relationship with him, she'd start to feel like a kept woman. Matthew's father had kept a woman on the side, as had many of her grandfather's friends. People from that world—Matthew's world—thought differently about people and relationships.

"I need someone to go with me," Matthew said. "These things are always attended in couples. If you'll come, I'll cover your expenses."

Put like that, it sounded reasonable. Yet there was resistance to the idea deep in her chest. Having a temporary physical relationship with Matthew while staying in Charleston was one thing, but becoming entangled in his world of wealth and privilege…it scared her.

She tucked her legs beneath her and tried again. "I'm already living in your house, eating—"

"Susannah," he said, cutting her off, "you came to Charleston to do Flynn and me a favor. You've stayed on because we asked you to, again as a favor. And now *I'm asking if you'll help me out by attending a fundraising event as my guest.* You've done nothing but give since you got here. At the very least, let me buy you a dress to wear while you're doing one of those favors."

Oh, sweet Lord, he knew how to get what he wanted. *I'm asking if you'll help me out by attending a fundraising event as my guest.* How could she say no to such a small favor?

She let out a long breath. "It doesn't feel right." Attending the event or letting him buy the dress.

"But you'll do it." His confident, devastating smile spread across his face and she was lost.

"Okay," she said, and hoped she wouldn't regret this.

Eight

Matt stepped into the exclusive boutique, his hand at Susannah's waist ensuring she entered with him, even if it was reluctantly. Flynn was spending the day with his grandmother and Pamela so Matt could have a full day at TKG, and he'd slipped out to meet Susannah here during his lunch hour.

He was determined she would have something perfect, that she liked, and he had a feeling that if he left her alone, she'd prioritize economy over those factors. He'd never met a woman so determined not to be given anything.

His personal assistant was in her sixties and always wore the same severe outfits, so he'd gone to RJ's assistant this morning for advice on the best store to take Susannah. Brooke had been excellent, giving him choices and not once asking the obvious question of why he'd want the name of a women's clothing store—the precise reason he hadn't asked any of his sisters. He knew Brooke could be discreet.

The saleswoman glided over and gave them a welcoming smile. "How may I help?"

He moved Susannah infinitesimally forward with a hand at her back. "We'd like a cocktail gown. It's for an elite gathering, so quality is paramount."

He felt Susannah's invisible flinch at his not so subtle message about money being no object, but he was unrepentant. She deserved the best the store had to offer.

"Of course, sir," the saleswoman said. "If ma'am would follow me?"

As the other woman moved away, Susannah leaned over and whispered, "I still don't like this. I can buy my own dress."

"We've discussed this. I'll be happier if I buy it."

She shot him a resigned look before following the sales assistant deeper into the store.

In fact, there was something immensely satisfying in being able to give her this. Perhaps it was in his DNA—providing for his lover. Perhaps it was marking her as his own with expensive fabrics. Or perhaps it was as simple as wanting to give something back after all she'd given him and his son, to bring her joy.

The saleswoman reappeared and showed Matt to an upholstered chair with a good view of the curtain screening the generously sized change room where Susannah had apparently gone.

Within minutes, she tentatively stepped out, wearing a figure-hugging royal-blue dress that flared from her knees. His brain froze, and all he could do was stare—and hope he wasn't making a fool of himself. The color made her blue eyes bluer, highlighted her porcelain skin and the shape drew attention to each curve, making him wish they were home and he could explore them himself.

"I usually choose much simpler designs," she said. "But the saleswoman was fairly insistent about this one."

He cleared his throat before he could speak. "It's stunning."

She gave him an appreciative smile then slipped behind the curtain again. While she was gone, he tried to regulate his breathing. Who knew shopping for women's clothes would be this dangerous to his health?

A few minutes later she emerged in an oriental red sheath with a mandarin collar. Cut into the fabric was a large tear-drop shape that exposed the top of her cleavage. He restrained a groan.

"Not that one," he rasped. There was no way he wanted other men seeing her in that dress. They'd be imagining her out of it. The way he was right now.

"Yes, I don't think red is my color," she said, surveying it in the mirror.

"Sweetheart, if red was any more your color, I'd have to pick myself up off the floor. I only meant it might be too sexy for the Barclays' fundraiser."

She looked down at the hole over most of her décolletage and grinned. "You're probably right."

She disappeared and returned in a floating dress that had an overlay of sheer blush pink fabric. The bodice was fitted, then it fell in soft drapes to below her knees. It was pure Susannah. Fresh and free and feminine. Sweet, yet sexy as all hell.

She turned in front of the mirror, looking at it from all angles and he watched her, heart thundering as if it would explode. If he'd wanted her before, seeing her in a different environment, in these clothes, the need was more than anything he'd ever experienced.

Her gaze flicked to his in the mirror, and he could see she was surprised by the dress, liked it.

"That's the one," he said.

She arched an eyebrow. "Do I get some say?"

"Of course," he said, knowing he was calling her bluff. "Do you like it?"

"Why, yes, I do," she said with an overly innocent smile. "Thank you for asking."

She twisted to find the price tag, but he leaped to his feet and clasped her hand before she could read it. "Don't look. Just let me buy it for you."

Their gazes held and he could feel the battle she waged inside herself. It had been momentous for her to accept him buying the dress in the first place, he knew that. She was obviously more used to giving than receiving. But to not even know the amount she'd be indebted to him for would take a leap of faith.

Finally she nodded, and he felt a surge of masculine satisfaction.

Once they'd told the saleswoman of their decision and he'd paid, they were back out on the pavement, the dress wrapped in tissue paper and in a bag that was looped around his fingers.

"Is there anything else you need?" He knew accessories were important, but wasn't sure on the details. Matching shoes, perhaps?

"A gelato," she said with certainty.

As the words registered, he did a double take. This woman never stopped surprising him. He tried—but failed—to keep a grin from emerging. "You need a gelato?"

"There's a store on the next block that sells the best in the state." Her face lit with enthusiasm, which was undeniably infectious. "Let me buy you one."

He couldn't remember the last time he'd gone out for gelato. It seemed too whimsical a thing to do. There was a container of strawberry ice cream in the freezer at home for Flynn, but it wasn't something he would take a serving of for himself.

However, he recognized the nature of her offer—accepting his purchase of the dress had been uncomfortable, and she was trying to reestablish the balance by giving him something back. It might be only a small gift in return, but the spirit of the exchange would allow her to retain some dignity.

He took her hand and interlaced their fingers. "A gelato would be good."

She smiled broadly and led the way. As they walked down the street, hand in hand, an odd feeling crept over him—the people passing by would think he and Susannah were a couple. In a proper relationship. And, stranger still, he didn't mind the feeling. He hadn't been on the lookout for someone new in his life, but he rather liked the feeling of having a gorgeous woman by his side.

Susannah herself was only here temporarily, and besides, he had a feeling that when she entered a long-term relationship, she'd want it all—love and marriage. Neither of which he would ever offer a woman again. Been there, done that, paid the price. Dealing with falling out of love with his wife, the mother of his child, had been the hardest thing he'd ever done. The pain as he and Grace had sorted through the wreckage of their marriage wasn't something he'd ever let be repeated.

But maybe at some point in the future, he should consider a longer term relationship. Obviously he'd keep it separate from Flynn—the last thing that kid needed was a procession of Matt's girlfriends to attach to then lose. Yet he couldn't help but remember Susannah's comment over breakfast her first morning in his house.

You can't live just for your work and Flynn. You have needs, too, Matthew.

Maybe after things settled down with The Kincaid Group and Flynn was one hundred percent better, he'd think about finding someone amenable to a quiet, part-time relationship.

"There it is," Susannah said, pointing to a storefront with a bright yellow-and-white striped awning. "Have you been here before?"

"Can't remember it." He looked at the people casually ordering inside. "Then again, I'm not sure I've lined up for ice cream since I was a kid." Until Susannah had converted him to desserts, he'd been more of a cheese-platter guy. Now he was about to eat a serving of sugar in the middle of the day.

A young man with a white paper hat sauntered down to their end of the counter. "What can I get you folks?"

"We'll need to try a couple of samples first," Susannah said. "It's my friend's first time."

"No problem." He reached for a cup of small plastic spoons. "Which ones?"

Susannah turned and looked up at him expectantly. Matt dug his hands into his pockets and surveyed the variety of flavors—everything from tiramisu to mango. While he read the labels, he indicated that Susannah should go ahead and order, so she asked for a double serving of pink grapefruit, no cone.

"I'll try the grapefruit," Matt said to the young guy, who then scooped a small spoon into the pale pink ice confection and handed it over the counter.

It touched his taste buds with an explosion of flavor—sharp tang and sweet simultaneously. The effect woke up every cell in his body. "I'll have that one," he said.

Susannah laid a delicate hand on his forearm. "You can't have the first one you taste, Matthew. Try another couple first."

He'd always adhered to the principle that you took what you wanted, but this was Susannah's excursion so he deferred to her plan. "The passion fruit and the amaretto."

The guy behind the counter handed him two more spoons. Both were good, but neither had the startling effect of the first one.

"A double serving of the grapefruit in a cup," he said.

They took their gelato and Matt looked around at the tables. "Inside or outside?" he asked.

"Outside," she said without hesitation. "It's gloriously warm for February and I don't want to waste it."

He held the door open for her, remembering the day she'd wanted to eat breakfast in the courtyard. And how she'd looked like a goddess with her face turned to the early morning sun. He'd been spellbound.

"You really like being outside, don't you?"

They found an empty picnic-style table on the paved area to the side of the store and sat down. A spoon loaded with pink gelato disappeared into her mouth, and then emerged empty from between closed lips. He waited while she swallowed, feeling his blood begin to heat.

A dreamy expression filled her eyes. "Sunshine and breeze, Matthew. You can't beat them."

"You know," he said without thinking, "that's a good way to describe you."

She paused with the spoon halfway to her mouth and an adorable line appeared between her brows. "What is?"

"You've swept into my life like a fresh breeze. And wherever you are, it's like there's sunshine." As soon as the words were out of his mouth, he felt stupid and wanted to snatch them back. Spouting bad lines of pseudopoetry? RJ would laugh his head off.

But Susannah simply smiled. "Thank you, that's a lovely thing to say."

She took another spoonful of gelato and he followed suit, watching her as he ate. There was something about Susannah that sparkled from within, made him want to understand as much as he could about what made her tick.

"Will you tell me something personal if I ask?"

"Depends." She smiled, tucking a pale silken strand of hair behind her ears. "Why not try me?"

"Was it as easy to give up Flynn in reality as you've said?" Since Flynn's health scare, when a little devil had been on Matt's shoulder, taunting him with the possibility of losing his son, he'd wondered about Susannah's act of giving Flynn to him in the first place. "I just can't imagine handing him to someone."

Absently she stirred the gelato in her cup. "It was nothing like what you'd go through now if you lost him," she said quietly, bringing her gaze back to him. "I knew from the start what I was doing. In my mind, I always thought of him as your baby. Yours and Grace's."

He sat back in his seat as she ate more of her gelato. That sounded reasonable in theory, but putting it into practice was surely a different story. "You never thought about changing your mind?"

"If you and Grace had changed your minds—" she paused,

as if choosing her words carefully "—and said I could have kept him, I would have been over the moon. But he was your baby from the start, so I didn't dream of a future with him."

"You're amazing," he said and meant it. Susannah Parrish possessed the most unselfish heart he'd come across.

She stared down at her paper cup for long moments and when she looked up at him again, her eyes glistened. "When I was sixteen, I lost a baby."

All the air left his lungs as the weight of her loss hit him squarely in the chest. He reached across the table and grasped her hand. "I'm sorry."

She squeezed his fingers. "It was an accidental pregnancy, but as soon as I knew, I loved that baby with everything inside me."

Susannah pushed her cup to the side of the metal picnic table. She hadn't spoken about that dear baby since he'd died. The whole period in her life wasn't something she let herself dwell on. Usually. But Matthew was so easy to talk to, and he needed to hear this, to understand.

"I got pregnant because I was angry at my grandparents."

His head tilted to the side. "Their tug-of-war for you?"

"Yes, but it was more than that. Looking back, I was such a good kid. But it was never enough for them. There were constant lectures about being 'a lady,' and expectations I would perform better next time and be the proper social accessory. I was easy prey for a teenage boy." Her hands circled her throat. "I met him at one of my grandparents' parties and in my one act of teenage rebellion I went with him out to the secluded gardens and, inevitably, became pregnant."

With understanding in his eyes, he shook his head. "It might have been only one rebellion, but it was a doozy."

"We told our parents and though no one was thrilled, his parents were downright manipulative. They demanded I sign a contract to place the baby for adoption as soon as it was born so nothing would interfere with the glorious future they had planned for their son."

She clearly remembered the feeling of being overwhelmed by a rich family who stuck together. One who thought they could get whatever they wanted by pushing hard enough. Matthew's family seemed nice, but her experience of families with inherited wealth had been frightening—they thought and operated differently than other people. Flynn would experience that as an insider—the Kincaids would stick by him through thick and thin—but she would never get involved with a family like that. It had been the reason she'd been reluctant at first to get involved with Grace's surrogacy proposal. But seeing the strength of Grace's need, and her own mother's financial desperation, had convinced her it was the right thing to do. Still, she'd taken the contract Grace had given her to a lawyer before signing it to make sure she was fully protected in case things went pear-shaped.

To the wealthy, outsiders were always expendable to some degree. Just like her mother had been with her father's family.

She glanced at Matthew and saw the disapproval of how she'd been treated in his narrowed eyes. Despite being part of one of those families, he was a good man, but the powerful bonds with his family were evident in everything he did. As was how accustomed he was to getting what he wanted through money and influence.

"That was unforgivable of them," he said.

Tears pricked at the back of her eyes, both from what had happened back then, and for Matthew's support now. "My mother thought so, as well. She wasn't happy that I was pregnant so young, but she was thrilled about having a grandchild. I refused to sign that contact. I was keeping him, no matter what."

"What happened?" he asked, voice deep with concern.

"He was born too early. They said that sometimes happens when the mother is so young—there was no other explanation, no other reason. Good news for being able to carry Flynn years later, but it didn't help when I was a teenager and wanted answers." Her eyes drifted closed, as if to protect her against the pain. Yet that merely provided a blank slate for the memories. "The doctors worked hard to help him, and he made it to three weeks old, but his little lungs and organs simply weren't developed enough to handle this life. We never even brought him home from the hospital."

"Oh, Susannah, I'm sorry." He stood and pulled her out of her seat and into his arms. "What was his name?"

"William," she said against his chest. "After my dad."

He stroked a hand over her hair. "A good name."

Despite wanting to stay in his arms and soak up the support he offered, she pulled back and drew him down to the seat beside her. It was important he hear this.

"Matthew, I told you this story to show you the difference. I was a mess of grief when I lost William. And I still think about how my life would be if he'd lived. But Flynn was always meant to be yours. I won't deny that it was a wrench to give him up, but nothing like losing William."

He nodded and cupped her cheek. "Because you'd let yourself love William."

"Yes," she whispered. "I reminded myself all the time that Flynn belonged to you."

A ball of emotion lodged in his throat. "I don't know if I've ever said thank you for him. I know we said some things at the hospital about how grateful we were, but I never sat down like this, looked you in the eye and said it." He reached for her hands and clasped them tightly between his. "Thank you, Susannah Parrish. You did a beautiful thing in giving us our baby."

The sincerity in his bottomless green eyes touched a secret place inside her. "One thing I learned from losing William is that you can't put a price on the gift of life. It's infinitely precious. And I was glad, deep in my soul, to be able to give you and Grace that gift."

"I believe that of you." He leaned forward and placed a kiss on the top of her head. "What about the future? You've had two babies, but you didn't get to keep either of them. Will you have another?"

"I'd love to raise a baby. Or two or three." A vision rose of a little girl who matched Flynn, with Matthew's coloring and a dimple in her chin. She wore a purple cotton dress with a big bow at the front and held out her chubby arms. The picture was so clear she ached to draw the girl close. Matthew's voice dragged her from the dreamlike trance.

"You'll be a fabulous mother."

Horrified by the direction of her thoughts, she looked away. This was a temporary situation. She was going back to Georgia in a few days. If she let herself become enamored by fantasies, she'd wind up making bad decisions.

"Did you see they sell the gelato by tub, as well?" she said brightly, changing the direction of the conversation without any subtlety. "We could take some home to Flynn. What's his favorite?"

"Strawberry." Matthew rose from his seat, either not noticing or choosing not to comment on the abrupt change of subject. "But I'll get a tub of pink grapefruit as well for us." He dropped his voice. "I think it will taste even better tonight in bed."

Nine

Walking through the entranceway of the Barclays' mansion on Matthew's tuxedo-clad arm transported Susannah back ten years. The scene was awash with soft light and everything sparkled as these events always did, from the cocktail dresses of the female guests, to the gleaming marble and cut-glass chandeliers.

She'd attended similar events as a teenager with her grandparents, where they'd dress her up and parade her around. Their son—her father—was gone, and their two daughters had moved interstate, so her grandparents had relished the chance for a substitute child to use as a social accessory. The trip on the way had been full of instructions.

Don't scratch your nose.

Don't touch your hair and ruin the hairdresser's work.

Do smile (but only in the aloof, sophisticated style they'd made her practice).

Do seem interested in everything people tell you, but never laugh too hard or shriek. Not that she remembered shrieking; she'd been a quiet girl, but her grandparents left nothing to chance. She was there representing them, and her behavior was of vital importance.

Going home to her mother again where she could be herself had always been a relief. She could even scratch her nose if she felt the need.

She'd sometimes wondered whether her grandparents knew anything about her at all, or only saw a dress-up doll they could mold and shape to the image they wanted.

A shiver passed across her skin as she thought about meeting them here tonight, but they had a holiday place in Florida they used in January and February. And their friends hadn't seen her since she was a teenager, so hopefully none would recognize her as an adult.

"Are you okay?" Matthew asked close to her ear. "You seem a little strained."

She smiled up at him. "I'm good." Tonight was important to him; he needed her to help. As fate would have it, she was here again, being someone else's accessory, but this time she'd chosen the role. She could use all the skills her grandparents had taught her, ones that had then been refined during her work in public relations, for Matthew's benefit.

"What's your plan?" she asked him.

He cast a glance around the room, looking as reluctant to be here as she was. "Find my target, sell him on TKG and get out."

She chuckled. "How about a more subtle approach?"

"What do you suggest?" he asked, grabbing two glasses of champagne from a passing waiter.

"We mingle, work the room a bit, perhaps laying ground-work for future new business, then when an opportunity that feels natural arises with the client you're targeting, you chat with him and build a relationship."

"So less brash than my usual method?" His eyebrow arched at an amused angle.

"With many businesspeople, your forthright approach would

be pitch-perfect. But the people here will respond better to good manners and subtlety."

"Good point." His arm moved out from under her hand and slid around her waist. "Okay, let's do it."

An older woman with a heavy necklace Susannah knew was made of real diamonds and sapphires finished talking to the people who'd arrived before them and made her way over.

"Good evening, I'm Lydia Barclay, your hostess."

"Nice to meet you, ma'am," Matthew said. "I'm Matthew Kincaid, and this is Susannah Parrish."

"Kincaid?" Her eyes narrowed as her gaze raked him up and down. "You must be Elizabeth's son. We're on the board of the Arts Trust together."

"She speaks highly of you," Matthew said smoothly and flashed his devastating smile.

Mrs. Barclay fluttered her eyelashes, apparently charmed. "Let me introduce you to my dear friends, Mr. and Mrs. Raleigh."

Over the next twenty minutes, they slowly mingled with other guests and Susannah relaxed into her role. She remembered an occasional person from parties she'd been to years ago, but she was relieved that no one recognized her as an adult, avoiding any messy questions about her family. Perhaps they'd never looked at her properly when she was a teenager—just seen that her grandparents had a "well behaved" girl with them.

The irony almost made her laugh. She'd been prized as much then for slipping into someone else's role as she was now—being the replacement for Grace in Matthew's house. But now wasn't the time for reflection. She had a job to do. She pushed the thoughts aside and smiled, taking the hand of the next wealthy socialite who was being introduced to her.

Matt shook the hand of the man before him, his other hand firmly at Susannah's waist. Since Grace's death, he'd taken his mother anywhere he needed a plus one, so this was strange in

some ways. But mainly it felt right. Susannah was a natural—
conversing with everyone she met, putting them at ease, finding
common ground. He was pretty much following in her wake.
She must be great in her role as public-relations manager at the
bank she worked for—maybe he should mention her to Laurel,
in case his sister was looking for new staff for her PR team at
TKG.

And—he smiled inside—if she took a job in Charleston, there
would be no need for her to leave his bed. He pulled her a little
closer to his side, immeasurably pleased by the idea.

As the couple they'd been talking to moved away, Matt
leaned down to speak near Susannah's ear, allowing his lips to
brush her lobe. "Thank you for coming tonight."

She shivered and turned her face up to him, her clear blue
eyes captivating. "You're welcome."

"Though I'm not sure if I should be thanking you or not for
wearing that dress. It's been driving me crazy." He had plans
for that dress later. Of peeling her out of it and spending hours
exploring the skin it currently covered.

"You chose it," she said sweetly.

Then he saw Larrimore. Dead ahead but walking toward him.
He was talking to another man and hadn't seen them yet and by
moving a few inches to the right, Matt was able to put himself in
their walking path without being too obvious. Subtlety. He was
going to play this Susannah's way since he hadn't had any luck
with Larrimore so far. Just as the men walked past Susannah's
shoulder, he casually looked up and caught the eye of his quarry.
The friend walked on, but Larrimore stopped and nodded.

"Mr. Larrimore, good to see you again," he said, extending
a hand. "May I introduce you to Susannah Parrish?"

As he spoke the words, Susannah stiffened and leaned back
into his hand at her waist, as if her instincts were telling her to
get away. The other man's face turned a deep red and he made
no move to take Matt's offered hand. Matt dropped it, looking

from one to the other, trying to understand the dynamics that had sprung up.

"Parrish?" Larrimore said from between his teeth.

Susannah seemed to be stirred into action by the word—she drew a deep breath and lifted her chin. Then she said one word.

"Grandfather."

Matt's mind reeled. Arnold Larrimore was Susannah's *grandfather*?

The other man grabbed Matt's arm and steered him into a semiprivate alcove. "New plan, Kincaid."

"I'm listening," he said warily, watching Susannah over Larrimore's shoulder. Her face was pale, but she was following them, so he stayed put for the moment.

"That girl broke her grandmother's heart," he said irritably, his eyes reminding Matt of a boxer's in the ring. "You get her to reconcile with my wife and The Kincaid Group gets all Larrimore Industries' business."

Susannah had paused behind her grandfather—close enough to hear, but not to declare her presence. Her eyes were huge in her porcelain face. He remembered her telling him about her grandparents' treatment of her mother, of their underhanded appeals for her to live with them, and of their cruel refusal to help when she needed money for her mother. Her trembling hand lifted to circle her throat, her thoughts plain on her face. She was wondering if he was going to sell her out for the sake of his business.

He glanced back to Larrimore, his heart hardening. "No deal, Larrimore. If your wife—or you—want a relationship with Susannah, you'll have to ask her yourself. But a little friendly advice—she'll probably be more receptive if you ask her directly instead of trying to manipulate her from behind the scenes."

Without waiting for a reply, he reached for Susannah's hand and headed for the door. To hell with subtlety.

Stunned, Susannah allowed herself to be led away. She hadn't expected Matthew to offer her on a platter, but he desperately needed new business for his company. And if he was willing to go out of his way to attend this event tonight just to see her grandfather, then Larrimore Industries would have been a major client for TKG. Under the circumstances, she'd at least expected him to negotiate something more palatable—to look for a win-win.

Yet, here they were, outside the Barclays' mansion, climbing into one of the courtesy cars that would take them to the airstrip where the TKG jet was waiting.

As they settled in the backseat, she laid a hand on Matthew's tense jaw. "Thank you."

"Don't thank me," he said, pulling her closer and tucking her under his arm. "I should have said more to him. Done more."

"What you said was perfect." Utterly perfect. He'd stood up to her grandfather for her—defended her in a way she couldn't remember ever being defended before. Her heart glowed.

"You weren't exaggerating about the old man. To talk about you as if you weren't there, to attempt to trade you like a commodity…" He shook his head, apparently unable to finish the sentence.

She knew she should feel as affronted about her grandfather's behavior as Matthew was. But she didn't. She'd expected no more from him.

Matthew's reaction however…that had been amazing.

Could she give him something of equal value back? If he was prepared to lose the account that he needed for the family business for her, could she put up with visiting her grandparents a couple of times to let him get the deal back? Her body tensed in dissent, but she knew what she had to do. For Matthew.

She pulled away to face him in the dim interior. "I want you to call him and tell him you'll take the deal."

His eyes spat fire. "Like hell I will."

"You need the account," she pointed out.

"Susannah, after he ignored your pleas for money when you and your mother needed him, I wouldn't touch that man's account with a barge pole. But I don't want to talk about him any-more." The car slowed as they reached the airstrip. "We have the night off, my mother is with Flynn and we have the company jet." He stepped out of the car then offered her his hand.

"What do you have in mind?" she asked when they were standing on the tarmac.

The breeze blew her hair around her face and he smoothed it back. "How about I surprise you? Once the pilot gets clearance on a new flight plan, we can go."

She grinned, ready for anything if it involved this man. "Sounds great."

When the jet landed, Susannah had lost track of time. She'd been too absorbed in Matthew and the stories he'd been telling about growing up as one of five children. Seemed the Kincaid kids had been a bit of a handful, but Elizabeth had been more than up to the job.

She peeked out the window; it was hard to see much in the late-night darkness, but they were definitely outside the city area. "Where are we?"

"Willis Hall, not far from Hartsville. My father left it to me."

She turned from the window. "A house with its own airstrip?"

"It's a relatively small strip—the company jet doesn't need as much length as bigger craft. And my grandfather was always fond of cutting out the middleman," he said, unbuckling and picking up his jacket. He'd discarded the cuff links from his dress shirt and rolled up his sleeves to expose his wrists. Ever since she'd first seen those wrists and hands stirring a pot of chili beans, the sight of them made her breath catch. She knew that was an overreaction to a body part, but nothing about her attraction to Matthew had made sense from the day she'd ar-rived.

The pilot popped around the door. "You're clear to disem-bark, Mr. Kincaid."

"Thank you, Lachlan," Matthew said, before sliding his arms

into his jacket and guiding Susannah to the door the pilot had opened. They stood for a moment at the top of the steps, looking over toward a grand, two-story antebellum plantation-style house, its tall windows gleaming in the light of the full moon.

She sighed, trying to imagine living in a place so magical for vacations as a child. "Did your father bring you here often?"

"It was my grandfather's vacation home. My mother often brought us out on school holidays to spend time with the extended family. Dad was usually *working*." With the inflection he gave the word "working," it was clear he now thought his father had been with his second family during those holidays. He rubbed a finger across his forehead. "I don't think I've been out in fifteen years."

He climbed down the short set of stairs then turned and held out his hand to help her down—help she appreciated since the steps were harder to navigate in her heels.

On the ground, Matthew took her hand and guided her across the private airstrip toward what looked like a small cottage. "I thought since our night was cut short and Flynn is with Mom, it would be a good time to finally check the place out again."

The night air was cold and quickly seeped through the pink shawl she wore. She shivered and Matthew took off his tuxedo jacket and sat it on her shoulders. His fingers lingered and she shivered again, this time from his nearness.

She looked around at the silhouettes of the trees and stars in the sky, taking in as much as she could discern in the moonlight. If he hadn't been out in fifteen years, then Grace had never been here. A selfish corner of her heart liked that there was something Matthew was sharing just with her.

Though, that also meant Flynn hadn't seen the place. "You didn't come here when you inherited it?"

He shrugged casually. "The will reading was less than two months ago and Flynn was sick with the virus back then. I wouldn't leave him. My PA rang the couple who had been looking after this place and told them to keep doing whatever they'd been doing in the short-term, and I'd continue their salaries. Once things had settled I'd planned to come out and have a look then decide what to do with it."

"What about the pilot?" she asked, glancing back to the plane.

Matthew took out his keys and opened the door to the small building beside the strip. "This staff cottage has been used by pilots and other employees for decades." He flicked a switch and a sitting room was flooded with light. "The couple who look after the house keep it stocked with supplies and entertainments. It's better than the pilot's lounge he was at earlier this evening."

There was a Jeep in a garage beside the cottage, and after taking the key from a hook in the kitchen and snagging a coat for himself from another hook, Matthew guided her to the passenger seat. There was something surreal about coming out to such an isolated spot late at night, and she had to wonder why he'd really suggested it. There must have been other chances for him to check on his inheritance before now.

The short drive, passing the dark shapes of sprawling oaks, was like something from a fairy tale, and when they pulled up in front of an elegant porch, dominated by tall, white Grecian-style columns, she couldn't contain a sigh of wonder.

"Have you thought about what you want to do with the place?" she asked.

"Not really." Instead of climbing out, he turned to face her. "I was close to my grandparents, and when Mom would bring us out on vacations, I was in heaven, just running around and playing all day. I thought I could pass those experiences on to Flynn and make it our vacation home."

He came around to her door and opened it for her and they made their way to the deep front porch. "Then again, maybe I'll sell it," he said as he unlocked the front door.

She looked around at the first room they entered, a large reception room with family portraits in dark frames on cream walls and an assortment of trophies and other mementos on the mantel. "You don't think it's important to keep it in the family?"

"I recently discovered that my father had a different view of what family means than I do." His shoulders rolled back. "So, no, I don't feel a whole lot of obligation about keeping his family's traditions."

The betrayal was still obviously raw for him and she wished there was some way to ease that ache, even though she knew it was something he'd have to work through on his own.

As they walked through the rooms, she was surprised how sparkling and fresh the house was. She'd expected something a little more rustic.

"Your caretakers keep it looking like this all the time?" she asked, turning in a circle.

"Much of it looks the way it did when Grandpa was alive. Since it was only a vacation home, it's always had someone coming in once a week and keeping it ready for the family to drop in."

But one question replayed in her mind. She stopped him with a hand on his forearm. "Matthew, why did you bring me out here tonight?"

"I'm not sure," he said, looking down at her hand as it lay on the dark fabric of his tuxedo coat. Then he laid his large, warm hand over hers, sending sparks dancing across her skin. "I wanted to see it again. And to share that with you."

She bit down on a smile. He genuinely wanted to share this part of himself, of his history, with her. Yet, she could see he was conflicted about his inheritance by the lines that appeared around his eyes. He had a deep attachment to this place, and wanted that for Flynn, but was resisting it because he was still angry at his father. The complexities of this man called to her.

He lifted her hand from his forearm and turned it over, then kissed her palm gently, slowly, and the sweet pressure began to build inside her. He smiled into her eyes—he knew the effect it was having, then he tucked her hand into the crook of his arm.

"There's a sitting room through here with a fireplace," he

said. "I'm hoping part of the caretaker's duties was to keep it ready."

They found the sitting room, with its buttery-yellow walls and dark wood furniture, and Matthew went over to an old wood-burning fireplace that was already packed with kindling and split logs. He found the matches on a nearby ledge and hunkered down to reposition the twigs and scrunched newspaper. The fabric of his black trousers pulled taut over his powerful thighs. As he struck the match, it hissed then caught, and he threw it into the kindling. In the glittering light of the new fire, his cheekbones were accentuated, his profile becoming darkly mysterious.

She moved closer and put her hands out in front of the small flame, welcoming the heat it already generated, wanting to be closer to Matthew's heat, too.

"The house was mainly used in the summer, so fireplaces are all we have for heating," he said, holding his hands out to the warmth, as well.

"You realize I can't see the rest of the house now." She turned, giving her back a chance closer to the flames. "I'm not moving from this fireplace."

The look he gave her heated her skin, even from a distance. "I could be happy with that arrangement." He moved a few paces and took a thick blanket from the back of a chaise longue, then an armload of cushions.

He sauntered back and dropped the cushions haphazardly on the floor and held up the blanket. "I take it that you've heard about the best way to keep warm in the cold?"

"Central heating?"

His mouth twitched. "When there is no central heating."

"Then you might need to explain."

"Body heat." He took her hand and slowly kissed each finger in turn, then the palm. "Clothes off, skin on skin, wrapped in a blanket."

"Are you making a pass at me, Mr. Kincaid?" she asked a little breathlessly.

"No, ma'am." His mouth scorched a path down the inside of her wrist. "I'm solely concerned for your comfort and health."

Her skin flared hotter under his mouth than from the fireplace and, without thinking, she thrust the fingers of her other hand through his short, silky hair. But it wasn't enough. She wanted more.

She tugged her hand away from under his mouth and brought his face up to hers. Pulse soaring, she kissed him hungrily, her lips, her tongue urging him to take what he wanted. He seemed to understand. One hand slid up from her waist, cupping a sensitized breast, gently massaging his way until he found the peak, then brushing it with the back of his hand through the fabric of her dress.

A surge of need overtook her and she shrugged out of his tuxedo jacket, letting it fall to the mess of cushions at their feet and his coat quickly followed.

He reached behind her and unzipped the dress. "You took my breath away in this dress tonight." He pressed an openmouthed kiss to the bare shoulder he uncovered. "But I can't wait another second to see you out of it."

As he slid the fabric down her body and his darkened eyes followed its path, her skin quivered. The desire in his eyes hadn't dimmed from the first time they'd made love. If anything, it increased every time, matching her own growing need for him—each time together offered new opportunities to explore, to create responses, to feel. She couldn't imagine ever tiring of touching his body, of being touched by him.

She worked his shirttails free then unbuttoned the white dress shirt, pushing it over his broad shoulders and down muscled arms. The firelight flickered patterns on his chest, accentuating the ridges of muscle, making the skin shimmer like gold. She ran the pads of her fingers across his collarbone, scraping her nails lightly down his sternum.

"Don't move," she said. "Just give me a few minutes." Matthew was usually so intent on his mission to give her pleasure, and she was normally so absorbed in the sensations he evoked, that she didn't get enough time to tease him the way he teased her.

"Anything you want," he said.

She unbuttoned his trousers, lowering the zipper extra slow, watching his face—his eyes drifted closed and the ridged muscles of his abdomen clenched tight. He held himself completely still, though he was vibrating with the effort of doing it. She hooked her thumbs under the waistband of the trousers and boxers beneath, and lowered them at a leisurely pace, going down on one knee as she took them to his ankles. He lifted one foot then the other so she could slide the shiny shoe and sock off then tug each leg of his trousers away. Still he didn't move.

Her ascent was just as slow, her hands stroking over the rough hairs of his legs, tracing the strong muscles. When she reached the top of his thighs, she wrapped a hand around him and kissed the velvet skin. As he groaned, she felt him sway a little then his knees locked.

"Damn, Susannah," he said through gritted teeth. "You're killing me."

She smiled up at him and found his wallet in the trousers then located the protection she knew he'd have hidden inside. She tore open the wrapper then rolled it slowly over him, placing another delicate kiss at the top. She continued her progress up his body, kissing his abdomen, shaping the curve of his buttocks with her palms, until she was again standing straight.

"I'm all yours," she said with satisfaction, leaning into him.

His eyes flared and, with hands on either side of her head, he kissed her with a primitive hunger. Her heart thumped an erratic beat; her body was drugged by his essence, completely at his mercy.

When he drew away, his breathing was labored and he rested

his forehead on hers. "Thank heavens you were done, because my control was on its last threads."

He wrapped his arms around her and kissed her again. The passion built impossibly fast, and she tugged at the shoulder straps of her bra, wanting, *needing* his touch across all of her skin. Sensing her urgency, he discarded her bra and panties with efficiency, then wrapped the blanket around them both. The musk of his naked skin filled her head, his dark taste was on her tongue, his hard body pressed against hers—he was assaulting her senses on every level. And she wanted everything he had to give.

He pulled her down to the cushions, readjusting the blanket to keep her covered, every movement causing their bodies to slide against each other, driving her to the edge of sanity. Her breath was erratic, too fast to control.

He shifted, pinning her on her back, pressing her into the cushions with a heavy, delicious weight. Desire tugged deep inside her and she arched to meet him, tucking her ankles at the back of his hard thighs. The blanket fell away, but there was no need for it anymore—the heat they were generating rivaled a bushfire. In one long movement, he slid inside her, filling her lusciously, completely, and a deep, wrenching groan was torn from his throat. Yet, as he leaned over her, he stilled, his green gaze locked on her eyes.

"Matthew," she whispered, "this wanting, it's…" She didn't know how to finish, how to describe the overwhelming need she felt for him, all the time.

He flexed his hips and squeezed his eyes shut. "I know," he said in a pained voice. "It's more—you're more—than anything."

He shifted again, and she couldn't think enough to form more words, all she could do was feel the decadence of having him moving inside her. She gripped his shoulders as he increased the pace, arched her hips to meet his long, fluid thrusts, lost herself in the haze of rising pleasure. Rising higher as if she was floating off the floor. His rhythm sending her higher still, out to the clouds, higher. Then his hand reached between them and found the pulsing core of her and she exploded into a thousand fragments, spinning out into the universe, Matthew's name on her lips.

Within moments, he followed her, shouting her name, his movements slowing until he slumped above her, spent.

He rolled to his side, taking her with him, and she rested her head on his heaving chest, clinging to him like a life raft while she found her way back to reality.

When her mind cleared, minutes or hours later, she lay warmed by the fire and his skin, and he pulled the blanket up over her shoulders and tucked her head under his chin. It was a moment so perfect that she dared not move an inch, not wanting to spoil the beauty of it.

Then Matthew stretched, and his fingers drifted down her arm. "Stay," he said against her hair.

The Earth tilted and jarred beneath her as that one word reverberated in her head.

Ten

Susannah stilled. Surely she'd misheard. Misunderstood. "Pardon?"

"Stay with me," he coaxed, pulling her closer. "With me and Flynn."

She went a little dizzy at the thought. If Matthew wanted her with him, could she actually walk away? From the man who made her heart leap whenever she saw him, who ignited a flaming passion deep inside, who was asking her to stay? From the little boy she loved more than life, her own son?

"You said this would be temporary," she said warily. "No illusions, no one would get hurt."

"But it's working. You've fitted into our lives seamlessly, and," he said, his voice lowering, "I like you here."

Her pulse skipped, even though she couldn't afford to be distracted. He thought she'd fitted in seamlessly? Of course she had—she'd been playing a role. Grace's role. "Matthew, I can't see this working out long-term." For more reasons that she could even name.

"Why not? You couldn't be more perfect for Flynn—you love him, I've seen it in your eyes." He lifted her chin with a knuckle. "You're his mother. And things between us are pretty damn fine."

Slowly she sat up, pulling one end of the blanket around her to shield her from the cold—and from the allure of his suggestion. "I can't stay with a man who's still in love with someone else," she said, despite it making her heart ache to say it aloud.

He frowned, then his eyes widened as if he'd realized her meaning and he sat up in a mirror of her pose. "You think I'm still in love with Grace?"

She bit down on her lip, knowing she had to push the point if he was to understand her reasoning. "I can see you are."

"How can you see it?" he asked incredulously.

"Your house is practically a shrine to her." The photos on every wall, her bedroom that hadn't been touched since she died. "And it's in the way you almost flinch every time her name is mentioned. She affects you."

"It's not love," he said tightly, his gaze flicking to the fire. "It's guilt."

Guilt? She hesitated, her brain scrambling to reevaluate everything she knew about Matthew and Grace. "Why would you feel guilty?"

He scrubbed both hands through his hair and turned his face to the ceiling before looking back to her and meeting her gaze. "When Grace died, we were considering a divorce."

Her breath hitched in her throat. Grace and Matthew Kincaid had been talking about a divorce? She wouldn't have believed it if she'd heard it from anyone but Matthew himself. "You seemed like the perfect couple."

"We were college sweethearts and we'd thought back then that what we had would last forever." He rubbed a hand down his face and suddenly looked weary. "But life doesn't always unfold the way you expect it to."

She took his hand. "What happened?"

"Nothing drastic," he said, glancing down at their interlaced fingers. "We married straight out of college. Grace didn't want a job because we'd planned to start a family. But when she didn't become pregnant as soon as she'd hoped, her desire for a baby quickly turned into desperation for one. Maybe not having a job let her dwell on it too much, maybe I didn't support her the way I should have, but it was all she wanted to talk about, all she could think about."

"I knew she was keen, but I hadn't realized it was that strong." Whenever she'd met with Grace, they'd talked about babies, but it had seemed appropriate when their connection was the surrogacy. She hadn't guessed that Grace would be the same everywhere.

"I tried to be understanding—I wanted children, too, and I knew the need was stronger for her. But it took a toll on our marriage. All we talked about was babies, and eventually, we stopped knowing each other. There was no room to talk about our day, or our dreams about anything else." His tone was fairly neutral, but there was a deep pain in his eyes—the hurt from the breakdown of his marriage still lived inside him. "By the time Flynn came along, the damage was done. The only thing we had in common was him. That was enough for the first year, when everything revolved around the baby, but at some point, we realized we were strangers who shared a house and a son."

"Oh, Matthew," she said, her heart bleeding for them both.

"We started to discuss a divorce and even touched on how we'd share custody of Flynn. Then I pushed too far," he said, his voice becoming rough for the first time.

She moved closer, so their knees were touching, wanting to give him as much support as he'd given her so many times over the last few weeks. "Tell me."

"I thought she needed some time away to make sure divorce was what she wanted. I left the house every day for work, but she was home all day, and really only spoke to her parents, me and Flynn. Separating was such a big decision—life changing—

I wanted her to have really thought about it and be sure. For both of us to be sure."

"Grace didn't want to go?" she asked with a sinking feeling in her stomach.

He swallowed hard, then again before continuing. "She was worried because she'd never been away from Flynn for a night. I thought that was even more of a reason for her to have a break. Time to focus on herself and think about our marriage. I'd always been a hands-on father, so Flynn and I would be fine for a weekend."

Her stomach clenched tight. Despite knowing the story had to end badly, part of her still kept hoping Matthew and Flynn could be spared somehow. "I'm almost afraid to ask."

"The TKG jet was already booked, so I chartered a private plane to take her to her parents' place for the weekend and pretty much pushed her out the door." His eyes closed and he pressed fingers to the lids, as if trying to erase the picture in his mind.

She remembered the day she'd returned to Charleston and Matthew had told her Grace had died—he'd said it had happened in a small plane crash. "Something happened to the plane."

"It went down over the water." He flinched, eyes squinting, as if it was happening in front of him. "It took them days to retrieve her body."

She felt physically sick just imagining that day. "Oh, poor Grace."

"She never would have gone if it wasn't for me," he said, his voice a rough whisper. He turned to watch the flickering of the fire and when he turned back, his eyes held more anguish than she'd thought was humanly possible. "It was my idea, I'd chartered the plane, I'd pushed her to go. It was my fault Flynn lost his mother, her parents lost their only child, and a beautiful soul lost her life."

Seeing his naked pain almost made her lose control of the tears that threatened, but he needed her now. She gripped his fingers tight. "Matthew, it was an accident. There's no one to blame. Certainly not you."

"I failed her in the most primal of ways—I didn't protect my wife." His mouth twisted, the skin around his lips so pale. "The only thing I had left to offer her was to keep the secret about being Flynn's biological mother, and to honor her where I could."

"That's why the house feels like a shrine to her." He couldn't bear to move anything away because of the guilt.

He shrugged one shoulder. "For Flynn, too—so he had reminders of her as much as possible."

"You're not still in love with her," she said, finally understanding.

He slowly shook his head. "I wasn't in love with her when she died. I'm sure she wasn't in love with me by then, either."

She wriggled to his side and he wrapped his arms around her. For a long time, neither of them moved more than to give a light caress, neither spoke.

"Stay with me," he whispered.

He was tearing her in two. He might not still be in love with Grace, but he hadn't moved on. Having a temporary relationship with him was one thing, but staying indefinitely? Changing her job and moving interstate for a man who was living in the past and would only ever see her as a replacement for his dead wife? The wife whose death filled him with guilt. Since she'd been in Charleston, she'd been tagging along in Matthew's life like an accessory—attending the Barclays' fundraiser, letting him buy her a dress, drinking fancy wines, fitting into his family's schedule visiting the hospital, cooking family meals. She'd been glad to do what she could, to help. But it had just been the list of tasks that had needed doing. It wasn't about her. It had been the person Matthew had needed her to be, so she'd slotted in.

It was no foundation for a relationship, even if she felt more for him than she'd expected.

She hated society fundraisers, hated being part of the world her grandparents and the Kincaids inhabited—they prioritized money and power, and thought family secrets were par for the course. She couldn't stay in that environment. Yet she couldn't walk away from this man. Or Flynn. What other option was there?

"Tell me, Matthew, what are you really suggesting?"

"If you need a ring to stay, I can do that," he said, the muscles in his neck taut with resistance to the idea.

The blood in her veins turned cold. "You're proposing marriage?" She could barely believe he'd said the words, no matter how reluctantly.

"If you need that," he repeated. "It might be better for Flynn anyway."

Something inside her withered. He thought that she—that any woman—could be happy to be offered marriage "if she needed that"?

"You don't think marriage should be about love and commitment?" Things that would make the union solid and able to weather storms.

"Susannah, I have to be honest. I'm not ready to love again. I don't think I'll ever be ready, but that doesn't change the fact that I want you to stay."

As she looked into his deep green eyes, the pieces finally fitted together. "You don't think you *deserve* love again, do you?"

His eyes slid away. "How about we just keep it simple? You stay with Flynn and me, and we'll all be happy."

Matthew looked down at Susannah's sweet face with no idea what was going on in her head. All he knew was that she was overthinking this. Why fix what wasn't broken? This was working, so they should leave things as they were.

"Matthew, I can't stay."

Before he could answer, his cell buzzed and he reached for his trousers on the floor to find it. The ringtone was the one he'd programmed for immediate family—if one of them was calling this late, it must be important. "We're not finished on this subject," he said as he thumbed the answer button.

"Hello," he said, his eyes still on Susannah as she chewed on her lip.

"Matt, it's Laurel." The tension that vibrated in his sister's voice had him sitting up straight, heart in his mouth.

"Is it Flynn?" Even knowing Laurel wasn't with Flynn tonight, his son was always the first place his mind went when he worried.

"Flynn's fine," she said quickly. "I'm here with him now."

Laurel was at his house late at night—that couldn't be good. "Then where's Mom?"

"The police have taken her in for questioning."

His mother had been taken by the police? His stomach plunged into free fall. "Questioning about what?"

"About Dad's murder," she said, her voice wavering.

His temples began throbbing in a heavy drumbeat. His mother was the last person on Earth who would have anything to do with a murder, let alone her own husband's—surely even the police could see that?

"I'm leaving now," he said reaching for his trousers.

He disconnected and tugged his trousers up his legs. "We have to go back."

"Is your mother in trouble?" Susannah asked, her eyes round and full of concern.

God, he hoped not. But who knew what the justice system would do? "They've taken her in for questioning about Dad's murder."

Her face paled and he offered her a quick reassuring smile. The fire had burned down but he couldn't leave it alight with no one in the house. He looked around and found a fire blanket discreetly hanging in an alcove nearby and ripped it open. Making a mental note to send someone out to replace the safety blanket, he smothered the fire.

Susannah zipped up her dress, frowning. "I've only met your

mother a couple of times, but that sounds crazy. She's not capable of something as violent. As horrific."

"Of course she isn't. Any fool could see that." He grabbed his shirt, shoved his arms down the sleeves and left the sides hang open, unbuttoned. "The detectives are wasting time by interviewing her while the killer walks the streets of Charleston."

He let out an oath as they hurried out the door to the plane.

Susannah followed Matthew through his front door and slipped off her heels. The trip back had been tense and he'd spent much of it on the phone to a lawyer and his siblings. RJ, Kara and Lily were already at the station or on their way, and Matthew's unspoken words were clear—he hated being so far away when his family needed him. She understood. The Kincaids were a family who stuck together and were always there for each other, and yet...they were a family of privilege, secrets and lies. Not a life she could ever be part of.

When they stepped into the parlor, they found a beautiful woman with long, dark auburn hair and green eyes—the picture of Matthew's mother.

"Susannah, this is my sister Laurel," Matthew said brusquely. "Laurel, this is Susannah Parrish."

Laurel held out a hand. "I wish we were meeting under better circumstances, but nice to meet you, anyway." She had tension around her eyes, but her tone was unfailingly polite.

"Likewise," Susannah said, then stepped back to let the siblings talk.

Matthew rubbed the muscles at the back of his neck. "Flynn's asleep?"

"Since before I got here. He won't know anything's happened."

"Thank goodness for small mercies. I don't know why they had to do this at night."

"When I arrived, Detective McDonough and his partner were still here—they'd waited with Mom till she could leave. They said some new evidence had come to light just today, and they were following it up."

"New evidence?" He threw up a hand, palm out. "It's ludicrous to think there could be evidence against her."

Laurel flicked her hair over a shoulder. "I did happen to mention that once or twice."

Matthew showed the first glimmer of a smile since he'd taken Laurel's call. "I bet you did. As I'm sure the lawyers will, too. Have you heard from Mom since they took her?"

"No, but Kara rang when she arrived at the station and said they were all there. Mom's still being questioned. Matt, I—"

He gave a quick nod. "Me, too." He turned to Susannah, reaching for her hand and interlacing their fingers. "Would you mind staying here with Flynn while Laurel and I go down to the police station?"

"Of course I will." She'd been about to offer anyway. "And let me know if there's anything else I can do to help."

He tugged her closer and cupped her cheek with his palm, apparently not caring that Laurel was witnessing the gesture. "Hopefully we won't be long, but even if they drag it out, we should be back before he wakes up."

"Don't worry about me," she said, hoping to at least relieve him of one concern. "We'll be fine. I just hope your mother is okay."

He looked down at her for one beat, then two, the worry for his mother in his eyes, but also the fire that had been there when they'd made love still burned. Then, with no warning, his head swooped down and he kissed her, one hand sliding into her hair, the other behind her back. Helpless, she leaned into him, into the kiss.

Then he pulled back and met her gaze. "Thanks for staying with him."

He turned to Laurel, indicating his rumpled tuxedo with a hand. "I'll just get changed and we'll leave."

He strode for the stairs then took them two at a time, and Susannah dared to peek at Laurel. Matthew had just pretty much announced to his family that they were sleeping together. Now he'd asked her to stay, secrecy was obviously not high on his agenda anymore.

Laurel smiled. "Thank you from me, too."

"Really, I don't mind staying with Flynn."

"Not for that," Laurel said, stepping closer so she could drop her voice. "Matt's my baby brother and he's had a rough time the last few years. Anything that makes him happy gets a ringing endorsement from me."

Susannah felt the blush creep up from her chest to her throat. It was sweet of Laurel to say that but her relationship with Matthew wasn't what Laurel had probably imagined.

She'd be going in a few days, as soon as her leave was up. Despite Matthew's request to stay, there was no way she could.

Matthew came running back down, buttoning a clean shirt as he cleared the stairs, threw a quick kiss on Susannah's cheek, then she was suddenly alone.

She woke on the couch with a start. After a quick shower, she'd been waiting in the parlor for Matthew's return but when she opened her eyes, it was Flynn who stood before her, clutching his favorite teddy, the corners of his mouth turned down.

Fear had her wide-awake in an instant, but she kept her voice calm. "What's the matter, sweetie?"

"I had a bad dream," he said, his bottom lip trembling.

Her chest clenching at his sad little face, she held out her arm and he climbed onto the couch with her, snuggling his warm little back into her chest. She pulled a throw rug from the back of the couch over both of them.

"What was the dream about?" she asked gently.

"I don't mer'ember."

She racked her brain for ideas to deal with childhood bad dreams, but came back to Flynn's own suggestion from when he was in hospital. "Would you like me to sing an Elvis song?"

He nodded, his messy hair brushing under her chin as he did. Holding him a little bit tighter, she sang a verse of "Teddy Bear."

"Sudi?" he said, tipping his head back in an attempt to see her face. "Can I call you Mommy?"

Her heart fell like a stone into her stomach. She and Matthew had tried so hard to be clear with Flynn about her role. Matthew had taken Flynn aside when he first arrived home from hospital and explained that Susannah was only staying temporarily. Then during the week they'd been sure to regularly drop phrases into conversation like, "When Susannah goes home next week," and "During my special little vacation here," to reinforce the message. Obviously their efforts hadn't been clear enough.

Carefully she sat up, bringing him with her, and sat him on her knee. "Sweetie, we've talked about this. You know I'm not your mommy."

"But, maybe you are." His face was serious, as if he'd had an idea that had possibly missed her notice.

She was almost afraid to ask, but forewarned was forearmed. "Why would you think so?"

"You live in our house," he said, his solemn eyes barely blinking.

"I don't really live here. I'm just staying for a little vacation." Though she knew that distinction might be lost on a three-year-old.

Undeterred, he pressed on. "You cook for us like a mommy."

"That's only because your daddy can't cook. In some families, it's the daddy who cooks. And in your family, Pamela makes most of your meals, doesn't she?"

Reluctantly he nodded. Then he perked up. "Daddy kisses you like a mommy."

She could have slapped herself. They thought they'd been so careful, not kissing anywhere Flynn could see them. Apparently their attempts at being discreet had failed.

Although, perhaps Flynn had been on the lookout as he collected his list of evidence. Now his list encompassed that she kissed like a mommy, sang like one, cooked like one, lived in their house and kissed the daddy.

And the worst part was he was *right*.

She'd slipped into the role of wife and mother so easily. But it wasn't *her* role. And neither Kincaid saw her as anything more than that role.

"I think it's time we put you back to bed," she said, moving him onto the couch beside her. "You can talk about this tomorrow with your dad."

His smile drooped and it broke her heart. Everything inside her wanted to say that she would be his mommy. That she *was* his mommy.

But Flynn deserved a mother who had a proper relationship with his father, where there was love and marriage and plans of forever. It was the only way to create a secure family unit for the little boy. One day Matthew would be ready to move on, and he'd find the perfect mother for Flynn. But Matthew wasn't ready yet and, therefore, it wasn't her.

Now she just had to tell Matthew.

Eleven

When Matthew finally arrived home from the police station, the sun was peeking over the horizon. Dark circles underlined his eyes and his every movement conveyed exhaustion. Susannah walked over to where he was closing the door behind him, her entire body vibrating with tension about what she would have to say, knowing she would be adding to the stress lining his face.

He pulled her into an embrace, slumping a little of his weight onto her shoulders, and let out a deep sigh. She wanted nothing more than to take him upstairs and hold him while he slept, but that was not on the agenda—now or ever. She closed her eyes and saw Flynn's little face, solemnly asking if he could call her Mommy. This couldn't wait. So she simply held him in her arms, and wished things could be different.

He straightened and yawned and she stepped back, folding her arms tightly under her breasts. "How's your mother?"

"Tired. Upset." He speared his fingers through his short hair. "But they've finished questioning her and Laurel's taking her home."

She had only met Elizabeth a couple of times but she'd liked her, and hated to think of her going through something so awful—being questioned at a police station, being a suspect in a murder investigation, or the horror of knowing your husband had been murdered. She repressed a shiver.

"Have they eliminated her from suspicion now?"

"I'm not sure what they've decided. Our lawyers have told us not to worry, which is a little hard to achieve. Detective Mc-Donough told Mom not to leave town while they further their investigations. Which could mean they still suspect her, or could have been a parting shot to keep us all on our toes."

"Matthew," she said, then paused to moisten her lips, "I'm sorry about the timing, but there's something important I need to tell you."

He checked his watch then glanced at the window where the sun's first rays were shining. Turning back to her, he opened his mouth and she knew he was about to ask if it could wait, but something of her anguish must have shown on her face because he rubbed his eyes and said, "Sure, shoot."

Part of her wanted to jump at the reprieve he'd been about to offer, to delay the inevitable heartache, but that would be cowardly and only make things worse for Flynn. For everyone. "Thank you. It's already waited too long."

His eyes were wary as they regarded her, then he nodded. "This looks like a conversation I'll need to pay attention to. Let me get a coffee first." He headed through to the kitchen and asked, "Do you want one?" over his shoulder.

She was already wired enough without the caffeine. "No, thanks."

Belly churning, she watched his hands work efficiently and methodically filling the machine with coffee grounds before turning it on. His eyes were preoccupied, weary, and she remembered this was a man who'd lost his wife and father in a twelve-month period, whose son had suffered a major illness, and whose mother had as good as been accused of murder. And now she was about to add to his burden. *I'm sorry, Matthew.*

Once his mug was full and steaming, he leaned back against the counter and drank. Then he leveled his gaze at her. "Is this about our conversation at the farmhouse?"

"No." She felt a tear escape and roll down her cheek. "And yes."

"Hey," he said, setting his mug down and pulling her against his chest. "What's happened?"

You happened, she wanted to say. *My life was fine then Flynn fell sick and you called me and now nothing's the same.* Despite Flynn's health improving, it was too late—she'd been drawn into their lives and could barely see a way out past the entanglements, past the caring.

She rested her cheek against his chest and focused on the half-empty mug on the counter beside them. "Flynn woke during the night and we had a talk."

He lifted her chin with his thumb, his eyes one hundred percent alert now. "What kind of talk?"

"He's been collecting more evidence that I'm his new mother," she said, trying not to wince as she remembered Flynn's earnest little face.

Matthew's arm stiffened around her. "What's he got?"

"I live here, I cook and—" she drew in a trembling breath "—I kiss the daddy."

He closed his eyes and swore. "I had no idea he'd seen us."

"Matthew, it's gone too far. Flynn's already going to be disappointed when I leave. I have to go today, before he can ask again."

He shook his head, dismissing the idea. "Flynn wants you to stay—that only strengthens my case." He kissed her cheek, the tip of her nose. "You fit in here. Stay with us."

How easy it would be to say yes, to stay here forever, to lose herself in their lives. She knew she couldn't stay as a replacement, but her heart ached to do exactly that, despite the price....

She couldn't think straight in his arms—the very reason she'd become so entangled in his life in the first place. Calling on every ounce of willpower she possessed, she extracted herself from his embrace and leaned back against the opposing counter. The cool air stung her skin where Matthew's body heat had warmed her only seconds ago.

"The thing is I fit in here a little *too* well."

"How can you fit in too well?" he asked, his eyes narrowing.

She swallowed, trying to moisten her parched throat. "It's like you and Flynn have just been waiting for someone to fill the Grace-shaped hole in your family. I tick all the boxes—there's an attraction between us, I'm Flynn's biological mother, I cook."

He snorted. "How can it be a bad thing that we meld together as a family?"

She wrapped her arms around her middle and held herself tight as if she could stop herself from falling to pieces in front of him. "Because when I eventually have a family of my own, it will be somewhere I'm wanted for *myself*." Her eyes were stinging, and she tried to stop the tears from forming. "My worth in this house is primarily as a replacement."

His eyes widened. Blazed. "That's ridiculous."

"I know you didn't mean it to happen this way, and that it's partly my fault, but neither of you know *me*." Was it so wrong to want to be seen for herself? Wanted for herself? She cast around for a way to explain. "When people start a relationship, or a family, it's like the edges of their joining are elastic, and they move out around the things both people bring to that relationship. But nothing changed here. I fitted in the spaces that were already vacant. There's nothing about me here."

"That's crazy, Susannah. To start with, your desserts were new," he said with a little grin.

"Grace cooked, Pamela cooked." She lifted one shoulder and let it drop again. "I continued the tradition. That my dishes were different hardly matters."

He scrubbed his fingers through his hair, frustration shining in his eyes. "I don't even know what you're talking about. I *know* you're not Grace."

Her bottom lip quivered but she wouldn't let the emotion overtake her, not until she was on her own. "I don't think anyone here can be sure of what they know," she said slowly. "Everything is smoke and mirrors—you're living in the past because you can't let go of your guilt, your father had secrets, you have secrets. I'll bet there are other secrets in your family yet to come out."

His eyes hardened. "You know why I can't tell people about Flynn. I swore to Grace I wouldn't tell a soul. And even if I could break it, her parents would be destroyed if they found out—all it would take would be one person who knows to slip up. You and I are as far as the information can ever go."

"I do, Matthew, I understand." She could feel the tears that welled in her eyes begin to spill over, and she swiped at them. "But you have to understand that I need to leave today, both for my own sake and for Flynn—before he gets any more attached."

He grabbed his mug and cast the remains of his coffee down the sink, then turned to face her again, hands low on hips. "So you're just walking away? From Flynn?"

Had he forgotten what he'd asked of her? Nothing as simple as taking another week's leave. He'd asked her to confront a mother's deepest instinct and decide whether she'd stay with the son she'd borne. Yes, she'd originally felt the baby had been his and Grace's, but that was before she'd spent time with Flynn.

"I have to, Matthew," she whispered, suddenly cold all over. "Please don't make this harder."

He raised his eyebrows pointedly. "If it's hard, then maybe it's wrong."

She squeezed her eyes shut—she couldn't do this anymore. Couldn't keep discussing why she had to go. It hurt far too much.

"I'll say goodbye to Flynn this morning," she said, looking

out the window. "And I'll send him a couple of letters and presents from Georgia so the cut isn't too abrupt."

"What about me?" he asked bitterly. "How are you going to ease the break for me?"

"The same way I'll ease it for myself. Time." She choked in a breath. "I'll miss you, Matthew." She couldn't deny it, even if she wanted to.

His face softened, and he pulled her roughly against him. "I'll miss you, too."

She melted into him and for the last time, just let herself feel him against her. Let herself smell the scent of his skin through his shirt. Feel the day-old stubble against her temple. He leaned down and gave her a lingering kiss that tasted of coffee but felt like sadness. She needed to pull away, yet she couldn't make herself. And then she realized why.

She'd gone and fallen in love with him. Her stomach swooped low.

He was right. If it was hard, then it was probably wrong—it *shouldn't* be easy to leave the man you loved. But it only made things worse. It was an unrequited love—Matthew had made no secret of the fact that he'd never let himself love again. If she'd been the woman to change his stance, he'd have changed it already.

And, even if he could love her, Matthew didn't see her, the real her. If she stayed, she'd forever be living Grace's life, not her own. A life as a Kincaid in a world she'd escaped once as a teenager.

Drawing a shaky breath, she pulled away and dashed for her bedroom to pack. Hot tears streamed down her face freely. If she didn't go today, she might settle for this half life and stay forever.

A few hours later, Matt watched Susannah climb into a taxi in his driveway, his chest ripping open. Everything was good with her here—they fitted together, their strengths complemented each other, he couldn't imagine he'd ever have enough of her in his bed and Flynn adored her.

But that wasn't enough for this woman. Susannah Parrish wanted it all. More than he had to give. His temples pounded. He'd given his heart away once and it had been decimated when things had collapsed between him and Grace. Realizing they'd fallen out of love, that all his dreams of the future for his marriage and their little family were gone, had been almost more than he could bear. He'd never offer his heart again.

And Susannah wouldn't settle for anything less.

When she'd stood up to his brothers at the hospital, he'd admired her refusal to back down, her stubbornness. And though he was desperate to make her stay, a little part of him still had to admire her commitment to what she wanted.

Flynn was inside with his grandmother. He'd cried when they told him Susannah was leaving, but the promise of postcards and presents from Georgia had mollified him somewhat. The taxi crawled down the driveway and paused before turning onto his quiet street. Susannah looked up and he caught her gaze. Her face was pinched as she refused to let herself cry. Damn it. *Why was she doing this?*

She thought he didn't see her? Every time he closed his eyes, it was her smile that appeared. She'd invaded his dreams at night, his thoughts during the day. How could she think he didn't see her?

The taxi moved off down the street and he forcefully locked away everything he was feeling. He couldn't afford to fall apart—he had a little boy depending on him.

He thumbed the keyless lock on his car, climbed in and headed for the TKG building. The first order of business was to explain to RJ why he'd lost the Larrimore's account last night. Not something he'd been looking forward to, but compared with Susannah leaving, it no longer seemed to matter as much.

He picked up two coffees from their favorite coffee shop on

the way, wishing it was late enough in the day for Scotch instead.

"Good morning, Brooke," he said to RJ's secretary. "Is my brother in?"

Brooke looked up from her computer screen and smiled. "Good morning, Matthew. I just took him a pile of papers to sign, so he'll probably be glad for the interruption."

RJ was sitting at his desk and stretched his arms over his head when Matt knocked on the open door. "You've come bearing gifts. Excellent."

Matt walked across to the desk and put a steaming cup of coffee in front of him. "Thought we could use the extra caffeine today."

RJ had been at the police station by the time Matt had arrived last night, and had probably had as much sleep as he'd had—none.

"Have you spoken to Mom today?" RJ asked after taking a sip of the dark brew.

Matt nodded. "She's at my place. She's still a little shaken, but seems fine. She insisted on staying with Flynn to give her something to do."

Matt never would have asked her to do it—he'd have preferred to keep her wrapped up in cotton wool today. Perhaps send her off to a spa to be spoiled for a few hours. But his mother had rung early and insisted looking after Flynn was what she wanted. She said seeing Flynn healthy put everything else that was going on into perspective.

RJ put the coffee on his desk and frowned at it. "She was with him last night when they took her in, wasn't she?"

Matt nodded. Time to come clean. "I went to the Barclays' fundraiser. Which is what I need to talk to you about."

"You were hoping to tie things down with Larrimore, weren't you?"

Matt's blood simmered thinking about Larrimore's offer last night to deliver Susannah in exchange for the account. He should have said or done more, but at the time, his first priority had been getting Susannah out of there. He took a swig of his coffee and drained the cup. The next time he met the old man, things would be different. He had no idea what he'd do, but someone needed to bring the man down a peg.

He crumpled his empty cup and pitched it into the wastebasket. "The deal's off the table."

RJ swore. "Did he give a reason for canceling?"

"I ended it," Matt said evenly, confident he'd done the right thing.

RJ's jaw dropped. "Why the hell did you do that?"

"Turns out Larrimore is Susannah's grandfather. Due to some history between them, she's estranged herself." Rightly so—the man was a bully. And Matthew would never let anyone hurt Susannah, grandfather or not, potential client or not. "When he saw her with me last night, he offered a new deal—I get Susannah to make nice and we get their business."

"You sided with her," RJ surmised, raising his brows.

"Beyond the point that I'm not willing to manipulate people to get an account, she had a solid reason for estranging herself in the first place."

"You're pretty tight with this Susannah. What's your plan there?"

Despite his heart beating like a freight train, Matt schooled his features to be neutral. "No plan. She's gone."

"That surprises me," RJ said, leaning back and interlocking his fingers behind his head. "That day at the hospital, there was definitely something between you."

Something? What had sparked with Susannah had been more than something, more than he could have dreamed. A tidal wave of anguish threatened to crash over him and he steeled himself against its power. "There might have been, but it's over."

"Is this about Grace? You're still hooked on her?"

Matt looked up sharply. Seemed Susannah wasn't the only one who'd thought that. He heaved out a breath. He owed his brother the truth. "Grace and I were talking about a divorce when she died."

RJ dropped his arms and sat up straight. "Lord. I had no idea."

"She was going away for the weekend to think about it." The guilt still burned in his gut, but the story was a little easier told a second time. Had lost the sharpest edges, thanks to Susannah's gentle listening. "We had to make sure it was what we really wanted."

RJ's head tilted to the side, his eyes incredulous. "All this time I thought you'd put your life on hold because you were still in love with her."

Matt frowned. "What do you mean, I'd put my life on hold?"

"You walk around like, I don't know, your insides are bound tight or something." RJ winced, clearly uncomfortable, but willing to proceed anyway. "The only time there seems to be a spark of life in you is when you're with Flynn. Kara said to me once that your eyes say you're closed for business."

It's like you and Flynn have just been waiting for someone to fill the Grace-shaped hole in your family.

Waiting.

The room closed in on him until he couldn't breathe. He ran a finger around the collar of his shirt. *Had* he put his life on hold? Waiting for...waiting for what?

Abruptly he stood and headed for the watercooler in the corner of RJ's office and poured himself a drink. Susannah had accused him of thinking he didn't deserve to love again. Deep down, he knew that was true to some extent. But added to that, he could see that because Grace died when they were talking about a divorce, he'd never had closure. He'd been in limbo about the end of their relationship.

He'd been unable to grieve his wife as a man in love, and hadn't been granted divorce papers the way a man leaving a relationship would. With neither avenue open, he'd stood still. Stagnant.

He turned to find his brother watching him warily. "I really have had my life on hold, haven't I?"

RJ nodded, clearly relieved the awkward part of the conversation was over. "Have you opened the letter Dad left you yet?"

When their father's will had been read, they'd all been handed a letter their father had written. Each of Reginald's five children, his wife, his mistress and his mistress's two sons. Matt had watched RJ open his straightaway but he simply couldn't bring himself to do the same. He'd been too angry. If his father had been standing in front of him instead of lying in his grave, he'd have walked away, too angry to talk to him—he hadn't wanted to talk to him via a letter, either.

He rubbed his fingers across his forehead. Maybe it was time he gave his father a hearing.

"I'll catch you later," he said to his brother on the way out the door.

Back in his office, Matt slid open the second drawer of his desk and reached below the papers there to find the envelope he hadn't seen since the day his father's will had been read. He hadn't wanted the letter at his house, in his private life, so he'd thrown it at the bottom of this drawer and tried to forget about it.

But despite his anger at his father, it was time to read the man's final words to him.

Dear Matthew,

I hesitate to write this letter, because I know of all my children, you'll be the most disappointed in me. And perhaps you have the right to judge me harshly. You know how hard it is to be a father, how much we want to do the best by our children, how we want to give them the world.

The difference between us is you've become a better father to Flynn than I could ever have hoped to be to any of my children. In the short time you've had that little boy, you've devoted yourself to him, then, after losing Grace, you've been all things to your son.

I'm proud of you. More proud than I could say to your face. You've become a fine man, a good father.

I wish I'd been half the father to you, to all my children, that you are to Flynn. I've failed Jack the worst, but I've kept this secret from you all these years, and left you to find out after I've gone.

All I can ask for now is forgiveness. I have no excuses. All I can offer is my apology and to tell you that if you can't forgive me, I'll understand. And that I'll still love you and be proud of you.

Love,
Dad

A great, thick ball of emotion clogged his throat, and he struggled to get control. This hadn't been what he'd expected. If he'd thought about what was in the letter at all, he'd have predicted a bunch of excuses and a request to play nice with Jack and Alan.

Instead it was full of love and...and admiration. The grief he'd put a stopper on since the day of the will reading burned the backs of his eyes. But he was no role model for fatherhood. He'd just screwed up again by letting Flynn get attached to Susannah then scaring her off.

Susannah.

She'd said it was all smoke and mirrors with him. His father had secrets and he'd had secrets. She was right.

He'd been angry at his father for not telling them that he'd fathered a child before he'd married their mother, yet here he was, keeping Flynn's biological mother a secret.

He stalked to the window, leaning an arm on the frame.

"I'm sorry, Grace," he whispered to the white clouds hovering over Charleston, "but I can't do it anymore. I can't let Flynn grow up with secrets, too."

To be the man his father had thought he was, he had to step

up to the plate. He needed to tell his family that Susannah was Flynn's biological mother, and she needed to be there to hear it. To be acknowledged by them.

In three strides, he was back at his desk, phone in hand. He dialed Susannah's cell and waited. She should have touched down in Georgia by now. How would she react to hearing from him again, and so soon? Would she refuse to come? His pulse resounded in his ears.

It rang five times before she picked up, which gave him a few moments to plan what he wanted to say. But when he heard her voice, the sweet sound flowed around and through him and his mind froze. All he could think about was her blue eyes, the way her blond hair would be falling around her shoulders, her lips parted to say his name.

Susannah stood in the hall outside her apartment, keys in one hand, her carry-on suitcase in the other, her cell phone wedged between her shoulder and ear as she tried to unlock the door.

"Hello?" she repeated. She should have checked the display screen when she answered, but her hands were full and she was in a rush to get inside, so she'd just thumbed the answer button.

It had been a horror flight home. The plane had traveled smoothly, but she'd spent the entire time praying she'd made the right decision, knowing she'd spend the rest of her life convincing herself she'd done the right thing to leave Matthew. To leave Flynn. The key turned in the lock and she pushed through, but still the person on the other end of the phone didn't speak.

"Hello?" she said again, dropping her suitcase and shutting the door. She was about to hang up, when a voice familiar and dear said her name.

Her heart clenched and twisted. "Matthew." Then her brain caught up. "Is it Flynn? Has something happened?"

"He's fine. He's home with my mother."

"Oh, thank God," she said, relieved beyond measure.

"But I would like you to come back to Charleston for something."

She squeezed her eyes shut and leaned against the back of her couch. If he asked her to go back to him, would she have the strength to refuse again?

"Matthew—" But he interrupted her.

"I can't let Flynn grow up with secrets," he said, his voice firm. "I'm going to tell my family that Grace wasn't his biological mother. That you are. And I'd like you to be there when I tell them."

Stunned, she moved to the front of the couch and sank down into the overstuffed cushions. "Why?"

"I think it's only fair that you're acknowledged when I tell them."

"No, why are you telling them at all? You said you could never break that vow to Grace."

"My obligations to Flynn outweigh my responsibility to Grace. I have to do what's right by him, and the right thing is for him to know everything as soon as he's ready."

He was really going to tell them. Then tell Flynn when the boy was ready.

Flynn would always know she was his biological mother.

A flower of hope, of love, bloomed in her chest, but before it became too big, she needed to close it down. Exposing this secret would make everything so much more complex. How would Flynn feel? Would it make things harder for him, to have another mother who didn't live with him and his daddy? Would Matthew want her to keep in touch with Flynn? And where would that leave her relationship with Matthew—it had been hard enough to walk away once, could she do it over and over?

She pinched the bridge of her nose, trying to make sense of her swirling thoughts, and of Matthew's change of heart. "That must have been a hard decision."

"Not once I had a couple of things pointed out to me." His

voice was almost rueful, yet the tension it held was too strong for that.

She knew she had no right to ask, but until a few hours ago, she'd been privy to his innermost thoughts, so the words tumbled out. "By who?"

"You. RJ. My father," he said, and before she could question how he'd had advice from his father, he asked, "Will you come?"

Could she do it? *Should* she? Walk back into the Kincaids' world for a day. Be near the man she loved but couldn't have. Be acknowledged as the mother of a little boy she loved, but would never be a proper mother to.

Once this information came out, she and Matthew would need time to discuss the ramifications, and plan how they wanted to handle the future for Flynn, so she guessed they'd have to meet at some point, anyway.

Weary and overwhelmed, she rubbed her eyes with a trembling hand. "When are you going to tell them?"

"This Sunday. My family has lunch together every Sunday, so they'll all be there. In fact, it'll be the first time I've been since Flynn went to hospital."

She could think of nothing worse than facing the Kincaids when they learned she was the biological mother of their grandson and nephew. Memories crowded in—her grandparents' displeasure at everything she did. The agony of facing the family of the boy she'd been pregnant to as a teenager. How overpowered she'd felt. She lifted her chin. She was a different person now. This time she would stand up, not only for Matthew, but for Flynn and herself.

To get her voice to work, she had to swallow hard. "I'll be there."

She disconnected and—once again—hoped to heaven she'd done the right thing. For all their sakes.

Twelve

As he waited for Susannah at the airport arrivals gate for the second time in a month, Matt found himself tapping his thighs with his thumbs, nervous as all hell. It had only been a matter of days since he'd seen her last, yet it felt like an eternity. His arms were desperate to hold her, to keep her here by his side.

At three in the morning as he'd lain awake, aching for her, optimism had surfaced and he'd wondered if she missed him this much, too. If her torment was half as strong as his, maybe she'd reconsidered and would stay this time.

She emerged through the door; the long blond hair that had curtained their faces when she'd leaned down to him was around her shoulders. The lips that had scorched his body were painted blush-pink and pressed together in a flat line. The crystalline-blue eyes that had darkened with passion when she looked at him were searching the crowd.

She was carrying a large handbag. Not the small carry-on suitcase she'd had last time—she really was planning to return to Georgia tonight. His stomach withered as disappointment surged.

When her gaze landed on him, he stilled, looking for a clue as to her thoughts. She gave away none beyond some nerves of her own in the way she touched her hair. He made his way over and kissed the silken skin of her cheek. Two inches to the right of where he wanted to kiss, but she'd withdrawn the right.

"Did you have a good flight?" he asked, annoyed that his voice sounded more like a rasp.

"Yes, thank you."

So formal. This woman who'd loved his body with such passion. The contrast between what they'd had and how things now stood between them was gut-wrenching. He placed a hand at the small of her back and guided her to the exit nearest his car.

Just outside the door, her step faltered. She looked up at him, a small line between her brows. "Matthew, I've been thinking about Grace's parents since you rang. If you tell everyone about me, then how will they...?"

He guessed her mind. He'd been worried, too. "I've told them." It had been important to him that they hear before his own family. "I visited them yesterday and told them everything. About how devastated Grace had been about not having a child of her own blood, and why she'd wanted all the details of the egg donation to be kept secret. How devoted she'd been to Flynn and how proud they could be of her. And how much Flynn loves them." He hadn't wanted doubts on any of these points.

"How did they take it?"

"There were tears," he admitted as they threaded their way through lines of parked cars. "But I think after they get over the shock they'll be okay. I explained that they would always be Flynn's grandparents, and I had no intention of restricting their access. They're too important to Flynn to ever jeopardize that."

"You're a good man, Matthew Kincaid," she said quietly.

He swore under his breath. A good man, but not good enough to stay with. She still believed the ridiculous idea that she was a replacement for Grace, and nothing he said seemed to convince her otherwise.

They arrived at his car and he opened the passenger door for her. She stepped in and he closed the door.

As he slid into the driver's seat, she said, "You might be interested to know that I had a call from my grandmother last night."

He paused before starting the ignition. "Did you take the call?"

"Against all my instincts," she said with a little smile, and some of the strain between them melted away.

"Then why answer it?"

She paused, tucking her hair behind her ears. "Remember what my grandfather said at the Barclays'?"

"That you broke your grandmother's heart." It had been a low blow and Matt was still furious thinking about it. He reached for her hand and held it between his. "If you ask me, they reaped what they sowed."

"Maybe," she said, looking down at their joined hands. "But my father put up with his parents because he believed in forgiveness. And he must have loved them, too."

"If he'd stood up to them sooner, you might not have had to endure their control games and manipulations."

"From what my grandmother said—and didn't say—I think I might have been the first person to stand up to them. They're rich, they have social position and my grandfather is a bully. People have let them get away with a lot."

"But not you." His chest swelled, he was so incredibly proud of her in this moment.

She gave him a beautiful smile, obviously picking up on the genuine emotion in his voice. "We might be able to come to a new understanding." Her smile faded and her gaze was earnest as it met his. "Another thing she said was that she wasn't happy with the deal my grandfather put to you at the Barclays', and to make up for it, she told Granddaddy to give Larrimore Industries' business to your company. He'll be calling you tomorrow."

He couldn't help the grin that spread across his face. "I'd have liked to have been a fly on the wall when she told him to do that. I think I'll enjoy taking his call." Not wanting to lose the more relaxed mood, an idea formed in his head. "We've got a bit of time before the family lunch, and Flynn is already there with Mom and Pamela. Is there anything you want to do?"

"How much time do we have?"

He checked his watch. "About an hour, give or take."

She bit down on a smile. "Have you heard of John's Point?"

He hadn't been to the little lookout for years, and couldn't see any particular appeal for a visit. He'd hoped she'd suggest somewhere more private. Intimate. But she was here today at his request, so the least he could do was drop by if she wanted to see it.

"Sure," he said and started the car.

They spent the drive talking about Flynn's health and the Elvis songs he'd conned people into singing recently. In the days since Susannah had left, Matt had missed many things about her, but this kind of easy conversation was perhaps one he'd missed the most.

When they arrived at the small viewing platform on the rocky outcrop, her eyes lit up and the effect was mesmerizing. She undid her seat belt and climbed out before he could get around to open her door.

"What is it about this place?" he asked as he clicked the keyless lock.

The wind whipped her hair around her face. "When I was a girl, my father used to bring me here."

She began to climb the path and he followed behind. "So it reminds you of your father?"

"Yes." She turned and looked at him over her shoulder, grinning. "And no."

Matthew chuckled. They reached the top, a little-known lookout with a panoramic view over Charleston and out to sea. "You like the view?"

"Sure, the view's great," she said over her shoulder.

He could live an entire life with Susannah Parrish and never tire of trying to figure out what was going on in her mind. "That's not why you wanted to come."

"Nope," she said and walked to the rail and stretched out her arms. The strong wind smoothed the hair from her face, pressed her dress against her curves. Her eyes drifted closed and her mouth tugged wide in a smile of deep pleasure.

"I used to come here often when I lived in Charleston," she said, her eyes still closed. "Every week, if I could manage it."

"You came for the wind," he said, as it finally made sense. He remembered the look of joy on her face that morning in his courtyard. "You have a thing for the wind."

"I do," she said without embarrassment. "It revitalizes me. Some people like adrenaline sports, some like the water. I like the breeze in my hair, against my skin."

"I have to admit, I like seeing you with the breeze in your hair." She was magnificent. Like a goddess.

She opened one eye and smiled at him. "Come and try it." She held out a hand and without thinking, he took it, stepping up onto the bottom rung of the railing, and leaning forward so it took his weight. She moved behind him and lifted his arms to the side before taking up her own position again.

"Now close your eyes," she said, not looking at him. "And pretend you're alone with the breeze."

Feeling a little foolish, he followed her instructions and was amazed to find that within seconds, the world faded away and almost his entire focus was taken by the current of air that pressed against him. *Almost* his entire focus. Because he never lost the awareness of Susannah. He reached out his fingertips and found her hand, entangling them together. Hers didn't respond at first, then they quickly wrapped around his, tightly. He opened his eyes and glanced over. She was looking at him and he could see straight into her heart, and he finally understood something in his conscious mind that he had always known, soul deep.

Susannah was no woman's replacement.

She'd been right that he had seen her that way on some level. He'd used it as a defense against falling in love with her because he couldn't stand the thought of things going the same way they had with Grace. But nothing with Susannah would go the same way, because Susannah was nothing like Grace. Whatever happened between them would be unique and belonging to them alone.

He wanted that. Wanted everything that came of being with her.

"Susannah," he said, his voice rough with all he hadn't said.

"No, Matthew. Please don't say it again. I can't stay." Her eyes filled with tears. Tears he'd caused.

Everything inside him wanted to rise up and revolt, to refuse to accept. But no matter how many times he asked, she kept giving the same answer. He wouldn't beg, and even if he did, he doubted it would make any difference.

He dropped his arms and straightened. Despite the canyon-size ache inside, he had to keep himself together or he'd never get through the next few hours with his family.

He checked his watch. "It's probably time we got to my mother's."

The drive to the Kincaid mansion was silent. Why had she done something as foolish as take him to John's Point? At the airport, things had been too formal, almost abrupt. But they'd settled in to being able to carry a conversation. Then she'd ruined that and could kick herself for making things more difficult for him just before he had to confront his family.

They pulled up in front of an elaborately embellished Federal mansion with a gorgeous porch and outbuildings to the side.

While she gaped at the beauty of the building, Matthew came around and opened her door.

A swarm of butterflies fluttered in her belly. What would his family think of her? Would they judge her to be good enough to be the mother of their precious nephew and grandson? They'd seemed to like her when she was a friend, but things would be different now. This was Flynn's family, and despite having met most of them before, she wanted to do the right thing. Make the right impression, for Flynn's sake.

Matthew took her hand as she stepped out, and guided her in with a warm palm at the small of her back. As they walked through the door, her gut clenched tight. Suddenly she was alone. And small. Just like when she was a child visiting her grandparents or accompanying them to their friends' homes. Big, impressive houses where the cream of society lived.

People waiting to judge her and find her lacking.

Noises floated on the air from a room farther away—a large family laughing, talking, glassware clinking. She was reminded of her mother visiting the Larrimores' for the first time—the beginning of their campaign of exclusion and snubbing.

Matthew leaned down to her ear, his breath warm as it feathered over her cheek. "Everything okay?"

She looked up into his brilliant green eyes and the world tilted to correct itself and she was back to being herself again. "Everything's fine," she said.

Except that she'd never have him. Another difference between her arrival here and her mother's at the Larrimore mansion became clear—her father had been besotted and had proposed with romance and genuine passion. Matthew had offered her a ring "if she needed it." The ache inside was almost unbearable. She shut it away—dwelling on it wouldn't change a thing, it would only make today harder to live through.

They entered a large, exquisitely decorated room and Elizabeth and RJ smiled as they came over to greet her. Matthew introduced her to Lily and her fiancé, Daniel, then Kara and

Laurel came into the room, glasses of iced tea in their hands, deep in conversation. They saw her and came over to kiss her cheek, both with mischievous grins—Laurel had obviously told Kara about the kiss she'd witnessed the night Elizabeth had been taken in for questioning.

Elizabeth slid her hand in the crook of Matthew's arm. "You said you had something to tell us?" Her eyes were wide, hopeful, and Susannah had a bad feeling. His family thought this was going to be a happy announcement, perhaps even an engagement…

"I do. Where's Flynn?"

Elizabeth waved an arm toward the door. "In the kitchen house with Pamela. She'll keep him out there till we come for him."

"Thanks." Susannah saw the tension lurking in his eyes when he glanced at her, but his face was calm and composed when his gaze returned to his family. "Perhaps if we all sit down?"

"Shall I get the champagne?" Laurel asked.

Matthew winced, finally understanding their expectations, and his shoulders seemed to take on an even heavier weight. "It's not that sort of news."

There were some rumblings in the group. "Then what the hell kind of news is it?" RJ asked, clearly speaking for them all.

"Let's go in here," Matthew said, indicating the less-formal family room. Buzzing with curious anticipation, his family filed in, sitting on couches, Kara on the corner of a coffee table, RJ on the armrest of one couch.

"There's something I should have told you before now," he began. His shoulders were tense. Standing a few feet to the side of him, Susannah knew this was tearing him up inside because he felt he was betraying Grace, but he was going to do it, anyway. Because he thought it was the right thing to do. She'd never loved him more. She wanted to lace her fingers through his to offer support, but knew it would give the wrong impression to his family, and they were already suspicious more existed between Matthew and her than friendship.

Instead she moved an infinitesimal step closer and he looked up. She gave him an encouraging smile, and some of the tension melted from his features.

He turned back to his family. "You all know Grace was unable to carry a baby to term. What you don't know is that Susannah was the surrogate who carried Flynn."

There were a couple of gasps, and a few comments about not having told them sooner, but he continued on. "There's more. When Grace and I were having difficulty conceiving..." He drew in a long breath through a tight jaw. His back was ramrod straight. This was the moment of truth—he was breaking a vow he'd made to his dead wife. Matthew wasn't the kind of man who made vows easily, she knew. And he'd break them even less easily. Uncaring of the consequences this time, she moved to his side, freely giving whatever she could. His hand snaked out and wrapped around hers, squeezing her fingers tight. When he continued, his voice was even and strong. No one—who wasn't having their fingers squeezed to within an inch of their health— would guess this was hard for him.

"We found that Grace's eggs weren't able to be used. She went to Susannah again for help, and Susannah's eggs were used instead. Susannah is Flynn's biological mother."

There was silence in the room. Not a comment or clink of glass, or movement. Matthew's grasp on her fingers didn't ease. Despite wondering how his family was reacting to the news, to her, she kept her gaze on Matthew. He needed her.

"The reason Susannah has been here recently is when Flynn was in danger of needing a bone-marrow transplant, I wasn't an ideal donor because of my penicillin allergy. I called Susannah, and she graciously said she'd come to Charleston and do whatever we needed. She's been here on standby. In case Flynn needed her bone marrow."

Elizabeth was the first to move. She sprang out of her seat

and claimed Susannah in a fierce hug. "You did that for my grandson?"

"Well," Susannah stammered, surprised, "I didn't need to do anything in the end."

"But you came. And you were willing." Elizabeth stepped away, tears shining in her eyes. "Thank you."

RJ was next to grab her in a bear hug. "We all love that kid. Thanks for being here for him."

She was hugged and thanked by each Kincaid in turn, becoming a little disoriented and wobbly, but then, still in a hug from one of his sisters, a familiar hand clasped hers and she was grounded again, anchored in uneven waters. She glanced around the group, and something struck her. This family was unlike any of the society families she'd met with her grandparents. And they were nothing like her grandparents themselves. She'd been so wary of the Kincaids, so caught up in her expectations of wealthy, powerful families, that she'd allowed herself to be prejudiced. That was unfair. They were a warm, loving family.

"But why was this such a secret?" Elizabeth said when they'd settled again. "Why hide who Susannah is?"

Susannah turned to Elizabeth before Matthew could speak. This was one time she could save him the anguish of answering. "He was honoring Grace's wishes, and that took a lot of courage."

Matthew looked at her, and there was such emotion in his eyes that her heart missed a beat.

"You know," Elizabeth said, "I think lunch might be ready. Let's go into the dining room." More was said, but Susannah couldn't hear anything besides a background buzz. She was watching Matthew. He didn't move until the room was quiet, then he took her hand. "Will you come with me out into the garden?"

She knew he was going to ask her to stay here in Charleston. The way he'd almost asked earlier. Yet nothing had changed between them. She still loved him. He still wanted her, she had no doubt, but not the way she needed him to want her. If she had to refuse him again, she might just fall apart.

She was about to deflect the question, when he added, "I promise I won't ask you to stay again."

What else did they have to say to each other? Yet it was such a simple request and he was standing before her so tall and solid and *Matthew* that she couldn't find it inside herself to say no. A few more stolen moments together before her evening flight could hardly make things worse than they were.

With emotion clogging her throat, she nodded, and followed him out. They were deep in the elaborate gardens, a long way from the house when he stopped walking and turned to her.

"I need to say something to you, and you won't want to believe it, but please just listen anyway."

"Okay," she said warily.

There was silence for a long moment and she watched a line form between his brows, the dip of his Adam's apple. "You think I only see you as a replacement for Grace and you were probably right at the start."

"I didn't help, by trying to fit into your lives seamlessly."

"That was a blessing. At that time, with Flynn so unwell, I appreciated that more than I can say."

"But it meant you never saw me."

"I saw you," he said huskily. "I see you now."

"Matthew—"

"You're the woman who intuitively found my favorite place in the house to be alone."

She frowned, then understanding dawned as clear as the blue sky above them. "The wine cellar."

"The cellar has been the only place I can be me in that house. Sometimes I've needed that for five minutes. Not a father or a husband or, more recently, a widower. Just me. And you went there for the same reason, didn't you?"

"Yes," she whispered.

"And I didn't mind being there with you. Sharing it with you."

She went to speak again, but he placed a finger over her lips. "You're the woman who throws her arms out to the sky just to feel the breeze against her face. Who introduced me to pink grapefruit gelato and who cooks decadent desserts. Who has a strange fascination with my wrists and hands."

A smile wobbled on her lips. "I thought I was being subtle."

"You were. But I was watching you closely." He tenderly smoothed the hair back from her face. "I couldn't take my eyes off you. I still can't."

This was breaking her heart. She blinked, not knowing which way to turn, what to do or say. "Why are you making this more difficult?"

"You're the woman who stood up to her grandparents and forced them to treat her properly," he said as if she hadn't spoken. "Maybe the only person who's done that to the Larrimores, and they've come back to you and I'll bet money they'll be in your life again, but on your terms."

That was one charge she couldn't accept. She shook her head. "I'm not sure—"

He put the finger back over her lips. "You were magnificent in your strength with them."

A painful pressure was building behind her breastbone and she pushed a hand to it to ease the ache. It made no difference. "Please, Matthew." Her eyes burned with unshed tears.

"I see you, Susannah," he said with fierce certainty. "Maybe at the start I was foolish enough to let you slip into Grace's role in our family, but you're no replacement. You're Susannah, and I see you."

A tear slipped down her cheek. "Matthew…"

"Most important of all you're the woman I love."

Her heart turned over in her chest as she hardly dared to believe. "You said—"

"I swore I'd never love again," he said, cutting her off then he winced. "A stupid, stupid thing to say, to even think. I was trying to save myself from the hurt of the breakdown in my relationship with Grace, but being without you for these past few days...that's been worse than any pain I was trying to avoid."

"For me, too," she said, her lips quivering, happiness swelling within.

"Tell me one thing. Do you love me? Because if you don't, I swear I'll—"

With a tentative hand, she reached out and stroked the side of his face. "I love you, Matthew, almost more than my heart can bear."

"Susannah," he said in a thick voice, and crushed her in his arms. "I said I wouldn't ask you to stay, and I was serious." He stepped back, just holding her hands between his. "I want much more than you to merely stay. Marry me."

A shiver of delight ran down her spine then worked its way outward, till she was trembling all over. He saw the real her. He was willing to accept his love for her. It was too much...

"Marry me, Susannah Parrish, and make a life with me and Flynn." His brilliant green eyes were full of love and yearning. "And when I say make a life with us, I mean just that. Not the life we have now, but one we create together, that reflects all three of us. We can live anywhere, do anything. As long as we do it together."

"Yes," she said, but it only came out as a faint rasp. So she drew in a long breath and said it again, making sure it was as strong and sure as she felt. "Yes, Matthew Kincaid, I'll marry you. There's nothing in this world that could make me happier than to create a life with you and Flynn."

He picked her up and turned them in a circle before releasing her and kissing her. Everything inside her danced—the air was warmer on her skin, the sun shone more brightly. Matthew, *her Matthew,* loved her. Wanted to build a life with her.

Then she drew away. "And I promise you, I won't let Flynn

forget Grace. She loved him, and he needs to know that. But I have a question for you."

"Ask me anything," he said, emotion shining in his eyes.

"Since you've been watching me this closely and seem to know so much about me, did you know I'm pregnant with your child?"

His eyes widened and his jaw slackened. Then a grin split his face and he picked her up again. Laughter bubbled up her throat and out.

"I'd planned to tell you today, but I knew it was going to be hard for you to explain to your family about Flynn, so I wanted to let you do that first. I—"

"I don't care when you were going to tell me, as long as you did." He kissed her. "Flynn will be beside himself to have a little brother or sister."

She bit down on her smile, trying to be serious for a moment. "Matthew, I'm not very far along, so do you mind if we don't tell anyone yet?"

"Frankly that's one secret I'd be glad to keep for now."

And then he leaned down and kissed her with all the passion and honesty she'd ever hoped for.

* * * * *

Turn the page for an exclusive short story

by USA TODAY bestselling author
Day Leclaire.

THE KINCAIDS: JACK AND NIKKI, PART II
Day Leclaire

This was a mistake. This was a mistake. This was a *huge* mistake.

Nikki Thomas pushed the door to her office shut, tempted to lock it, as well. Unfortunately if someone dropped by, she'd be forced to explain, something she was unwilling to do. If only she hadn't made that outrageous bid at the bachelor charity auction for Read and Write, a local nonprofit organization that supported literacy in everyone from five to ninety-five. If only the man she'd bid on had been anyone other than Jack Sinclair.

But she had bid on Jack Sinclair, the most despised man in all Charleston, South Carolina. Jack Sinclair, the Kincaid bastard. Jack Sinclair, the direct competitor of The Kincaid Group, the firm she worked for as a corporate investigator. Jack Sinclair, the man who'd taken her in his arms one short month ago and kissed her senseless. Kissed her in a way she'd never, ever been kissed before. Kissed her in a way she wanted to be kissed again.

Soon.

Working up her courage, she crossed to her desk and placed

the call on her cell phone, preferring not to use the company landline to contact "the enemy." A moment later, a woman answered, clearly an admin. "Please connect me to Jack Sinclair," Nikki requested briskly.

"Certainly. May I ask who's calling and what it's regarding?"

"Nikki Thomas." That was the easy part. Answering the other question was the not-so-easy part and a ball of tension formed in the pit of her stomach. How could she be so cool and collected when it came to her job, and such a mess when it came to personal relationships? It didn't make any sense. "It's regarding… It's regarding an appointment Jack and I were forced to postpone." Okay, that would work. Enough information to get past the dragon at the gate, but not so much it caused undue comment.

"I'd be happy to help you with that appointment. I have Mr. Sinclair's calendar right here."

Damn. Not enough info to get past the dragon. "Thank you, but he asked that I speak to him directly. If you could just let him know I'm on the line?"

"Of course, Ms. Thomas."

Several minutes of silence ensued, long enough that the urge to simply hang up almost had her pressing the disconnect button at least half a dozen times. Before she could give in to impulse, Jack's dark, distinctive voice sounded in her ear. "Nikki?"

She closed her eyes, fighting back a shiver. If a voice could be a food, his would be dark, creamy Belgian chocolate, the sort that melted on the tongue and gave that delicious sensation of bittersweet richness. She fought to keep her voice calm and level, to hide the almost overwhelming need for a hit of the chocolate she was imagining.

"Hi, Jack." For some reason her voice came out low. Sultry.

"I thought you'd changed your mind about our date." His voice also sounded low. Sexy.

She managed a quick laugh. "Hey, I won you fair and square.

I'm not about to change my mind." Especially not after that mind-blowing kiss they'd shared.

"Paid top dollar for me, as I recall."

"A thousand of those top dollars, as *I* recall."

"I'll try to make it worth every penny. I gather you're ready to collect what you've won?"

His tone sounded lightly flirtatious suggesting she'd caught him alone in his office with a few minutes on his hands. A soft squeak came through the line, the sort of sound a desk chair made when tipped back. An image of him sprang to life. Corporate Jack, feet resting on the edge of his desk, wearing an expensive, tailored suit in a dense brown color that matched his hair, with a narrow pinstripe in a robin's egg blue to match his eyes. The shirt...? A crisp taupe with an expensive tie that picked up on the blue again. From what little she knew of him, he'd have loosened the knot of his tie, giving him an edge that blended business with a worldly casualness. A lion in his prime, secure in his position and able to overcome any threat. Heaven help her!

She hastened to answer his question. "I am ready to collect my winnings. I believe that's a night of dinner and dancing." She moistened her lips, going for broke. "Not to mention, a wish of my choice."

His soft chuckle had her practically melting in her chair. "Foolish on my part to throw that into the bargain. Do you want your wish, too, or just a date?"

Tempting. Oh, so tempting. "I think we'll stick with dinner and dancing for the time being."

"Is this weekend convenient?"

She made a pretense of flipping through her calendar book, though she doubted it fooled him. "Actually that would be perfect."

"Shall we say Saturday? I'll pick you up at six."

"Great." A knock sounded on her door, distracting her. "I'll see you then, Jack."

His laugh rang in her ear, stirring the most outrageous sensations. "You've forgotten one small detail."

Matthew Kincaid, Director of New Business for The Kincaid Group, stood in the doorway, and she waved him in, dismayed by his presence. Not someone she wanted to overhear this particular conversation. "What detail have I forgotten?" she asked Jack.

"Where do I pick you up?"

"Oh, right." She rattled off the address. "I'll see you then."

"Someone just walked into your office, didn't they?"

"Is it that obvious?" she asked, wry humor sliding through the question.

"I can hear it in your voice. As tempted as I am to tease you about it, I'll play the part of the gentleman and let you go. See you Saturday."

"I look forward to it." She disconnected the call and turned her attention to Matthew and smiled. "Hey, stranger. Good to see you back at work. How's Flynn doing?"

His expression relaxed into a grin. He'd suffered one of the most terrifying ordeals any parent could face when his three-year-old son had developed aplastic anemia following a strong viral infection. Fortunately, the medication Flynn received to treat the disease worked. If it hadn't, his biological mother, Susannah, was waiting in the wings to donate her bone marrow. Her timely appearance had also led to a romance between her and Matthew, one soon heading to the altar. "Better and better, thanks."

"I hear congratulations are in order." She smiled with sincere pleasure. "I couldn't be happier for you and Susannah."

"I'm still in shock. A happy sort of shock, since it's still sinking in."

"I hope you'll bring her by and introduce us. From everything I've heard, your fiancée is a special woman."

"She is that."

"So, what's up? Did you have something you needed me to do for you?"

"A potential client I'd like you to check out." He handed her a file. "I definitely don't want to turn away business if I can help it. But I also want to be smart about it."

"Understandable." She flipped open the file and scanned the details. "I'll get right on this. When do you need to get back to them?"

"Monday."

"No problem. I'll have it to you by Friday."

He hesitated, warning that she probably wouldn't like the next topic of conversation. Sure enough, he asked, "I don't suppose that was Jack Sinclair you were talking to? I heard you mention his name when I first knocked."

Nikki lifted a shoulder in a casual shrug. "I won dinner with him at the Read and Write literacy auction. We've had a little trouble coordinating our schedules."

"So, you're not dating him?"

A tiny flare of temper curled through her at the intrusion into her private affairs, but she kept her voice calm and even. "This will be our first." She tilted her head to one side. "Is that a problem?"

"Could be." He lowered his voice. "You know who he is, Nikki. The damage he's already caused the family. The damage he could cause The Kincaid Group. You work here, which makes you as vulnerable as the rest of us if he takes over and decides to clean house."

"I doubt that will happen. RJ's in line to—"

"You're right. RJ *is* in line to step into Dad's shoes. But considering Sinclair owns forty-five percent of TKG stock, there's no guarantee it'll happen. I guess the board will decide that during the annual meeting in June." His green eyes narrowed. "But now that I think about it, you might be in a position to help."

She stiffened. Did he know her secret? Is that why he was

asking for her help? No, no. It wasn't possible. No one knew. She forced herself to relax. "What can I do?" she asked simply.

"You're going out with him on this date, right?" He kept his gaze trained on her, his expression reflecting his determination. "Maybe he'll say something to you, give you some idea about his intentions."

"That doesn't make sense, Matthew. Why would he confide in me?"

"He doesn't know you work for us, right? Maybe you could bring up the subject, see if Sinclair says anything that might help us figure out his plans."

She shook her head even before he finished speaking. "Please don't ask me to spy for you. I don't do business that way."

"Think about it, Nikki. Think long and hard." He planted his hands on her desk and leaned in, not in a threatening way, more as a way to underscore his conviction. "While you're enjoying dinner with Sinclair, listen to him. Get a feel for the man. Is he someone you want in charge of TKG? He's our competitor. There's no way he won't attempt to fold TKG into Carolina Shipping. If I'm wrong and you think he's on the up-and-up, fine. But if you get the impression he's as ruthless as we've heard…"

She hesitated, then nodded. "I'll think about it, Matthew. No promises."

"Fair enough."

But the idea of spying on Jack Sinclair made her squirm despite feeling a strong allegiance to the Kincaids, particularly to Reginald Kincaid, who'd literally saved her professional reputation when her ex-fiancé had ripped it to shreds. Still… Would it be so awful to just listen to Jack and ask a few questions to draw him out? And if Jack happened to say something helpful, was there really any harm in passing it along? She blew out a sigh, knowing full well what she'd do, that she'd use whatever investigative skills available to help the Kincaids.

Nikki closed her eyes, letting go of what might have been. Letting go of possibilities. It was a darn shame. In the short time she'd spent with Jack, they'd hit it off. Not to mention the key element that had kept her fantasizing about him for a solid month.

Jack really was a fantastic kisser.

Jack arrived at Nikki's door promptly at six. To his surprise, he realized he was looking forward to seeing her again, to discovering if the attraction he'd felt the night of the bachelor auction remained, or if it had faded in the month since they'd been apart. One thing that continued to linger in his memory was that kiss they'd shared.

He couldn't remember the last time he'd felt such an explosive reaction to a woman, nor experienced such a deep, unremitting want. Even after so long he continued to puzzle over it, unable to explain what made her so different from other women he'd known. He was simply forced to accept one indisputable fact. He wanted her, wanted her more than anyone else he'd ever kissed. She represented a tantalizing interlude to call to mind whenever the stress of business—or the Kincaids—grew too severe, which was just about every damn day.

He released a short, mocking laugh, calling himself every kind of fool. He'd built a brief encounter up in his mind, fantasizing it into something it wasn't, and never could be. Ridiculous, really.

Tonight, he'd escort the very attractive Nikki Thomas to his home for a candlelit evening of dinner and dancing. They might exchange another kiss or two. He doubted it would go anywhere from there. Then he'd return her safely to her doorstep. And that would be the end of that. Maybe at some point down the road she'd call about this ridiculous wish he'd promised to grant. Chances were, she wouldn't bother. It had been more in the way of a joke. After that, he'd get down to the serious business of destroying the Kincaids, before they could destroy him. Story over.

He found a parking space close to her Rainbow Row house,

a miracle in itself, and exited his Aston Martin Volante. He approached the front door and knocked, surprised when it swung open almost immediately. It was then that Jack realized three very important facts.

One. His fantasies had been all wrong. Nikki Thomas was far more beautiful than he remembered.

Two. If the evening ended any other way than with her in his bed, he might just go insane.

And three. One night with her couldn't possibly come close to satisfying him.

She stood before him in a flirty little dress, the brilliant sapphire-blue perfectly matching the color of her eyes. She wore her hair up in a loose knot, a few wayward tendrils escaping to caress the creamy skin of her neck—creamy skin he wanted to taste. Badly.

"Right on time. I like that about a man," she said with a warm smile.

"Almost as much as I appreciate promptness in a woman."

"Sounds like we're in agreement." Her smile grew, drawing his attention to the lush mouth he planned to consume at his earliest possible opportunity. "At least on this point."

"An excellent start."

Taking his hand in hers, she leaned in and kissed the corner of his mouth. Instantly the want he'd been holding in check slammed through him. Without a word, he yanked her close, took her mouth with a passion that caused wildfire to burst into flames between them. He didn't even remember slamming the door closed or maneuvering her backward, just felt the dull thud when they hit the wall and her soft gasp that allowed him to slip inside her warm, sweet mouth.

He half expected her to protest the taking. Instead her arms wound around his neck and she tugged him closer, her soft moan threatening to unman him. His hands swept over her, tracing the impressive curves her dress displayed. Naked. He wanted her naked and under him. To hell with dinner. Instead they'd consume each other. Make love here and now.

Before he could act, she spun away, drawing in a deep, shaky breath. "Okay, that answers that question." She snatched up a knee-length black wool coat that hid every scrap of her from view. "Shall we go?" she asked, though he caught a ripple of turbulence racing through her words.

"No. Stay." It was all he could manage.

She took a swift step away from him, a deep feminine vulnerability darkening her eyes. "I don't think that's smart."

Before he could stop her, she opened the door and stepped out into the brisk February breeze, leaving him no choice but to follow. He waited while she locked her front door and fought to regain his self-control, shocked by the lack of it. The cold helped clear his head and when she turned, he was able to gesture toward the Aston Martin with something approaching normalcy. She paused on the sidewalk to admire the sleek lines of the ruby-red car.

"Impressive." She spared him a swift look, one that held the shocked echo of the kiss they'd just shared. Well, at least he wasn't the only one. Thank God for that much. "All of Charleston will know it's you whether you're coming or going."

He inclined his head. "That's the idea." He opened the passenger door, admiring the graceful way Nikki slid in. Admiring even more the flash of long, toned legs, accentuated by a pair of mile-high heels. He was fast creating a Nikki "to do" list and seeing her naked in those heels just topped it. "You haven't asked where we're going," he commented as soon as he'd climbed behind the steering wheel.

"I like surprises. Most of the time, at least."

"Let's hope that kiss was one of the surprises you liked. Most of the time."

She hesitated for an unnerving moment, then admitted, "I think you can safely put a check in the 'like' box." She moistened her lips in a way that suggested she could still taste him. "Will I like this next surprise?"

"I hope so, though there's no way it can compare to kissing you." The engine started with a low, muted roar. "This surprise has to do with tonight's venue. To be honest, I considered taking you home."

"And where is home?"

"Greenville."

Her brows shot up. "That's a mile or so down the road."

"About two hundred of them," he confirmed. "But then I decided we'd spend the entire date driving and as much as I'd enjoy talking to you, I'd prefer putting those hours to a much better use."

Her magnificent eyes narrowed. "And to what use do you plan to put them?"

He slowed for a red light and pulled to a stop before responding. "With you in my arms." He flicked her a quick glance before the light changed. She didn't bother to conceal a certain level of wariness and he forced himself to throttle back when every part of him demanded he punch the gas. "Dancing, of course. Naturally that meant a change of venue was in order."

"Naturally."

"But I still wanted to take you home. So…"

"So?" she prompted.

"We'll settle for my home away from home. Since my company is based in Charleston, it's impractical to commute to and from Greenville every day."

"Makes sense." She leaned back against her seat, continuing to regard him through narrowed eyes.

"What?" he asked.

"Just trying to decide what sort of place you'd own."

"Here…or in Greenville?"

She waved a hand through the air. "Oh, the Greenville one is easy."

Bull. "And what sort of place do you think I'd own in Green-ville?"

"A magnificent plantation," she answered promptly. "Gracious Southern living at its best. A blend of past and present, beautifully restored. And I imagine the interior is a blend, as well, antiques mated with classic contemporary. Am I close?"

"Damn." She was better than he'd anticipated.

She chuckled. "I'm good at reading people."

"I'll consider myself forewarned."

"But I forgot the most important part."

"Which is?"

"You'd want to put your own mark on the place in some way. Probably a way that had your interior decorator most unhappy."

"Now I'm seriously impressed." And he was. "What about my Charleston place?"

"Mmm. More difficult," she admitted. "I'm guessing it would need to be large enough to entertain. Considering the car you drive, you like a bit of flash. Yet, elegant flash. You wouldn't settle for anything that didn't have a view of the water. I'm thinking you went in the opposite direction with your Charleston home. Modern. Contemporary. All the comforts, but less Old World. Am I close?"

"No."

"Well, shoot." Her luscious mouth turned downward, tempting him beyond reason to kiss her again. "Where did I go wrong?"

"You didn't. You weren't close, you're dead-on. Again." He spared her a swift glance. "You researched me, didn't you?"

Her blatant surprise answered for her, even before she shook her head in automatic denial. "I really didn't. It's a game I used to play with my father. He's a cop. Was a cop," she corrected.

"That's right. You mentioned he's in law enforcement." Then her correction sank in. "*Was* in law enforcement?"

"Died in the line of duty," she explained with painful brevity.

"I'm sorry."

"So was my family." She made an effort to throw off the shadows. "When I was little we'd play this game where we'd see strangers at a restaurant or in the park and we'd try to figure out things about them based on what we observed. Sometimes my father would go over and identify himself in order to see how close we'd come."

"People didn't mind?"

"You know, they never did. Dad just had this way about him. He could put people at their ease." She tossed him a broad grin. "Or scare them spitless. You didn't dare lie to my father. He could smell it a mile away. He'd just stare at you with those cop's eyes of his and the truth would come tumbling out, willy-nilly."

"Sounds like a man I'd have enjoyed getting to know."

She tilted her head in his direction. "No secrets to hide? He was hell on secrets, I can tell you."

"None worth mentioning," he replied smoothly.

"Huh. I think you're a first."

"In what way?"

"I don't think I've ever met a man without secrets."

They'd arrived at his oceanfront home, saving him from commenting further. It was exactly as she'd described. Instead of pulling into the garage, he parked by the walkway leading to the front steps. Ankle-high lights edged the curving ribbon of slate, tucked discreetly into the strip of garden that bracketed each side. Short, neatly trimmed bushes stood sentry duty along the edge of the garden and Nikki suspected that in the spring and summer a wealth of flowers added color and texture.

He opened the door for her and she stepped into a large, open foyer. On the far side, a great room cascaded toward the back of the house where a wall of windows overlooked the ocean. An enormous stone fireplace occupied one end of the space, complete with cheerfully crackling fire. Comfortable sofas and wing chairs grouped themselves in a loose semicircle around the hearth. Nearby, a table covered in snowy-white linen had been placed in front of the glass wall in preparation for their meal.

"Would you care for a drink?" he asked.

"Yes, please." She wandered deeper into the great room. "This is a gorgeous place, Jack. Perfect for entertaining."

"It's also perfect for intimate dinners for two." He handed her a glass of wine, the deep ruby color combining with the scent of berry, spice and herbs. "Thank you for bidding on me. I hope you'll find the evening well worth what you paid."

"I'm sure I will." She touched her glass to his, the crystal singing melodically. She took a sip of the creamy wine and smiled in appreciation. "I don't think I've tasted anything quite like it."

"It's a Spanish Termanthia I discovered a few years ago. A little exotic. But the spices in the Cantonese meal we're having tonight pair well with it."

"Sounds delicious."

As it was. The meal was catered, the waitstaff gliding in and out so efficiently, she barely noticed their presence. The conversation never lagged. The diciest moment came when he asked what she did for a living.

"I'm a corporate investigator," she answered, keeping her tone easy and off-the-cuff. "I specialize in background checks, illegal activities on the part of employees, corporate espionage. That sort of thing."

"Interesting." She'd captured his interest. "Do you also work the financial end of things?"

"Sometimes, though that's not my primary area of expertise. We have a CPA to handle that aspect, though I often work in conjunction with him. If he suspects fraudulent billing on the part of a supplier, I might go undercover and look into it. But for the most part my job involves a lot of computer time and pushing paper around." She helped herself to a final bite of stir-fry before deliberating nudging the plate aside. If she ate any more she risked exploding, but man, it had been good. "What about you? You own Carolina Shipping, right?"

"So, you did research me."

She picked up her wineglass and swirled the contents. "Which sounds worse, that I researched you…or that I listened to local gossip?" She drank, returned the glass to the table and relaxed back in her chair. "It's hard to go anywhere these days without hearing about you and the Kincaids."

"So, you know who I am."

"Yes. And I know about your connection to the Kincaid family."

His mouth tightened. "Congratulations. You win the award for finding the most polite way of calling me Reginald Kincaid's bastard I've ever heard. I'm surprised, knowing who I am, that you still came tonight."

She lifted an eyebrow, decided to be blunt. "Was I supposed to cancel because you're a bastard?"

"I wouldn't have been surprised."

She gave him a direct look. "The only way I would have canceled is if you'd been a bastard in actuality rather than in birth. Does that clarify the matter?"

"I believe it does."

He fell silent while their plates were whisked away. Then he stood and held out his hand. Unresisting, she took it, allowed him to tug her from her chair. She stepped into his arms without any hesitation and lifted her face to his. Where before their kiss had been frantic and beyond passionate, now it was slow and leisurely. The flames were there, no question about that, but carefully banked toward a long, slow burn.

She could taste the wine they'd consumed, taste the delicate blend of spices that had flavored their dinner and now flavored their kiss. This time when his hands skimmed over her curves, they were thorough rather than desperate, inching the gauge of her need to steadily higher and higher levels. Aware that they were fast approaching the point of no return, she pulled back and stared up at him.

He wasn't handsome in the conventional sense. His features were too hard for that, hacked into strong, ruthless lines by birth and circumstances that had toughened him through trial by fire. And yet, he appealed on some elemental level, male to female. He called to her, filled her with a longing she'd never experienced before, left her trembling with a feminine vulnerability that terrified her. He must have read some of her reaction because he cupped her face with a gentleness she'd never have guessed him capable of.

"I requested that they put dessert in the refrigerator for later," he informed her. "If you'd prefer it now...?"

"Not a chance. I'm stuffed." Then she keyed in on what he'd said and eyed him uncertainly. "Later?"

A small flame kindled in his gaze. "How does key-lime tart sound...for breakfast?"

She exhaled a long sigh of hesitation. "Complicated."

"Is that a yes, or a no?"

She closed her eyes and faced the truth. Whatever was going on between them was long past complicated. Not that it changed anything. She looked at him. Wanted him. And felt her helpless surrender. "That's a yes. In fact, it's a hell, yes."

* * * * *

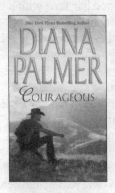